DANTE ALIGHIERI was born in Florence, Italy, in 1265. His early poetry falls into the tradition of love poetry that passed from the Provençal to such Italian poets as Guido Cavalcanti, Dante's friend and mentor. Dante's first major work was the *Vita Nuova (New Life),* 1293–1294. This sequence of lyrics, sonnets, and prose narrative describes his love, first earthly, then spiritual, for Beatrice, whom he had first seen as a child of nine, and who had died when Dante was twenty-five.

Dante married about 1285, served Florence in battle, and rose to a position of leadership in the bitter factional politics of that city-state. In 1300 he and the other city magistrates found it necessary to banish leaders from both the Black and White factions, including Dante's friend Cavalcanti, a fellow White. But after the Blacks seized control of Florence in 1301, Dante himself was tried in absentia and was banished from the city on pain of death. He never returned to Florence.

In exile he wrote his *Convivio,* or *Banquet,* a kind of poetic compendium of medieval philosophy, as well as a political treatise, *Monarchia.* He probably began his *Comedy* (later to be called the *Divine Comedy* and consisting of three parts, the *Inferno,* the *Purgatorio,* and the *Paradiso*) around 1307 or 1308. On a diplomatic mission to Venice in 1321, Dante fell ill, and returned to Ravenna, where he died.

"Dante's basic, quintessential clarity has largely been captured, and for the first time in English. . . . At long last, an English Dante which . . . should satisfy Italianists, and medievalists, and readers of poetry."—*Burton Raffel,* The Denver Quarterly

"Exactly what we have waited for these years, a Dante with clarity, eloquence, terror, and profoundly moving depths."
—*Robert Fagles, Princeton University*

"A miracle. A lesson in the art of translation and a model (an encyclopedia) for poets. The full range and richness of American English is displayed as perhaps never before."—*Charles Simic*

The Divine Comedy of
DANTE ALIGHIERI

PARADISO

A Verse Translation

with an Introduction

by Allen Mandelbaum

Notes by Anthony Oldcorn
and Daniel Feldman,
with Giuseppe Di Scipio

Drawings by Barry Moser

BANTAM CLASSIC

THE DIVINE COMEDY: PARADISO
A Bantam Book

PUBLISHING HISTORY

The Divine Comedy of Dante Alighieri, translated by Allen Mandelbaum, is published in hardcover by the University of California Press: *Volume I, Inferno* (1980); *Volume II, Purgatorio* (1981); *Volume III, Paradiso* (1982). Of the three separate volumes of commentary under the general editorship of Allen Mandelbaum, Anthony Oldcorn, and Charles Ross, *Volume I: The California Lectura Dantis: Inferno* was published by the University of California Press in 1998. For information, please address University of California Press, 2223 Fulton St., Berkeley, CA 94720.

Bantam Classic edition published February 1986
Bantam Classic reissue edition / August 2004

Published by
Bantam Dell
A Division of Random House, Inc.
New York, New York

ISBN 0-553-21204-4

Manufactured in the United States of America
Published simultaneously in Canada

BVGM   38

This translation of the PARADISO *is inscribed to*
Toni Burbank and Stanley Holwitz,
whose DOPPIO LUME S'ADDUA

CONTENTS

INTRODUCTION

P*aradiso* is a poem of spectacle, of wheeling shapes that enter and exit, form, re-form, and dis-form; of voices that discourse out of their faceless flames; of letters and words spelled out across the heavens by living lights in flight; of flames that shape the remarkable Eagle; of the vast amphitheater of the Celestial Rose in the tenth and final heaven, the Empyrean, where the blessed range in carefully orchestrated ranks.

That expanse is such that when, some two-thirds of the way through Paradise, the voyager turns his gaze back and downward toward the earth, he sees (XXII, 134–135 and 148–152):

> *... this globe in such a way that I*
> *smiled at its scrawny image ...*

> *And all the seven heavens showed to me*
> *their magnitudes, their speeds, the distances*
> *of each from each. The little threshing floor*
> *that so incites our savagery was all—*
> *from hills to river mouths—revealed to me ...*

Such cosmic expanse and order does admit of likeness to spacious waters (I, 112–117):

> *Therefore, these natures move to different ports*
> *across the mighty sea of being, each*
> *given the impulse that will bear it on.*
> *This impulse carries fire to the moon;*
> *this is the motive force in mortal creatures;*
> *this binds the earth together, makes it one.*

But that expanse does not allow us solitude or intimacy—with one exception: our intimate entry into the making of the poem, into the atelier, forge, foundry, workshop, mind and heart, of the maker-orchestrator.

Here we find the exilic despair that was so imperative a source of the energies and exhilaration of a work unlike anything Dante had completed before. That despair forms the bitter part of the burden of the prophecy he hears from his ancestor, Cacciaguida, at the center of *Paradiso* (XVII, 55–60):

> *"You shall leave everything you love most dearly:*
> *this is the arrow that the bow of exile*
> *shoots first. You are to know the bitter taste*
> *of others' bread, how salt it is, and know*
> *how hard a path it is for one who goes*
> *descending and ascending others' stairs."*

And here we find the pride that this terminal *cantica* engenders, Dante's sense of the uniqueness of this work as against any wrought prior to him (II, 7–9 and XIX, 7–9):

> *The waves I take were never sailed before;*
> *Minerva breathes, Apollo pilots me,*
> *and the nine Muses show to me the Bears.*

> *And what I now must tell has never been*
> *reported by a voice, inscribed by ink,*
> *never conceived by the imagination...*

There is pride—and there is the nakedly buoyant, joyous presumption, and even fleeting complacency, of one who contemplates not only from the heights (as in XXII, 148–152, above) but also savors the height itself (XI, 1–12):

> *O senseless cares of mortals, how deceiving*
> *are syllogistic reasonings that bring*
> *your wings to flight so low, to earthly things!*
> *One studied law and one the Aphorisms*

of the physicians; one was set on priesthood
and one, through force or fraud, on rulership;
one meant to plunder, one to politick;
one labored, tangled in delights of flesh,
and one was fully bent on indolence;
while I, delivered from our servitude
to all these things, was in the height of heaven
with Beatrice, so gloriously welcomed.

And in Dante's envisioning of this ever-widening expanse—so unlike the ever-narrowing hellish voyage to the deepest pit, and the hopeful, ever-narrowing voyage to the Mount of Purgatory's summit—we are asked to share the travail of the writer, the constraints and limits of speech and memory, as he struggles with magnitudes. Time and time again, the very scribe who tells us (X, 22–27):

Now, reader, do not leave your bench, but stay
to think on that of which you have foretaste;
you will have much delight before you tire.
I have prepared your fare; now feed yourself,
because that matter of which I am made
the scribe calls all my care unto itself.

also asks us to enter—intimately—into his cares and concerns at his own bench. But each of the chimings on obstacles and barriers, on the immensity of the task, on its impossibility, only serves to magnify the dimensions and intensity of the vision—whether it be the vision of the smile of Beatrice, or of the happiness of St. Peter coming to greet Beatrice, or of the mystery of the Incarnation.

The full force of these visions rests in and rises from the temporal shapes and duration of fabulation in the *Comedy,* a long poem, long in the time of its making ("this work so shared by heaven and by earth/ that it has made me lean through these long years," XXV, 2–3). But Dante's leaps and lapses in the making of *Paradiso,* the gyres and wheelings of his dervishing desk, do offer, in themselves, another "strange sight" (XXXIII,

136), an extraordinary spectacle, a vision of the cunning yet transparent place of Dante's own incarnating (I, 4–9; XXIII, 55–63; XXIV, 25–27; XXX, 22–33; XXXIII, 55–57, 58–63, 106–108, 121–123):

> I was within the heaven that receives
> more of His light; and I saw things that he
> who from that height descends, forgets or can
> not speak; for nearing its desired end,
> our intellect sinks into an abyss
> so deep that memory fails to follow it.
>
> If all the tongues that Polyhymnia
> together with her sisters made most rich
> with sweetest milk, should come now to assist
> my singing of the holy smile that lit
> the holy face of Beatrice, the truth
> would not be reached—not its one-thousandth part.
> And thus, in representing Paradise,
> the sacred poem has to leap across,
> as does a man who finds his path cut off.
>
> My pen leaps over it; I do not write:
> our fantasy and, all the more so, speech
> are far too gross for painting folds so deep.
>
> I yield: I am defeated at this passage
> more than a comic or a tragic poet
> has ever been by a barrier in his theme;
> for like the sun that strikes the frailest eyes,
> so does the memory of her sweet smile
> deprive me of the use of my own mind.
> From that first day when, in this life, I saw
> her face, until I had this vision, no
> thing ever cut the sequence of my song,
> but now I must desist from this pursuit,
> in verses, of her loveliness, just as
> each artist who has reached his limit must.
> From that point on, what I could see was greater

than speech can show: at such a sight, it fails—
and memory fails when faced with such excess.

As one who sees within a dream, and, later,
the passion that had been imprinted stays,
but nothing of the rest returns to mind,
such am I, for my vision almost fades
completely, yet it still distills within
my heart the sweetness that was born of it.

What little I recall is to be told,
from this point on, in words more weak than those
of one whose infant tongue still bathes at the breast.

How incomplete is speech, how weak, when set
against my thought! And this, to what I saw
is such—to call it little is too much.

Much, of course, is tellable, is chartable. We, seated at our benches, intent on Dante's dervishing, may have at hand both the *Paradiso* and a gazetteer for sedentaries therefor, a gazetteer with seven entries for the seven heavenly bodies that were considered planets (and Dante will also call the planets stars)—Moon, Mercury, Venus, Sun, Mars, Jupiter, Saturn. Three additional entries would cover the Eighth Heaven or Sphere of the Fixed Stars, those stars that are invariant in their position in relation to each other; the Ninth Heaven, the "swiftest of the spheres" (I, 123) and "matter's largest sphere" (XXX, 38), the Primum Mobile, the primal source of motion for all the eight spheres that lie below and within it; and the Tenth Heaven, the Empyrean, a Christian addition to the gazetteer, a heaven not envisioned by Ptolemy, Alfraganus, or Alpetragius. This gazetteer—except for the entry under the Empyrean—may well be subject to the cavil muttered by another exile, Osip Mandelstam: "The Middle Ages...did not fit into the Ptolemaic system: they took refuge there."

But Dante's refuge is also ours: a way to scan his journey in space, riprap or calculated scaffold, a frame of composition in which he and we can rest, as he labors at the fundamental, experimental, scribal trial and task: invention. We can see the invented becoming memory as it is made, and we can also see Dante outreading readers, conjuring his being remembered in a future. The energy of his invention informs the words of Mandelstam:

> Dante is an antimodernist. His contemporaneity is inexhaustible, measureless, and unending.... It is unthinkable to read the cantos of Dante without aiming them in the direction of the present day. They were made for that. They are missiles for capturing the future. They demand the commentary of the *futurum*.

We, bruised by this incredibly cruel century, are part, a small part of that future, and Dante is concerned for his place among us. That concern and desire are momentarily shadowed by his fear that too much truth may offend the readers of his own age. But that shadow is quickly dispelled; for Dante to compromise his words would lose, for him, fame, honor, audience, in the future (XVII, 118–120):

> *"Yet if I am a timid friend of truth,*
> *I fear that I may lose my life among*
> *those who will call this present, ancient times."*

Thus, he holds fast to Cacciaguida's injunction (XVII, 127–134):

> *"Nevertheless, all falsehood set aside,*
> *let all that you have seen be manifest,*
> *and let them scratch wherever it may itch.*
> *For if, at the first taste, your words molest,*
> *they will, when they have been digested, end*
> *as living nourishment. As does the wind,*
> *so shall your outcry do—the wind that sends*
> *its roughest blows against the highest peaks . . ."*

We, too, as part of the future, are asked by Dante to measure our fitness as readers, to measure our hungering for the fare that he calls the "bread of angels" (II, 1–6 and 10–15):

O you who are within your little bark,
eager to listen, following behind
my ship that, singing, crosses to deep seas,
turn back to see your shores again: do not
attempt to sail the seas I sail; you may,
by losing sight of me, be left astray.

You other few who turned your minds in time
unto the bread of angels, which provides
men here with life—but hungering for more—
you may indeed commit your vessel to
the deep salt-sea, keeping your course within
my wake, ahead of where waves smooth again.

In a literal sense, we may fall short. For to have turned to the "bread of angels" means, in the most probable "translation" of Dante's metaphorical use of biblical manna, to have begun the study of speculative theology. Such study is less than frequent today, such disciplined recognition and schooling of a hungering that can only be fully appeased with the enlightenment found in the beatific vision proper to the angels—and perhaps not even to them.

But the "bread of angels" as object of the hungering of the mind for meaning involves "a reachless goal," a search that must for us, here—and even for the Seraphim there—collide with mystery (XXI, 91–99):

"But even Heaven's most enlightened soul,
that Seraph with his eye most set on God,
could not provide the why, not satisfy
what you have asked; for deep in the abyss
of the Eternal Ordinance, it is
cut off from all created beings' vision.
And to the mortal world, when you return,

> *tell this, lest men continue to trespass*
> *and set their steps toward such a reachless goal."*

And if "we cannot satisfy/ our mind unless it is enlightened by/ the truth beyond whose boundary no truth lies" (IV, 124–126), then Dante would accord with Stevens's assessment of our earthly situation: "It can never be satisfied, the mind, never."

That collision with mystery, that dissatisfaction of the mind—we do know. It is from this earth that we turn to the "bread of angels," and upon this earth that Dante envisions. That "bread" is also the bread of desire and of the forms that longing engenders. It is the manna that all of us receive in act and memory, the manna of days and nights of grace that lies beyond any algebra of merits.

Now we can set aside the gazetteer. Now we can share the hungering. We, in this future, may lack the resolution and independence of Dante, but we certainly share his metamorphic vicissitudes, the mutabilities of a man who defines himself as one "who by my very nature am/ given to every sort of change" (V, 98–99). And when the changing Dante appropriates, it is not only the mediators of antiquity, the gods and muses of his invocations, whom he calls upon; he also appropriates our age, the future angels of Rilke and of Stevens; and he even appropriates the still nameless poets of the future (I, 34–36):

> *Great fire can follow a small spark: there may*
> *be better voices after me to pray*
> *to Cyrrha's god for aid—that he may answer.*

That future also includes the future of the poet after the completion of the poem. For though Dante's *Paradiso* is completed near the end of his life, his poem is not equatable with his life. And in the opening of the final canto we are to share the sense of poetry as prayer—as vocative that pleads not only for the present need to reach, to see, but also for help in persevering, in living after the envisioning. The prayer of Bernard of Clairvaux to Mary, "Virgin mother, daughter of your Son," after fixing her place as centerpoint in universal time, turns to the needs of *"this* man," Dante (XXXIII, 19–36):

> *"In you compassion is, in you is pity,*
> *in you is generosity, in you*
> *is every goodness found in any creature.*
> *This man—who from the deepest hollow in*
> *the universe, up to this height, has seen*
> *the lives of spirits, one by one—now pleads*
> *with you, through grace, to grant him so much virtue*
> *that he may lift his vision higher still—*
> *may lift it toward the ultimate salvation.*
> *And I, who never burned for my own vision*
> *more than I burn for his, do offer you*
> *all of my prayers—and pray that they may not*
> *fall short—that, with your prayers, you may disperse*
> *all of the clouds of his mortality*
> *so that the Highest Joy be his to see.*
> *This, too, o Queen, who can do what you would,*
> *I ask of you: that after such a vision,*
> *his sentiments preserve their perseverance."*

That Saint Bernard should be the speaker here, and that this prayer should occupy so privileged a place in *Paradiso*—these attest to the complex conjoining in Dante of two often diverging paths: the path of intellect and the path of love.

Dante inhabits and inherits the extraordinary intellectual edifice, foreshadowed a century earlier by Abelard, that finds its culmination in the university life and institutions of thirteenth-century Paris. His Ulysses in the *Inferno* may indeed represent Dante's recoiling from the very limits that the ultimate exaltation of intellect may reach, extend, transgress.

Against Abelard and that nascent reason-able tradition stood his ferocious adversary Bernard, emblem of the rich expansion of the language of God-directed love, in which the theologians outdo all poets before—and often including—Dante. That line exalts affection, the ardor of God-seeking.

Aquinas had already charted the erotics of knowing with enduring precision: he had already wed intellect and affect. But in Aquinas, Dante could never have found so central a place for the feminine protagonist of affect: Mary. And in Aquinas, he could certainly not have found his incarnate Beatrice. Beatrice, of course, also shares the modes of argumentation, the instruments of the "other"—intellectual—tradition. If not Theology or Sacred Science itself, she is a confident theologian. But she is, too, a feminine apparition—yet not an icon or idol. She is the living daughter of Memory and Affection.

Mary herself, before Bernard's prayer, had been evoked by Dante in the present tense of the writer writing of his life on our earth, outside the poem of Paradise, in lines that are no less memorable than Bernard's prayer to Mary: "The name of that fair flower which I always/ invoke, at morning and at evening..." (XXIII, 88–89), where that fair flower is Mary, the Rosa Mystica, the Mary of the Rosary and "the Rose in which the Word of God became/ flesh" (XXIII, 73–74).

And when Dante evokes Beatrice in Canto XXIII, he finally brings to bear on her two earthly likenesses most dear to him, the maternal and the ornithological, here joined to his stupendous string of dawn and pre-dawn scenes (XXIII, 1–15):

As does the bird, among beloved branches,
when, through the night that hides things from us, she
has rested near the nest of her sweet fledglings
and, on an open branch, anticipates
the time when she can see their longed-for faces
and find the food with which to feed them—chore
that pleases her, however hard her labors—
as she awaits the sun with warm affection,
steadfastly watching for the dawn to break:
so did my lady stand, erect, intent,
turned toward that part of heaven under which
the sun is given to less haste; so that,
as I saw her in longing and suspense,

I grew to be as one who, while he wants
what is not his, is satisfied with hope.

Along the way to Beatrice as bird among "beloved branches," along the way to Bernard's prayer, we are asked to share the work of a maker who is ever conscious that the praise and enactment of music or dance are auto-celebrations of the movement of verse itself (even as Milton was in praising Harry Lawes, or Hopkins in praising the "colossal smile" of Henry Purcell, or Fray Luis in praising Salinas). A maker conscious, too, that verse can mime the movement of the soul in joyous love (XIV, 19–24):

As dancers in a ring, when drawn and driven
by greater gladness, lift at times their voices
and dance their dance with more exuberance,
so, when they heard that prompt, devout request,
the blessed circles showed new joyousness
in wheeling dance and in amazing song.

That "amazing song" is sung in a poem that, may, in program, claim to be a timeless poem. *Paradiso* may be intent on the vision of the everlasting, a poem that sees—apparently— what are the simultaneous presences of the blessed in the Empyrean stretched out over time and space only to accommodate Dante's earthly eyes (IV, 37–45):

"They showed themselves to you here not because
this is their sphere, but as a sign for you
that in the Empyrean their place is lowest.
Such signs are suited to your mind, since from
the senses only can it apprehend
what then becomes fit for the intellect.
And this is why the Bible condescends
to human powers, assigning feet and hands
to God, but meaning something else instead."

Yet Dante does not hesitate to glory in the timing mechanism of the clock and in seeing in its machinery the movement of music, of dance, of the time-borne verse line itself, and of the spirit's growth in love (X, 139–148 and XXIV, 13–18):

Then, like a clock that calls us at the hour
in which the bride of God, on waking, sings
matins to her Bridegroom, encouraging
His love (when each clock-part both drives and draws),
chiming the sounds with notes so sweet that those
with spirit well-disposed feel their love grow;
so did I see the wheel that moved in glory
go round and render voice to voice with such
sweetness and such accord that they can not
be known except where joy is everlasting.

And just as, in a clock's machinery,
to one who watches them, the wheels turn so
that, while the first wheel seems to rest, the last
wheel flies; so did those circling dancers—as
they danced to different measures, swift and slow—
make me a judge of what their riches were.

And on the way to Bernard's prayer we will also find that our sympathy with Dante's metamorphic nature has been instructed in one specific way of change within his book of changes: the use of multiple possibilities as instruments and way stations in the conversion of the self to an integral presence (not unakin to Saint Augustine's: "Love made me what I am, that I may be what I was not before"). Variety and vicissitude—even exile—may be the apprenticeship and bondage needed before the freedom of oneness can be reached. (And perhaps this mode of metamorphosis is not that un-Ovidian. Did not Ovid himself beseech a "seamless" way in his incipit?

My soul would sing of metamorphoses,
but since, o gods, you were the source of these
bodies becoming other bodies, breathe
your breath into my book of changes: may
the song I sing be seamless as its way
weaves from the world's beginning to our day.)

To that end, the *"io sol uno,"* "I myself/ alone," of *Inferno* (II, 3–4) extends through "I crown and miter you over yourself" of *Purgatorio* (XXVII, 142) to—now in a political context—Dante's best party as his own "self" at the end of the prophecy by Cacciaguida, Dante's ancestor (XVII, 61–69):

> *"And what will be most hard for you to bear*
> *will be the scheming, senseless company*
> *that is to share your fall into this valley;*
> *against you they will be insane, completely*
> *ungrateful and profane; and yet, soon after,*
> *not you but they will have their brows bloodred.*
> *Of their insensate acts, the proof will be*
> *in the effects; and thus, your honor will*
> *be best kept if your party is your self."*

That self finds an almost obsessively narcissistic model in the image of the Three-in-One of the Trinity toward the end of Canto XXXIII (124–126):

> *Eternal Light, You only dwell within*
> *Yourself, and only You know You; Self-knowing,*
> *Self-known, You love and smile upon Yourself!*

But the vast population of the *Comedy* is proof against the claustrophobia of that model, as is Dante's gratefulness in the *Paradiso* to the otherness of Beatrice. Her otherness made possible his engendering the *Paradiso,* even as the otherness of Virgil nurtured the making of *Inferno* and *Purgatorio.* The Paradisiac gratitude of Dante to Beatrice stands in a diptych with his valediction to Virgil *(Purg.* XXX, 43–54), even as her silent smile complements the silent smile of Virgil in the Earthly Paradise, in *Purgatorio,* XXVIII, 147 *(Par.* XXXI, 79–93):

> *"O lady, you in whom my hope gains strength,*
> *you who, for my salvation, have allowed*
> *your footsteps to be left in Hell, in all*
> *the things that I have seen, I recognize*

the grace and benefit that I, depending
upon your power and goodness, have received.
You drew me out from slavery to freedom
by all those paths, by all those means that were
within your power. Do, in me, preserve
your generosity, so that my soul,
which you have healed, when it is set loose from
my body, be a soul that you will welcome."
So did I pray. And she, however far
away she seemed, smiled, and she looked at me.
Then she turned back to the eternal fountain.

Even as the smile of Beatrice and Dante's gratitude were—earlier—condensed in one of the rare passages in *Paradiso* where Dante is likened to a dreamer (XXIII, 49–54):

I was as one who, waking from a dream
he has forgotten, tries in vain to bring
that vision back into his memory,
when I heard what she offered me, deserving
of so much gratitude that it can never
be canceled from the book that tells the past.

———

I am no less indebted now, completing this translation of the *Comedy,* to those already acknowledged in the *Inferno* and *Purgatorio* volumes, not least to Laury Magnus, whose *"anima ... più di me degna"* overlooked one who was "drawn and driven" from the *"selva oscura"* through to "new trees ... renewed when they bring forth new boughs."

But the *Paradiso* translation was completed under somewhat charred circumstances. In this time, those who have *"[i]mparadisa[to] la mia mente"* and my gazetteer were: Gigliola and Donatella Nocera and their parents in Siracusa, where their Ortygia offered me a blessed stay; Pieraldo Vola in Rome; and Olga and Vittore Branca in Venice. West of the Mississippi, there were the Zwickers and Stangs of St. Louis, the Bassoffs of Boulder, the Richardsons and Feldmans of

Denver, the Estesses and Bernards of Houston, and Nanette Heiman of San Francisco. Eastward of the Mississippi: the Alcalays; Leonard and Rayma Feldman; Leon and Peggy Gold; Gale Sigal and Walter Stiller; K. S. Rust; the Austers; Henry Weinfield and Joyce Block; Thomas Harrison; Leon Gottfried; Anthony Oldcorn, Charles Ross, Teodolinda Barolini, and Giuseppe Di Scipio, colleagues whose work on the *Lectura Dantis* volumes freed me for these ten spheres; the Hanses; the Marianis; and Joseph Marbach, a truly Hippocratic physician *"che natura/ a li animali fé ch'ell' ha più cari."*

After the death of my mother, Leah Gordon Mandelbaum, at the completion of this work, Ely Pilchik provided unexpected Paradisiac consolation, as did shared readings with my seminar at the Graduate Center.

The visit of Mario Luzi to the States—so warmly abetted by Jon Snyder and Francesca Valente—focused much for us both in mulling on magma and metamorphosis. Anne Greenberg, Cecilia Hunt, and Daniel Feldman nurtured editorially beyond anything my *ruminare* and *vanare* could conjure. For Barry Moser, Michael Bixler, Czeslaw Jan Grycz, and myself, the road of this bookmaking has indeed been such that *dicer, cor,* and labor "shared one way." The most tenacious tutelary spirits, whose "double lights" gave me the strength to see The End, share the dedication of this book; New York to Los Angeles spans much less than their *magnificenza* does.

In Valbonne and Mougins, Elisa and Nicholas, grandchildren whose "differing voices join to sound sweet music," were joined in turn by Margherita, Jonathan, and Anne in amply providing the "bread of angels."

The Graduate Center   Allen Mandelbaum
of the City University of New York
May, 1984

PARADISO

PARADISO

CANTO I

La gloria di colui che tutto move
    per l'universo penetra, e risplende
in una parte più e meno altrove.

Nel ciel che più de la sua luce prende   4
fu' io, e vidi cose che ridire
né sa né può chi di là sù discende;

perché appressando sé al suo disire,   7
nostro intelletto si profonda tanto,
che dietro la memoria non può ire.

Veramente quant' io del regno santo   10
ne la mia mente potei far tesoro,
sarà ora materia del mio canto.

O buono Appollo, a l'ultimo lavoro   13
fammi del tuo valor sì fatto vaso,
come dimandi a dar l'amato alloro.

Infino a qui l'un giogo di Parnaso   16
assai mi fu; ma or con amendue
m'è uopo intrar ne l'aringo rimaso.

Entra nel petto mio, e spira tue   19
sì come quando Marsïa traesti
de la vagina de le membra sue.

O divina virtù, se mi ti presti   22
tanto che l'ombra del beato regno
segnata nel mio capo io manifesti,

vedra'mi al piè del tuo diletto legno   25
venire, e coronarmi de le foglie
che la materia e tu mi farai degno.

Sì rade volte, padre, se ne coglie   28
per trïunfare o cesare o poeta,
colpa e vergogna de l'umane voglie,

Proem and Invocation to Apollo. Dante's passing beyond the human, beyond the earth, in heavenward ascent with Beatrice. His wonder. Beatrice on the Empyrean and the order of the universe.

The glory of the One who moves all things
   permeates the universe and glows
in one part more and in another less.

   I was within the heaven that receives   4
more of His light; and I saw things that he
who from that height descends, forgets or can

   not speak; for nearing its desired end,   7
our intellect sinks into an abyss
so deep that memory fails to follow it.

   Nevertheless, as much as I, within   10
my mind, could treasure of the holy kingdom
shall now become the matter of my song.

   O good Apollo, for this final task   13
make me the vessel of your excellence,
what you, to merit your loved laurel, ask.

   Until this point, one of Parnassus' peaks   16
sufficed for me; but now I face the test,
the agon that is left; I need both crests.

   Enter into my breast; within me breathe   19
the very power you made manifest
when you drew Marsyas out from his limbs' sheath.

   O godly force, if you so lend yourself   22
to me, that I might show the shadow of
the blessed realm inscribed within my mind,

   then you would see me underneath the tree   25
you love; there I shall take as crown the leaves
of which my theme and you shall make me worthy.

   So seldom, father, are those garlands gathered 28
for triumph of a ruler or a poet—
a sign of fault or shame in human wills—

che parturir letizia in su la lieta 31
delfica deïtà dovria la fronda
peneia, quando alcun di sé asseta.

Poca favilla gran fiamma seconda: 34
forse di retro a me con miglior voci
si pregherà perché Cirra risponda.

Surge ai mortali per diverse foci 37
la lucerna del mondo; ma da quella
che quattro cerchi giugne con tre croci,

con miglior corso e con migliore stella 40
esce congiunta, e la mondana cera
più a suo modo tempera e suggella.

Fatto avea di là mane e di qua sera 43
tal foce, e quasi tutto era là bianco
quello emisperio, e l'altra parte nera,

quando Beatrice in sul sinistro fianco 46
vidi rivolta e riguardar nel sole:
aguglia sì non li s'affisse unquanco.

E sì come secondo raggio suole 49
uscir del primo e risalire in suso,
pur come pelegrin che tornar vuole,

così de l'atto suo, per li occhi infuso 52
ne l'imagine mia, il mio si fece,
e fissi li occhi al sole oltre nostr' uso.

Molto è licito là, che qui non lece 55
a le nostre virtù, mercé del loco
fatto per proprio de l'umana spece.

Io nol soffersi molto, né sì poco, 58
ch'io nol vedessi sfavillar dintorno,
com' ferro che bogliente esce del foco;

e di sùbito parve giorno a giorno 61
essere aggiunto, come quei che puote
avesse il ciel d'un altro sole addorno.

Beatrice tutta ne l'etterne rote 64
fissa con li occhi stava; e io in lei
le luci fissi, di là sù rimote.

Nel suo aspetto tal dentro mi fei, 67
qual si fé Glauco nel gustar de l'erba
che 'l fé consorto in mar de li altri dèi.

that when Peneian branches can incite 31
someone to long and thirst for them, delight
must fill the happy Delphic deity.

Great fire can follow a small spark: there may 34
be better voices after me to pray
to Cyrrha's god for aid—that he may answer.

The lantern of the world approaches mortals 37
by varied paths: but on that way which links
four circles with three crosses, it emerges

joined to a better constellation and 40
along a better course, and it can temper
and stamp the world's wax more in its own manner.

Its entry from that point of the horizon 43
brought morning there and evening here; almost
all of that hemisphere was white—while ours

was dark—when I saw Beatrice turn round 46
and left, that she might see the sun: no eagle
has ever stared so steadily at it.

And as a second ray will issue from 49
the first and reascend, much like a pilgrim
who seeks his home again, so on her action,

fed by my eyes to my imagination, 52
my action drew, and on the sun I set
my sight more than we usually do.

More is permitted to our powers there 55
than is permitted here, by virtue of
that place, made for mankind as its true home.

I did not bear it long, but not so briefly 58
as not to see it sparkling round about,
like molten iron emerging from the fire;

and suddenly it seemed that day had been 61
added to day, as if the One who can
had graced the heavens with a second sun.

The eyes of Beatrice were all intent 64
on the eternal circles; from the sun,
I turned aside: I set my eyes on her.

In watching her, within me I was changed 67
as Glaucus changed, tasting the herb that made
him a companion of the other sea gods.

Trasumanar significar *per verba*   70
non si poria; però l'essemplo basti
a cui esperïenza grazia serba.

S'i' era sol di me quel che creasti   73
novellamente, amor che 'l ciel governi,
tu 'l sai, che col tuo lume mi levasti.

Quando la rota che tu sempiterni   76
desiderato, a sé mi fece atteso
con l'armonia che temperi e discerni,

parvemi tanto allor del cielo acceso   79
de la fiamma del sol, che pioggia o fiume
lago non fece alcun tanto disteso.

La novità del suono e 'l grande lume   82
di lor cagion m'accesero un disio
mai non sentito di cotanto acume.

Ond' ella, che vedea me sì com' io,   85
a quïetarmi l'animo commosso,
pria ch'io a dimandar, la bocca aprio

e cominciò: "Tu stesso ti fai grosso   88
col falso imaginar, sì che non vedi
ciò che vedresti se l'avessi scosso.

Tu non se' in terra, sì come tu credi;   91
ma folgore, fuggendo il proprio sito,
non corse come tu ch'ad esso riedi."

S'io fui del primo dubbio disvestito   94
per le sorrise parolette brevi,
dentro ad un nuovo più fu' inretito

e dissi: "Già contento *requievi*   97
di grande ammirazion; ma ora ammiro
com' io trascenda questi corpi levi."

Ond' ella, appresso d'un pïo sospiro,   100
li occhi drizzò ver' me con quel sembiante
che madre fa sovra figlio deliro,

e cominciò: "Le cose tutte quante   103
hanno ordine tra loro, e questo è forma
che l'universo a Dio fa simigliante.

Qui veggion l'alte creature l'orma   106
de l'etterno valore, il qual è fine
al quale è fatta la toccata norma.

Passing beyond the human cannot be   70
worded: let Glaucus serve as simile—
until grace grant you the experience.

Whether I only was the part of me   73
that You created last, You—governing
the heavens—know: it was Your light that raised me.

When that wheel which You make eternal through   76
the heavens' longing for You drew me with
the harmony You temper and distinguish,

the fire of the sun then seemed to me   79
to kindle so much of the sky, that rain
or river never formed so broad a lake.

The newness of the sound and the great light   82
incited me to learn their cause—I was
more keen than I had ever been before.

And she who read me as I read myself,   85
to quiet the commotion in my mind,
opened her lips before I opened mine

to ask, and she began: "You make yourself   88
obtuse with false imagining; you can
not see what you would see if you dispelled it.

You are not on the earth as you believe;   91
but lightning, flying from its own abode,
is less swift than you are, returning home."

While I was freed from my first doubt by these   94
brief words she smiled to me, I was yet caught
in new perplexity. I said: "I was

content already; after such great wonder,   97
I rested. But again I wonder how
my body rises past these lighter bodies."

At which, after a sigh of pity, she   100
settled her eyes on me with the same look
a mother casts upon a raving child,

and she began: "All things, among themselves,   103
possess an order; and this order is
the form that makes the universe like God.

Here do the higher beings see the imprint   106
of the Eternal Worth, which is the end
to which the pattern I have mentioned tends.

Ne l'ordine ch'io dico sono accline   109
tutte nature, per diverse sorti,
più al principio loro e men vicine;

onde si muovono a diversi porti   112
per lo gran mar de l'essere, e ciascuna
con istinto a lei dato che la porti.

Questi ne porta il foco inver' la luna;   115
questi ne' cor mortali è permotore;
questi la terra in sé stringe e aduna;

né pur le creature che son fore   118
d'intelligenza quest' arco saetta,
ma quelle c'hanno intelletto e amore.

La provedenza, che cotanto assetta,   121
del suo lume fa 'l ciel sempre quïeto
nel qual si volge quel c'ha maggior fretta;

e ora lì, come a sito decreto,   124
cen porta la virtù di quella corda
che ciò che scocca drizza in segno lieto.

Vero è che, come forma non s'accorda   127
molte fïate a l'intenzion de l'arte,
perch' a risponder la materia è sorda,

così da qesto corso si diparte   130
talor la creatura, c'ha podere
di piegar, così pinta, in altra parte;

e sì come veder si può cadere   133
foco di nube, sì l'impeto primo
l'atterra torto da falso piacere.

Non dei più ammirar, se bene stimo,   136
lo tuo salir, se non come d'un rivo
se d'alto monte scende giuso ad imo.

Maraviglia sarebbe in te se, privo   139
d'impedimento, giù ti fossi assiso,
com' a terra quïete in foco vivo."

Quinci rivolse inver' lo cielo il viso.   142

Within that order, every nature has   109
its bent, according to a different station,
nearer or less near to its origin.

Therefore, these natures move to different ports   112
across the mighty sea of being, each
given the impulse that will bear it on.

This impulse carries fire to the moon: 115
this is the motive force in mortal creatures:
this binds the earth together, makes it one.

Not only does the shaft shot from this bow   118
strike creatures lacking intellect, but those
who have intelligence, and who can love.

The Providence that has arrayed all this   121
forever quiets—with Its light—that heaven
in which the swiftest of the spheres revolves;

to there, as toward a destined place, we now   124
are carried by the power of the bow
that always aims its shaft at a glad mark.

Yet it is true that, even as a shape   127
may, often, not accord with art's intent,
since matter may be unresponsive, deaf,

so, from this course, the creature strays at times   130
because he has the power, once impelled,
to swerve elsewhere; as lightning from a cloud

is seen to fall, so does the first impulse,   133
when man has been diverted by false pleasure,
turn him toward earth. You should—if I am right—

not feel more marvel at your climbing than   136
you would were you considering a stream
that from a mountain's height falls to its base.

It would be cause for wonder in you if,   139
no longer hindered, you remained below,
as if, on earth, a living flame stood still."

Then she again turned her gaze heavenward.   142

Beatrice

The Sun

CANTO II

O voi che siete in piccioletta barca,
   desiderosi d'ascoltar, seguiti
dietro al mio legno che cantando varca,

   tornate a riveder li vostri liti: 4
non vi mettete in pelago, ché forse,
perdendo me, rimarreste smarriti.

   L'acqua ch'io prendo già mai non si corse;   7
Minerva spira, e conducemi Appollo,
e nove Muse mi dimostran l'Orse.

   Voialtri pochi che drizzaste il collo   10
per tempo al pan de li angeli, del quale
vivesi qui ma non sen vien satollo,

   metter potete ben per l'alto sale   13
vostro navigio, servando mio solco
dinanzi a l'acqua che ritorna equale.

   Que' glorïosi che passaro al Colco   16
non s'ammiraron come voi farete,
quando Iasón vider fatto bifolco.

   La concreata e perpetüa sete   19
del deïforme regno cen portava
veloci quasi come 'l ciel vedete.

   Beatrice in suso, e io in lei guardava;   22
e forse in tanto in quanto un quadrel posa
e vola e da la noce si dischiava,

   giunto mi vidi ove mirabil cosa   25
mi torse il viso a sé; e però quella
cui non potea mia cura essere ascosa,

   volta ver' me, sì lieta come bella,   28
"Drizza la mente in Dio grata," mi disse,
"che n'ha congiunti con la prima stella."

Address to the reader. Arrival in the First Heaven, the Sphere of the Moon. Beatrice's vigorous confutation of Dante, who thinks that rarity and density are the causes of the spots we see on the body of the Moon.

O you who are within your little bark,
   eager to listen, following behind
my ship that, singing, crosses to deep seas,

   turn back to see your shores again: do not   4
attempt to sail the seas I sail: you may,
by losing sight of me, be left astray.

   The waves I take were never sailed before;   7
Minerva breathes, Apollo pilots me,
and the nine Muses show to me the Bears.

   You other few who turned your minds in time   10
unto the bread of angels, which provides
men here with life—but hungering for more—

   you may indeed commit your vessel to   13
the deep salt-sea, keeping your course within
my wake, ahead of where waves smooth again.

   Those men of glory, those who crossed to Colchis,   16
when they saw Jason turn into a ploughman
were less amazed than you will be amazed.

   The thirst that is innate and everlasting—   19
thirst for the godly realm—bore us away
as swiftly as the heavens that you see.

   Beatrice gazed upward. I watched her.   22
But in a span perhaps no longer than
an arrow takes to strike, to fly, to leave

   the bow, I reached a place where I could see   25
that something wonderful drew me; and she
from whom my need could not be hidden, turned

   to me (her gladness matched her loveliness):   28
"Direct your mind to God in gratefulness,"
she said; "He has brought us to the first star."

Parev' a me che nube ne coprisse   31
lucida, spessa, solida e pulita,
quasi adamante che lo sol ferisse.

Per entro sé l'etterna margarita   34
ne ricevette, com' acqua recepe
raggio di luce permanendo unita.

S'io era corpo, e qui non si concepe   37
com' una dimensione altra patio,
ch'esser convien se corpo in corpo repe,

accender ne dovria più il disio   40
di veder quella essenza in che si vede
come nostra natura e Dio s'unio.

Lì si vedrà ciò che tenem per fede,   43
non dimostrato, ma fia per sé noto
a guisa del ver primo che l'uom crede.

Io rispuosi: "Madonna, sì devoto   46
com' esser posso più, ringrazio lui
lo qual dal mortal mondo m'ha remoto.

Ma ditemi: che son li segni bui   49
di questo corpo, che là giuso in terra
fan di Cain favoleggiare altrui?"

Ella sorrise alquanto, e poi "S'elli erra   52
l'oppinïon," mi disse, "d'i mortali
dove chiave di senso non diserra,

certo non ti dovrien punger li strali   55
d'ammirazione omai, poi dietro ai sensi
vedi che la ragione ha corte l'ali.

Ma dimmi quel che tu da te ne pensi."   58
E io: "Ciò che n'appar qua sù diverso
credo che fanno i corpi rari e densi."

Ed ella: "Certo assai vedrai sommerso   61
nel falso il creder tuo, se bene ascolti
l'argomentar ch'io li farò avverso.

La spera ottava vi dimostra molti   64
lumi, li quali e nel quale e nel quanto
notar si posson di diversi volti.

Se raro e denso ciò facesser tanto,   67
una sola virtù sarebbe in tutti,
più e men distribuita e altrettanto.

It seemed to me that we were covered by   31
a brilliant, solid, dense, and stainless cloud,
much like a diamond that the sun has struck.

Into itself, the everlasting pearl   34
received us, just as water will accept
a ray of light and yet remain intact.

If I was body (and on earth we can   37
not see how things material can share
one space—the case, when body enters body),

then should our longing be still more inflamed   40
to see that Essence in which we discern
how God and human nature were made one.

What we hold here by faith, shall there be seen,   43
not demonstrated but directly known,
even as the first truth that man believes.

I answered: "With the most devotion I   46
can summon, I thank Him who has brought me
far from the mortal world. But now tell me:

what are the dark marks on this planet's body   49
that there below, on earth, have made men tell
the tale of Cain?" She smiled somewhat, and then

she said: "If the opinion mortals hold   52
falls into error when the senses' key
cannot unlock the truth, you should not be

struck by the arrows of amazement once   55
you recognize that reason, even when
supported by the senses, has short wings.

But tell me what you think of it yourself."   58
And I: "What seems to us diverse up here
is caused—I think—by matter dense and rare."

And she: "You certainly will see that your   61
belief is deeply sunk in error if
you listen carefully as I rebut it.

The eighth sphere offers many lights to you,   64
and you can tell that they, in quality
and size, are stars with different visages.

If rarity and density alone   67
caused this, then all the stars would share one power
distributed in lesser, greater, or

Virtù diverse esser convegnon frutti   70
di princìpi formali, e quei, for ch'uno,
seguiterieno a tua ragion distrutti.

Ancor, se raro fosse di quel bruno   73
cagion che tu dimandi, o d'oltre in parte
fora di sua materia sì digiuno

esto pianeto, o, sì come comparte   76
lo grasso e 'l magro un corpo, così questo
nel suo volume cangerebbe carte.

Se 'l primo fosse, fora manifesto   79
ne l'eclissi del sol, per trasparere
lo lume come in altro raro ingesto.

Questo non è: però è da vedere   82
de l'altro; e s'elli avvien ch'io l'altro cassi,
falsificato fia lo tuo parere.

S'elli è che questo raro non trapassi,   85
esser conviene un termine da onde
lo suo contrario più passar non lassi;

e indi l'altrui raggio si rifonde   88
così come color torna per vetro
lo qual di retro a sé piombo nasconde.

Or dirai tu ch'el si dimostra tetro   91
ivi lo raggio più che in altre parti,
per esser lì refratto più a retro.

Da questa instanza può deliberarti   94
esperïenza, se già mai la provi,
ch'esser suol fonte ai rivi di vostr' arti.

Tre specchi prenderai; e i due rimovi   97
da te d'un modo, e l'altro, più rimosso,
tr'ambo li primi li occhi tuoi ritrovi.

Rivolto ad essi, fa che dopo il dosso   100
ti stea un lume che i tre specchi accenda
e torni a te da tutti ripercosso.

Ben che nel quanto tanto non si stenda   103
la vista più lontana, lì vedrai
come convien ch'igualmente risplenda.

Or, come ai colpi de li caldi rai   106
de la neve riman nudo il suggetto
e dal colore e dal freddo primai,

in equal force. But different powers must   70
be fruits of different formal principles;
were you correct, one only would be left,

   the rest, destroyed. And more, were rarity   73
the cause of the dim spots you question, then
in part this planet would lack matter through

   and through, or else as, in a body, lean   76
and fat can alternate, so would this planet
alternate the pages in its volume.

   To validate the first case, in the sun's   79
eclipse, the light would have to show through, just
as when it crosses matter that is slender.

   This is not so; therefore we must consider   82
the latter case—if I annul that too,
then your opinion surely is confuted.

   If rarity does not run through and through   85
the moon, then there must be a limit where
thickness does not allow the light to pass;

   from there, the rays of sun would be thrown back,   88
just as, from glass that hides lead at its back,
a ray of colored light returns, reflected.

   Now you will say that where a ray has been   91
reflected from a section farther back,
that ray will show itself to be more dim.

   Yet an experiment, were you to try it,   94
could free you from your cavil—and the source
of your arts' course springs from experiment.

   Taking three mirrors, place a pair of them   97
at equal distance from you; set the third
midway between those two, but farther back.

   Then, turning toward them, at your back have placed   100
a light that kindles those three mirrors and
returns to you, reflected by them all.

   Although the image in the farthest glass   103
will be of lesser size, there you will see
that it must match the brightness of the rest.

   Now, just as the sub-matter of the snow,   106
beneath the blows of the warm rays, is stripped
of both its former color and its cold,

  così rimaso te ne l'intelletto   109
voglio informar di luce sì vivace,
che ti tremolerà nel suo aspetto.

  Dentro dal ciel de la divina pace   112
si gira un corpo ne la cui virtute
l'esser di tutto suo contento giace.

  Lo ciel seguente, c'ha tante vedute,   115
quell' esser parte per diverse essenze,
da lui distratte e da lui contenute.

  Li altri giron per varie differenze   118
le distinzion che dentro da sé hanno
dispongono a lor fini e lor semenze.

  Questi organi del mondo così vanno,   121
come tu vedi omai, di grado in grado,
che di sù prendono e di sotto fanno.

  Riguarda bene omai sì com' io vado   124
per questo loco al vero che disiri,
sì che poi sappi sol tener lo guado.

  Lo moto e la virtù d'i santi giri,   127
come dal fabbro l'arte del martello,
da' beati motor convien che spiri;

  e 'l ciel cui tanti lumi fanno bello,   130
de la mente profonda che lui volve
prende l'image e fassene suggello.

  E come l'alma dentro a vostra polve   133
per differenti membra e conformate
a diverse potenze si risolve,

  così l'intelligenza sua bontate   136
multiplicata per le stelle spiega,
girando sé sovra sua unitate.

  Virtù diverso fa diversa lega   139
col prezïoso corpo ch'ella avviva,
nel qual, sì come vita in voi, si lega.

  Per la natura lieta onde deriva,   142
la virtù mista per lo corpo luce
come letizia per pupilla viva.

  Da essa vien ciò che da luce a luce   145
par differente, non da denso e raro;
essa è formal principio che produce,

    conforme a sua bontà, lo turbo e 'l chiaro."   148

so is your mind left bare of error; I   109
would offer now to you a new form, light
so living that it trembles in your sight.

Within the heaven of the godly peace   112
revolves a body in whose power lies
the being of all things that it enfolds.

The sphere that follows, where so much is shown,   115
to varied essences bestows that being,
to stars distinct and yet contained in it.

The other spheres, in ways diverse, direct   118
the diverse powers they possess, so that
these forces can bear fruit, attain their aims.

So do these organs of the universe   121
proceed, as you now see, from stage to stage,
receiving from above and acting downward.

Now do attend to how I pass by way   124
of reason to the truth you want that—then—
you may learn how to cross the ford alone.

The force and motion of the holy spheres   127
must be inspired by the blessed movers,
just as the smith imparts the hammer's art;

and so, from the deep Mind that makes it wheel,   130
the sphere that many lights adorn receives
that stamp of which it then becomes the seal.

And as the soul within your dust is shared   133
by different organs, each most suited to
a different potency, so does that Mind

unfold and multiply its bounty through   136
the varied heavens, though that Intellect
itself revolves upon its unity.

With the dear body that it quickens and   139
with which, as life in you, it too is bound,
each different power forms a different compound.

Because of the glad nature of its source,   142
the power mingled with a sphere shines forth,
as gladness, through the living pupil, shines.

From this, and not from matter rare or dense,   145
derive the differences from light to light;
this is the forming principle, producing,

conforming with its worth, the dark, the bright."   148

CANTO III

Quel sol che pria d'amor mi scaldò 'l petto,
   di bella verità m'avea scoverto,
provando e riprovando, il dolce aspetto;

   e io, per confessar corretto e certo   4
me stesso, tanto quanto si convenne
leva' il capo a proferer più erto;

   ma visïone apparve che ritenne   7
a sé me tanto stretto, per vedersi,
che di mia confession non mi sovvenne.

   Quali per vetri trasparenti e tersi,   10
o ver per acque nitide e tranquille,
non sì profonde che i fondi sien persi.

   tornan d'i nostri visi le postille   13
debili sì, che perla in bianca fronte
non vien men forte a le nostre pupille;

   tali vid' io più facce a parlar pronte;   16
per ch'io dentro a l'error contrario corsi
a quel ch'accese amor tra l'omo e 'l fonte.

   Sùbito sì com' io di lor m'accorsi,   19
quelle stimando specchiati sembianti,
per veder di cui fosser, li occhi torsi;

   e nulla vidi, e ritorsili avanti   22
dritti nel lume de la dolce guida,
che, sorridendo, ardea ne li occhi santi.

   "Non ti maravigliar perch' io sorrida,"   25
mi disse, "appresso il tuo püeril coto,
poi sopra 'l vero ancor lo piè non fida,

   ma te rivolve, come suole, a vòto: 28
vere sustanze son ciò che tu vedi,
qui rilegate per manco di voto.

The First Heaven: the Sphere of the Moon. Dante's first vision of the blessed. Piccarda Donati. Her explanation of the souls' place in the sphere assigned to them by God. The Moon as site of those whose vows gave way before violence. The empress Constance. Disappearance of the souls.

That sun which first had warmed my breast with love
had now revealed to me, confuting, proving,
the gentle face of truth, its loveliness;

   and I, in order to declare myself 4
corrected and convinced, lifted my head
as high as my confessional required.

   But a new vision showed itself to me; 7
the grip in which it held me was so fast
that I did not remember to confess.

   Just as, returning through transparent, clean 10
glass, or through waters calm and crystalline
(so shallow that they scarcely can reflect),

   the mirrored image of our faces meets 13
our pupils with no greater force than that
a pearl has when displayed on a white forehead—

   so faint, the many faces I saw keen 16
to speak: thus, my mistake was contrary
to that which led the man to love the fountain.

   As soon as I had noticed them, thinking 19
that what I saw were merely mirrorings,
I turned around to see who they might be;

   and I saw nothing; and I let my sight 22
turn back to meet the light of my dear guide,
who, as she smiled, glowed in her holy eyes.

   "There is no need to wonder if I smile," 25
she said, "because you reason like a child;
your steps do not yet rest upon the truth;

   your mind misguides you into emptiness: 28
what you are seeing are true substances,
placed here because their vows were not fulfilled.

Però parla con esse e odi e credi;   31
ché la verace luce che le appaga
da sé non lascia lor torcer li piedi."

E io a l'ombra che parea più vaga   34
di ragionar, drizza'mi, e cominciai,
quasi com' uom cui troppa voglia smaga:

"O ben creato spirito, che a' rai   37
di vita etterna la dolcezza senti
che, non gustata, non s'intende mai.

grazïoso mi fia se mi contenti   40
del nome tuo e de la vostra sorte."
Ond' ella, pronta e con occhi ridenti:

"La nostra carità non serra porte   43
a giusta voglia, se non come quella
che vuol simile a sé tutta sua corte.

I' fui nel mondo vergine sorella;   46
e se la mente tua ben sé riguarda,
non mi ti celerà l'esser più bella.

ma riconoscerai ch'i' son Piccarda,   49
che, posta qui con questi altri beati,
beata sono in la spera più tarda.

Li nostri affetti, che solo infiammati   52
son nel piacer de lo Spirito Santo,
letizian del suo ordine formati.

E questa sorte che par giù cotanto,   55
però n'è data, perché fuor negletti
li nostri voti, e vòti in alcun canto."

Ond' io a lei: "Ne' mirabili aspetti   58
vostri risplende non so che divino
che vi trasmuta da' primi concetti:

però non fui a rimembrar festino;   61
ma or m'aiuta ciò che tu mi dici,
sì che raffigurar m'è più latino.

Ma dimmi: voi che siete qui felici,   64
disiderate voi più alto loco
per più vedere e per più farvi amici?"

Con quelle altr' ombre pria sorrise un poco;   67
da indi mi rispuose tanto lieta,
ch'arder parea d'amor nel primo foco:

Thus, speak and listen; trust what they will say: 31
the truthful light in which they find their peace
will not allow their steps to turn astray."

Then I turned to the shade that seemed most anxious   34
to speak, and I began as would a man
bewildered by desire too intense:

"O spirit born to goodness, you who feel,   37
beneath the rays of the eternal life,
that sweetness which cannot be known unless

it is experienced, it would be gracious   40
of you to let me know your name and fate."
At this, unhesitant, with smiling eyes:

"Our charity will never lock its gates   43
against just will; our love is like the Love
that would have all Its court be like Itself.

Within the world I was a nun, a virgin;   46
and if your mind attends and recollects,
my greater beauty here will not conceal me,

and you will recognize me as Piccarda,   49
who, placed here with the other blessed ones,
am blessed within the slowest of the spheres.

Our sentiments, which only serve the flame   52
that is the pleasure of the Holy Ghost,
delight in their conforming to His order.

And we are to be found within a sphere   55
this low, because we have neglected vows,
so that in some respect we were deficient."

And I to her: "Within your wonderful   58
semblance there is something divine that glows,
transforming the appearance you once showed:

therefore, my recognizing you was slow;   61
but what you now have told me is of help;
I can identify you much more clearly.

But tell me: though you're happy here, do you   64
desire a higher place in order to
see more and to be still more close to Him?"

Together with her fellow shades she smiled   67
at first; then she replied to me with such
gladness, like one who burns with love's first flame:

"Frate, la nostra volontà quïeta   70
virtù di carità, che fa volerne
sol quel ch'avemo, e d'altro non ci asseta.

Se disïassimo esser più superne,   73
foran discordi li nostri disiri
dal voler di colui che ne cerne;

che vedrai non capere in questi giri,   76
s'essere in carità è qui *necesse,*
e se la sua natura ben rimiri.

Anzi è formale ad esto beato *esse*   79
tenersi dentro a la divina voglia,
per ch'una fansi nostre voglie stesse;

sì che, some noi sem di soglia in soglia   82
per questo regno, a tutto il regno piace
com' a lo re che 'n suo voler ne 'nvoglia.

E 'n la sua volontade è nostra pace: 85
ell' è quel mare al qual tutto si move
ciò ch'ella crïa o che natura face."

Chiaro mi fu allor come ogne dove   88
in cielo è paradiso, *etsi* la grazia
del sommo ben d'un modo non vi piove.

Ma sì com' elli avvien, s'un cibo sazia   91
e d'un altro rimane ancor la gola,
che quel si chere e di quel si ringrazia,

così fec' io con atto e con parola,   94
per apprender da lei qual fu la tela
onde non trasse infino a co la spuola.

"Perfetta vita e alto merto inciela   97
donna più sù," mi disse, "a la cui norma
nel vostro mondo giù si veste e vela,

perché fino al morir si vegghi e dorma   100
con quello sposo ch'ogne voto accetta
che caritate a suo piacer conforma.

Dal mondo, per seguirla, giovinetta   103
fuggi'mi, e nel suo abito mi chiusi
e promisi la via de la sua setta.

Uomini poi, a mal più ch'a bene usi,   106
fuor mi rapiron de la dolce chiostra:
Iddio si sa qual poi mia vita fusi.

"Brother, the power of love appeases our   70
will so—we only long for what we have;
we do not thirst for greater blessedness.

Should we desire a higher sphere than ours,   73
then our desires would be discordant with
the will of Him who has assigned us here,

but you'll see no such discord in these spheres; 76
to live in love is—here—necessity,
if you think on love's nature carefully.

The essence of this blessed life consists   79
in keeping to the boundaries of God's will,
through which our wills become one single will;

so that, as we are ranged from step to step   82
throughout this kingdom, all this kingdom wills
that which will please the King whose will is rule.

And in His will there is our peace: that sea   85
to which all beings move—the beings He
creates or nature makes—such as His will."

Then it was clear to me how every place   88
in Heaven is in Paradise, though grace
does not rain equally from the High Good.

But just as, when our hunger has been sated   91
with one food, we still long to taste the other—
while thankful for the first, we crave the latter—

so was I in my words and in my gestures,   94
asking to learn from her what was the web
of which her shuttle had not reached the end.

"A perfect life," she said, "and her high merit   97
enheaven, up above, a woman whose
rule governs those who, in your world, would wear

nuns' dress and veil, so that, until their death, 100
they wake and sleep with that Spouse who accepts
all vows that love conforms unto His pleasure.

Still young, I fled the world to follow her;   103
and, in her order's habit, I enclosed
myself and promised my life to her rule.

Then men more used to malice than to good   106
took me—violently—from my sweet cloister:
God knows what, after that, my life became.

E quest' altro splendor che ti si mostra   109
da la mia destra parte e che s'accende
di tutto il lume de la spera nostra,

ciò ch'io dico di me, di sé intende;   112
sorella fu, e così le fu tolta
di capo l'ombra de le sacre bende.

Ma poi che pur al mondo fu rivolta   115
contra suo grado e contra buona usanza,
non fu dal vel del cor già mai disciolta.

Quest' è la luce de la gran Costanza   118
che del secondo vento di Soave
generò 'l terzo e l'ultima possanza."

Così parlommi, e poi cominciò *"Ave,*   121
Maria" cantando, e cantando vanio
come per acqua cupa cosa grave.

La vista mia, che tanto lei seguio   124
quanto possibil fu, poi che la perse,
volsesi al segno di maggior disio,

e a Beatrice tutta si converse;   127
ma quella folgorò nel mïo sguardo
si che da prima il viso non sofferse;

e ciò mi fece a dimandar più tardo.   130

This other radiance that shows itself   109
to you at my right hand, a brightness kindled
by all the light that fills our heaven—she

    has understood what I have said: she was   112
a sister, and from her head, too, by force,
the shadow of the sacred veil was taken.

    But though she had been turned back to the world 115
against her will, against all honest practice,
the veil upon her heart was never loosed.

    This is the splendor of the great Costanza,   118
who from the Swabians' second gust engendered
the one who was their third and final power."

    This said, she then began to sing *"Ave   121
Maria"* and, while singing, vanished as
a weighty thing will vanish in deep water.

    My sight, which followed her as long as it   124
was able to, once she was out of view,
returned to where its greater longing lay,

    and it was wholly bent on Beatrice;   127
but she then struck my eyes with so much brightness
that I, at first, could not withstand her force;

    and that made me delay my questioning.   130

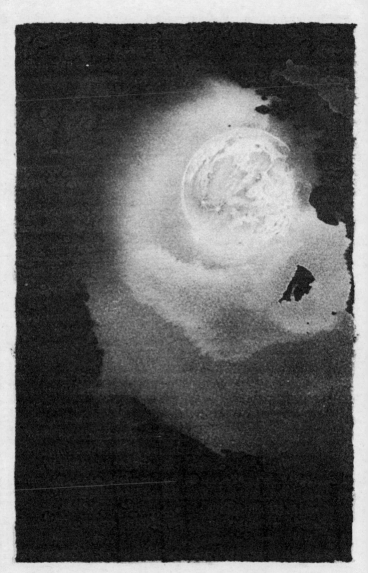

The First Star

CANTO IV

I ntra due cibi, distanti e moventi
 d'un modo, prima si morria di fame,
che liber' omo l'un recasse ai denti;

   sì si starebbe un agno intra due brame   4
di fieri lupi, igualmente temendo;
sì si starebbe un cane intra due dame:

   per che, s'i' mi tacea, me non riprendo,   7
da li miei dubbi d'un modo sospinto,
poi ch'era necessario, né commendo.

   Io mi tacea, ma 'l mio disir dipinto   10
m'era nel viso, e 'l dimandar con ello,
più caldo assai che per parlar distinto.

   Fé sì Beatrice qual fé Danïello,   13
Nabuccodonosor levando d'ira,
che l'avea fatto ingiustamente fello;

   e disse: "Io veggio ben come ti tira   16
uno e altro disio, sì che tua cura
sé stessa lega sì che fuor non spira.

   Tu argomenti: 'Se 'l buon voler dura,   19
la vïolenza altrui per qual ragione
di meritar mi scema la misura?'

   Ancor di dubitar ti dà cagione   22
parer tornarsi l'anime a le stelle,
secondo la sentenza di Platone.

   Queste son le question che nel tuo *velle*   25
pontano igualmente; e però pria
tratterò quella che più ha di felle.

   D'i Serafin colui che più s'india,   28
Moïsè, Samuel, e quel Giovanni
che prender vuoli, io dico, non Maria,

Still the First Heaven: the Sphere of the Moon. Dante's two questions. Beatrice's first answer: the true place of the souls in the Empyrean; how their appearance in lower spheres is suited to Dante's limited apprehension. Her second answer: violence and unfulfilled vows, absolute and relative will. Dante's further query. Beatrice's dazzling gaze.

B efore a man bit into one of two
foods equally removed and tempting, he
would die of hunger if his choice were free;

so would a lamb stand motionless between   4
the cravings of two savage wolves, in fear
of both; so would a dog between two deer;

thus, I need neither blame nor praise myself   7
when both my doubts compelled me equally:
what kept me silent was necessity.

I did not speak, but in my face were seen   10
longing and questioning, more ardent than
if spoken words had made them evident.

Then Beatrice did just as Daniel did,   13
when he appeased Nebuchadnezzar's anger,
the rage that made the king unjustly fierce.

She said: "I see how both desires draw you,   16
so that your anxiousness to know is self-
entangled and cannot express itself.

You reason: 'If my will to good persists,   19
why should the violence of others cause
the measure of my merit to be less?'

And you are also led to doubt because   22
the doctrine Plato taught would find support
by souls' appearing to return to the stars.

These are the questions that, within your will,   25
press equally for answers; therefore, I
shall treat the most insidious question first.

Neither the Seraph closest unto God,   28
nor Moses, Samuel, nor either John—
whichever one you will—nor Mary has,

    non hanno in altro cielo i loro scanni   31
che questi spirti che mo t'appariro,
né hanno a l'esser lor più o meno anni;

    ma tutti fanno bello il primo giro,   34
e differentemente han dolce vita
per sentir più e men l'etterno spiro.

    Qui si mostraro, non perché sortita   37
sia questa spera lor, ma per far segno
de la celestïal c'ha men salita.

    Cosi parlar conviensi al vostro ingegno,   40
però che solo da sensato apprende
ciò che fa poscia d'intelletto degno.

    Per questo la Scrittura condescende   43
a vostra facultate, e piedi e mano
attribuisce a Dio e altro intende;

    e Santa Chiesa con aspetto umano   46
Gabrïel e Michel vi rappresenta,
e l'altro che Tobia rifece sano.

    Quel che Timeo de l'anime argomenta   49
non è simile a ciò che qui si vede,
però che, come dice, par che senta.

    Dice che l'alma a la sua stella riede,   52
credendo quella quindi esser decisa
quando natura per forma la diede;

    e forse sua sentenza è d'altra guisa   55
che la voce non suona, ed esser puote
con intenzion da non esser derisa.

    S'elli intende tornare a queste ruote   58
l'onor de la influenza e 'l biasmo, forse
in alcun vero suo arco percuote.

    Questo principio, male inteso, torse   61
già tutto il mondo quasi, sì che Giove,
Mercurio e Marte a nominar trascorse.

    L'altra dubitazion che ti commove   64
ha men velen, però che sua malizia
non ti poria menar da me altrove.

    Parere ingiusta la nostra giustizia   67
ne li occhi d'i mortali, è argomento
di fede e non d'eretica nequizia.

I say, their place in any other heaven   31
than that which houses those souls you just saw,
nor will their blessedness last any longer.

But all those souls grace the Empyrean;   34
and each of them has gentle life—though some
sense the Eternal Spirit more, some less.

They showed themselves to you here not because   37
this is their sphere, but as a sign for you
that in the Empyrean their place is lowest.

Such signs are suited to your mind, since from   40
the senses only can it apprehend
what then becomes fit for the intellect.

And this is why the Bible condescends   43
to human powers, assigning feet and hands
to God, but meaning something else instead.

And Gabriel and Michael and the angel   46
who healed the eyes of Tobit are portrayed
by Holy Church with human visages.

That which Timaeus said in reasoning   49
of souls does not describe what you have seen,
since it would seem that as he speaks he thinks.

He says the soul returns to that same star   52
from which—so he believes—it had been taken
when nature sent that soul as form to body;

but his opinion is, perhaps, to be   55
taken in other guise than his words speak,
intending something not to be derided.

If to these spheres he wanted to attribute   58
honor and blame for what they influence,
perhaps his arrow reaches something true.

This principle, ill-understood, misled   61
almost all of the world once, so that Jove
and Mercury and Mars gave names to stars.

The other doubt that agitates you is   64
less poisonous; for its insidiousness
is not such as to lead you far from me.

To mortal eyes our justice seems unjust;   67
that this is so, should serve as evidence
for faith—not heresy's depravity.

Ma perché puote vostro accorgimento   70
ben penetrare a questa veritate,
come disiri, ti farò contento.

Se vïolenza è quando quel che pate   73
nïente conferisce a quel che sforza,
non fuor quest' alme per essa scusate:

ché volontà, se non vuol, non s'ammorza,   76
ma fa come natura face in foco,
se mille volte vïolenza il torza.

Per che, s'ella si piega assai o poco,   79
segue la forza; e così queste fero
possendo rifuggir nel santo loco.

Se fosse stato lor volere intero,   82
come tenne Lorenzo in su la grada,
e fece Muzio a la sua man severo,

così l'avria ripinte per la strada   85
ond' eran tratte, come fuoro sciolte;
ma così salda voglia è troppo rada.

E per queste parole, se ricolte   88
l'hai come dei, è l'argomento casso
che t'avria fatto noia ancor più volte.

Ma or ti s'attraversa un altro passo   91
dinanzi a li occhi, tal che per te stesso
non usciresti: pria saresti lasso.

Io t'ho per certo ne la mente messo   94
ch'alma beata non poria mentire,
però ch'è sempre al primo vero appresso;

e poi potesti da Piccarda udire   97
che l'affezion del vel Costanza tenne;
sì ch'ella par qui meco contradire.

Molte fïate già, frate, addivenne   100
che, per fuggir periglio, contra grato
si fé di quel che far non si convenne;

come Almeone, che, di ciò pregato   103
dal padre suo, la propria madre spense,
per non perder pietà si fé spietato.

A questo punto voglio che tu pense   106
che la forza al voler si mischia, e fanno
sì che scusar non si posson l'offense.

But that your intellect may penetrate   70
more carefully into your other query,
I shall—as you desire—explain it clearly.

If violence means that the one who suffers   73
has not abetted force in any way,
then there is no excuse these souls can claim:

for will, if it resists, is never spent,   76
but acts as nature acts when fire ascends,
though force—a thousand times—tries to compel.

So that, when will has yielded much or little,   79
it has abetted force—as these souls did:
they could have fled back to their holy shelter.

Had their will been as whole as that which held   82
Lawrence fast to the grate and that which made
of Mucius one who judged his own hand, then

once freed, they would have willed to find the faith   85
from which they had been dragged; but it is all
too seldom that a will is so intact.

And through these words, if you have grasped their bent,   88
you can eliminate the argument
that would have troubled you again—and often.

But now another obstacle obstructs   91
your sight; you cannot overcome it by
yourself—it is too wearying to try.

I've set it in your mind as something certain   94
that souls in blessedness can never lie,
since they are always near the Primal Truth.

But from Piccarda you were also able   97
to hear how Constance kept her love of the veil:
and here Piccarda seems to contradict me.

Before this—brother—it has often happened   100
that, to flee menace, men unwillingly
did what should not be done; so did Alcmaeon,

to meet the wishes of his father, kill   103
his mother—not to fail in filial
piety, he acted ruthlessly.

At that point—I would have you see—the force   106
to which one yielded mingles with one's will;
and no excuse can pardon their joint act.

Voglia assoluta non consente al danno;   109
ma consentevi in tanto in quanto teme,
se si ritrae, cadere in più affanno.

Però, quando Piccarda quello spreme,   112
de la voglia assoluta intende, e io
de l'altra; sì che ver diciamo insieme."

Cotal fu l'ondeggiar del santo rio   115
ch'uscì del fonte ond' ogne ver deriva;
tal puose in pace uno e altro disio.

"O amanza del primo amante, o diva,"   118
diss' io appresso, "il cui parlar m'inonda
e scalda sì, che più m'avviva,

non è l'affezion mia tanto profonda,   121
che basti a render voi grazia per grazia;
ma quei che vede e puote ciò risponda.

Io veggio ben che già mai non si sazia   124
nostro intelletto, se 'l ver non lo illustra
di fuor dal qual nessun vero si spazia.

Posasi in esso, come fera in lustra,   127
tosto che giunto l'ha; e giugner puollo:
se non, ciascun disio sarebbe *frustra*.

Nasce per quello, a guisa di rampollo,   130
a piè del vero il dubbio; ed è natura
ch'al sommo pinge noi di collo in collo.

Questo m'invita, questo m'assicura   133
con reverenza, donna, a dimandarvi
d'un'altra verità che m'è oscura.

Io vo' saper se l'uom può sodisfarvi   136
ai voti manchi sì con altri beni,
ch'a la vostra statera non sien parvi."

Beatrice mi guardò con li occhi pieni   139
di faville d'amor così divini,
che, vinta, mia virtute diè le reni,

e quasi mi perdei con li occhi chini.   142

Absolute will does not concur in wrong;   109
but the contingent will, through fear that its
resistance might bring greater harm, consents.

Therefore, Piccarda means the absolute   112
will when she speaks, and I the relative;
so that the two of us have spoken truth."

Such was the rippling of the holy stream   115
issuing from the fountain from which springs
all truth: it set to rest both of my longings.

Then I said: "O beloved of the First   118
Lover, o you—divine—whose speech so floods
and warms me that I feel more and more life,

however deep my gratefulness, it can   121
not match your grace with grace enough; but He
who sees and can—may He grant recompense.

I now see well: we cannot satisfy   124
our mind unless it is enlightened by
the truth beyond whose boundary no truth lies.

Mind, reaching that truth, rests within it as   127
a beast within its lair; mind can attain
that truth—if not, all our desires were vain.

Therefore, our doubting blossoms like a shoot   130
out from the root of truth; this natural
urge spurs us toward the peak, from height to height.

Lady, my knowing why we doubt, invites,   133
sustains, my reverent asking you about
another truth that is obscure to me.

I want to know if, in your eyes, one can   136
amend for unkept vows with other acts—
good works your balance will not find too scant."

Then Beatrice looked at me with eyes so full   139
of sparks of love, eyes so divine that my
own force of sight was overcome, took flight,

and, eyes downcast, I almost lost my senses.   142

CANTO V

S'io ti fiammeggio nel caldo d'amore
di là dal modo che 'n terra si vede,
sì che del viso tuo vinco il valore,

non ti maravigliar, ché ciò procede   4
da perfetto veder, che, come apprende,
così nel bene appreso move il piede.

Io veggio ben sì come già resplende   7
ne l'intelletto tuo l'etterna luce,
che, vista, sola e sempre amore accende;

e s'altra cosa vostro amor seduce,   10
non è se non di quella alcun vestigio,
mal conosciuto, che quivi traluce.

Tu vuo' saper se con altro servigio,   13
per manco voto, si può render tanto
che l'anima sicuri di letigio."

Sì cominciò Beatrice questo canto;   16
e sì com' uom che suo parlar non spezza,
continüò così 'l processo santo:

"Lo maggior don che Dio per sua larghezza   19
fesse creando, e a la sua bontate
più conformato, e quel ch'e' più apprezza,

fu de la volontà la libertate;   22
di che le creature intelligenti,
e tutte e sole, fuore e son dotate.

Or ti parrà, se tu quinci argomenti,   25
l'alto valor del voto, s'è sì fatto
che Dio consenta quando tu consenti;

ché, nel fermar tra Dio e l'omo il patto,   28
vittima fassi di questo tesoro,
tal quale io dico; e fassi col suo atto.

Still the First Heaven: the Sphere of the Moon. Beatrice on the cause of her own radiance, and then on the possibility of recompensing for unfulfilled vows. Ascent to the Second Heaven, the Sphere of Mercury. Encounter with the shades there. The nameless holy form whose discourse will constitute the next canto and reveal him to be Justinian.

I f in the fire of love I seem to flame
  beyond the measure visible on earth,
so that I overcome your vision's force,

    you need not wonder; I am so because   4
of my perfected vision—as I grasp
the good, so I approach the good in act.

    Indeed I see that in your intellect   7
now shines the never-ending light; once seen,
that light, alone and always, kindles love;

    and if a lesser thing allure your love,   10
it is a vestige of that light which—though
imperfectly—gleams through that lesser thing.

    You wish to know if, through a righteous act, 13
one can repair a promise unfulfilled,
so that the soul and God are reconciled."

    So Beatrice began this canto, and   16
as one who does not interrupt her speech,
so did her holy reasoning proceed:

    "The greatest gift the magnanimity   19
of God, as He created, gave, the gift
most suited to His goodness, gift that He

    most prizes, was the freedom of the will;   22
those beings that have intellect—all these
and none but these—received and do receive

    this gift: thus you may draw, as consequence, 25
the high worth of a vow, when what is pledged
with your consent encounters God's consent;

    for when a pact is drawn between a man   28
and God, then through free will, a man gives up
what I have called his treasure, his free will.

Dunque che render puossi per ristoro?   31
Se credi bene usar quel c'hai offerto,
di maltolletto vuo' far buon lavoro.

Tu se' omai del maggior punto certo;   34
ma perché Santa Chiesa in ciò dispensa,
che par contra lo ver ch'i' t'ho scoverto,

convienti ancor sedere un poco a mensa,   37
però che 'l cibo rigido c'hai preso,
richiede ancora aiuto a tua dispensa.

Apri la mente a quel ch'io ti paleso   40
e fermalvi entro; ché non fa scïenza,
sanza lo ritenere, avere inteso.

Due cose si convegnono a l'essenza   43
di questo sacrificio: l'una è quella
di che si fa; l'altr' è la convenenza.

Quest' ultima già mai non si cancella   46
se non servata; e intorno di lei
sì preciso di sopra si favella:

però necessitato fu a li Ebrei   49
pur l'offerere, ancor ch'alcuna offerta
si permutasse, come saver dei.

L'altra, che per materia t'è aperta,   52
puote ben esser tal, che non si falla
se con altra materia si converta.

Ma non trasmuti carco a la sua spalla   55
per suo arbitrio alcun, sanza la volta
e de la chiave bianca e de la gialla;

e ogne permutanza credi stolta,   58
se la cosa dimessa in la sorpresa
come 'l quattro nel sei non è raccolta.

Però qualunque cosa tanto pesa   61
per suo valor che tragga ogne bilancia,
sodisfar non si può con altra spesa.

Non prendan li mortali il voto a ciancia;   64
siate fedeli, e a ciò far non bieci,
come Ieptè a la sua prima mancia;

cui più si convenia dicer 'Mal feci,'   67
che, servando, far peggio; e così stolto
ritrovar puoi il gran duca de' Greci,

What, then, can be a fitting compensation?   31
To use again what you had offered, would
mean seeking to do good with ill-got gains.

By now you understand the major point;   34
but since the Holy Church gives dispensations—
which seems in contrast with the truth I stated—

you need to sit at table somewhat longer: 37
the food that you have taken was tough food—
it still needs help, if you are to digest it.

Open your mind to what I shall disclose,   40
and hold it fast within you; he who hears,
but does not hold what he has heard, learns nothing.

Two things are of the essence when one vows   43
a sacrifice: the matter of the pledge
and then the formal compact one accepts.

This last can never be annulled until   46
the compact is fulfilled: it is of this
that I have spoken to you so precisely.

Therefore, the Hebrews found it necessary   49
to bring their offerings, although—as you
must know—some of their offerings might be altered.

As for the matter of the vow—discussed   52
above—it may be such that if one shifts
to other matter, one commits no sin.

But let none shift the burden on his shoulder   55
through his own judgment, without waiting for
the turning of the white and yellow keys;

and let him see that any change is senseless,   58
unless the thing one sets aside can be
contained in one's new weight, as four in six.

Thus, when the matter of a vow has so   61
much weight and worth that it tips every scale,
no other weight can serve as substitute.

Let mortals never take a vow in jest;   64
be faithful and yet circumspect, not rash
as Jephthah was, in offering his first gift;

he should have said, 'I did amiss,' and not   67
done worse by keeping faith. And you can find
that same stupidity in the Greeks' chief—

onde pianse Efigènia il suo bel volto,   70
e fé pianger di sé i folli e i savi
ch'udir parlar di così fatto cólto.

Siate, Cristiani, a muovervi più gravi: 73
non siate come penna ad ogne vento,
e non crediate ch'ogne acqua vi lavi.

Avete il novo e 'l vecchio Testamento,   76
e 'l pastor de la Chiesa che vi guida;
questo vi basti a vostro salvamento.

Se mala cupidigia altro vi grida,   79
uomini siate, e non pecore matte,
sì che 'l Giudeo di voi tra voi non rida!

Non fate com' agnel che lascia il latte   82
de la sua madre, e semplice e lascivo
seco medesmo a suo piacer combatte!"

Così Beatrice a me com' ïo scrivo;   85
poi si rivolse tutta disïante
a quella parte ove 'l mondo è più vivo.

Lo suo tacere e 'l trasmutar sembiante   88
puoser silenzio al mio cupido ingegno,
che già nuove questioni avea davante;

e sì come saetta che nel segno   91
percuote pria che sia la corda queta,
così corremmo nel secondo regno.

Quivi la donna mia vid' io sì lieta,   94
come nel lume di quel ciel si mise,
che più lucente se ne fé 'l pianeta.

E se la stella si cambiò e rise,   97
qual mi fec'io che pur da mia natura
trasmutabile son per tutte guise!

Come 'n peschiera ch'è tranquilla e pura   100
traggonsi i pesci a ciò che vien di fori
per modo che lo stimin lor pastura,

sì vid' io ben più di mille splendori   103
trarsi ver' noi, e in ciascun s'udia:
"Ecco chi crescerà li nostri amori."

E sì come ciascuno a noi venìa,   106
vedeasi l'ombra piena di letizia
nel folgór chiaro che di lei uscia.

when her fair face made Iphigenia grieve   70
and made the wise and made the foolish weep
for her when they heard tell of such a rite.

Christians, proceed with greater gravity: 73
do not be like a feather at each wind,
nor think that all immersions wash you clean.

You have both Testaments, the Old and New,   76
you have the shepherd of the Church to guide you;
you need no more than this for your salvation.

If evil greed would summon you elsewhere,   79
be men, and not like sheep gone mad, so that
the Jew who lives among you not deride you!

Do not act like the foolish, wanton lamb   82
that leaves its mother's milk and, heedless, wants
to war against—and harm—its very self!"

These words of Beatrice I here transcribe;   85
and then she turned—her longing at the full—
to where the world is more alive with light.

Her silence and the change in her appearance   88
imposed a silence on my avid mind,
which now was ready to address new questions;

and even as an arrow that has struck   91
the mark before the bow-cord comes to rest,
so did we race to reach the second realm.

When she had passed into that heaven's light,   94
I saw my lady filled with so much gladness
that, at her joy, the planet grew more bright.

And if the planet changed and smiled, what then   97
did I—who by my very nature am
given to every sort of change—become?

As in a fish-pool that is calm and clear,   100
the fish draw close to anything that nears
from outside, if it seems to be their fare,

such were the far more than a thousand splendors   103
I saw approaching us, and each declared:
"Here now is one who will increase our loves."

And even as each shade approached, one saw,   106
because of the bright radiance it sent forth,
the joyousness with which that shade was filled.

Pensa, lettor, se quel che qui s'inizia 109
non procedesse, come tu avresti
di più savere angosciosa carizia;

e per te vederai come da questi 112
m'era in disio d'udir lor condizioni,
sì come a li occhi mi fur manifesti.

"O bene nato a cui veder li troni 115
del trïunfo etternal concede grazia
prima che la milizia s'abbandoni,

del lume che per tutto il ciel si spazia 118
noi semo accesi; e però, se disii
di noi chiarirti, a tuo piacer ti sazia."

Così da un di quelli spirti pii 121
detto mi fu; e da Beatrice: "Dì, dì
sicuramente, e credi come a dii."

"Io veggio ben sì come tu t'annidi 124
nel proprio lume, e che de li occhi il traggi,
perch' e' corusca sì come tu ridi;

ma non so chi tu se', né perché aggi, 127
anima degna, il grado de la spera
che si vela a' mortai con altrui raggi."

Questo diss' io diritto a la lumera 130
che pria m'avea parlato; ond' ella fessi
lucente più assai di quel ch'ell' era.

Sì come il sol che si cela elli stessi 133
per troppa luce, come 'l caldo ha róse
le temperanze d'i vapori spessi,

per più letizia sì mi si nascose 136
dentro al suo raggio la figura santa;
e così chiusa chiusa mi rispuose

nel modo che 'l seguente canto canta. 139

Consider, reader, what your misery   109
and need to know still more would be if, at
this point, what I began did not go on;

    and you will—unassisted—feel how I   112
longed so to hear those shades narrate their state
as soon as they appeared before my eyes.

    "O you born unto gladness, whom God's grace   115
allows to see the thrones of the eternal
triumph before your war of life is ended,

    the light that kindles us is that same light   118
which spreads through all of heaven; thus, if you
would know us, sate yourself as you may please."

    So did one of those pious spirits speak   121
to me. And Beatrice then urged: "Speak, speak
confidently; trust them as you trust gods."

    "I see—plainly—how you have nested in   124
your own light; see—you draw it from your eyes—
because it glistens even as you smile;

    but I do not know who you are or why,   127
good soul, your rank is in a sphere concealed
from mortals by another planet's rays."

    I said this as I stood turned toward the light 130
that first addressed me; and at this, it glowed
more radiantly than it had before.

    Just as the sun, when heat has worn away   133
thick mists that moderate its rays, conceals
itself from sight through an excess of light,

    so did that holy form, through excess gladness, 136
conceal himself from me within his rays;
and so concealed, concealed, he answered me

    even as the next canto is to sing.   139

The Never-Ending Light

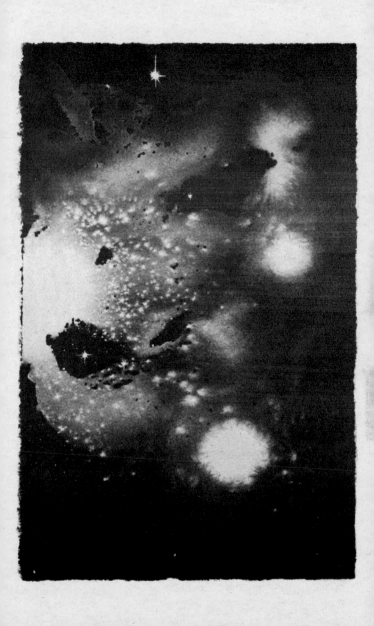

CANTO VI

P oscia che Costantin l'aquila volse
    contr' al corso del ciel, ch'ella seguio
dietro a l'antico che Lavina tolse,

    cento e cent' anni e più l'uccel di Dio   4
ne lo stremo d'Europa si ritenne,
vicino a' monti de' quai prima uscìo;

    e sotto l'ombra de le sacre penne   7
governò 'l mondo lì di mano in mano,
e, sì cangiando, in su la mia pervenne.

    Cesare fui e son Iustinïano,   10
che, per voler del primo amor ch'i' sento,
d'entro le leggi trassi il troppo e 'l vano.

    E prima ch'io a l'ovra fossi attento,   13
una natura in Cristo esser, non piùe,
credea, e di tal fede era contento;

    ma 'l benedetto Agapito, che fue   16
sommo pastore, a la fede sincera
mi dirizzò con le parole sue.

    Io li credetti; e ciò che 'n sua fede era,   19
vegg' io or chiaro sì, come tu vedi
ogne contradizione e falsa e vera.

    Tosto che con la Chiesa mossi i piedi,   22
a Dio per grazia piacque di spirarmi
l'alto lavoro, e tutto 'n lui mi diedi;

    e al mio Belisar commendai l'armi,   25
cui la destra del ciel fu sì congiunta,
che segno fu ch'i' dovessi posarmi.

    Or qui a la question prima s'appunta   28
la mia risposta; ma sua condizione
mi stringe a seguitare alcuna giunta,

After Constantine had turned the Eagle
counter to heaven's course, the course it took
behind the ancient one who wed Lavinia,

one hundred and one hundred years and more,   4
the bird of God remained near Europe's borders,
close to the peaks from which it first emerged;

beneath the shadow of the sacred wings,   · 7
it ruled the world, from hand to hand, until
that governing—changing—became my task.

Caesar I was and am Justinian,   10
who, through the will of Primal Love I feel,
removed the vain and needless from the laws.

Before I grew attentive to this labor,   13
I held that but one nature—and no more—
was Christ's—and in that faith, I was content;

but then the blessed Agapetus, he   16
who was chief shepherd, with his words turned me
to that faith which has truth and purity.

I did believe him, and now clearly see   19
his faith, as you with contradictories
can see that one is true and one is false.

As soon as my steps shared the Church's path,   22
God, of His grace, inspired my high task
as pleased Him. I was fully drawn to that.

Entrusting to my Belisarius   25
my arms, I found a sign for me to rest
from war: Heaven's right hand so favored him.

My answer to the question you first asked   28
ends here, and yet the nature of this answer
leads me to add a sequel, so that you

    perché tu veggi con quanta ragione   31
si move contr' al sacrosanto segno
e chi 'l s'appropria e chi a lui s'oppone.

    Vedi quanta virtù l'ha fatto degno   34
di reverenza; e cominciò da l'ora
che Pallante morì per darli regno.

    Tu sai ch'el fece in Alba sua dimora   37
per trecento anni e oltre, infino al fine
che i tre a' tre pugnar per lui ancora.

    E sai ch'el fé dal mal de le Sabine   40
al dolor di Lucrezia in sette regi,
vincendo intorno le genti vicine.

    Sai quel ch'el fé portato da li egregi   43
Romani incontro a Brenno, incontro a Pirro,
incontro a li altri principi e collegi;

    onde Torquato e Quinzio, che dal cirro   46
negletto fu nomato, i Deci e' Fabi
ebber la fama che volontier mirro.

    Esso atterrò l'orgoglio de li Aràbi   49
che di retro ad Anibale passaro
l'alpestre rocce, Po, di che tu labi.

    Sott' esso giovanetti trïunfaro   52
Scipïone e Pompeo; e a quel colle
sotto 'l qual tu nascesti parve amaro.

    Poi, presso al tempo che tutto 'l ciel volle   55
redur lo mondo a suo modo sereno,
Cesare per voler di Roma il tolle.

    E quel che fé da Varo infino a Reno,   58
Isàra vide ed Era e vide Senna
e ogne valle onde Rodano è pieno.

    Quel che fé poi ch'elli uscì di Ravenna   61
e saltò Rubicon, fu di tal volo,
che nol seguiteria lingua né penna.

    Inver' la Spagna rivolse lo stuolo,   64
poi ver' Durazzo, e Farsalia percosse
sì ch'al Nil caldo si sentì del duolo.

    Antandro e Simeonta, onde si mosse,   67
rivide e là dov' Ettore si cuba;
e mal per Tolomeo poscia si scosse.

    may see with how much reason they attack   31
the sacred standard—those who seem to act
on its behalf and those opposing it.

    See what great virtue made that Eagle worthy   34
of reverence, beginning from that hour
when Pallas died that it might gain a kingdom.

    You know that for three hundred years and more,   37
it lived in Alba, until, at the end,
three still fought three, contending for that standard.

    You know how, under seven kings, it conquered   40
its neighbors—in the era reaching from
wronged Sabine women to Lucrece's grief—

    and what it did when carried by courageous   43
Romans, who hurried to encounter Brennus,
Pyrrhus, and other principates and cities.

    Through this, Torquatus, Quinctius (who is named   46
for his disheveled hair), the Decii,
and Fabii gained the fame I gladly honor.

    That standard brought the pride of Arabs low   49
when they had followed Hannibal across
those Alpine rocks from which, Po, you descend.

    Beneath that standard, Scipio, Pompey—   52
though young—triumphed; and to that hill beneath
which you were born, that standard seemed most harsh.

    Then, near the time when Heaven wished to bring   55
all of the world to Heaven's way—serene—
Caesar, as Rome had willed, took up that standard.

    And what it did from Var to Rhine was seen   58
by the Isère, Saône, and Seine and all
the valley-floors whose rivers feed the Rhone.

    And what it did, once it had left Ravenna   61
and leaped the Rubicon, was such a flight
as neither tongue nor writing can describe.

    That standard led the legions on to Spain,   64
then toward Durazzo, and it struck Pharsalia
so hard that the warm Nile could feel that hurt.

    It saw again its source, Antandros and   67
Simois, and the place where Hector lies;
then roused itself—the worse for Ptolemy.

Da indi scese folgorando a Iuba;   70
onde si volse nel vostro occidente,
ove sentia la pompeana tuba.

Di quel che fé col baiulo seguente,   73
Bruto con Cassio ne l'inferno latra,
e Modena e Perugia fu dolente.

Piangene ancor la trista Cleopatra,   76
che, fuggendoli innanzi, dal colubro
la morte prese subitana e atra.

Con costui corse infino al lito rubro;   79
con costui puose il mondo in tanta pace,
che fu serrato a Giano il suo delubro.

Ma ciò che 'l segno che parlar mi face   82
fatto avea prima e poi era fatturo
per lo regno mortal ch'a lui soggiace,

diventa in apparenza poco e scuro,   85
se in mano al terzo Cesare si mira
con occhio chiaro e con affetto puro;

ché la viva giustizia che mi spira,   88
li concedette, in mano a quel ch'i' dico,
gloria di far vendetta a la sua ira.

Or qui t'ammira in ciò ch'io ti replìco: 91
poscia con Tito a far vendetta corse
de la vendetta del peccato antico.

E quando il dente longobardo morse   94
la Santa Chiesa, sotto le sue ali
Carlo Magno, vincendo, la soccorse.

Omai puoi giudicar di quei cotali   97
ch'io accusai di sopra e di lor falli,
che son cagion di tutti vostri mali.

L'uno al pubblico segno i gigli gialli   100
oppone, e l'altro appropria quello a parte,
sì ch'è forte a veder chi più si falli.

Faccian li Ghibellin, faccian lor arte   103
sott' altro segno, ché mal segue quello
sempre chi la giustizia e lui diparte;

e non l'abbatta esto Carlo novello   106
coi Guelfi suoi, ma tema de li artigli
ch'a più alto leon trasser lo vello.

From Egypt, lightning-like, it fell on Juba;   70
and then it hurried to the west of you,
where it could hear the trumpet of Pompey.

Because of what that standard did, with him   73
who bore it next, Brutus and Cassius howl
in Hell, and grief seized Modena, Perugia.

Because of it, sad Cleopatra weeps   76
still; as she fled that standard, from the asp
she drew a sudden and atrocious death.

And, with that very bearer, it then reached   79
the Red Sea shore: with him, that emblem brought
the world such peace that Janus' shrine was shut.

But what the standard that has made me speak   82
had done before or then was yet to do
throughout the mortal realm where it holds rule,

comes to seem faint and insignificant   85
if one, with clear sight and pure sentiment,
sees what it did in the third Caesar's hand;

for the true Justice that inspires me   88
granted to it—in that next Caesar's hand—
the glory of avenging His own wrath.

Now marvel here at what I show to you: 91
with Titus—afterward—it hurried toward
avenging vengeance for the ancient sin.

And when the Lombard tooth bit Holy Church,   94
then Charlemagne, under the Eagle's wings,
through victories he gained, brought help to her.

Now you can judge those I condemned above,   97
and judge how such men have offended, have
become the origin of all your evils.

For some oppose the universal emblem   100
with yellow lilies; others claim that emblem
for party: it is hard to see who is worse.

Let Ghibellines pursue their undertakings   103
beneath another sign, for those who sever
this sign and justice are bad followers.

And let not this new Charles strike at it with   106
his Guelphs—but let him fear the claws that stripped
a more courageous lion of its hide.

Molte fïate già pianser li figli   109
per la colpa del padre, e non si creda
che Dio trasmuti l'armi per suoi gigli!

Questa picciola stella si correda   112
d'i buoni spirti che son stati attivi
perché onore e fama li succeda:

e quando li disiri poggian quivi,   115
sì disvïando, pur convien che i raggi
del vero amore in sù poggin men vivi.

Ma nel commensurar d'i nostri gaggi   118
col merto è parte di nostra letizia,
perché non li vedem minor né maggi.

Quindi addolcisce la viva giustizia   121
in noi l'affetto sì, che non si puote
torcer già mai ad alcuna nequizia.

Diverse voci fanno dolci note;   124
così diversi scanni in nostra vita
rendon dolce armonia tra queste rote.

E dentro a la presente margarita   127
luce la luce di Romeo, di cui
fu l'ovra grande e bella mal gradita.

Ma i Provenzai che fecer contra lui   130
non hanno riso; e però mal cammina
qual si fa danno del ben fare altrui.

Quattro figlie ebbe, e ciascuna reina,   133
Ramondo Beringhiere, e ciò li fece
Romeo, persona umìle e peregrina.

E poi il mosser le parole biece   136
a dimandar ragione a questo giusto,
che li assegnò sette e cinque per diece,

indi partissi povero e vetusto;   139
e se 'l mondo sapesse il cor ch'elli ebbe
mendicando sua vita a frusto a frusto,

assai lo loda, e più lo loderebbe."   142

The sons have often wept for a father's fault;   109
and let this son not think that God will change
the emblem of His force for Charles's lilies.

This little planet is adorned with spirits   112
whose acts were righteous, but who acted for
the honor and the fame that they would gain:

and when desires tend toward earthly ends,   115
then, so deflected, rays of the true love
mount toward the life above with lesser force.

But part of our delight is measuring   118
rewards against our merit, and we see
that our rewards are neither less nor more.

Thus does the Living Justice make so sweet   121
the sentiments in us, that we are free
of any turning toward iniquity.

Differing voices join to sound sweet music;   124
so do the different orders in our life
render sweet harmony among these spheres.

And in this very pearl there also shines   127
the light of Romeo, of one whose acts,
though great and noble, met ungratefulness.

And yet those Provençals who schemed against him   130
had little chance to laugh, for he who finds
harm to himself in others' righteous acts

takes the wrong path. Of Raymond Berenger's   133
four daughters, each became a queen—and this,
poor and a stranger, Romeo accomplished.

Then Berenger was moved by vicious tongues   136
to ask this just man for accounting—one
who, given ten, gave Raymond five and seven.

And Romeo, the poor, the old, departed;   139
and were the world to know the heart he had
while begging, crust by crust, for his life-bread,

it—though it praise him now—would praise him more."

CANTO VII

O *sanna, sanctus Deus sabaòth,*
    superillustrans claritate tua
felices ignes horum malacòth!"

Così, volgendosi a la nota sua,   4
fu viso a me cantare essa sustanza,
sopra la qual doppio lume s'addua;

    ed essa e l'altre mossero a sua danza,   7
e quasi velocissime faville
mi si velar di sùbita distanza.

    Io dubitava e dicea "Dille, dille!"   10
fra me, "dille" dicea, "a la mia donna
che mi diseta con le dolci stille."

    Ma quella reverenza che s'indonna   13
di tutto me, pur per *Be* e per *ice,*
mi richinava come l'uom ch'assonna.

    Poco sofferse me cotal Beatrice   16
e cominciò, raggiandomi d'un riso
tal, che nel foco faria l'uom felice:

    "Secondo mio infallibile avviso,   19
come giusta vendetta giustamente
punita fosse, t'ha in pensier miso;

    ma io ti solverò tosto la mente;   22
e tu ascolta, ché le mie parole
di gran sentenza ti faran presente.

    Per non soffrire a la virtù che vole   25
freno a suo prode, quell' uom che non nacque,
dannando sé, dannò tutta sua prole;

    onde l'umana specie inferma giacque   28
giù per secoli molti in grande errore,
fin ch'al Verbo di Dio discender piacque

Still the Second Heaven: the Sphere of Mercury. Disapperance of Justinian and his fellow spirits in the wake of hymning and dancing. Beatrice's explanations of Justinian's references to Christ's death as God's just vengeance and the destruction of Jerusalem as vengeance for just vengeance; human corruptibility; the mysteries of Salvation and Resurrection.

*H*osanna, sanctus Deus sabaòth,
   superillustrans claritate tua
felices ignes horum malacòth!"

   Thus, even as he wheeled to his own music,   4
I saw that substance sing, that spirit-flame
above whom double lights were twinned; and he

   and his companions moved within their dance,   7
and as if they were swiftest sparks, they sped
out of my sight because of sudden distance.

   I was perplexed, and to myself, I said: 10
"Tell her! Tell her! Tell her, the lady who
can slake my thirst with her sweet drops"; and yet

   the reverence that possesses all of me,   13
even on hearing only *Be* and *ice,*
had bowed my head—I seemed a man asleep.

   But Beatrice soon ended that; for she   16
began to smile at me so brightly that,
even in fire, a man would still feel glad.

   "According to my never-erring judgment,   19
the question that perplexes you is how
just vengeance can deserve just punishment;

   but I shall quickly free your mind from doubt;   22
and listen carefully; the words I speak
will bring the gift of a great truth in reach.

   Since he could not endure the helpful curb   25
on his willpower, the man who was not born,
damning himself, damned all his progeny.

   For this, mankind lay sick, in the abyss   28
of a great error, for long centuries,
until the Word of God willed to descend

 u' la natura, che dal suo fattore   31
s'era allungata, unì a sé in persona
con l'atto sol del suo etterno amore.

 Or drizza il viso a quel ch'or si ragiona: 34
questa natura al suo fattore unita,
qual fu creata, fu sincera e buona;

 ma per sé stessa pur fu ella sbandita   37
di paradiso, però che si torse
da via di verità e da sua vita.

 La pena dunque che la croce porse   40
s'a la natura assunta si misura,
nulla già mai sì giustamente morse;

 e così nulla fu di tanta ingiura,   43
guardando a la persona che sofferse,
in che era contratta tal natura.

 Però d'un atto uscir cose diverse: 46
ch'a Dio e a' Giudei piacque una morte;
per lei tremò la terra e 'l ciel s'aperse.

 Non ti dee oramai parer più forte,   49
quando si dice che giusta vendetta
poscia vengiata fu da giusta corte.

 Ma io veggi' or la tua mente ristretta   52
di pensiero in pensier dentro ad un nodo,
del qual con gran disio solver s'aspetta.

 Tu dici: 'Ben discerno ciò ch'i' odo;   55
ma perché Dio volesse, m'è occulto,
a nostra redenzion pur questo modo.'

 Questo decreto, frate, sta sepulto   58
a li occhi di ciascuno il cui ingegno
ne la fiamma d'amor non è adulto.

 Veramente, però ch'a questo segno   61
molto si mira e poco si discerne,
dirò perché tal modo fu più degno.

 La divina bontà, che da sé sperne   64
ogne livore, ardendo in sé, sfavilla
sì che dispiega le bellezze etterne.

 Ciò che da lei sanza mezzo distilla   67
non ha poi fine, perché non si move
la sua imprenta quand' ella sigilla.

to where the nature that was sundered from 31
its Maker was united to His person
by the sole act of His eternal Love.

Now set your sight on what derives from that. 34
This nature, thus united to its Maker,
was good and pure, even as when created;

but in itself, this nature had been banished 37
from paradise, because it turned aside
from its own path, from truth, from its own life.

Thus, if the penalty the Cross inflicted 40
is measured by the nature He assumed,
no one has ever been so justly stung;

yet none was ever done so great a wrong, 43
if we regard the Person made to suffer,
He who had gathered in Himself that nature.

Thus, from one action, issued differing things: 46
God and the Jews were pleased by one same death;
earth trembled for that death and Heaven opened.

You need no longer find it difficult 49
to understand when it is said that just
vengeance was then avenged by a just court.

But I now see your understanding tangled 52
by thought on thought into a knot, from which,
with much desire, your mind awaits release.

You say: 'What I have heard is clear to me; 55
but this is hidden from me—why God willed
precisely this pathway for our redemption.'

Brother, this ordinance is buried from 58
the eyes of everyone whose intellect
has not matured within the flame of love.

Nevertheless, since there is much attempting 61
to find this point, but little understanding,
I shall tell why that way was the most fitting.

The Godly Goodness that has banished every 64
envy from Its own Self, burns in Itself;
and sparkling so, It shows eternal beauties.

All that derives directly from this Goodness 67
is everlasting, since the seal of Goodness
impresses an imprint that never alters.

Ciò che da essa sanza mezzo piove   70
libero è tutto, perché non soggiace
a la virtute de le cose nove.

Più l'è conforme, e però più le piace;   73
ché l'ardor santo ch'ogne cosa raggia,
ne la più somigliante è più vivace.

Di tutte queste dote s'avvantaggia   76
l'umana creatura, e s'una manca,
di sua nobilità convien che caggia.

Solo il peccato è quel che la disfranca   79
e falla dissimìle al sommo bene,
per che del lume suo poco s'imbianca;

e in sua dignità mai non rivene,   82
se non rïempie, dove colpa vòta,
contra mal dilettar con giuste pene.

Vostra natura, quando peccò *tota*   85
nel seme suo, da queste dignitadi,
come di paradiso, fu remota;

né ricovrar potiensi, se tu badi   88
ben sottilmente, per alcuna via,
sanza passar per un di questi guadi:

o che Dio solo per sua cortesia   91
dimesso avesse, o che l'uom per sé isso
avesse sodisfatto a sua follia.

Ficca mo l'occhio per entro l'abisso   94
de l'etterno consiglio, quanto puoi
al mio parlar distrettamente fisso.

Non potea l'uomo ne' termini suoi   97
mai sodisfar, per non potere ir giuso
con umiltate obedïendo poi,

quanto disobediendo intese ir suso;   100
e questa è la cagion per che l'uom fue
da poter sodisfar per sé dischiuso.

Dunque a Dio convenia con le vie sue   103
riparar l'omo a sua intera vita,
dico con l'una, o ver con amendue.

Ma perché l'ovra tanto è più gradita   106
da l'operante, quanto più appresenta
de la bontà del core ond' ell' è uscita,

Whatever rains from It immediately   70
is fully free, for it is not constrained
by any influence of other things.

Even as it conforms to that Goodness,   73
so does it please It more; the Sacred Ardor
that gleams in all things is most bright within

those things most like Itself. The human being   76
has all these gifts, but if it loses one,
then its nobility has been undone.

Only man's sin annuls man's liberty,   79
makes him unlike the Highest Good, so that,
in him, the brightness of Its light is dimmed;

and man cannot regain his dignity   82
unless, where sin left emptiness, man fills
that void with just amends for evil pleasure.

For when your nature sinned so totally   85
within its seed, then, from these dignities,
just as from Paradise, that nature parted;

and they could never be regained—if you   88
consider carefully—by any way
that did not pass across one of these fords:

either through nothing other than His mercy,   91
God had to pardon man, or of himself
man had to proffer payment for his folly.

Now fix your eyes on the profundity   94
of the Eternal Counsel; heed as closely
as you are able to, my reasoning.

Man, in his limits, could not recompense;   97
for no obedience, no humility,
he offered later could have been so deep

that it could match the heights he meant to reach   100
through disobedience; man lacked the power
to offer satisfaction by himself.

Thus there was need for God, through His own ways,   103
to bring man back to life intact—I mean
by one way or by both. But since a deed

pleases its doer more, the more it shows   106
the goodness of the heart from which it springs,
the Godly Goodness that imprints the world

la divina bontà che 'l mondo imprenta,   109
di proceder per tutte le sue vie,
a rilevarvi suso, fu contenta.

Né tra l'ultima notte e 'l primo die   112
sì alto o sì magnifico processo,
o per l'una o per l'altra, fu o fie: ·

ché più largo fu Dio a dar sé stesso   115
per far l'uom sufficiente a rilevarsi,
che s'elli avesse sol da sé dimesso;

e tutti li altri modi erano scarsi   118
a la giustizia, se 'l Figliuol di Dio
non fosse umilïato ad incarnarsi.

Or per empierti bene ogne disio,   121
ritorno a dichiararti in alcun loco,
perché tu veggi lì così com' io.

Tu dici: 'Io veggio l'acqua, io veggio il foco,   124
l'aere e la terra e tutte lor misture
venire a corruzione, e durar poco;

e queste cose pur furon creature;   127
per che, se ciò ch'è detto è stato vero,
esser dovrien da corruzion sicure.'

Li angeli, frate, e 'l paese sincero   130
nel qual tu se', dir si posson creati,
sì come sono, in loro essere intero;

ma li alimenti che tu hai nomati   133
e quelle cose che di lor si fanno
da creata virtù sono informati.

Creata fu la materia ch'elli hanno;   136
creata fu la virtù informante
in queste stelle che 'ntorno a lor vanno.

L'anima d'ogne bruto e de le piante   139
di complession potenzïata tira
lo raggio e 'l moto de le luci sante;

ma vostra vita sanza mezzo spira   142
la somma beninanza, e la innamora
di sé sì che poi sempre la disira.

E quinci puoi argomentare ancora   145
vostra resurrezion, se tu ripensi
come l'umana carne fessi allora

che li primi parenti intrambo fensi."   148

was happy to proceed through both Its ways 109
to raise you up again. Nor has there been,
nor will there be, between the final night

and the first day, a chain of actions so 112
lofty and so magnificent as He
enacted when He followed His two ways;

for God showed greater generosity 115
in giving His own self that man might be
able to rise, than if He simply pardoned;

for every other means fell short of justice, 118
except the way whereby the Son of God
humbled Himself when He became incarnate.

Now to give all your wishes full content, 121
I go back to explain one point, so that
you, too, may see it plainly, as I do.

You say: 'I see that water, see that fire 124
and air and earth and all that they compose
come to corruption, and endure so briefly;

and yet these, too, were things created; if 127
what has been said above is true, then these
things never should be subject to corruption.'

Brother, the angels and the pure country 130
where you are now—these may be said to be
created, as they are, in all their being;

whereas the elements that you have mentioned, 133
as well as those things that are made from them,
receive their form from a created power.

The matter they contain had been created, 136
just as within the stars that wheel about them,
the power to give form had been created.

The rays and motion of the holy lights 139
draw forth the soul of every animal
and plant from matter able to take form;

but your life is breathed forth immediately 142
by the Chief Good, who so enamors it
of His own Self that it desires Him always.

So reasoning, you also can deduce 145
your resurrection; you need but remember
the way in which your human flesh was fashioned

when both of the first parents were created." 148

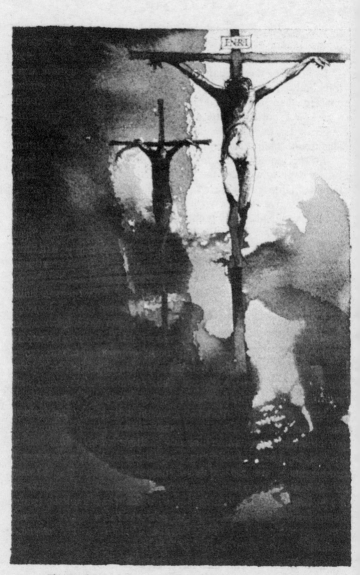

The Crucifixion

CANTO VIII

Solea creder lo mondo in suo periclo
che la bella Ciprigna il folle amore
raggiasse, volta nel terzo epiciclo;

    per che non pur a lei faceano onore   4
di sacrificio e di votivo grido
le genti antiche ne l'antico errore;

    ma Dïone onoravano e Cupido,   7
quella per madre sua, questo per figlio,
e dicean ch'el sedette in grembo a Dido;

    e da costei ond' io principio piglio   10
pigliavano il vocabol de la stella
che 'l sol vagheggia or da coppa or da ciglio.

    Io non m'accorsi del salire in ella;   13
ma d'esservi entro mi fé assai fede
la donna mia ch'i' vidi far più bella.

    E come in fiamma favilla si vede,   16
e come in voce voce si discerne,
quand' una è ferma e altra va e riede,

    vid' io in essa luce altre lucerne   19
muoversi in giro più e men correnti,
al modo, credo, di lor viste interne.

    Di fredda nube non disceser venti,   22
o visibili o no, tanto festini,
che non paressero impediti e lenti

    a chi avesse quei lumi divini   25
veduti a noi venir, lasciando il giro
pria cominciato in li alti Serafini;

    e dentro a quei che più innanzi appariro   28
sonava *"Osanna"* sì, che unque pio
di rïudir non fui sanza disiro.

Origin of the planet Venus's name. Ascent to the Third Heaven, the Sphere of Venus. Charles Martel. His discourse on fathers and sons and the vicissitudes of heredity, and then on the need to respect men's natural dispositions.

T he world, when still in peril, thought that, wheeling,
    in the third epicycle, Cyprian
the fair sent down her rays of frenzied love,

    so that, in ancient error, ancient peoples   4
not only honored her with sacrifices
and votive cries, but honored, too, Dïone

    and Cupid, one as mother, one as son   7
of Cyprian, and told how Cupid sat
in Dido's lap; and gave the name of her

    with whom I have begun this canto, to   10
the planet that is courted by the sun,
at times behind her and at times in front.

    I did not notice my ascent to it,   13
yet I was sure I was in Venus when
I saw my lady grow more beautiful.

    And just as, in a flame, a spark is seen,   16
and as, in plainsong, voice in voice is heard—
one holds the note, the other comes and goes—

    I saw in that light other wheeling lamps,   19
some more and some less swift, yet in accord,
I think, with what their inner vision was.

    Winds, seen or unseen, never have descended   22
so swiftly from cold clouds as not to seem
impeded, slow, to any who had seen

    those godly lights approaching us, halting   25
the circling dance those spirits had begun
within the heaven of high Seraphim;

    and a *"Hosanna"* sounded from within   28
their front ranks—such that I have never been
without desire to hear it sound again.

Indi si fece l'un più presso a noi   31
e solo incominciò: "Tutti sem presti
al tuo piacer, perché di noi ti gioi.

Noi ci volgiam coi principi celesti   34
d'un giro e d'un girare e d'una sete,
ai quali tu del mondo già dicesti:

   'Voi che 'ntendendo il terzo ciel movete';   37
e sem sì pien d'amor, che, per piacerti,
non fia men dolce un poco di quïete."

Poscia che li occhi miei si fuoro offerti   40
a la mia donna reverenti, ed essa
fatti li avea di sé contenti e certi,

   rivolsersi a la luce che promessa   43
tanto s'avea, e "Deh, chi siete?" fue
la voce mia di grande affetto impressa.

E quanta e qual vid' io lei far piùe   46
per allegrezza nova che s'accrebbe,
quando parlai, a l'allegrezze sue!

Così fatta, mi disse: "Il mondo m'ebbe   49
giù poco tempo; e se più fosse stato,
molto sarà di mal, che non sarebbe.

La mia letizia mi ti tien celato   52
che mi raggia dintorno e mi nasconde
quasi animal di sua seta fasciato.

Assai m'amasti, e avesti ben onde;   55
che s'io fossi giù stato, io ti mostrava
di mio amor più oltre che le fronde.

Quella sinistra riva che si lava   58
di Rodano poi ch'è misto con Sorga,
per suo segnore a tempo m'aspettava,

   e quel corno d'Ausonia che s'imborga   61
di Bari e di Gaeta e di Catona,
da ove Tronto e Verde in mare sgorga.

Fulgeami già in fronte la corona   64
di quella terra che 'l Danubio riga
poi che le ripe tedesche abbandona.

E la bella Trinacria, che caliga   67
tra Pachino e Peloro, sopra 'l golfo
che riceve da Euro maggior briga,

Then one drew nearer us, and he began 31
alone: "We all are ready at your pleasure,
so that you may receive delight from us.

One circle and one circling and one thirst 34
are ours as we revolve with the celestial
Princes whom, from the world, you once invoked:

'You who, through understanding, move the third 37
heaven.' Our love is so complete—to bring
you joy, brief respite will not be less sweet."

After my eyes had turned with reverence 40
to see my lady, after her consent
had brought them reassurance and content,

they turned back to the light that promised me 43
so much; and, "Tell me, who are you," I asked
in a voice stamped with loving sentiment.

And how much larger, brighter did I see 46
that spirit grow when, as I spoke, it felt
new gladness added to its gladnesses!

Thus changed, it then replied: "The world held me 49
briefly below; but had my stay been longer,
much evil that will be, would not have been.

My happiness, surrounding me with rays, 52
keeps me concealed from you; it hides me like
a creature that is swathed in its own silk.

You loved me much and had good cause for that; 55
for had I stayed below, I should have showed
you more of my love than the leaves alone.

The left bank that the Rhone bathes after it 58
has mingled with the waters of the Sorgue,
awaited me in due time as its lord,

as did Ausonia's horn, which—south of where 61
the Tronto and the Verde reach the sea—
Catona, Bari, and Gaeta border.

Upon my brow a crown already shone— 64
the crown of that land where the Danube flows
when it has left behind its German shores.

And fair Trinacria, whom ashes (these 67
result from surging sulphur, not Typhoeus)
cover between Pachynus and Pelorus,

    non per Tifeo ma per nascente solfo,   70
attesi avrebbe li suoi regi ancora,
nati per me di Carlo e di Ridolfo,

    se mala segnoria, che sempre accora   73
li popoli suggetti, non avesse
mosso Palermo a gridar: 'Mora, mora!'

    E se mio frate questo antivedesse,   76
l'avara povertà di Catalogna
già fuggeria, perché non li offendesse;

    ché veramente proveder bisogna   79
per lui, o per altrui, sì ch'a sua barca
carcata più d'incarco non si pogna.

    La sua natura, che di larga parca   82
discese, avria mestier di tal milizia
che non curasse di mettere in arca."

    "Però ch'i' credo che l'alta letizia   85
che 'l tuo parlar m'infonde, segnor mio,
là 've ogne ben si termina e s'inizia,

    per te si veggia come la vegg' io,   88
grata m'è più; e anco quest' ho caro
perché 'l discerni rimirando in Dio.

    Fatto m'hai lieto, e così mi fa chiaro,   91
poi che, parlando, a dubitar m'hai mosso
com' esser può, di dolce seme, amaro."

    Questo io a lui; ed elli a me: "S'io posso   94
mostrarti un vero, a quel che tu dimandi
terrai lo viso come tien lo dosso.

    Lo ben che tutto il regno che tu scandi   97
volge e contenta, fa esser virtute
sua provedenza in questi corpi grandi.

    E non pur le nature provedute   100
sono in la mente ch'è da sé perfetta,
ma esse insieme con la lor salute:

    per che quantunque quest' arco saetta   103
disposto cade a proveduto fine,
sì come cosa in suo segno diretta.

    Se ciò non fosse, il ciel che tu cammine   106
producerebbe sì li suoi effetti,
che non sarebbero arti, ma ruine;

along the gulf that Eurus vexes most,   70
would still await its rulers born—through me—
from Charles and Rudolph, if ill sovereignty,

which always hurts the heart of subject peoples,   73
had not provoked Palermo to cry out:
'Die! Die!' And if my brother could foresee

what ill-rule brings, he would already flee   76
from Catalonia's grasping poverty,
aware that it may cause him injury;

for truly there is need for either him   79
or others to prevent his loaded boat
from having to take on still greater loads.

His niggard nature is descended from   82
one who was generous; and he needs soldiers
who are not bent on filling up their coffers."

"My lord, since I believe that you perceive   85
completely—where all good begins and ends—
the joy I see within myself on hearing

your words to me, my joy is felt more freely;   88
and I joy, too, in knowing you are blessed,
since you perceived this as you gazed at God.

You made me glad; so may you clear the doubt   91
that rose in me when you—before—described
how from a gentle seed, harsh fruit derives."

These were my words to him, and he replied: 94
"If I can show one certain truth to you,
you will confront what now is at your back.

The Good that moves and makes content the realm   97
through which you now ascend, makes providence
act as a force in these great heavens' bodies;

and in the Mind that, in itself, is perfect,   100
not only are the natures of His creatures
but their well-being, too, provided for;

and thus, whatever this bow shoots must fall   103
according to a providential end,
just like a shaft directed to its target.

Were this not so, the heavens you traverse   106
would bring about effects in such a way
that they would not be things of art but shards.

e ciò esser non può, se li 'ntelletti   109
che muovon queste stelle non son manchi,
e manco il primo, che non li ha perfetti.

  Vuo' tu che questo ver più ti s'imbianchi?"   112
E io "Non già; ché impossibil veggio
che la natura, in quel ch'è uopo, stanchi."

  Ond' elli ancora: "Or dì: sarebbe il peggio   115
per l'omo in terra, se non fosse cive?"
"Sì," rispuos' io; "e qui ragion non cheggio."

  "E puot' elli esser, se giù non si vive   118
diversamente per diversi offici?
Non, se 'l maestro vostro ben vi scrive."

  Sì venne deducendo infino a quici;   121
poscia conchiuse: "Dunque esser diverse
convien di vostri effetti le radici:

  per ch'un nasce Solone e altro Serse,   124
altro Melchisedèch e altro quello
che, volando per l'aere, il figlio perse.

  La circular natura, ch'è suggello   127
a la cera mortal, fa ben sua arte,
ma non distingue l'un da l'altro ostello.

  Quinci addivien ch'Esaù si diparte   130
per seme da Iacòb; e vien Quirino
da sì vil padre, che si rende a Marte.

  Natura generata il suo cammino   133
simil farebbe sempre a' generanti,
se non vincesse il proveder divino.

  Or quel che t'era dietro t'è davanti: 136
ma perché sappi che di te mi giova,
un corollario voglio che t'ammanti.

  Sempre natura, se fortuna trova   139
discorde a sé, com' ogne altra semente
fuor di sua regïon, fa mala prova.

  E se 'l mondo là giù ponesse mente   142
al fondamento che natura pone,
seguendo lui, avria buona la gente.

  Ma voi torcete a la religïone   145
tal che fia nato a cignersi la spada,
e fate re di tal ch'è da sermone;

  onde la traccia vostra è fuor di strada."   148

That cannot be unless the Minds that move 109
these planets are defective and, defective,
the First Mind, which had failed to make them perfect.

Would you have this truth still more clear to you?" 112
I: "No. I see it is impossible
for nature to fall short of what is needed."

He added: "Tell me, would a man on earth 115
be worse if he were not a citizen?"
"Yes," I replied, "and here I need no proof."

"Can there be citizens if men below 118
are not diverse, with diverse duties? No,
if what your master writes is accurate."

Until this point that shade went on, deducing; 121
then he concluded: "Thus, the roots from which
your tasks proceed must needs be different:

so, one is born a Solon, one a Xerxes, 124
and one a Melchizedek, and another,
he who flew through the air and lost his son.

Revolving nature, serving as a seal 127
for mortal wax, plies well its art, but it
does not distinguish one house from another.

Thus, even from the seed, Esau takes leave 130
of Jacob; and because he had a father
so base, they said Quirinus was Mars' son.

Engendered natures would forever take 133
the path of those who had engendered them,
did not Divine provision intervene.

Now that which stood behind you, stands in front: 136
but so that you may know the joy you give me,
I now would cloak you with a corollary.

Where Nature comes upon discrepant fortune, 139
like any seed outside its proper region,
Nature will always yield results awry.

But if the world below would set its mind 142
on the foundation Nature lays as base
to follow, it would have its people worthy.

But you twist to religion one whose birth 145
made him more fit to gird a sword, and make
a king of one more fit for sermoning,

so that the track you take is off the road." 148

CANTO IX

D a poi che Carlo tuo, bella Clemenza,
  m'ebbe chiarito, mi narrò li 'nganni
che ricever dovea la sua semenza;

    ma disse: "Taci e lascia muover li anni";   4
sì ch'io non posso dir se non che pianto
giusto verrà di retro ai vostri danni.

    E già la vita di quel lume santo   7
rivolta s'era al Sol che la rïempie
come quel ben ch'a ogne cosa è tanto.

    Ahi anime ingannate e fatture empie,   10
che da sì fatto ben torcete i cuori,
drizzando in vanità le vostre tempie!

    Ed ecco un altro di quelli splendori   13
ver' me si fece, e 'l suo voler piacermi
significava nel chiarir di fori.

    Li occhi di Beatrice, ch'eran fermi   16
sovra me, come pria, di caro assenso
al mio disio certificato fermi.

    "Deh, metti al mio voler tosto compenso,   19
beato spirto," dissi, "e fammi prova
ch'i' possa in te refletter quel ch'io penso!"

    Onde la luce che m'era ancor nova,   22
del suo profondo, ond' ella pria cantava,
seguette come a cui di ben far giova:

    "In quella parte de la terra prava   25
italica che siede tra Rïalto
e le fontane di Brenta e di Piava,

    si leva un colle, e non surge molt' alto,   28
là onde scese già una facella
che fece a la contrada un grande assalto.

*The Third Heaven: the Sphere of Venus. The prophecy of Charles
Martel. Cunizza da Romano and her prophecy. Folco of Marseille, who
points out Rahab, and then denounces contemporary ecclesiastics and
prophesies the regeneration of the Church.*

Fair Clemence, after I had been enlightened
   by your dear Charles, he told me how his seed
would be defrauded, but he said: "Be silent

   and let the years revolve." All I can say   4
is this: lament for vengeance well-deserved
will follow on the wrongs you are to suffer.

   And now the life-soul of that holy light   7
turned to the Sun that fills it even as
the Goodness that suffices for all things.

   Ah, souls seduced and creatures without reverence,   10
who twist your hearts away from such a Good,
who let your brows be bent on emptiness!

   And here another of those splendors moved   13
toward me; and by its brightening without,
it showed its wish to please me. Beatrice,

   whose eyes were fixed on me, as they had been   16
before, gave me the precious certainty
that she consented to my need to speak.

   "Pray, blessed, spirit, may you remedy—   19
quickly—my wish to know," I said. "Give me
proof that you can reflect the thoughts I think."

   At which that light, one still unknown to me,   22
out of the depth from which it sang before,
continued as if it rejoiced in kindness:

   "In that part of indecent Italy   25
that lies between Rialto and the springs
from which the Brenta and the Piave stream,

   rises a hill—of no great height—from which   28
a firebrand descended, and it brought
much injury to all the land about.

D'una radice nacqui e io ed ella: 31
Cunizza fui chiamata, e qui refulgo
perché mi vinse il lume d'esta stella;

　　ma lietamente a me medesma indulgo   34
la cagion di mia sorte, e non mi noia;
che parria forse forte al vostro vulgo.

Di questa luculenta e cara gioia   37
del nostro cielo che più m'è propinqua,
grande fama rimase; e pria che moia,

　　questo centesimo anno ancor s'incinqua: 40
vedi se far si dee l'omo eccellente,
sì ch'altra vita la prima relinqua.

E ciò non pensa la turba presente   43
che Tagliamento e Adice richiude,
né per esser battuta ancor si pente;

　　ma tosto fia che Padova al palude   46
cangerà l'acqua che Vicenza bagna,
per essere al dover le genti crude;

　　e dove Sile e Cagnan s'accompagna,   49
tal signoreggia e va con la testa alta,
che già per lui carpir si fa la ragna.

Piangerà Feltro ancora la difalta   52
de l'empio suo pastor, che sarà sconcia
sì, che per simil non s'entrò in malta.

Troppo sarebbe larga la bigoncia   55
che ricevesse il sangue ferrarese,
e stanco chi 'l pesasse a oncia a oncia,

　　che donerà questo prete cortese   58
per mostrarsi di parte; e cotai doni
conformi fieno al viver del paese.

Sù sono specchi, voi dicete Troni,   61
onde refulge a noi Dio giudicante;
sì che questi parlar ne paion buoni."

Qui si tacette; e fecemi sembiante   64
che fosse ad altro volta, per la rota
in che si mise com' era davante.

L'altra letizia, che m'era già nota   67
per cara cosa, mi si fece in vista
qual fin balasso in che lo sol percuota.

Both he and I were born of one same root: 31
Cunizza was my name, and I shine here
because this planet's radiance conquered me.

But in myself I pardon happily   34
the reason for my fate; I do not grieve—
and vulgar minds may find this hard to see.

Of the resplendent, precious jewel that stands   37
most close to me within our heaven, much
fame still remains and will not die away

before this hundredth year returns five times: 40
see then if man should not seek excellence—
that his first life bequeath another life.

And this, the rabble that is now enclosed   43
between the Adige and Tagliamento
does not consider, nor does it repent

despite its scourgings; and since it would shun   46
its duty, at the marsh the Paduans
will stain the river-course that bathes Vicenza;

and where the Sile and Cagnano flow   49
in company, one lords it, arrogant;
the net to catch him is already set.

Feltre shall yet lament the treachery   52
of her indecent shepherd—act so filthy
that for the like none ever entered prison.

The vat to hold the blood of the Ferrarese   55
would be too large indeed, and weary he
who weighs it ounce by ounce—the vat that he,

generous priest, will offer up to show   58
fidelity to his Guelph party; and
such gifts will suit the customs of that land.

Above are mirrors—Thrones is what you call them—   61
and from them God in judgment shines on us;
and thus we think it right to say such things."

Here she was silent and appeared to me   64
to turn toward other things, reentering
the wheeling dance where she had been before.

The other joy, already known to me   67
as precious, then appeared before my eyes
like a pure ruby struck by the sun's rays.

　　Per letiziar là sù fulgor s'acquista,　　　　　　　　70
sì come riso qui; ma giù s'abbuia
l'ombra di fuor, come la mente è trista.

　　"Dio vede tutto, e tuo veder s'inluia,"　　　　　　73
diss' io, "beato spirto, sì che nulla
voglia di sé a te puot' esser fuia.

　　Dunque la voce tua, che 'l ciel trastulla　　　　76
sempre col canto di quei fuochi pii
che di sei ali facen la coculla,

　　perché non satisface a' miei disii?　　　　　　　79
Già non attendere' io tua dimanda,
s'io m'intuassi, come tu t'inmii."

　　"La maggior valle in che l'acqua si spanda,"　　82
incominciaro allor le sue parole,
"fuor di quel mar che la terra inghirlanda,

　　tra ' discordanti liti contra 'l sole　　　　　　85
tanto sen va, che fa meridïano
là dove l'orizzonte pria far suole.

　　Di quella valle fu' io litorano　　　　　　　　88
tra Ebro e Macra, che per cammin corto
parte lo Genovese dal Toscano.

　　Ad un occaso quasi e ad un orto　　　　　　　91
Buggea siede e la terra ond' io fui,
che fé del sangue suo già caldo il porto.

　　Folco mi disse quella gente a cui　　　　　　94
fu noto il nome mio; e questo cielo
di me s'imprenta, com' io fe' di lui;

　　ché più non arse la figlia di Belo,　　　　　　97
noiando e a Sicheo e a Creusa,
di me, infin che si convenne al pelo;

　　né quella Rodopëa che delusa　　　　　　　100
fu da Demofoonte, né Alcide
quando Iole nel core ebbe rinchiusa.

　　Non però qui si pente, ma si ride,　　　　　　103
non de la colpa, ch'a mente non torna,
ma del valor ch'ordinò e provide.

　　Qui si rimira ne l'arte ch'addorna　　　　　　106
cotanto affetto, e discernesi 'l bene
per che 'l mondo di sù quel di giù torna.

On high, joy is made manifest by brightness,   70
as, here on earth, by smiles; but down below,
the shade grows darker when the mind feels sorrow.

"God can see all," I said, "and, blessed spirit,   73
your vision is contained in Him, so that
no wish can ever hide itself from you.

Your voice has always made the heavens glad,   76
as has the singing of the pious fires
that make themselves a cowl of their six wings:

why then do you not satisfy my longings?   79
I would not have to wait for your request
if I could enter you as you do me."

"The widest valley into which the waters   82
spread from the sea that girds the world," his words
began, "between discrepant shores, extends

eastward so far against the sun, that when   85
those waters end at the meridian,
that point—when they began—was the horizon.

I lived along the shoreline of that valley   88
between the Ebro and the Magra, whose
brief course divides the Genoese and Tuscans.

Beneath the same sunset, the same sunrise,   91
lie both Bougie and my own city, which
once warmed its harbor with its very blood.

Those men to whom my name was known, called me   94
Folco; and even as this sphere receives
my imprint, so was I impressed with its;

for even Belus' daughter, wronging both   97
Sychaeus and Creusa, did not burn
more than I did, as long as I was young;

nor did the Rhodopean woman whom   100
Demophoön deceived, nor did Alcides
when he enclosed Iole in his heart.

Yet one does not repent here; here one smiles—   103
not for the fault, which we do not recall,
but for the Power that fashioned and foresaw.

For here we contemplate the art adorned   106
by such great love, and we discern the good
through which the world above forms that below.

Ma perché tutte le tue voglie piene   109
ten porti che son nate in questa spera,
procedere ancor oltre mi convene.

Tu vuo' saper chi è in questa lumera   112
che qui appresso me così scintilla
come raggio di sole in acqua mera.

Or sappi che là entro si tranquilla   115
Raab; e a nostr' ordine congiunta,
di lei nel sommo grado si sigilla.

Da questo cielo, in cui l'ombra s'appunta   118
che 'l vostro mondo face, pria ch'altr' alma
del trïunfo di Cristo fu assunta.

Ben si convenne lei lasciar per palma   121
in alcun cielo de l'alta vittoria
che s'acquistò con l'una e l'altra palma,

perch' ella favorò la prima gloria   124
di Iosüè in su la Terra Santa,
che poco tocca al papa la memoria.

La tua città, che di colui è pianta   127
che pria volse le spalle al suo fattore
e di cui è la 'nvidia tanto pianta,

produce e spande il maladetto fiore   130
c'ha disvïate le pecore e li agni,
però che fatto ha lupo del pastore.

Per questo l'Evangelio e i dottor magni   133
son derelitti, e solo ai Decretali
si studia, sì che pare a' lor vivagni.

A questo intende il papa e ' cardinali;   136
non vanno i lor pensieri a Nazarette,
là dove Gabrïello aperse l'ali.

Ma Vaticano e l'altre parti elette   139
di Roma che son state cimitero
a la milizia che Pietro seguette,

tosto libere fien de l'avoltero."   142

But so that all your longings born within   109
this sphere may be completely satisfied
when you bear them away, I must continue.

You wish to know what spirit is within   112
the light that here beside me sparkles so,
as would a ray of sun in limpid water.

Know then that Rahab lives serenely in   115
that light, and since her presence joins our order,
she seals that order in the highest rank.

This heaven, where the shadow cast by earth   118
comes to a point, had Rahab as the first
soul to be taken up when Christ triumphed.

And it was right to leave her in this heaven   121
as trophy of the lofty victory
that Christ won, palm on palm, upon the cross,

for she had favored the initial glory   124
of Joshua within the Holy Land—
which seldom touches the Pope's memory.

Your city, which was planted by that one   127
who was the first to turn against his Maker,
the one whose envy cost us many tears—

produces and distributes the damned flower   130
that turns both sheep and lambs from the true course,
for of the shepherd it has made a wolf.

For this the Gospel and the great Church Fathers   133
are set aside and only the Decretals
are studied—as their margins clearly show.

On these the pope and cardinals are intent.   136
Their thoughts are never bent on Nazareth,
where Gabriel's open wings were reverent.

And yet the hill of Vatican as well   139
as other noble parts of Rome that were
the cemetery for Peter's soldiery

will soon be freed from priests' adultery."   142

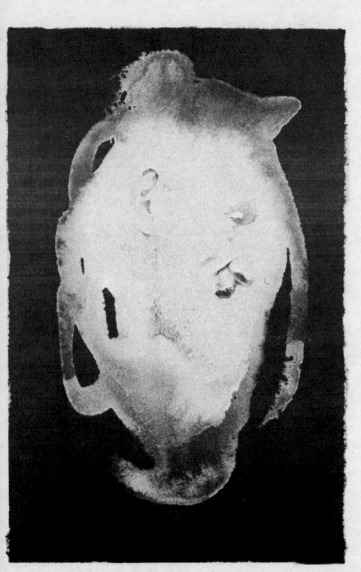

Thomas Aquinas and the Other 11 Lights

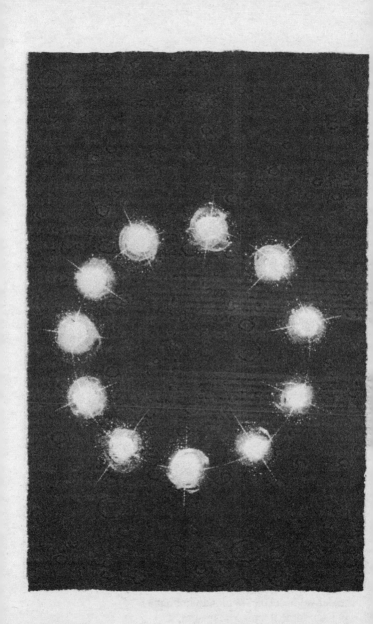

CANTO X

Guardando nel suo Figlio con l'Amore
che l'uno e l'altro etternalmente spira,
lo primo e ineffabile Valore

quanto per mente e per loco si gira   4
con tant' ordine fé, ch'esser non puote
sanza gustar di lui chi ciò rimira.

Leva dunque, lettore, a l'alte rote   7
meco la vista, dritto a quella parte
dove l'un moto e l'altro si percuote;

e lì comincia a vagheggiar ne l'arte   10
di quel maestro che dentro a sé l'ama,
tanto che mai da lei l'occhio non parte.

Vedi come da indi si dirama   13
l'oblico cerchio che i pianeti porta,
per sodisfare al mondo che li chiama.

Che se la strada lor non fosse torta,   16
molta virtù nel ciel sarebbe in vano,
e quasi ogne potenza qua giù morta;

e se dal dritto più o men lontano   19
fosse 'l partire, assai sarebbe manco
e giù e sù de l'ordine mondano.

Or ti riman, lettor, sovra 'l tuo banco,   22
dietro pensando a ciò che si preliba,
s'esser vuoi lieto assai prima che stanco.

Messo t'ho innanzi; omai per te ti ciba;   25
ché a sé torce tutta la mia cura
quella materia ond' io son fatto scriba.

Lo ministro maggior de la natura,   28
che del valor del ciel lo mondo imprenta
e col suo lume il tempo ne misura,

Divine wisdom and the harmony of Creation. Ascent to the Fourth Heaven, the Sphere of the Sun. Thanksgiving to God. St. Thomas and the other eleven spirits, who form a crown around Beatrice and Dante.

Gazing upon His Son with that Love which
  One and the Other breathe eternally,
the Power—first and inexpressible—

  made everything that wheels through mind and space　4
so orderly that one who contemplates
that harmony cannot but taste of Him.

  Then, reader, lift your eyes with me to see　7
the high wheels; gaze directly at that part
where the one motion strikes against the other;

  and there begin to look with longing at　10
that Master's art, which in Himself he loves
so much that his eye never parts from it.

  See there the circle branching from that cross-point　13
obliquely: zodiac to bear the planets
that satisfy the world in need of them.

  For if the planets' path were not aslant,　16
much of the heavens' virtue would be wasted
and almost every power on earth be dead;

  and if the zodiac swerved more or less　19
far from the straight course, then earth's harmony
would be defective in both hemispheres.

  Now, reader, do not leave your bench, but stay　22
to think on that of which you have foretaste;
you will have much delight before you tire.

  I have prepared your fare; now feed yourself,　25
because that matter of which I am made
the scribe calls all my care unto itself.

  The greatest minister of nature—he　28
who imprints earth with heaven's worth and, with
his light, provides the measurement for time—

con quella parte che sù si rammenta   31
congiunto, si girava per le spire
in che più tosto ognora s'appresenta;

e io era con lui; ma del salire   34
non m'accors' io, se non com' uom s'accorge,
anzi 'l primo pensier, del suo venire.

E Bëatrice quella che sì scorge   37
di bene in meglio, sì subitamente
che l'atto suo per tempo non si sporge.

Quant' esser convenia da sé lucente   40
quel ch'era dentro al sol dov' io entra'mi,
non per color, ma per lume parvente!

Perch' io lo 'ngegno e l'arte e l'uso chiami,   43
sì nol direi che mai s'imaginasse;
ma creder puossi e di veder si brami.

E se le fantasie nostre son basse   46
a tanta altezza, non è maraviglia;
ché sopra 'l sol non fu occhio ch'andasse.

Tal era quivi la quarta famiglia   49
de l'alto Padre, che sempre la sazia,
mostrando come spira e come figlia.

E Bëatrice cominciò: "Ringrazia,   52
ringrazia il Sol de li angeli, ch'a questo
sensibil t'ha levato per sua grazia."

Cor di mortal non fu mai sì digesto   55
a divozione e a rendersi a Dio
con tutto 'l suo gradir cotanto presto,

come a quelle parole mi fec' io;   58
e sì tutto 'l mio amore in lui si mise,
che Bëatrice eclissò ne l'oblio.

Non le dispiacque, ma sì se ne rise,   61
che lo splendor de li occhi suoi ridenti
mia mente unita in più cose divise.

Io vidi più folgór vivi e vincenti   64
far di noi centro e di sé far corona,
più dolci in voce che in vista lucenti:

così cinger la figlia di Latona   67
vedem talvolta, quando l'aere è pregno,
sì che ritenga il fil che fa la zona.

    since he was in conjunction with the part   31
I noted, now was wheeling through the spirals
where he appears more early every day.

    And I was with him, but no more aware   34
of the ascent than one can be aware
of any sudden thought before it starts.

    The one who guides me so from good to better   37
is Beatrice, and on our path her acts
have so much swiftness that they span no time.

    How bright within themselves must be the lights   40
I saw on entering the Sun, for they
were known to me by splendor, not by color!

    Though I should call on talent, craft, and practice, 43
my telling cannot help them be imagined;
but you can trust—and may you long to see it.

    And if our fantasies fall short before   46
such heights, there is no need to wonder; for
no eye has seen light brighter than the Sun's.

    Such was the sphere of His fourth family,   49
whom the High Father always satisfies,
showing how He engenders and breathes forth.

    And Beatrice began: "Give thanks, give thanks   52
to Him, the angels' Sun, who, through His grace,
has lifted you to this embodied sun."

    No mortal heart was ever so disposed   55
to worship, or so quick to yield itself
to God with all its gratefulness, as I

    was when I heard those words, and all my love   58
was so intent on Him that Beatrice
was then eclipsed within forgetfulness.

    And she was not displeased, but smiled at this,   61
so that the splendor of her smiling eyes
divided my rapt mind between two objects.

    And I saw many lights, alive, most bright;   64
we formed the center, they became a crown,
their voices even sweeter than their splendor:

    just so, at times, we see Latona's daughter   67
circled when saturated air holds fast
the thread that forms the girdle of her halo.

Ne la corte del cielo, ond' io rivegno,   70
si trovan molte gioie care e belle
tanto che non si posson trar del regno;

    e 'l canto di quei lumi era di quelle;   73
chi non s'impenna sì che là sù voli,
dal muto aspetti quindi le novelle.

    Poi, sì cantando, quelli ardenti soli   76
si fuor girati intorno a noi tre volte,
come stelle vicine a' fermi poli,

    donne mi parver, non da ballo sciolte,   79
ma che s'arrestin tacite, ascoltando
fin che le nove note hanno ricolte.

    E dentro a l'un senti' cominciar: "Quando   82
lo raggio de la grazia, onde s'accende
verace amore e che poi cresce amando,

    multiplicato in te tanto resplende,   85
che ti conduce su per quella scala
u' sanza risalir nessun discende;

    qual ti negasse il vin de la sua fiala   88
per la tua sete, in libertà non fora
se non com' acqua ch'al mar non si cala.

    Tu vuo' saper di quai piante s'infiora   91
questa ghirlanda che 'ntorno vagheggia
la bella donna ch'al ciel t'avvalora.

    Io fui de li agni de la santa greggia   94
che Domenico mena per cammino
u' ben s'impingua se non si vaneggia.

    Questi che m'è a destra più vicino,   97
frate e maestro fummi, ed esso Alberto
è di Cologna, e io Thomas d' Aquino.

    Se sì di tutti li altri esser vuo' certo,   100
di retro al mio parlar ten vien col viso
girando su per lo beato serto.

    Quell' altro fiammeggiare esce del riso   103
di Grazïan, che l'uno e l'altro foro
aiutò sì che piace in paradiso.

    L'altro ch'appresso addorna il nostro coro,   106
quel Pietro fu che con la poverella
offerse a Santa Chiesa suo tesoro.

In Heaven's court, from which I have returned,   70
one finds so many fair and precious gems
that are not to be taken from that kingdom:
     one of those gems, the song those splendors sang.   73
He who does not take wings to reach that realm,
may wait for tidings of it from the mute.

After those ardent suns, while singing so,   76
had wheeled three times around us, even as
stars that are close to the fixed poles, they seemed
     to me like women who, though not released   79
from dancing, pause in silence, listening
until new notes invite to new dancing.

And from within one light I heard begin: 82
"Because the ray of grace, from which true love
is kindled first and then, in loving, grows,
     shines with such splendor, multiplied, in you,   85
that it has led you up the stair that none
descends who will not climb that stair again,
     whoever would refuse to quench your thirst   88
with wine from his flask, would be no more free
than water that does not flow toward the sea.

You want to know what plants bloom in this garland   91
that, circling, contemplates with love the fair
lady who strengthens your ascent to heaven.

I was a lamb among the holy flock   94
that Dominic leads on the path where one
may fatten well if one does not stray off.

He who is nearest on my right was both   97
my brother and my teacher: from Cologne,
Albert, and I am Thomas of Aquino.

If you would know who all the others are,   100
then even as I speak let your eyes follow,
making their way around the holy wreath.

That next flame issues from the smile of Gratian,   103
who served one and the other court of law
so well that his work pleases Paradise.

That other, who adorns our choir next—   106
he was that Peter who, like the poor widow,
offered his treasure to the Holy Church.

La quinta luce, ch'è tra noi più bella,   109
spira di tale amor, che tutto 'l mondo
là giù ne gola di saper novella:
    entro v'è l'alta mente u' sì profondo   112
saver fu messo, che, se 'l vero è vero,
a veder tanto non surse il secondo.
    Appresso vedi il lume di quel cero   115
che giù in carne più a dentro vide
l'angelica natura e 'l ministero.
    Ne l'altra piccioletta luce ride   118
quello avvocato de' tempi cristiani
del cui latino Augustin si provide.
    Or se tu l'occhio de la mente trani   121
di luce in luce dietro a le mie lode,
già de l'ottava con sete rimani.
    Per vedere ogne ben dentro vi gode   124
l'anima santa che 'l mondo fallace
fa manifesto a chi di lei ben ode.
    Lo corpo ond' ella fu cacciata giace   127
giuso in Cieldauro; ed essa da martiro
e da essilio venne a questa pace.
    Vedi oltre fiammeggiar l'ardente spiro   130
d'Isidoro, di Beda e di Riccardo,
che a considerar fu più che viro.
    Questi onde a me ritorna il tuo riguardo,   133
è 'l lume d'uno spirto che 'n pensieri
gravi a morir li parve venir tardo:
    essa è luce etterna di Sigieri,   136
che, leggendo nel Vico de li Strami,
silogizzò invidïosi veri."
    Indi, come orologio che ne chiami   139
ne l'ora che la sposa di Dio surge
a mattinar lo sposo perché l'ami,
    che l'una parte e l'altra tira e urge,   142
tin tin sonando con sì dolce nota,
che 'l ben disposto spirto d'amor turge;
    così vid' ïo la gloriosa rota   145
muoversi e render voce a voce in tempra
e in dolcezza ch'esser non pò nota
    se non colà dove gioir s'insempra.   148

The fifth light, and the fairest light among us,   109
breathes forth such love that all the world below
hungers for tidings of it; in that flame

there is the lofty mind where such profound   112
wisdom was placed that, if the truth be true,
no other ever rose with so much vision.

Next you can see the radiance of that candle   115
which, in the flesh, below, beheld most deeply
the angels' nature and their ministry.

Within the other little light there smiles   118
that champion of the Christian centuries
whose narrative was used by Augustine.

Now, if your mind's eye, following my praising,   121
was drawn from light to light, you must already
be thirsting for the eighth: within that light,

because he saw the Greatest Good, rejoices   124
the blessed soul who makes the world's deceit
most plain to all who hear him carefully.

The flesh from which his soul was banished lies   127
below, within Cieldauro, and he came
from martyrdom and exile to this peace.

Beyond, you see, flaming, the ardent spirits   130
of Isidore and Bede and Richard—he
whose meditation made him more than man.

This light from whom your gaze returns to me   133
contains a spirit whose oppressive thoughts
made him see death as coming much too slowly:

it is the everlasting light of Siger,   136
who when he lectured in the Street of Straw,
demonstrated truths that earned him envy."

Then, like a clock that calls us at the hour   139
in which the Bride of God, on waking, sings
matins to her Bridegroom, encouraging

His love (when each clock-part both drives and draws),   142
chiming the sounds with notes so sweet that those
with spirit well-disposed feel their love grow;

so did I see the wheel that moved in glory   145
go round and render voice to voice with such
sweetness and such accord that they can not

be known except where joy is everlasting.   148

CANTO XI

O insensata cura de' mortali,
  quanto son difettivi silogismi
quei che ti fanno in basso batter l'ali!

  Chi dietro a *iura* e chi ad amforismi   4
sen giva, e chi seguendo sacerdozio,
e chi regnar per forza o per sofismi,

  e chi rubare e chi civil negozio,   7
chi nel diletto de la carne involto
s'affaticava e chi si dava a l'ozio,

  quando, da tutte queste cose sciolto,   10
con Bëatrice m'era suso in cielo
cotanto glorïosamente accolto.

  Poi che ciascuno fu tornato ne lo   13
punto del cerchio in che avanti s'era,
fermossi, come a candellier candelo.

  E io senti' dentro a quella lumera   16
che pria m'avea parlato, sorridendo
incominciar, faccendosi più mera:

  "Così com' io del suo raggio resplendo,   19
sì, riguardando ne la luce etterna,
li tuoi pensieri onde cagioni apprendo.

  Tu dubbi, e hai voler che si ricerna   22
in sì aperta e 'n sì distesa lingua
lo dicer mio, ch'al tuo sentir si sterna,

  ove dinanzi dissi: 'U' ben s'impingua,'   25
e là u' dissi: 'Non nacque il secondo';
e qui è uopo che ben si distingua.

  La provedenza, che governa il mondo   28
con quel consiglio nel quale ogne aspetto
creato è vinto pria che vada al fondo,

The Fourth Heaven: the Sphere of the Sun. The senseless cares of mortals. The long clarification by St. Thomas of his comment on his own order, the Dominicans. His telling of the life of St. Francis, who wed Poverty and founded the Franciscans.

O senseless cares of mortals, how deceiving
    are syllogistic reasonings that bring
your wings to flight so low, to earthly things!

    One studied law and one the *Aphorisms*   4
of the physicians; one was set on priesthood
and one, through force or fraud, on rulership;

    one meant to plunder, one to politick;   7
one labored, tangled in delights of flesh,
and one was fully bent on indolence;

    while I, delivered from our servitude   10
to all these things, was in the height of heaven
with Beatrice, so gloriously welcomed.

    After each of those spirits had returned   13
to that place in the ring where it had been,
it halted, like a candle in its stand.

    And from within the splendor that had spoken   16
to me before, I heard him, as he smiled—
become more radiant, more pure—begin:

    "Even as I grow bright within Its rays,   19
so, as I gaze at the Eternal Light,
I can perceive your thoughts and see their cause.

    You are in doubt; you want an explanation   22
in language that is open and expanded,
so clear that it contents your understanding

    of two points: where I said, 'They fatten well,'   25
and where I said, 'No other ever rose'—
and here one has to make a clear distinction.

    The Providence that rules the world with wisdom   28
so fathomless that creatures' intellects
are vanquished and can never probe its depth,

    però che andasse ver' lo suo diletto   31
la sposa di colui ch'ad alte grida
disposò lei col sangue benedetto,

    in sé sicura e anche a lui più fida,   34
due principi ordinò in suo favore,
che quinci e quindi le fosser per guida.

    L'un fu tutto serafico in ardore;   37
l'altro per sapïenza in terra fue
di cherubica luce uno splendore.

    De l'un dirò, però che d'amendue   40
si dice l'un pregiando, qual ch'om prende,
perch' ad un fine fur l'opere sue.

    Intra Tupino e l'acqua che discende   43
del colle eletto dal beato Ubaldo,
fertile costa d'alto monte pende,

    onde Perugia sente freddo e caldo   46
da Porta Sole; e di rietro le piange
per grave giogo Nocera con Gualdo.

    Di questa costa, là dov' ella frange   47
più sua rattezza, nacque al mondo un sole,
come fa questo talvolta di Gange.

    Però chi d'esso loco fa parole,   52
non dica Ascesi, ché direbbe corto,
ma Orïente, se proprio dir vuole.

    Non era ancor molto lontan da l'orto,   55
ch'el cominciò a far sentir la terra
de la sua gran virtute alcun conforto;

    ché per tal donna, giovinetto, in guerra   58
del padre corse, a cui, come a la morte,
la porta del piacer nessun diserra;

    e dinanzi a la sua spirital corte   61
et coram patre le si fece unito;
poscia di dì in dì l'amò più forte.

    Questa, privata del primo marito,   64
millecent' anni e più dispetta e scura
fino a costui si stette sanza invito;

    né valse udir che la trovò sicura   67
con Amiclate, al suon de la sua voce,
colui ch'a tutto 'l mondo fé paura;

so that the Bride of Him who, with loud cries,   31
had wed her with His blessed blood, might meet
her Love with more fidelity and more

assurance in herself, on her behalf   34
commanded that there be two princes, one
on this side, one on that side, as her guides.

One prince was all seraphic in his ardor;   37
the other, for his wisdom, had possessed
the splendor of cherubic light on earth.

I shall devote my tale to one, because   40
in praising either prince one praises both:
the labors of the two were toward one goal.

Between Topino's stream and that which flows   43
down from the hill the blessed Ubaldo chose,
from a high peak there hangs a fertile slope;

from there Perugia feels both heat and cold   46
at Porta Sole, while behind it sorrow
Nocera and Gualdo under their hard yoke.

From this hillside, where it abates its rise,   49
a sun was born into the world, much like
this sun when it is climbing from the Ganges.

Therefore let him who names this site not say   52
Ascesi, which would be to say too little,
but *Orient,* if he would name it rightly.

That sun was not yet very distant from   55
his rising, when he caused the earth to take
some comfort from his mighty influence;

for even as a youth, he ran to war   58
against his father, on behalf of her—
the lady unto whom, just as to death,

none willingly unlocks the door; before   61
his spiritual court *et coram patre,*
he wed her; day by day he loved her more.

She was bereft of her first husband; scorned,   64
obscure, for some eleven hundred years,
until that sun came, she had had no suitor.

Nor did it help her when men heard that he   67
who made earth tremble found her unafraid—
serene, with Amyclas—when he addressed her;

né valse esser costante né feroce,   70
sì che, dove Maria rimase giuso,
ella con Cristo pianse in su la croce.

Ma perch' io non proceda troppo chiuso,   73
Francesco e Povertà per questi amanti
prendi oramai nel mio parlar diffuso.

La lor concordia e i lor lieti sembianti,   76
amore e maraviglia e dolce sguardo
facieno esser cagion di pensier santi;

tanto che 'l venerabile Bernardo   79
si scalzò prima, e dietro a tanta pace
corse e, correndo, li parve esser tardo.

Oh ignota ricchezza! oh ben ferace!   82
Scalzasi Egidio, scalzasi Silvestro
dietro a lo sposo, sì la sposa piace.

Indi sen va quel padre e quel maestro   85
con la sua donna e con quella famiglia
che già legava l'umile capestro.

Né li gravò viltà di cuor le ciglia   88
per esser fi' di Pietro Bernardone,
né per parer dispetto a maraviglia;

ma regalmente sua dura intenzione   91
ad Innocenzio aperse, e da lui ebbe
primo sigillo a sua religïone.

Poi che la gente poverella crebbe   94
dietro a costui, la cui mirabil vita
meglio in gloria del ciel si canterebbe,

di seconda corona redimita   97
fu per Onorio da l'Etterno Spiro
la santa voglia d'esto archimandrita.

E poi che, per la sete del martiro,   100
ne la presenza del Soldan superba
predicò Cristo e li altri che 'l seguiro,

e per trovare a conversione acerba   103
troppo la gente e per non stare indarno,
redissi al frutto de l'italica erba,

nel crudo sasso intra Tevero e Arno   106
da Cristo prese l'ultimo sigillo,
che le sue membra due anni portarno.

nor did her constancy and courage help   70
when she, even when Mary stayed below,
suffered with Christ upon the cross. But so

that I not tell my tale too darkly, you   73
may now take Francis and take Poverty
to be the lovers meant in my recounting.

Their harmony and their glad looks, their love   76
and wonder and their gentle contemplation,
served others as a source of holy thoughts;

so much so, that the venerable Bernard   79
went barefoot first; he hurried toward such peace;
and though he ran, he thought his pace too slow.

O wealth unknown! O good that is so fruitful!   82
Egidius goes barefoot, and Sylvester,
behind the groom—the bride delights them so.

Then Francis—father, master—goes his way   85
with both his lady and his family,
the lowly cord already round their waists.

Nor did he lower his eyes in shame because   88
he was the son of Pietro Bernardone,
nor for the scorn and wonder he aroused;

but like a sovereign, he disclosed in full—   91
to Innocent—the sternness of his rule;
from him he had the first seal of his order.

And after many of the poor had followed   94
Francis, whose wondrous life were better sung
by glory's choir in the Empyrean,

the sacred purpose of this chief of shepherds   97
was then encircled with a second crown
by the Eternal Spirit through Honorius.

And after, in his thirst for martyrdom,   100
within the presence of the haughty Sultan,
he preached of Christ and those who followed Him.

But, finding hearers who were too unripe   103
to be converted, he—not wasting time—
returned to harvest the Italian fields;

there, on the naked crag between the Arno   106
and Tiber, he received the final seal
from Christ; and this, his limbs bore for two years.

Quando a colui ch'a tanto ben sortillo 109
piacque di trarlo suso a la mercede
ch'el meritò nel suo farsi pusillo,

a' frati suoi, sì com' a giuste rede, 112
raccomandò la donna su più cara,
e comandò che l'amassero a fede;

e del suo grembo l'anima preclara 115
mover si volle, tornando al suo regno,
e al suo corpo non volle altra bara.

Pensa oramai qual fu colui che degno 118
collega fu a mantener la barca
di Pietro in alto mar per dritto segno;

e questo fu il nostro patrïarca; 121
per che qual segue lui, com' el comanda,
discerner puoi che buone merce carca.

Ma 'l suo peculio di nova vivanda 124
è fatto ghiotto, sì ch'esser non puote
che per diversi salti non si spanda;

e quanto le sue pecore remote 127
e vagabunde più da esso vanno,
più tornano a l'ovil di latte vòte.

Ben son di quelle che temono 'l danno 130
e stringonsi al pastor; ma son sì poche,
che le cappe fornisce poco panno.

Or, se le mie parole non son fioche, 133
se la tua audïenza è stata attenta,
se ciò ch'è detto a la mente revoche,

in parte fia la tua voglia contenta, 136
perché vedrai la pianta onde si scheggia,
e vedra' il corrègger che argomenta

'U' ben s'impingua, se non si vaneggia.' " 139

When He who destined Francis to such goodness   109
was pleased to draw him up to the reward
that he had won through his humility,

    then to his brothers, as to rightful heirs,   112
Francis commended his most precious lady,
and he bade them to love her faithfully;

    and when, returning to its kingdom, his   115
bright soul wanted to set forth from her bosom,
it, for its body, asked no other bier.

    Consider now that man who was a colleague   118
worthy of Francis; with him, in high seas,
he kept the bark of Peter on true course.

    Such was our patriarch; thus you can see   121
that those who follow him as he commands,
as cargo carry worthy merchandise.

    But now his flock is grown so greedy for   124
new nourishment that it must wander far,
in search of strange and distant grazing lands;

    and as his sheep, remote and vagabond,   127
stray farther from his side, at their return
into the fold, their lack of milk is greater.

    Though there are some indeed who, fearing harm,   130
stay near the shepherd, they are few in number—
to cowl them would require little cloth.

    Now if my words are not too dim and distant,   133
if you have listened carefully to them,
if you can call to mind what has been said,

    then part of what you wish to know is answered,   136
for you will see the splinters on the plant
and see what my correction meant: 'Where one

    may fatten well, *if one does not stray off.*' "   139

Sts. Francis and Dominic

CANTO XII

Sì tosto come l'ultima parola
la benedetta fiamma per dir tolse,
a rotar cominciò la santa mola;

e nel suo giro tutta non si volse   4
prima ch'un'altra di cerchio la chiuse,
e moto a moto e canto a canto colse;

canto che tanto vince nostre muse,   7
nostre serene in quelle dolci tube,
quanto primo splendor quel ch'e' refuse.

Come se volgon per tenera nube   10
due archi paralelli e concolori,
quando Iunone a sua ancella iube,

nascendo di quel d'entro quel di fori,   13
a guisa del parlar di quella vaga
ch'amor consunse come sol vapori,

e fanno qui la gente esser presaga,   16
per lo patto che Dio con Noè puose,
del mondo che già mai più non s'allaga:

così di quelle sempiterne rose   19
volgiensi circa noi le due ghirlande,
e sì l'estrema a l'intima rispuose.

Poi che 'l tripudio e l'altra festa grande,   22
sì del cantare e sì del fiammeggiarsi
luce con luce gaudïose e blande,

insieme a punto e a voler quetarsi,   25
pur come li occhi ch'al piacer che i move
conviene insieme chiudere e levarsi;

del cor de l'una de le luci nove   28
si mosse voce, che l'ago a la stella
parer mi fece in volgermi al suo dove;

No sooner had the blessed flame begun
to speak its final word than the millstone
of holy lights began to turn, but it

was not yet done with one full revolution   4
before another ring surrounded it,
and motion matched with motion, song with song—

a song that, sung by those sweet instruments,   7
surpasses so our Muses and our Sirens
as firstlight does the light that is reflected.

Just as, concentric, like in color, two   10
rainbows will curve their way through a thin cloud
when Juno has commanded her handmaid,

the outer rainbow echoing the inner,   13
much like the voice of one—the wandering nymph—
whom love consumed as sun consumes the mist

(and those two bows let people here foretell,   16
by reason of the pact God made with Noah,
that flood will never strike the world again):

so the two garlands of those everlasting   19
roses circled around us, and so did
the outer circle mime the inner ring.

When dance and jubilation, festival   22
of song and flame that answered flame, of light
with light, of gladness and benevolence,

in one same instant, with one will, fell still   25
(just as the eyes, when moved by their desire,
can only close and open in accord),

then from the heart of one of the new lights   28
there came a voice, and as I turned toward it,
I seemed a needle turning to the polestar;

e cominciò: "L'amor che mi fa bella   31
mi tragge a ragionar de l'altro duca
per cui del mio sì ben ci si favella.

Degno è che, dov' è l'un, l'altro s'induca: 34
sì che, com' elli ad una militaro,
così la gloria loro insieme luca.

L'essercito di Cristo, che sì caro   37
costò a rïarmar, dietro a la 'nsegna
si movea tardo, sospeccioso e raro,

quando lo 'mperador che sempre regna   40
provide a la milizia, ch'era in forse,
per sola grazia, non per esser degna;

e, come è detto, a sua sposa soccorse   43
con due campioni, al cui fare, al cui dire
lo popol disvïato si raccorse.

In quella parte ove surge ad aprire   46
Zenfiro dolce le novelle fronde
di che si vede Europa rivestire,

non molto lungi al percuoter de l'onde   49
dietro a le quali, per la lunga foga,
lo sol talvolta ad ogne uom si nasconde,

siede la fortunata Calaroga   52
sotto la protezion del grande scudo
in che soggiace il leone e soggioga:

dentro vi nacque l'amoroso drudo   55
de la fede cristiana, il santo atleta
benigno a' suoi e a' nemici crudo;

e come fu creata, fu repleta   58
sì la sua mente di viva vertute
che, ne la madre, lei fece profeta.

Poi che le sponsalizie fuor compiute   61
al sacro fonte intra lui e la Fede,
u' si dotar di mutüa salute,

la donna che per lui l'assenso diede,   64
vide nel sonno il mirabile frutto
ch'uscir dovea di lui e de le rede;

e perché fosse qual era in costrutto,   67
quinci si mosse spirito a nomarlo
del possessivo di cui era tutto.

and it began: "The love that makes me fair   31
draws me to speak about the other leader
because of whom my own was so praised here.

Where one is, it is right to introduce   34
the other: side by side, they fought, so may
they share in glory and together gleam.

Christ's army, whose rearming cost so dearly,   37
was slow, uncertain of itself, and scanty
behind its ensign, when the Emperor

who rules forever helped his ranks in danger—   40
only out of His grace and not their merits.
And, as was said, He then sustained His bride,

providing her with two who could revive   43
a straggling people: champions who would
by doing and by preaching bring new life.

In that part of the West where gentle zephyr   46
rises to open those new leaves in which
Europe appears reclothed, not far from where,

behind the waves that beat upon the coast,   49
the sun, grown weary from its lengthy course,
at times conceals itself from all men's eyes—

there, Calaroga, blessed by fortune, sits   52
under the aegis of the mighty shield
on which the lion loses and prevails.

Within its walls was born the loving vassal   55
of Christian faith, the holy athlete, one
kind to his own and harsh to enemies;

no sooner was his mind created than   58
it was so full of living force that it,
still in his mother's womb, made her prophetic.

Then, at the sacred font, where Faith and he   61
brought mutual salvation as their dowry,
the rites of their espousal were complete.

The lady who had given the assent   64
for him saw, in a dream, astonishing
fruit that would spring from him and from his heirs.

And that his name might echo what he was,   67
a spirit moved from here to have him called
by the possessive of the One by whom

Domenico fu detto; e io ne parlo   70
sì come de l'agricola che Cristo
elesse a l'orto suo per aiutarlo.

Ben parve messo e famigliar di Cristo: 73
ché 'l primo amor che 'n lui fu manifesto,
fu al primo consiglio che diè Cristo.

Spesse fïate fu tacito e desto   76
trovato in terra da la sua nutrice,
come dicesse: 'Io son venuto a questo.'

Oh padre suo veramente Felice!   79
oh madre sua veramente Giovanna,
se, interpretata, val come si dice!

Non per lo mondo, per cui mo s'affanna   82
di retro ad Ostïense e a Taddeo,
ma per amor de la verace manna

in picciol tempo gran dottor si feo;   85
tal che si mise a circüir la vigna
che tosto imbianca, se 'l vignaio è reo.

E a la sedia che fu già benigna   88
più a' poveri giusti, non per lei,
ma per colui che siede, che traligna,

non dispensare o due o tre per sei,   91
non la fortuna di prima vacante,
non decimas, quae sunt pauperum Dei,

addimandò, ma contro al mondo errante   94
licenza di combatter per lo seme
del qual ti fascian ventiquattro piante.

Poi, con dottrina e con volere insieme,   97
con l'officio appostolico si mosse
quasi torrente ch'alta vena preme;

e ne li sterpi eretici percosse   100
l'impeto suo, più vivamente quivi
dove le resistenze eran più grosse.

Di lui si fecer poi diversi rivi   103
onde l'orto catolico si riga,
sì che i suoi arbuscelli stan più vivi.

Se tal fu l'una rota de la biga   106
in che la Santa Chiesa si difese
e vinse in campo la sua civil briga,

he was possessed completely. Dominic   70
became his name; I speak of him as one
whom Christ chose as the worker in His garden.

He seemed the fitting messenger and servant   73
of Christ: the very first love that he showed
was for the first injunction Christ had given.

His nurse would often find him on the ground,   76
alert and silent, in a way that said:
'It is for this that I have come.' Truly,

his father was Felice and his mother   79
Giovanna if her name, interpreted,
is in accord with what has been asserted.

Not for the world, for which men now travail   82
along Taddeo's way or Ostian's,
but through his love of the true manna, he

became, in a brief time, so great a teacher   85
that he began to oversee the vineyard
that withers when neglected by its keeper.

And from the seat that once was kinder to   88
the righteous poor (and now has gone astray,
not in itself, but in its occupant),

he did not ask to offer two or three   91
for six, nor for a vacant benefice,
nor *decimas, quae sunt pauperum Dei*—

but pleaded for the right to fight against   94
the erring world, to serve the seed from which
there grew the four-and-twenty plants that ring you.

Then he, with both his learning and his zeal,   97
and with his apostolic office, like
a torrent hurtled from a mountain source,

coursed, and his impetus, with greatest force,   100
struck where the thickets of the heretics
offered the most resistance. And from him

there sprang the streams with which the catholic   103
garden has found abundant watering,
so that its saplings have more life, more green.

If such was one wheel of the chariot   106
in which the Holy Church, in her defense,
taking the field, defeated enemies

ben ti dovrebbe assai esser palese   109
l'eccellenza de l'altra, di cui Tomma
dinanzi al mio venir fu sì cortese.

Ma l'orbita che fé la parte somma   112
di sua circunferenza, è derelitta,
sì ch'è la muffa dov' era la gromma.

La sua famiglia, che si mosse dritta   115
coi piedi a le sue orme, è tanto volta,
che quel dinanzi a quel di retro gitta;

e tosto si vedrà de la ricolta   118
de la mala coltura, quando il loglio
si lagnerà che l'arca li sia tolta.

Ben dico, chi cercasse a foglio a foglio   121
nostro volume, ancor troveria carta
u' leggerebbe 'I' mi son quel ch'i' soglio';

ma non fia da Casal né d'Acquasparta,   124
là onde vegnon tali a la scrittura,
ch'uno la fugge e altro la coarta.

Io son la vita di Bonaventura   127
da Bagnoregio, che ne' grandi offici
sempre pospuosi la sinistra cura.

Illuminato e Augustin son quici,   130
che fuor de' primi scalzi poverelli
che nel capestro a Dio si fero amici.

Ugo da San Vittore è qui con elli,   133
e Pietro Mangiadore e Pietro Spano,
lo qual giù luce in dodici libelli;

Natàn profeta e 'l metropolitano   136
Crisostomo e Anselmo e quel Donato
ch'a la prim' arte degnò porre mano.

Rabano è qui, e lucemi dallato   139
il calavrese abate Giovacchino
di spirito profetico dotato.

Ad inveggiar cotanto paladino   142
mi mosse l'infiammata cortesia
di fra Tommaso e 'l discreto latino;

e mosse meco questa compagnia."   145

within, then you must see the excellence   109
of him—the other wheel—whom Thomas praised
so graciously before I made my entry.

And yet the track traced by the outer rim   112
of that wheel is abandoned now—as in
a cask of wine when crust gives way to mold.

His family, which once advanced with steps   115
that followed his footprints, has now turned back:
its forward foot now seeks the foot that lags.

And soon we are to see, at harvest time,   118
the poor grain gathered, when the tares will be
denied a place within the bin—and weep.

I do admit that, if one were to search   121
our volume leaf by leaf, he might still read
one page with, 'I am as I always was';

but those of Acquasparta or Casale   124
who read our Rule are either given to
escaping it or making it too strict.

I am the living light of Bonaventure   127
of Bagnorea; in high offices
I always put the left-hand interests last.

Illuminato and Augustine are here;   130
they were among the first unshod poor brothers
to wear the cord, becoming friends of God.

Hugh of St. Victor, too, is here with them;   133
Peter of Spain, who, with his twelve books, glows
on earth below; and Peter Book-Devourer,

Nathan the prophet, Anselm, and Chrysostom   136
the Metropolitan, and that Donatus
who deigned to deal with that art which comes first.

Rabanus, too, is here; and at my side   139
shines the Calabrian Abbot Joachim,
who had the gift of the prophetic spirit.

To this—my praise of such a paladin—   142
the glowing courtesy and the discerning
language of Thomas urged me on and stirred,

with me, the souls that form this company."   145

CANTO XIII

Imagini, chi bene intender cupe
quel chi'i' or vidi—e ritegna l'image,
mentre ch'io dico, come ferma rupe—,

quindici stelle che 'n diverse plage   4
lo cielo avvivan di tanto sereno
che soperchia de l'aere ogne compage;

imagini quel carro a cu' il seno   7
basta del nostro cielo e notte e giorno,
sì ch'al volger del temo non vien meno;

imagini la bocca di quel corno   10
che si comincia in punta de lo stelo
a cui la prima rota va dintorno,

aver fatto di sé due segni in cielo,   13
qual fece la figliuola di Minoi
allora che sentì di morte il gelo;

e l'un ne l'altro aver li raggi suoi,   16
e amendue girarsi per maniera
che l'uno andasse al primo e l'altro al poi;

e avrà quasi l'ombra de la vera   19
costellazione e de la doppia danza
che circulava il punto dov' io era:

poi ch'è tanto di là da nostra usanza,   22
quanto di là dal mover de la Chiana
si move il ciel che tutti li altri avanza.

Lì si cantò non Bacco, non Peana,   25
ma tre persone in divina natura,
e in una persona essa e l'umana.

Compié 'l cantare e 'l volger sua misura;   28
e attesersi a noi quei santi lumi,
felicitando sé di cura in cura.

L et him imagine, who would rightly seize
　　what I saw now—and let him while I speak
retain that image like a steadfast rock—

　　in heaven's different parts, those fifteen stars　　　　4
that quicken heaven with such radiance
as to undo the air's opacities;

　　let him imagine, too, that Wain which stays　　　　7
within our heaven's bosom night and day,
so that its turning never leaves our sight;

　　let him imagine those two stars that form　　　　10
the mouth of that Horn which begins atop
the axle round which the first wheel revolves;

　　then see these join to form two signs in heaven—　　　13
just like the constellation that was shaped
by Minos' daughter when she felt death's chill—

　　two signs with corresponding radii,　　　　16
revolving so that one sign moves in one
direction, and the other in a second;

　　and he will have a shadow—as it were—　　　　19
of the true constellation, the double dance
that circled round the point where I was standing:

　　a shadow—since its truth exceeds our senses,　　　22
just as the swiftest of all heavens is
more swift than the Chiana's sluggishness.

　　They sang no Bacchus there, they sang no Paean,　　25
but sang three Persons in the divine nature,
and in one Person the divine and human.

　　The singing and the dance fulfilled their measure;　　28
and then those holy lights gave heed to us,
rejoicing as they turned from task to task.

Ruppe il silenzio ne' concordi numi   31
poscia la luce in che mirabil vita
del poverel di Dio narrata fumi,

    e disse: "Quando l'una paglia è trita,   34
quando la sua semenza è già riposta,
a batter l'altra dolce amor m'invita.

    Tu credi che nel petto onde la costa   37
si trasse per formar la bella guancia
il cui palato a tutto 'l mondo costa,

    e in quel che, forato da la lancia,   40
e prima e poscia tanto sodisfece,
che d'ogne colpa vince la bilancia,

    quantunque a la natura umana lece   43
aver di lume, tutto fosse infuso
da quel valor che l'uno e l'altro fece;

    e però miri a ciò ch'io dissi suso,   46
quando narrai che non ebbe 'l secondo
lo ben che ne la quinta luce è chiuso.

    Or apri li occhi a quel ch'io ti rispondo,   49
e vedräi il tuo credere e 'l mio dire
nel vero farsi come centro in tondo.

    Ciò che non more e ciò che può morire   52
non è se non splendor di quella idea
che partorisce, amando, il nostro Sire;

    ché quella viva luce che sì mea   55
dal suo lucente, che non si disuna
da lui né da l'amor ch'a lor s'intrea,

    per sua bontate il suo raggiare aduna,   58
quasi specchiato, in nove sussistenze,
etternalmente rimanendosi una.

    Quindi discende a l'ultime potenze   61
giù d'atto in atto, tanto divenendo,
che più non fa che brevi contingenze;

    e queste contingenze essere intendo   64
le cose generate, che produce
con seme e sanza seme il ciel movendo.

    La cera di costoro e chi la duce   67
non sta d'un modo; e però sotto 'l segno
idëale poi più e men traluce.

The silence of the blessed fellowship   31
was broken by the very light from which
I heard the wondrous life of God's poor man;

that light said: "Since one stalk is threshed, and since   34
its grain is in the granary already,
sweet love leads me to thresh the other stalk.

You think that any light which human nature   37
can rightfully possess was all infused
by that Force which had shaped both of these two:

the one out of whose chest was drawn the rib   40
from which was formed the lovely cheek whose palate
was then to prove so costly to the world;

and One whose chest was transfixed by the lance,   43
who satisfied all past and future sins,
outweighing them upon the scales of justice.

Therefore you wondered at my words when I—   46
before—said that no other ever vied
with that great soul enclosed in the fifth light.

Now let your eyes hold fast to my reply,   49
and you will see: truth centers both my speech
and your belief, just like a circle's center.

Both that which never dies and that which dies   52
are only the reflected light of that
Idea which our Sire, with Love, begets;

because the living Light that pours out so   55
from Its bright Source that It does not disjoin
from It or from the Love intrined with them,

through Its own goodness gathers up Its rays   58
within nine essences, as in a mirror,
Itself eternally remaining One.

From there, from act to act, light then descends   61
down to the last potentialities,
where it is such that it engenders nothing

but brief contingent things, by which I mean   64
the generated things the moving heavens
bring into being, with or without seed.

The wax of such things and what shapes that wax   67
are not immutable; and thus, beneath
Idea's stamp, light shines through more or less.

Ond' elli avvien ch'un medesimo legno, 70
secondo specie, meglio e peggio frutta;
e voi nascete con diverso ingegno.

Se fosse a punto la cera dedutta 73
e fosse il cielo in sua virtù supprema,
la luce del suggel parrebbe tutta;

ma la natura la dà sempre scema, 76
similemente operando a l'artista
ch'a l'abito de l'arte ha man che trema.

Però se 'l caldo amor la chiara vista 79
de la prima virtù dispone e segna,
tutta la perfezion quivi s'acquista.

Così fu fatta già la terra degna 82
di tutta l'animal perfezïone;
così fu fatta la Vergine pregna;

sì ch'io commendo tua oppinïone, 85
che l'umana natura mai non fue
né fia qual fu in quelle due persone.

Or s'i' non procedesse avanti pïue, 88
'Dunque, come costui fu sanza pare?'
comincerebber le parole tue.

Ma perché paia ben ciò che non pare, 91
pensa chi era, e la cagion che 'l mosse,
quando fu detto 'Chiedi,' a dimandare.

Non ho parlato sì, che tu non posse 94
ben veder ch'el fu re, che chiese senno
acciò che re sufficïente fosse;

non per sapere il numero in che enno 97
li motor di qua sù, o se *necesse*
con contingente mai *necesse* fenno;

non *si est dare primum motum esse,* 100
o se del mezzo cerchio far si puote
trïangol sì ch'un retto non avesse.

Onde, se ciò ch'io dissi e questo note, 103
regal prudenza è quel vedere impari
in che lo stral di mia intenzion percuote;

e se al "surse" drizzi li occhi chiari, 106
vedrai aver solamente respetto
ai regi, che son molti, e ' buon son rari.

Thus it can be that, in the selfsame species,   70
some trees bear better fruit and some bear worse,
and men are born with different temperaments.

For were the wax appropriately readied,   73
and were the heaven's power at its height,
the brightness of the seal would show completely;

but Nature always works defectively—   76
she passes on that light much like an artist
who knows his craft but has a hand that trembles.

Yet where the ardent Love prepares and stamps   79
the lucid Vision of the primal Power,
a being then acquires complete perfection.

In that way, earth was once made worthy of   82
the full perfection of a living being:
thus was the Virgin made to be with child.

So that I do approve of the opinion   85
you hold: that human nature never was
nor shall be what it was in those two persons.

Now if I said no more beyond this point,   88
your words might well begin, 'How is it, then,
with your assertion of his matchless vision?'

But so that the obscure can be made plain,   91
consider who he was, what was the cause
of his request when he was told, 'Do ask.'

My words did not prevent your seeing clearly   94
that it was as a king that he had asked
for wisdom that would serve his royal task—

and not to know the number of the angels   97
on high or, if combined with a contingent,
necesse ever can produce *necesse,*

or *si est dare primum motum esse,*   100
or if, within a semicircle, one
can draw a triangle with no right angle.

Thus, if you note both what I said and say,   103
by 'matchless vision' it is kingly prudence
my arrow of intention means to strike;

and if you turn clear eyes to that word 'rose,'   106
you'll see that it referred to kings alone—
kings, who are many, and the good are rare.

Con questa distinzion prendi 'l mio detto;   109
e così puote star con quel che credi
del primo padre e del nostro Diletto.

E questo ti sia sempre piombo a' piedi,   112
per farti mover lento com' uom lasso
e al sì al no che tu non vedi:

ché quelli è tra li stolti bene a basso,   115
che sanza distinzione afferma e nega
ne l'un così come ne l'altro passo;

perch' elli 'ncontra che più volte piega   118
l'oppinïon corrente in falsa parte,
e poi l'affetto l'intelletto lega.

Vie più che 'ndarno da riva si parte,   121
perchè non torna tal qual e' si move,
chi pesca per lo vero e non ha l'arte.

E di ciò sono al mondo aperte prove   124
Parmenide, Melisso e Brisso e molti,
li quali andaro e non sapëan dove;

sì fé Sabellio e Arrio e quelli stolti   127
che furon come spade a le Scritture
in render torti li diritti volti.

Non sien le genti, ancor, troppo sicure   130
a giudicar, sì come quei che stima
le biade in campo pria che sien mature;

ch'i' ho veduto tutto 'l verno prima   133
lo prun mostrarsi rigido e feroce,
poscia portar la rosa in su la cima;

e legno vidi già dritto e veloce   136
correr lo mar per tutto suo cammino,
perire al fine a l'intrar de la foce.

Non creda donna Berta e ser Martino,   139
per vedere un furare, altro offerere,
vederli dentro al consiglio divino;

ché quel può surgere, e quel può cadere."   142

Take what I said with this distinction then;   109
in that way it accords with what you thought
of the first father and of our Beloved.

And let this weigh as lead to slow your steps,   112
to make you move as would a weary man
to *yes* or *no* when you do not see clearly:

whether he would affirm or would deny,   115
he who decides without distinguishing
must be among the most obtuse of men;

opinion—hasty—often can incline   118
to the wrong side, and then affection for
one's own opinion binds, confines the mind.

Far worse than uselessly he leaves the shore   121
(more full of error than he was before)
who fishes for the truth but lacks the art.

Of this, Parmenides, Melissus, Bryson,   124
are clear proofs to the world, and many others
who went their way but knew not where it went;

so did Sabellius and Arius   127
and other fools—like concave blades that mirror—
who rendered crooked the straight face of Scriptures.

So, too, let men not be too confident   130
in judging—witness those who, in the field,
would count the ears before the corn is ripe;

for I have seen, all winter through, the brier   133
display itself as stiff and obstinate,
and later, on its summit, bear the rose;

and once I saw a ship sail straight and swift   136
through all its voyaging across the sea,
then perish at the end, at harbor entry.

Let not Dame Bertha or Master Martin think   139
that they have shared God's Counsel when they see
one rob and see another who donates:

the last may fall, the other may be saved."   142

The Resurrection

CANTO XIV

Dal centro al cerchio, e sì dal cerchio al centro
movesi l'acqua in un ritondo vaso,
secondo ch'è percosso fuori o dentro:

ne la mia mente fé sùbito caso   4
questo ch'io dico, sì come si tacque
la glorïosa vita di Tommaso,

per la similitudine che nacque   7
del suo parlare e di quel di Beatrice,
a cui sì cominciar, dopo lui, piacque:

"A costui fa mestieri, e nol vi dice   10
né con la voce né pensando ancora,
d'un altro vero andare a la radice.

Diteli se la luce onde s'infiora   13
vostra sustanza, rimarrà con voi
etternalmente sì com' ell' è ora;

e se rimane, dite come, poi   16
che sarete visibili rifatti,
esser porà ch'al veder non vi nòi."

Come, da più letizia pinti e tratti,   19
a la fïata quei che vanno a rota
levan la voce e rallegrano li atti,

così, a l'orazion pronta e divota,   22
li santi cerchi mostrar nova gioia
nel torneare e ne la mira nota.

Qual si lamenta perché qui si moia   25
per viver colà sù, non vide quive
lo refrigerio de l'etterna ploia.

Quell' uno e due e tre che sempre vive   28
e regna sempre in tre e 'n due e 'n uno,
non circunscritto, e tutto circunscrive,

Still the Fourth Heaven: the Sphere of the Sun. Beatrice's request to the spirits to resolve Dante's query concerning the radiance of the spirits after the Resurrection. Solomon's reply. Appearance of new spirits. Ascent to the Fifth Heaven, the Sphere of Mars. The vision of a cross and Christ. The rapture of Dante.

From rim to center, center out to rim,
  so does the water move in a round vessel,
as it is struck without, or struck within.

  What I am saying fell most suddenly   4
into my mind, as soon as Thomas's
glorious living flame fell silent, since

  between his speech and that of Beatrice,   7
a similarity was born. And she,
when he was done, was pleased to start with this:

  "He does not tell you of it—not with speech   10
nor in his thoughts as yet—but this man needs
to reach the root of still another truth.

  Do tell him if that light with which your soul   13
blossoms will stay with you eternally
even as it is now; and if it stays,

  do tell him how, when you are once again   16
made visible, it will be possible
for you to see such light and not be harmed."

  As dancers in a ring, when drawn and driven   19
by greater gladness, lift at times their voices
and dance their dance with more exuberance,

  so, when they heard that prompt, devout request,   22
the blessed circles showed new joyousness
in wheeling dance and in amazing song.

  Whoever weeps because on earth we die   25
that we may live on high, has never seen
eternal showers that bring refreshment there.

  That One and Two and Three who ever lives   28
and ever reigns in Three and Two and One,
not circumscribed and circumscribing all,

    tre volte era cantato da ciascuno   31
di quelli spiriti con tal melodia,
ch'ad ogne merto saria giusto muno.

    E io udi' ne la luce più dia   34
del minor cerchio una voce modesta,
forse qual fu da l'angelo a Maria,

    risponder: "Quanto fia lunga la festa   37
di paradiso, tanto il nostro amore
si raggerà dintorno cotal vesta.

    La sua chiarezza séguita l'ardore;   40
l'ardor la visïone, e quella è tanta,
quant' ha di grazia sovra suo valore.

    Come la carne glorïosa e santa   43
fia rivestita, la nostra persona
più grata fia per esser tutta quanta;

    per che s'accrescerà ciò che ne dona   46
di gratüito lume il sommo bene,
lume ch'a lui veder ne condiziona;

    onde la visïon crescer convene,   49
crescer l'ardor che di quella s'accende,
crescer lo raggio che da esso vene.

    Ma sì come carbon che fiamma rende,   52
e per vivo candor quella soverchia,
sì che la sua parvenza si difende;

    così questo folgór che già ne cerchia   55
fia vinto in apparenza da la carne
che tutto dì la terra ricoperchia;

    né potrà tanta luce affaticarne: 58
ché li organi del corpo saran forti
a tutto ciò che potrà dilettarne."

    Tanto mi parver sùbiti e accorti   61
e l'uno e l'altro coro a dicer "Amme!"
che ben mostrar disio d'i corpi morti:

    forse non pur per lor, ma per le mamme, 64
per li padri e per li altri che fuor cari
anzi che fosser sempiterne fiamme.

    Ed ecco intorno, di chiarezza pari,   67
nascere un lustro sopra quel che v'era,
per guisa d'orizzonte che rischiari.

was sung three times by each and all those souls   31
with such a melody that it would be
appropriate reward for every merit.

And I could hear within the smaller circle's   34
divinest light a modest voice (perhaps
much like the angel's voice in speech to Mary)

reply: "As long as the festivity   37
of Paradise shall be, so long shall our
love radiate around us such a garment.

Its brightness takes its measure from our ardor,   40
our ardor from our vision, which is measured
by what grace each receives beyond his merit.

When, glorified and sanctified, the flesh   43
is once again our dress, our persons shall,
in being all complete, please all the more;

therefore, whatever light gratuitous   46
the Highest Good gives us will be enhanced—
the light that will allow us to see Him;

that light will cause our vision to increase,   49
the ardor vision kindles to increase,
the brightness born of ardor to increase.

Yet even as a coal engenders flame,   52
but with intenser glow outshines it, so
that in that flame the coal persists, it shows,

so will the brightness that envelops us   55
be then surpassed in visibility
by reborn flesh, which earth now covers up.

Nor will we tire when faced with such bright light,   58
for then the body's organs will have force
enough for all in which we can delight."

One and the other choir seemed to me   61
so quick and keen to say "Amen" that they
showed clearly how they longed for their dead bodies—

not only for themselves, perhaps, but for   64
their mothers, fathers, and for others dear
to them before they were eternal flames.

And—look!—beyond the light already there,   67
an added luster rose around those rings,
even as a horizon brightening.

E sì come al salir di prima sera   70
comincian per lo ciel nove parvenze,
sì che la vista pare e non par vera,

   parvemi lì novelle sussistenze   73
cominciare a vedere, e fare un giro
di fuor da l'altre due circunferenze.

   Oh vero sfavillar del Santo Spiro!   76
come si fece sùbito e candente
a li occhi miei che, vinti, nol soffriro!

   Ma Bëatrice sì bella e ridente   79
mi si mostrò, che tra quelle vedute
si vuol lasciar che non seguir la mente.

   Quindi ripreser li occhi miei virtute   82
a rilevarsi; e vidimi translato
sol con mia donna in più alta salute.

   Ben m'accors' io ch'io era più levato,   85
per l'affocato riso de la stella,
che mi parea più roggio che l'usato.

   Con tutto 'l core e con quella favella   88
ch'è una in tutti, a Dio feci olocausto,
qual conveniesi a la grazia novella.

   E non er' anco del mio petto essausto   89
l'ardor del sacrificio, ch'io conobbi
esso litare stato accetto e fausto;

   ché con tanto lucore e tanto robbi   94
m'apparvero splendor dentro a due raggi,
ch'io dissi: "O Elïòs che sì li addobbi!"

   Come distinta da minori e maggi   97
lumi biancheggia tra ' poli del mondo
Galassia sì, che fa dubbiar ben saggi;

   sì costellati facean nel profondo   100
Marte quei raggi il venerabil segno
che fan giunture di quadranti in tondo.

   Qui vince la memoria mia lo 'ngegno;   103
ché quella croce lampeggiava Cristo,
sì ch'io non so trovare essempro degno;

   ma chi prende sua croce e segue Cristo,   106
ancor mi scuserà di quel ch'io lasso,
vedendo in quell' albor balenar Cristo.

    And even as, at the approach of evening,   70
new lights begin to show along the sky,
so that the sight seems and does not seem real,

    it seemed to me that I began to see   73
new spirits there, forming a ring beyond
the choirs with their two circumferences.

    O the true sparkling of the Holy Ghost—   76
how rapid and how radiant before
my eyes that, overcome, could not sustain it!

    But, smiling, Beatrice then showed to me   79
such loveliness—it must be left among
the visions that take flight from memory.

    From this my eyes regained the strength to look   82
above again; I saw myself translated
to higher blessedness, alone with my

    lady; and I was sure that I had risen   85
because the smiling star was red as fire—
beyond the customary red of Mars.

    With all my heart and in that language which   88
is one for all, for this new grace I gave
to God my holocaust, appropriate.

    Though in my breast that burning sacrifice   91
was not completed yet, I was aware
that it had been accepted and auspicious;

    for splendors, in two rays, appeared to me,   94
so radiant and fiery that I said:
"O Helios, you who adorn them thus!"

    As, graced with lesser and with larger lights   97
between the poles of the world, the Galaxy
gleams so that even sages are perplexed;

    so, constellated in the depth of Mars,   100
those rays described the venerable sign
a circle's quadrants form where they are joined.

    And here my memory defeats my wit: 103
Christ's flaming from that cross was such that I
can find no fit similitude for it.

    But he who takes his cross and follows Christ   106
will pardon me again for my omission—
my seeing Christ flash forth undid my force.

   Di corno in corno e tra la cima e 'l basso   109
si movien lumi, scintillando forte
nel congiugnersi insieme e nel trapasso:
   così si veggion qui diritte e torte,   112
veloci e tarde, rinovando vista,
le minuzie d'i corpi, lunghe e corte,
   moversi per lo raggio onde si lista   115
talvolta l'ombra che, per sua difesa,
la gente con ingegno e arte acquista.
   E come giga e arpa, in tempra tesa   118
di molte corde, fa dolce tintinno
a tal da cui la nota non è intesa,
   così da' lumi che lì m'apparinno   121
s'accogliea per la croce una melode
che mi rapiva, sanza intender l'inno.
   Ben m'accors' io ch'elli era d'alte lode,   124
però ch'a me venìa "Resurgi" e "Vinci"
come a colui che non intende e ode.
   Io m'innamorava tanto quinci,   127
che 'nfino a lì non alcuna cosa
che mi legasse con sì dolci vinci.
   Forse la mia parola par troppo osa,   130
posponendo il piacer de li occhi belli,
ne' quai mirando mio disio ha posa;
   ma chi s'avvede che i vivi suggelli   133
d'ogne bellezza più fanno più suso,
e ch'io non m'era lì rivolto a quelli,
   escusar puommi di quel ch'io m'accuso   136
per escusarmi, e vedermi dir vero:
ché 'l piacer santo non è qui dischiuso,
   perché si fa, montando, più sincero.   139

Lights moved along that cross from horn to horn 109
and from the summit to the base, and as
they met and passed, they sparkled, radiant:

so, straight and slant and quick and slow, one sees 112
on earth the particles of bodies, long
and short, in shifting shapes, that move along

the ray of light that sometimes streaks across 115
the shade that men devise with skill and art
to serve as their defense against the sun.

And just as harp and viol, whose many chords 118
are tempered, taut, produce sweet harmony
although each single note is not distinct,

so, from the lights that then appeared to me, 121
out from that cross there spread a melody
that held me rapt, although I could not tell

what hymn it was. I knew it sang high praise, 124
since I heard "Rise" and "Conquer," but I was
as one who hears but cannot seize the sense.

Yet I was so enchanted by the sound 127
that until then no thing had ever bound
me with such gentle bonds. My words may seem

presumptuous, as though I dared to deem 130
a lesser thing the lovely eyes that bring
to my desire, as it gazes, peace.

But he who notes that, in ascent, her eyes— 133
all beauty's living seals—gain force, and notes
that I had not yet turned to them in Mars,

can then excuse me—just as I accuse 136
myself, thus to excuse myself—and see
that I speak truly: here her holy beauty

is not denied—ascent makes it more perfect. 139

CANTO XV

Benigna volontade in che si liqua
sempre l'amor che drittamente spira,
come cupidità fa ne la iniqua,

silenzio puose a quella dolce lira,   4
e fece quïetar le sante corde
che la destra del cielo allenta e tira.

Come saranno a' giusti preghi sorde   7
quelle sustanze che, per darmi voglia
ch'io le pregassi, a tacer fur concorde?

Bene è che sanza termine si doglia   10
chi, per amor di cosa che non duri
etternalmente, quello amor si spoglia.

Quale per li seren tranquilli e puri   13
discorre ad ora ad or sùbito foco,
movendo li occhi che stavan sicuri,

e pare stella che tramuti loco,   16
se non che da la parte ond' e' s'accende
nulla sen perde, ed esso dura poco:

tale dal corno che 'n destro si stende   19
a piè di quella croce corse un astro
de la costellazion che lì resplende;

né si partì la gemma dal suo nastro,   22
ma per la lista radîal trascorse,
che parve foco dietro ad alabastro.

Sì pïa l'ombra d'Anchise si porse,   25
se fede merta nostra maggior musa,
quando in Eliso del figlio s'accorse.

"O sanguis meus, o superinfusa   28
gratia Deï, sicut tibi cui
bis unquam celi ianüa reclusa?"

Generous will—in which is manifest
always the love that breathes toward righteousness,
as in contorted will is greediness—

imposing silence on that gentle lyre,   4
brought quiet to the consecrated chords
that Heaven's right hand slackens and draws taut.

Can souls who prompted me to pray to them,   7
by falling silent all in unison,
be deaf to men's just prayers? Then he may grieve

indeed and endlessly—the man who leaves   10
behind such love and turns instead to seek
things that do not endure eternally.

As, through the pure and tranquil skies of night,   13
at times a sudden fire shoots, and moves
eyes that were motionless—a fire that seems

a star that shifts its place, except that in   16
that portion of the heavens where it flared,
nothing is lost, and its own course is short—

so, from the horn that stretches on the right,   19
down to the foot of that cross, a star ran
out of the constellation glowing there;

nor did that gem desert the cross's track,   22
but coursed along the radii, and seemed
just like a flame that alabaster screens.

With such affection did Anchises' shade   25
reach out (if we may trust our greatest muse)
when in Elysium he saw his son.

"O blood of mine—o the celestial grace   28
bestowed beyond all measure—unto whom
as unto you was Heaven's gate twice opened?"

Così quel lume: ond' io m'attesi a lui;   31
poscia rivolsi a la mia donna il viso,
e quinci e quindi stupefatto fui;

ché dentro a li occhi suoi ardeva un riso   34
tal, ch'io pensai co' miei toccar lo fondo
de la mia gloria e del mio paradiso.

Indi, a udire e a veder giocondo,   37
giunse lo spirto al suo principio cose,
ch'io non lo 'ntesi, sì parlò profondo;

né per elezïon mi si nascose,   40
ma per necessità, ché 'l suo concetto
al segno d'i mortal si soprapuose.

E quando l'arco de l'ardente affetto   43
fu sì sfogato, che 'l parlar discese
inver' lo segno del nostro intelletto,

la prima cosa che per me s'intese,   46
"Benedetto sia tu," fu, "trino e uno,
che nel mio seme se' tanto cortese!"

E seguì: "Grato e lontano digiuno,   49
tratto leggendo del magno volume
du' non si muta mai bianco né bruno,

solvuto hai, figlio, dentro a questo lume   52
in ch'io ti parlo, mercé di colei
ch'a l'alto volo ti vestì le piume.

Tu credi che a me tuo pensier mei   55
da quel ch'è primo, così come raia
da l'un, se si conosce, il cinque e 'l sei;

e però ch'io mi sia e perch' io paia   58
più gaudïoso a te, non mi domandi,
che alcun altro in questa turba gaia.

Tu credi 'l vero; ché i minori e' grandi   61
di questa vita miran ne lo speglio
in che, prima che pensi, il pensier pandi;

ma perché 'l sacro amore in che io veglio   64
con perpetüa vista e che m'asseta
di dolce disïar, s'adempia meglio,

la voce tua sicura, balda e lieta   67
suoni la volontà, suoni 'l disio,
a che la mia risposta è già decreta!"

That light said this; at which, I stared at him.   31
Then, looking back to see my lady, I,
on this side and on that, was stupefied;

    for in the smile that glowed within her eyes,   34
I thought that I—with mine—had touched the height
of both my blessedness and paradise.

    Then—and he was a joy to hear and see—   37
that spirit added to his first words things
that were too deep to meet my understanding.

    Not that he chose to hide his sense from me;   40
necessity compelled him; he conceived
beyond the mark a mortal mind can reach.

    And when his bow of burning sympathy   43
was slack enough to let his speech descend
to meet the limit of our intellect,

    these were the first words where I caught the sense: 46
"Blessed be you, both Three and One, who show
such favor to my seed." And he continued:

    "The long and happy hungering I drew   49
from reading that great volume where both black
and white are never changed, you—son—have now

    appeased within this light in which I speak   52
to you; for this, I owe my gratitude
to her who gave you wings for your high flight.

    You think your thoughts flow into me from Him   55
who is the First—as from the number one,
the five and six derive, if one is known—

    and so you do not ask me who I am   58
and why I seem more joyous to you than
all other spirits in this festive throng.

    Your thought is true, for both the small and great   61
of this life gaze into that mirror where,
before you think, your thoughts have been displayed.

    But that the sacred love in which I keep   64
my vigil with unending watchfulness,
the love that makes me thirst with sweet desire,

    be better satisfied, let your voice—bold,   67
assured, and glad—proclaim your will and longing,
to which my answer is decreed already."

Io mi volsi a Beatrice, e quella udio   70
pria ch'io parlassi, e arrisemi un cenno
che fece crescer l'ali al voler mio.

Poi cominciai così: "L'affetto e 'l senno,   73
come la prima equalità v'apparse,
d'un peso per ciascun di voi si fenno,

però che 'l sol che v'allumò e arse,   76
col caldo e con la luce è sì iguali,
che tutte simiglianze sono scarse.

Ma voglia e argomento ne' mortali,   79
per la cagion ch'a voi è manifesta,
diversamente son pennuti in ali;

ond' io, che son mortal, mi sento in questa   82
disagguaglianza, e però non ringrazio
se non col core a la paterna festa.

Ben supplico io a te, vivo topazio   85
che questa gioia prezïosa ingemmi,
perché mi facci del tuo nome sazio."

"O fronda mia in che io compiacemmi   88
pur aspettando, io fui la tua radice":
cotal principio, rispondendo, femmi.

Poscia mi disse: "Quel da cui si dice   91
tua cognazione e che cent' anni e piùe
girato ha 'l monte in la prima cornice,

mio figlio fu e tuo bisavol fue: 94
ben si convien che la lunga fatica
tu li raccorci con l'opere tue.

Fiorenza dentro da la cerchia antica,   97
ond' ella toglie ancora e terza e nona,
si stava in pace, sobria e pudica.

Non avea catenella, non corona,   100
non gonne contigiate, non cintura
che fosse a veder più che la persona.

Non faceva, nascendo, ancor paura   103
la figlia al padre, ché 'l tempo e la dote
non fuggien quinci e quindi la misura.

Non avea case di famiglia vòte;   106
non v'era giunto ancor Sardanapalo
a mostrar ciò che 'n camera si puote.

I turned to Beatrice, but she heard me 70
before I spoke; her smile to me was signal
that made the wings of my desire grow.

Then I began: "As soon as you beheld 73
the First Equality, both intellect
and love weighed equally for each of you,

because the Sun that brought you light and heat 76
possesses heat and light so equally
that no thing matches His equality;

whereas in mortals, word and sentiment— 79
to you, the cause of this is evident—
are wings whose featherings are disparate.

I—mortal—feel this inequality; 82
thus, it is only with my heart that I
can offer thanks for your paternal greeting.

Indeed I do beseech you, living topaz, 85
set in this precious jewel as a gem:
fulfill my longing—let me know your name."

"O you, my branch in whom I took delight 88
even awaiting you, I am your root,"
so he, in his reply to me, began,

then said: "The man who gave your family 91
its name, who for a century and more
has circled the first ledge of Purgatory,

was son to me and was your great-grandfather; 94
it is indeed appropriate for you
to shorten his long toil with your good works.

Florence, within her ancient ring of walls— 97
that ring from which she still draws tierce and nones—
sober and chaste, lived in tranquillity.

No necklace and no coronal were there, 100
and no embroidered gowns; there was no girdle
that caught the eye more than the one who wore it.

No daughter's birth brought fear unto her father, 103
for age and dowry then did not imbalance—
to this side and to that—the proper measure.

There were no families that bore no children; 106
and Sardanapalus was still a stranger—
not come as yet to teach in the bedchamber.

Non era vinto ancora Montemalo   109
dal vostro Uccellatoio, che, com' è vinto
nel montar sù, così sarà nel calo.

Bellincion Berti vid' io andar cinto   112
di cuoio e d'osso, e venir da lo specchio
la donna sua sanza 'l viso dipinto;

e vidi quel d'i Nerli e quel del Vecchio   115
esser contenti a la pelle scoperta,
e le sue donne al fuso e al pennecchio.

Oh fortunate! ciascuna era certa   118
de la sua sepultura, e ancor nulla
era per Francia nel letto diserta.

L'una vegghiava a studio de la culla,   121
e, consolando, usava l'idïoma
che prima i padri e le madri trastulla;

l'altra, traendo a la rocca la chioma,   124
favoleggiava con la sua famiglia
d'i Troiani, di Fiesole e di Roma.

Saria tenuta allor tal maraviglia   127
una Cianghella, un Lapo Salterello,
qual or saria Cincinnato e Corniglia.

A così riposato, a così bello   130
viver di cittadini, a così fida
cittadinanza, a così dolce ostello,

Maria mi diè, chiamata in alte grida;   133
e ne l'antico vostro Batisteo
insieme fui cristiano e Cacciaguida.

Moronto fu mio frate ed Eliseo;   136
mia donna venne a me di val di Pado,
e quindi il sopranome tuo si feo.

Poi seguitai lo 'mperador Currado;   139
ed el mi cinse de la sua milizia,
tanto per bene ovrar li venni in grado.

Dietro li andai incontro a la nequizia   142
di quella legge il cui popolo usurpa,
per colpa d'i pastor, vostra giustizia.

Quivi fu' io da quella gente turpa   145
disviluppato dal mondo fallace,
lo cui amor molt' anime deturpa;

e venni dal martiro a questa pace."   148

Not yet had your Uccellatoio's rise   109
outdone the rise of Monte Mario,
which, too, will be outdone in its decline.

I saw Bellincione Berti girt   112
with leather and with bone, and saw his wife
come from her mirror with her face unpainted.

I saw dei Nerli and del Vecchio   115
content to wear their suits of unlined skins,
and saw their wives at spindle and at spool.

O happy wives! Each one was sure of her   118
own burial place, and none—for France's sake—
as yet was left deserted in her bed.

One woman watched with loving care the cradle   121
and, as she soothed her infant, used the way
of speech with which fathers and mothers play;

another, as she drew threads from the distaff,   124
would tell, among her household, tales of Trojans,
and tales of Fiesole, and tales of Rome.

A Lapo Salterello, a Cianghella,   127
would then have stirred as much dismay as now
a Cincinnatus and Cornelia would.

To such a life—so tranquil and so lovely—   130
of citizens in true community,
into so sweet a dwelling place did Mary,

invoked in pains of birth, deliver me;   133
and I, within your ancient Baptistery,
at once became Christian and Cacciaguida.

Moronto was my brother, and Eliseo;   136
my wife came from the valley of the Po—
the surname that you bear was brought by her.

In later years I served the Emperor   139
Conrad—and my good works so gained his favor
that he gave me the girdle of his knighthood.

I followed him to war against the evil   142
of that law whose adherents have usurped—
this, through your Pastors' fault—your just possessions.

There, by that execrable race, I was   145
set free from fetters of the erring world,
the love of which defiles so many souls.

From martyrdom I came unto this peace."   148

The Evocation of Florence

CANTO XVI

O poca nostra nobiltà di sangue,
  se gloriar di te la gente fai
qua giù dove l'affetto nostro langue,

  mirabil cosa non mi sarà mai: 4
ché là dove appetito non si torce,
dico nel cielo, io me ne gloriai.

  Ben se' tu manto che tosto raccorce: 7
sì che, se non s'appon di dì in die,
lo tempo va dintorno con le force.

  Dal "voi" che prima a Roma s'offerie,   10
in che la sua famiglia men persevra,
ricominciaron le parole mie;

  onde Beatrice, ch'era un poco scevra,   13
ridendo, parve quella che tossio
al primo fallo scritto di Ginevra.

  Io cominciai: "Voi siete il padre mio;   16
voi mi date a parlar tutta baldezza;
voi mi levate sì, ch'i' son più ch'io.

  Per tanti rivi s'empie d'allegrezza   19
la mente mia, che di sé fa letizia
perché può sostener che non si spezza.

  Ditemi dunque, cara mia primizia,   22
quai fuor li vostri antichi e quai fuor li anni
che si segnaro in vostra püerizia;

  ditemi de l'ovil di San Giovanni   25
quanto era allora, e chi eran le genti
tra esso degne di più alti scanni."

  Come s'avviva a lo spirar d'i venti   28
carbone in fiamma, così vid' io quella
luce risplendere a' miei blandimenti;

Still the Fifth Heaven: the Sphere of Mars. Pride in birth. Dante's queries to Cacciaguida. Cacciaguida's replies: the date of his birth, his ancestors, the population and notable families of Florence in Cacciaguida's time.

If here below, where sentiment is far
　too weak to withstand error, I should see
men glorying in you, nobility

　of blood—a meager thing!—I should not wonder,　　4
for even where desire is not awry,
I mean in Heaven, I too felt such pride.

　You are indeed a cloak that soon wears out,　　7
so that if, day by day, we add no patch,
then circling time will trim you with its shears.

　My speech began again with *you,* the word　　10
that Rome was the first city to allow,
although her people seldom speak it now;

　at this word, Beatrice, somewhat apart,　　13
smiling, seemed like the woman who had coughed—
so goes the tale—at Guinevere's first fault.

　So did my speech begin: "You are my father;　　16
you hearten me to speak with confidence;
you raise me so that I am more than I.

　So many streams have filled my mind with gladness—　　19
so many, and such gladness, that mind must
rejoice that it can bear this and not burst.

　Then tell me, founder of my family,　　22
who were your ancestors and, in your boyhood,
what were the years the records registered;

　and tell me of the sheepfold of St. John—　　25
how numerous it was, who in that flock
were worthy of the highest offices."

　As at the breathing of the winds, a coal　　28
will quicken into flame, so I saw that
light glow at words that were affectionate;

e come a li occhi miei si fé più bella,   31
così con voce più dolce e soave,
ma non con questa moderna favella,

   dissemi: "Da quel dì che fu detto *'Ave'*   34
al parto in che mia madre, ch'è or santa,
s'alleviò di me ond' era grave,

   al suo Leon cinquecento cinquanta   37
e trenta fiate venne questo foco
a rinfiammarsi sotto la sua pianta.

   Li antichi miei e io nacqui nel loco   40
dove si truova pria l'ultimo sesto
da quei che corre il vostro annüal gioco.

   Basti d'i miei maggiori udirne questo: 43
chi ei si fosser e onde venner quivi,
più è tacer che ragionare onesto.

   Tutti color ch'a quel tempo eran ivi   46
da poter arme tra Marte e 'l Batista,
erano il quinto di quei ch'or son vivi.

   Ma la cittadinanza, ch'è or mista   49
di Campi, di Certaldo e di Fegghine,
pura vediesi ne l'ultimo artista.

   Oh quanto fora meglio esser vicine   52
quelle genti ch'io dico, e al Galluzzo
e a Trespiano aver vostro confine,

   che averle dentro e sostener lo puzzo   55
del villan d'Aguglion, di quel da Signa,
che già per barattare ha l'occhio aguzzo!

   Se la gente ch'al mondo più traligna   58
non fosse stata a Cesare noverca,
ma come madre a suo figlio benigna,

   tal fatto è fiorentino e cambia e merca,   61
che si sarebbe vòlto a Simifonti,
là dove andava l'avolo a la cerca;

   sariesi Montemurlo ancor de' Conti;   64
sarieno i Cerchi nel piovier d'Acone,
e forse in Valdigrieve i Buondelmonti.

   Sempre la confusion de le persone   67
principio fu del mal de la cittade,
come del vostro il cibo che s'appone;

    and as, before my eyes, it grew more fair,   31
so, with a voice more gentle and more sweet—
not in our modern speech—it said to me:

    "Down from that day when *Ave* was pronounced,   34
until my mother (blessed now), by giving
birth, eased the burden borne in bearing me,

    this fire of Mars had come five-hundred-fifty   37
and thirty more times to its Lion—there
to be rekindled underneath its paw.

    My ancestors and I were born just where   40
the runner in your yearly games first comes
upon the boundary of the final ward.

    That is enough concerning my forebears: 43
what were their names, from where they came—of that,
silence, not speech, is more appropriate.

    All those who, at that time, between the Baptist   46
and Mars, were capable of bearing arms,
numbered one fifth of those who live there now.

    But then the citizens, now mixed with Campi,   49
with the Certaldo, and with the Figline,
were pure down to the humblest artisan.

    Oh, it would be far better if you had   52
those whom I mention as your neighbors (and
your boundaries at Galuzzo and Trespiano),

    than to have them within, to bear the stench   55
of Aguglione's wretch and Signa's wretch,
whose sharp eyes now on barratry are set.

    If those who, in the world, go most astray   58
had not seen Caesar with stepmothers' eyes,
but, like a mother to her son, been kind,

    then one who has become a Florentine   61
trader and money changer would have stayed
in Semifonte, where his fathers peddled,

    the Counts would still be lords of Montemurlo,   64
the Cerchi would be in Acone's parish,
perhaps the Buondelmonti in Valdigreve.

    The mingling of the populations led   67
to evil in the city, even as
food piled on food destroys the body's health;

　　e cieco toro più avaccio cade   70
che cieco agnello; e molte volte taglia
più e meglio una che le cinque spade.

　　Se tu riguardi Luni e Orbisaglia   73
come sono ite, e come se ne vanno
di retro ad esse Chiusi e Sinigaglia,

　　udir come le schiatte si disfanno   76
non ti parrà nova cosa né forte,
poscia che le cittadi termine hanno.

　　Le vostre cose tutte hanno lor morte,   79
sì come voi; ma celasi in alcuna
che dura molto, e le vite son corte.

　　E come 'l volger del ciel de la luna   82
cuopre e discuopre i liti sanza posa,
così fa di Fiorenza la Fortuna:

　　per che non dee parer mirabil cosa   85
ciò ch'io dirò de li alti Fiorentini
onde è la fama nel tempo nascosa.

　　Io vidi li Ughi e vidi i Catellini,   88
Filippi, Greci, Ormanni e Alberichi,
già nel calare, illustri cittadini;

　　e vidi così grandi come antichi,   91
con quel de la Sannella, quel de l'Arca,
e Soldanieri e Ardinghi e Bostichi.

　　Sovra la porta ch'al presente è carca   94
di nova fellonia di tanto peso
che tosto fia iattura de la barca,

　　erano i Ravignani, ond' è disceso   97
il conte Guido e qualunque del nome
de l'alto Bellincione ha poscia preso.

　　Quel de la Pressa sapeva già come   100
regger si vuole, e avea Galigaio
dorata in casa sua già l'elsa e 'l pome.

　　Grand' era già la colonna del Vaio,   103
Sacchetti, Giuochi, Fifanti e Barucci
e Galli e quei ch'arrossan per lo staio.

　　Lo ceppo di che nacquero i Calfucci   106
era già grande, e già eran tratti
a le curule Sizii e Arrigucci.

the blind bull falls more quickly, more headlong,   70
than does the blind lamb; and the one blade can
often cut more and better than five swords.

    Consider Luni, Urbisaglia, how   73
they went to ruin (Sinigaglia follows,
and Chiusi, too, will soon have vanished); then,

    if you should hear of families undone,   76
you will find nothing strange or difficult
in that—since even cities meet their end.

    All things that you possess, possess their death,   79
just as you do; but in some things that last
long, death can hide from you whose lives are short.

    And even as the heaven of the moon,   82
revolving, respiteless, conceals and then
reveals the shores, so Fortune does with Florence;

    therefore, there is no cause for wonder in   85
what I shall tell of noble Florentines,
of those whose reputations time has hidden.

    I saw the Ughi, saw the Catellini,   88
Filippi, Greci, Ormanni, Alberichi,
famed citizens already in decline,

    and saw, as great as they were venerable,   91
dell'Arca with della Sannella, and
Ardinghi, Soldanieri, and Bostichi.

    Nearby the gate that now is burdened with   94
new treachery that weighs so heavily
that it will bring the vessel to shipwreck,

    there were the Ravignani, from whose line   97
Count Guido comes and all who—since—derive
their name from the illustrious Bellincione.

    And della Pressa knew already how   100
to rule; and Galigaio, in his house,
already had the gilded hilt and pommel.

    The stripe of Vair had mightiness already,   103
as did the Giuochi, Galli, and Barucci,
Fifanti, and Sacchetti, and those who

    blush for the bushel; and the stock from which   106
spring the Calfucci was already mighty,
and Sizzi and Arrigucci were already

Oh quali io vidi quei che son disfatti   109
per lor superbia! e le palle de l'oro
fiorian Fiorenza in tutt' i suoi gran fatti.

Così faceno i padri di coloro   112
che, sempre che la vostra chiesa vaca,
si fanno grassi stando a consistoro.

L'oltracotata schiatta che s'indraca   115
dietro a chi fugge, e a chi mostra 'l dente
o ver la borsa, com' agnel si placa,

già venìa sù, ma di picciola gente;   118
sì che non piacque ad Ubertin Donato
che poï il suocero il fé lor parente.

Già era 'l Caponsacco nel mercato   121
disceso giù da Fiesole, e già era
buon cittadino Giuda e Infangato.

Io dirò cosa incredibile e vera: 124
nel picciol cerchio s'entrava per porta
che si nomava da quei de la Pera.

Ciascun che de la bella insegna porta   127
del gran barone il cui nome e 'l cui pregio
la festa di Tommaso riconforta,

da esso ebbe milizia e privilegio;   130
avvegna che con popol si rauni
oggi colui che la fascia col fregio.

Già eran Gualterotti e Importuni;   133
e ancor saria Borgo più quïeto,
se di novi vicin fosser digiuni.

La casa di che nacque il vostro fleto,   136
per lo giusto disdegno che v'ha morti
e puose fine al vostro viver lieto,

era onorata, essa e suoi consorti: 139
o Buondelmonte, quanto mal fuggisti
le nozze süe per li altrui conforti!

Molti sarebber lieti, che son tristi,   142
se Dio t'avesse conceduto ad Ema
la prima volta ch'a città venisti.

Ma conveniesi, a quella pietra scema   145
che guarda 'l ponte, che Fiorenza fesse
vittima ne la sua pace postrema.

    raised to high office. Oh, how great were those   109
I saw—whom pride laid low! And the gold balls,
in all of her great actions, flowered Florence.

    Such were the ancestors of those who now,   112
whenever bishops' sees are vacant, grow
fat as they sit in church consistories.

    The breed—so arrogant and dragonlike   115
in chasing him who flees, but lamblike, meek
to him who shows his teeth or else his purse—

    was on the rise already, but of stock   118
so mean that Ubertin Donato, when
his father-in-law made him kin to them,

    was scarcely pleased. Already Caponsacco   121
had come from Fiesole down to the market;
already citizens of note were Giuda

    and Infangato. I shall tell a thing   124
incredible and true: the gateway through
the inner walls was named for the della Pera.

    All those whose arms bear part of the fair ensign   127
of the great baron—he whose memory
and worth are honored on the feast of Thomas—

    received knighthood and privilege from him,   130
though he whose coat of arms has fringed that ensign
has taken sides now with the populace.

    The Gualterotti and the Importuni   133
were there already; were the Borgo spared
new neighbors, it would still be tranquil there.

    The house of Amidei, with which your sorrows   136
began—by reason of its just resentment,
which ruined you and ended years of gladness—

    was honored then, as were its close companions.   139
O Buondelmonte, through another's counsel,
you fled your wedding pledge, and brought such evil!

    Many would now rejoice, who still lament,   142
if when you first approached the city, God
had given you unto the river Ema!

    But Florence, in her final peace, was fated   145
to offer up—unto that mutilated
stone guardian upon her bridge—a victim.

Con queste genti, e con altre con esse,   148
vid' io Fiorenza in sì fatto riposo,
che non avea cagione onde piangesse.

Con queste genti vid' io glorïoso   151
e giusto il popol suo, tanto che 'l giglio
non era ad asta mai posto a ritroso,

né per divisïon fatto vermiglio."   154

These were the families, and others with them: 148
the Florence that I saw—in such repose
that there was nothing to have caused her sorrow.

These were the families: with them I saw   151
her people so acclaimed and just, that on
her staff the lily never was reversed,

nor was it made bloodred by factious hatred."   154

CANTO XVII

Qual venne a Climenè, per accertarsi
  di ciò ch'avëa incontro a sé udito,
quei ch'ancor fa li padri ai figli scarsi;

  tal era io, e tal era sentito   4
e da Beatrice e da la santa lampa
che pria per me avea mutato sito.

  Per che mia donna "Manda fuor la vampa   7
del tuo disio," mi disse, "sì ch'ella esca
segnata bene de la interna stampa:

  non perché nostra conoscenza cresca   10
per tuo parlare, ma perché t'ausi
a dir la sete, sì che l'uom ti mesca."

  "O cara piota mia che sì t'insusi,   13
che, come veggion le terrene menti
non capere in trïangol due ottusi,

  così vedi le cose contingenti   16
anzi che sieno in sé, mirando il punto
a cui tutti li tempi son presenti;

  mentre ch'io era a Virgilio congiunto   19
su per lo monte che l'anime cura
e discendendo nel mondo defunto,

  dette mi fuor di mia vita futura   22
parole gravi, avvegna ch'io mi senta
ben tetragono ai colpi di ventura;

  per che la voglia mia saria contenta   25
d'intender qual fortuna mi s'appressa:
ché saetta previsa vien più lenta."

  Così diss' io a quella luce stessa   28
che pria m'avea parlato; e come volle
Beatrice, fu la mia voglia confessa.

Still the Fifth Heaven: the Sphere of Mars. Dante's asking Cacciaguida for word on what future awaits Dante. Cacciaguida's prophecy concerning Dante's exile and tribulations. Words of comfort from Cacciaguida, and his urging of Dante to fearless fulfillment of his poetic mission.

Like Phaethon (one who still makes fathers wary
of sons) when he had heard insinuations,
and he, to be assured, came to Clymene,

such was I and such was I seen to be   4
by Beatrice and by the holy lamp
that—earlier—had shifted place for me.

Therefore my lady said to me: "Display   7
the flame of your desire, that it may
be seen well-stamped with your internal seal,

not that we need to know what you'd reveal,   10
but that you learn the way that would disclose
your thirst, and you be quenched by what we pour."

"O my dear root, who, since you rise so high,   13
can see the Point in which all times are present—
for just as earthly minds are able to

see that two obtuse angles cannot be   16
contained in a triangle, you can see
contingent things before they come to be—

while I was in the company of Virgil,   19
both on the mountain that heals souls and when
descending to the dead world, what I heard

about my future life were grievous words—   22
although, against the blows of chance I feel
myself as firmly planted as a cube.

Thus my desire would be appeased if I   25
might know what fortune is approaching me:
the arrow one foresees arrives more gently."

So did I speak to the same living light   28
that spoke to me before; as Beatrice
had wished, what was my wish was now confessed.

Né per ambage, in che la gente folle   31
già s'inviscava pria che fosse anciso
l'Agnel di Dio che le peccata tolle,

ma per chiare parole e con preciso   34
latin rispuose quello amor paterno,
chiuso e parvente del suo proprio riso:

"La contingenza, che fuor del quaderno   37
de la vostra matera non si stende,
tutta è dipinta nel cospetto etterno;

necessità però quindi non prende   40
se non come dal viso in che si specchia
nave che per torrente giù discende.

Da indi, sì come viene ad orecchia   43
dolce armonia da organo, mi viene
a vista il tempo che ti s'apparecchia.

Qual si partio Ipolito d'Atene   46
per la spietata e perfida noverca,
tal di Fiorenza partir ti convene.

Questo si vuole e questo già si cerca,   49
e tosto verrà fatto a chi ciò pensa
là dove Cristo tutto dì si merca.

La colpa seguirà la parte offensa   52
in grido, come suol; ma la vendetta
fia testimonio al ver che la dispensa.

Tu lascerai ogne cosa diletta   55
più caramente; e questo è quello strale
che l'arco de lo essilio pria saetta.

Tu proverai sì come sa di sale   58
lo pane altrui, e come è duro calle
lo scendere e 'l salir per l'altrui scale.

E quel che più ti graverà le spalle,   61
sarà la compagnia malvagia e scempia
con la qual tu cadrai in questa valle;

che tutta ingrata, tutta matta ed empia   64
si farà contr' a te; ma, poco appresso,
ella, non tu, n'avrà rossa la tempia.

Di sua bestialitate il suo processo   67
farà la prova; sì ch'a te fia bello
averti fatta parte per te stesso.

Not with the maze of words that used to snare   31
the fools upon this earth before the Lamb
of God who takes away our sins was slain,

but with words plain and unambiguous,   34
that loving father, hidden, yet revealed
by his own smile, replied: "Contingency,

while not extending past the book in which   37
your world of matter has been writ, is yet
in the Eternal Vision all depicted

(but this does not imply necessity,   40
just as a ship that sails downstream is not
determined by the eye that watches it).

And from that Vision—just as from an organ   43
the ear receives a gentle harmony—
what time prepares for you appears to me.

Hippolytus was forced to leave his Athens   46
because of his stepmother, faithless, fierce;
and so must you depart from Florence: this

is willed already, sought for, soon to be   49
accomplished by the one who plans and plots
where—every day—Christ is both sold and bought.

The blame, as usual, will be cried out   52
against the injured party; but just vengeance
will serve as witness to the truth that wields it.

You shall leave everything you love most dearly: 55
this is the arrow that the bow of exile
shoots first. You are to know the bitter taste

of others' bread, how salt it is, and know   58
how hard a path it is for one who goes
descending and ascending others' stairs.

And what will be most hard for you to bear   61
will be the scheming, senseless company
that is to share your fall into this valley;

against you they will be insane, completely   64
ungrateful and profane; and yet, soon after,
not you but they will have their brows bloodred.

Of their insensate acts, the proof will be   67
in the effects; and thus, your honor will
be best kept if your party is your self.

Lo primo tuo refugio e 'l primo ostello   70
sarà la cortesia del gran Lombardo
che 'n su la scala porta il santo uccello;

   ch'in te avrà sì benigno riguardo,   73
che del fare e del chieder, tra voi due,
fia primo quel che tra li altri è più tardo.

Con lui vedrai colui che 'mpresso fue,   76
nascendo, sì da questa stella forte,
che notabili fier l'opere sue.

Non se ne son le genti ancora accorte   79
per la novella età, ché pur nove anni
son queste rote intorno di lui torte;

   ma pria che 'l Guasco l'alto Arrigo inganni,   82
parran faville de la sua virtute
in non curar d'argento né d'affanni.

Le sue magnificenze conosciute   85
saranno ancora, sì che ' suoi nemici
non ne potran tener le lingue mute.

A lui t'aspetta e a' suoi benefici;   88
per lui fia trasmutata molta gente,
cambiando condizion ricchi e mendici;

   e portera'ne scritto ne la mente   91
di lui, e nol dirai"; e disse cose
incredibili a quei che fier presente.

Poi giunse: "Figlio, queste son le chiose   94
di quel che ti fu detto; ecco le 'nsidie
che dietro a pochi giri son nascose.

Non vo' però ch'a' tuoi vicini invidie,   97
poscia che s'infutura la tua vita
via più là che 'l punir di lor perfidie."

Poi che, tacendo, si mostrò spedita   100
l'anima santa di metter la trama
in quella tela ch'io le porsi ordita,

   io cominciai, come colui che brama,   103
dubitando, consiglio da persona
che vede e vuol dirittamente e ama:

"Ben veggio, padre mio, sì come sprona   106
lo tempo verso me, per colpo darmi
tal, ch'è più grave a chi più s'abbandona;

Your first refuge and your first inn shall be   70
the courtesy of the great Lombard, he
who on the ladder bears the sacred bird;

and so benign will be his care for you   73
that, with you two, in giving and in asking,
that shall be first which is, with others, last.

You shall—beside him—see one who, at birth,   76
had so received the seal of this strong star
that what he does will be remarkable.

People have yet to notice him because   79
he is a boy—for nine years and no more
have these spheres wheeled around him—but before

the Gascon gulls the noble Henry, some   82
sparks will have marked the virtue of the Lombard:
hard labor and his disregard for silver.

His generosity is yet to be   85
so notable that even enemies
will never hope to treat it silently.

Put trust in him and in his benefits: 88
his gifts will bring much metamorphosis—
rich men and beggars will exchange their states.

What I tell you about him you will bear   91
inscribed within your mind—but hide it there";
and he told things beyond belief even

for those who will yet see them. Then he added: 94
"Son, these are glosses of what you had heard;
these are the snares that hide beneath brief years.

Yet I'd not have you envying your neighbors;   97
your life will long outlast the punishment
that is to fall upon their treacheries."

After that holy soul had, with his silence,   100
showed he was freed from putting in the woof
across the web whose warp I set for him,

I like a man who, doubting, craves for counsel   103
from one who sees and rightly wills and loves,
replied to him: "I clearly see, my father,

how time is hurrying toward me in order   106
to deal me such a blow as would be most
grievous for him who is not set for it;

per che di provedenza è buon ch'io m'armi,   109
sì che, se loco m'è tolto più caro,
io non perdessi li altri per miei carmi.

Giù per lo mondo sanza fine amaro,   112
e per lo monte del cui bel cacume
li occhi de la mia donna mi levaro,

e poscia per lo ciel, di lume in lume,   115
ho io appreso quel che s'io ridico,
a molti fia sapor di forte agrume;

e s'io al vero son timido amico,   118
temo di perder viver tra coloro
che questo tempo chiameranno antico."

La luce in che rideva il mio tesoro   121
ch'io trovai lì, si fé prima corusca,
quale a raggio di sole specchio d'oro;

indi rispuose: "Coscïenza fusca   124
o de la propria o de l'altrui vergogna
pur sentirà la tua parola brusca.

Ma nondimen, rimossa ogne menzogna,   127
tutta tua visïon fa manifesta;
e lascia pur grattar dov' è la rogna.

Ché se la voce tua sarà molesta   130
nel primo gusto, vital nodrimento
lascerà poi, quando sarà digesta.

Questo tuo grido farà come vento,   133
che le più alte cime più percuote;
e ciò non fa d'onor poco argomento.

Però ti son mostrate in queste rote,   136
nel monte e ne la valle dolorosa
pur l'anime che son di fama note,

che l'animo di quel ch'ode, non posa   139
né ferma fede per essempro ch'aia
la sua radice incognita e ascosa,

né per altro argomento che non paia."   142

    thus, it is right to arm myself with foresight,   109
that if I lose the place most dear, I may
not lose the rest through what my poems say.

    Down in the world of endless bitterness,   112
and on the mountain from whose lovely peak
I was drawn upward by my lady's eyes,

    and afterward, from light to light in Heaven,   115
I learned that which, if I retell it, must
for many have a taste too sharp, too harsh;

    yet if I am a timid friend of truth,   118
I fear that I may lose my life among
those who will call this present, ancient times."

    The light in which there smiled the treasure I   121
had found within it, first began to dazzle,
as would a golden mirror in the sun,

    then it replied: "A conscience that is dark—   124
either through its or through another's shame—
indeed will find that what you speak is harsh.

    Nevertheless, all falsehood set aside,   127
let all that you have seen be manifest,
and let them scratch wherever it may itch.

    For if, at the first taste, your words molest,   130
they will, when they have been digested, end
as living nourishment. As does the wind,

    so shall your outcry do—the wind that sends   133
its roughest blows against the highest peaks;
that is no little cause for claiming honor.

    Therefore, within these spheres, upon the mountain,   136
and in the dismal valley, you were shown
only those souls that unto fame are known—

    because the mind of one who hears will not   139
put doubt to rest, put trust in you, if given
examples with their roots unknown and hidden,

    or arguments too dim, too unapparent."   142

Diligite . . .

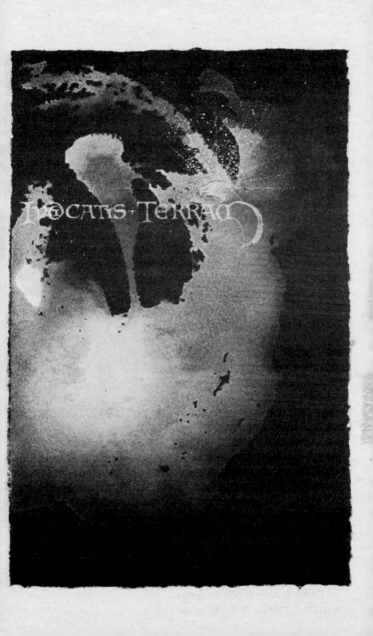

CANTO XVIII

Già si godeva solo del suo verbo
  quello specchio beato, e io gustava
lo mio, temprando col dolce l'acerbo;

  e quella donna ch'a Dio mi menava   4
disse: "Muta pensier; pensa ch'i' sono
presso a colui ch'ogne torto disgrava."

  Io mi rivolsi a l'amoroso suono   7
del mio conforto; e qual io allor vidi
ne li occhi santi amor, qui l'abbandono:

  non perch' io pur del mio parlar diffidi,   10
ma per la mente che non può redire
sovra sé tanto, s'altri non la guidi.

  Tanto poss' io di quel punto ridire,   13
che, rimirando lei, lo mio affetto
libero fu da ogne altro disire,

  fin che 'l piacere etterno, che diretto   16
raggiava in Bëatrice, dal bel viso
mi contentava col secondo aspetto.

  Vincendo me col lume d'un sorriso,   19
ella mi disse: "Volgiti e ascolta;
ché non pur ne' miei occhi è paradiso."

  Come si vede qui alcuna volta   22
l'affetto ne la vista, s'elli è tanto,
che da lui sia tutta l'anima tolta,

  così nel fiammeggiar del folgór santo,   25
a ch'io mi volsi, conobbi la voglia
in lui di ragionarmi ancora alquanto.

  El cominciò: "In questa quinta soglia   28
de l'albero che vive de la cima
e frutta sempre e mai non perde foglia,

B y now that blessed mirror was delighting
in its own inner words; I, tasting mine,
was tempering the bitter with the sweet.

But she, the lady leading me to God,   4
said: "Shift your thoughts: remember—I am close
to Him who lightens every unjust hurt."

Hearing the loving sound my solace spoke,   7
I turned. But here I have to leave untold
what love I saw within her holy eyes,

not just because I do not trust my speech,   10
but, too, because recall cannot retrieve
that much, unless Another is its guide.

This only—of that moment—can I tell: 13
that even as I gazed at her, my soul
was free from any other need as long

as the Eternal Loveliness that shone   16
on Beatrice directly, from her eyes,
contented me with the reflected light.

But, conquering my will with her smile's splendor,   19
she told me: "Turn to him and listen—for
not only in my eyes is Paradise."

As, here on earth, at times our sentiment,   22
if it be passionate enough to take
the soul entirely, shows in the face,

so, in the flaming of the holy fire   25
to which I turned, I saw that he desired
some further words with me. And he began:

"In this fifth resting place, upon the tree   28
that grows down from its crown and endlessly
bears fruit and never loses any leaves,

    spiriti son beati, che giù, prima   31
che venissero al ciel, fuor di gran voce,
sì ch'ogne musa ne sarebbe opima.

    Però mira ne' corni de la croce: 34
quello ch'io nomerò, lì farà l'atto
che fa in nube il suo foco veloce."

    Io vidi per la croce un lume tratto   37
dal nomar Iosuè, com' el si feo;
né mi fu noto il dir prima che 'l fatto.

    E al nome de l'alto Macabeo   40
vidi moversi un altro roteando,
e letizia era ferza del paleo.

    Così per Carlo Magno e per Orlando   43
due ne seguì lo mio attento sguardo,
com' occhio segue suo falcon volando.

    Poscia trasse Guiglielmo e Rinoardo   46
e 'l duca Gottifredi la mia vista
per quella croce, e Ruberto Guiscardo.

    Indi, tra l'altre luci mota e mista,   49
mostrommi l'alma che m'avea parlato
qual era tra i cantor del cielo artista.

    Io mi rivolsi dal mio destro lato   52
per vedere in Beatrice il mio dovere,
o per parlare o per atto, segnato;

    e vidi le sue luci tanto mere,   55
tanto gioconde, che la sua sembianza
vinceva li altri e l'ultimo solere.

    E come, per sentir più dilettanza   58
bene operando, l'uom di giorno in giorno
s'accorge che la sua virtute avanza,

    sì m'accors' io che 'l mio girare intorno   61
col cielo insieme avea cresciuto l'arco,
veggendo quel miracol più addorno.

    E qual è 'l trasmutare in picciol varco   64
di tempo in bianca donna, quando 'l volto
suo si discarchi di vergogna il carco,

    tal fu ne li occhi miei, quando fui vòlto,   67
per lo candor de la temprata stella
sesta, che dentro a sé m'avea ricolto.

are blessed souls that, down below, before   31
they came to heaven, were so notable
that any poem would be enriched by them.

Therefore look at the cross, along its horns: 34
those whom I name will race as swiftly as,
within a cloud, its rapid lightnings flash."

Then, just as soon as Joshua was named,   37
I saw a splendor thrust along the cross,
nor did I note the name before the act.

And at the name of noble Maccabeus,   40
I saw another flame wheel round itself,
and gladness was the whip that spurred that top.

So, too, for Charlemagne and Roland—my   43
attentive eye held fast to that pair like
a falconer who tracks his falcon's flight.

The next to draw my eyes along that cross   46
were William and Renouard and, too, Duke Godfrey
and Robert Guiscard. Then, when he had left me

and mingled with the other lights, the soul   49
who had addressed me showed his artistry,
singing among the singers in that sphere.

I turned to my right side to see if I   52
might see if Beatrice had signified
by word or gesture what I was to do

and saw such purity within her eyes,   55
such joy, that her appearance now surpassed
its guise at other times, even the last.

And as, by feeling greater joyousness   58
in doing good, a man becomes aware
that day by day his virtue is advancing,

so I became aware that my revolving   61
with heaven had increased its arc—by seeing
that miracle becoming still more brilliant.

And like the rapid change that one can see   64
in a pale woman's face when it has freed
itself from bearing bashful modesty,

such change I, turning, saw: the red of Mars   67
was gone—and now the temperate sixth star's
white heaven welcomed me into itself.

Io vidi in quella giovïal facella   70
lo sfavillar de l'amor che lì era
segnare a li occhi miei nostra favella.

   E come augelli surti di rivera,   73
quasi congratulando a lor pasture,
fanno di sé or tonda or altra schiera,

   sì dentro ai lumi sante creature   76
volitando cantavano, e faciensi
or D, or I, or L in sue figure.

   Prima, cantando, a sua nota moviensi;   79
poi, diventando l'un di questi segni,
un poco s'arrestavano e taciensi.

   O diva Pegasëa che li 'ngegni   82
fai glorïosi e rendili longevi,
ed essi teco le cittadi e ' regni,

   illustrami di te, sì ch'io rilevi   85
le lor figure com' io l'ho concette:
paia tua possa in questi versi brevi!

   Mostrarsi dunque in cinque volte sette   88
vocali e consonanti; e io notai
le parti sì, come mi parver dette.

   "DILIGITE IUSTITIAM," primai   91
fur verbo e nome di tutto 'l dipinto;
"QUI IUDICATIS TERRAM," fur sezzai.

   Poscia ne l'emme del vocabol quinto   94
rimasero ordinate; sì che Giove
pareva argento lì d'oro distinto.

   E vidi scendere altre luci dove   97
era il colmo de l'emme, e lì quetarsi
cantando, credo, il ben ch'a sé le move.

   Poi, come nel percuoter d'i ciocchi arsi   100
surgono innumerabili faville,
onde li stolti sogliono agurarsi,

   resurger parver quindi più di mille   103
luci e salir, qual assai e qual poco,
sì come 'l sol che l'accende sortille;

   e quïetata ciascuna in suo loco,   106
la testa e 'l collo d'un'aguglia vidi
rappresentare a quel distinto foco.

I saw within that torch of Jupiter   70
the sparkling of the love that it contained
design before my eyes the signs we speak.

   And just as birds that rise from riverbanks,   73
as if rejoicing after feeding there,
will form a round flock or another shape,

   so, in their lights, the saintly beings sang   76
and, in their flight, the figures that they spelled
were now a *D,* now *I,* and now an *L.*

   First, they moved to the rhythm of their song;   79
then, after they had finished forming one
letter, they halted for a while, in silence.

   O godly Pegasea, you who give   82
to genius glory and long life, as it,
through you, gives these to kingdoms and to cities,

   give me your light that I may emphasize   85
these signs as I inscribed them in my mind:
your power—may it appear in these brief lines!

   Those blessed spirits took the shape of five   88
times seven vowels and consonants, and I
noted the parts as they were spelled for me.

   DILIGITE IUSTITIAM were the verb   91
and noun that first appeared in that depiction;
QUI IUDICATIS TERRAM followed after.

   Then, having formed the *M* of the fifth word,   94
those spirits kept their order; Jupiter's
silver, at that point, seemed embossed with gold.

   And I saw other lights descending on   97
the apex of the *M* and, settling, singing—
I think—the Good that draws them to Itself.

   Then, as innumerable sparks rise up   100
when one strikes burning logs (and in those sparks
fools have a way of reading auguries),

   from that *M* seemed to surge more than a thousand   103
lights; and they climbed, some high, some low, just as
the Sun that kindles them assigned positions.

   With each light settled quietly in place,   106
I saw that the array of fire had shaped
the image of an eagle's head and neck.

Quei che dipinge lì, non ha chi 'l guidi;   109
ma esso guida, e da lui si rammenta
quella virtù ch'è forma per li nidi.

L'altra bëatitudo, che contenta   112
pareva prima d'ingigliarsi a l'emme,
con poco moto seguitò la 'mprenta.

O dolce stella, quali e quante gemme   115
mi dimostraro che nostra giustizia
effetto sia del ciel che tu ingemme!

Per ch'io prego la mente in che s'inizia   118
tuo moto e tua virtute, che rimiri
ond' esce il fummo che 'l tuo raggio vizia;

sì ch'un'altra fïata omai s'adiri   121
del comperare e vender dentro al templo
che si murò di segni e di martìri.

O milizia del ciel cu' io contemplo,   124
adora per color che sono in terra
tutti svïati dietro al malo essempio!

Già si solea con le spade far guerra;   127
ma or si fa togliendo or qui or quivi
lo pan che 'l pïo Padre a nessun serra.

Ma tu che sol per cancellare scrivi,   130
pensa che Pietro e Paulo, che moriro
per la vigna che guasti, ancor son vivi.

Ben puoi tu dire: "I' ho fermo 'l disiro   133
sì a colui che volle viver solo
e che per salti fu tratto al martiro,

ch'io non conosco il pescator né Polo."   136

He who paints there has no one as His guide: 109
He guides Himself; in Him we recognize
the shaping force that flows from nest to nest.

The other lights, who were, it seemed, content   112
at first to form a lily on the *M*,
moving a little, formed the eagle's frame.

O gentle star, what—and how many—gems   115
made plain to me that justice here on earth
depends upon the heaven you engem!

Therefore I pray the Mind in which begin   118
your motion and your force, to watch that place
which has produced the smoke that dims your rays,

that once again His anger fall upon   121
those who would buy and sell within that temple
whose walls were built by miracles and martyrs.

O hosts of Heaven whom I contemplate,   124
for all who, led by bad example, stray
within the life they live on earth, do pray!

Men once were used to waging war with swords;   127
now war means seizing here and there the bread
the tender Father would deny to none.

But you who only write to then erase,   130
remember this: Peter and Paul, who died
to save the vines you spoil, are still alive.

Well may you say: "My longing is so bent   133
on him who chose the solitary life
and for a dance was dragged to martyrdom—

I do not know the Fisherman or Paul."   136

CANTO XIX

Parea dinanzi a me con l'ali aperte
la bella image che nel dolce *frui*
liete facevan l'anime conserte;
    parea ciascuna rubinetto in cui   4
raggio di sole ardesse sì acceso,
che ne' miei occhi rifrangesse lui.
    E quel che mi convien ritrar testeso,   7
non portò voce mai, né scrisse incostro,
né fu per fantasia già mai compreso;
    ch'io vidi e anche udi' parlar lo rostro,   10
e sonar ne la voce e "io" e "mio,"
quand' era nel concetto e "noi" e "nostro."
    E cominciò: "Per esser giusto e pio   13
son io qui essaltato a quella gloria
che non si lascia vincere a disio;
    e in terra lasciai la mia memoria   16
sì fatta, che le genti lì malvage
commendan lei, ma non seguon la storia."
    Così un sol calor di molte brage   19
si fa sentir, come di molti amori
usciva solo un suon di quella image.
    Ond' io appresso: "O perpetüi fiori   22
de l'etterna letizia, che pur uno
parer mi fate tutti vostri odori,
    solvetemi, spirando, il gran digiuno   25
che lungamente m'ha tenuto in fame,
non trovandoli in terra cibo alcuno.
    Ben so io che, se 'n cielo altro reame   28
la divina giustizia fa suo specchio,
che 'l vostro non l'apprende con velame.

The handsome image those united souls,
  happy within their blessedness, were shaping,
appeared before me now with open wings.

　　Each soul seemed like a ruby—one in which　　4
a ray of sun burned so, that in my eyes,
it was the total sun that seemed reflected.

　　And what I now must tell has never been　　7
reported by a voice, inscribed by ink,
never conceived by the imagination;

　　for I did see the beak, did hear it speak　　10
and utter with its voice both *I* and *mine*
when *we* and *ours* were what, in thought, was meant.

　　And it began: "Because I was both just　　13
and merciful, I am exalted here
to glory no desire can surpass;

　　the memory I left on earth is such　　16
that even the malicious praise it there,
although they do not follow its example."

　　Thus one sole warmth is felt from many embers,　　19
even as from a multitude of loves
one voice alone rose from the Eagle's image.

　　To which I said: "O everlasting flowers　　22
of the eternal gladness, who make all
your fragrances appear to me as one,

　　do let your breath deliver me from that　　25
great fast which kept me hungering so long,
not finding any food for it on earth.

　　I know indeed that, though God's Justice has　　28
another realm in Heaven as Its mirror,
you here do not perceive it through a veil.

Sapete come attento io m'apparecchio   31
ad ascoltar; sapete qual è quello
dubbio che m'è digiun cotanto vecchio."

Quasi falcone ch'esce del cappello,   34
move la testa e con l'ali si plaude,
voglia mostrando e faccendosi bello,

vid' io farsi quel segno, che di laude   37
de la divina grazia era contesto,
con canti quai si sa chi là sù gaude.

Poi cominciò: "Colui che volse il sesto   40
a lo stremo del mondo, e dentro ad esso
distinse tanto occulto e manifesto,

non poté suo valor sì fare impresso   43
in tutto l'universo, che 'l suo verbo
non rimanesse in infinito eccesso.

E ciò fa certo che 'l primo superbo,   46
che fu la somma d'ogne creatura,
per non aspettar lume, cadde acerbo;

e quinci appar ch'ogne minor natura   49
è corto recettacolo a quel bene
che non ha fine e sé con sé misura.

Dunque vostra veduta, che convene   52
essere alcun de' raggi de la mente
di che tutte le cose son ripiene,

non pò da sua natura esser possente   55
tanto, che suo principio non discerna
molto di là da quel che l'è parvente.

Però ne la giustizia sempiterna   58
la vista che riceve il vostro mondo,
com' occhio per lo mare, entro s'interna;

che, ben che da la proda veggia il fondo,   61
in pelago nol vede; e nondimeno
èli, ma cela lui l'esser profondo.

Lume non è, se non vien dal sereno   64
che non si turba mai; anzi è tenèbra
od ombra de la carne o suo veleno.

Assai t'è mo aperta la latebra   67
che t'ascondeva la giustizia viva,
di che facei question cotanto crebra;

You know how keenly I prepare myself   31
to listen, and you know what is that doubt
which caused so old a hungering in me."

Just like a falcon set free from its hood,   34
which moves its head and flaps its wings, displaying
its eagerness and proud appearance, so

I saw that ensign do, that Eagle woven   37
of praises of God's grace, accompanied
by songs whose sense those up above enjoy.

Then it began: "The One who turned His compass   40
to mark the world's confines, and in them set
so many things concealed and things revealed,

could not imprint His Power into all   43
the universe without His Word remaining
in infinite excess of such a vessel.

In proof of this, the first proud being, he   46
who was the highest of all creatures, fell—
unripe because he did not wait for light.

Thus it is clear that every lesser nature   49
is—all the more—too meager a container
for endless Good, which is Its own sole measure.

In consequence of this, your vision—which   52
must be a ray of that Intelligence
with which all beings are infused—cannot

of its own nature find sufficient force   55
to see into its origin beyond
what God himself makes manifest to man;

therefore, the vision that your world receives   58
can penetrate into Eternal Justice
no more than eye can penetrate the sea;

for though, near shore, sight reaches the sea floor,   61
you cannot reach it in the open sea;
yet it is there, but hidden by the deep.

Only the light that shines from the clear heaven   64
can never be obscured—all else is darkness
or shadow of the flesh or fleshly poison.

Now is the hiding place of living Justice   67
laid open to you—where it had been hidden
while you addressed it with insistent questions.

ché tu dicevi: 'Un uom nasce a la riva   70
de l'Indo, e quivi non è chi ragioni
di Cristo né chi legga né chi scriva;

e tutti suoi voleri e atti buoni   73
sono, quanto ragione umana vede,
sanza peccato in vita o in sermoni.

Muore non battezzato e sanza fede: 76
ov' è questa giustizia che 'l condanna?
ov' è colpa sua, se ei non crede?'

Or tu chi se', che vuo' sedere a scranna,   79
per giudicar di lungi mille miglia
con la veduta corta d'una spanna?

Certo a colui che meco s'assottiglia,   82
se la Scrittura sovra voi non fosse,
da dubitar sarebbe a maraviglia.

Oh terreni animali! oh menti grosse!   85
La prima volontà, ch'è da sé buona,
da sé, ch'è sommo ben, mai non si mosse.

Cotanto è giusto quanto a lei consuona: 88
nullo creato bene a sé la tira,
ma essa, radïando, lui cagiona."

Quale sovresso il nido si rigira   91
poi c'ha pasciuti la cicogna i figli,
e come quel ch'è pasto la rimira;

cotal si fece, e sì levài i cigli,   94
la benedetta imagine, che l'ali
movea sospinte da tanti consigli.

Roteando cantava, e dicea: "Quali   97
son le mie note a te, che non le 'ntendi,
tal è il giudicio etterno a voi mortali."

Poi si quetaro quei lucenti incendi   100
de lo Spirito Santo ancor nel segno
che fé i Romani al mondo reverendi,

esso ricominciò: "A questo regno   103
non salì mai chi non credette 'n Cristo,
né pria né poi ch'el si chiavasse al legno.

Ma vedi: molti gridan 'Cristo, Cristo!'   106
che saranno in giudicio assai men *prope*
a lui, che tal che non conosce Cristo;

For you would say: 'A man is born along 70
the shoreline of the Indus River; none
is there to speak or teach or write of Christ.

And he, as far as human reason sees, 73
in all he seeks and all he does is good:
there is no sin within his life or speech.

And that man dies unbaptized, without faith. 76
Where is this justice then that would condemn him?
Where is his sin if he does not believe?'

Now who are you to sit upon the bench, 79
to judge events a thousand miles away,
when your own vision spans so brief a space?

Of course, for him who would be subtle with me, 82
were there no Scriptures to instruct you, then
there would be place for an array of questions.

O earthly animals, o minds obtuse! 85
The Primal Will, which of Itself is good,
from the Supreme Good—Its Self—never moved.

So much is just as does accord with It; 88
and so, created good can draw It to
itself—but It, rayed forth, causes such goods."

Just as, above the nest, the stork will circle 91
when she has fed her fledglings, and as he
whom she has fed looks up at her, so did

the blessed image do, and so did I, 94
the fledgling, while the Eagle moved its wings,
spurred on by many wills in unison.

Wheeling, the Eagle sang, then said: "Even 97
as are my songs to you—past understanding—
such is Eternal Judgment to you mortals."

After the Holy Ghost's bright flames fell silent 100
while still within the sign that made the Romans
revered throughout the world, again the Eagle

began: "No one without belief in Christ 103
has ever risen to this kingdom—either
before or after He was crucified.

But there are many who now cry 'Christ! Christ!' 106
who at the Final Judgment shall be far
less close to Him than one who knows not Christ;

e tai Cristian dannerà l'Etïope,   109
quando si partiranno i due collegi,
l'uno in etterno ricco e l'altro inòpe.

Che poran dir li Perse a' vostri regi,   112
come vedranno quel volume aperto
nel qual si scrivon tutti suoi dispregi?

Lì si vedrà, tra l'opere d'Alberto,   115
quella che tosto moverà la penna,
per che 'l regno di Praga fia diserto.

Lì si vedrà il duol che sovra Senna   118
induce, falseggiando la moneta,
quel che morrà di colpo di cotenna.

Lì si vedrà la superbia ch'asseta,   121
che fa lo Scotto e l'Inghilese folle,
sì che non può soffrir dentro a sua meta.

Vedrassi la lussuria e 'l viver molle   124
di quel di Spagna e di quel di Boemme,
che mai valor non conobbe né volle.

Vedrassi al Ciotto di Ierusalemme   127
segnata con un i la sua bontate,
quando 'l contrario segnerà un emme.

Vedrassi l'avarizia e la viltate   130
di quei che guarda l'isola del foco,
ove Anchise finì la lunga etate;

e a dare ad intender quanto è poco,   133
la sua scrittura fian lettere mozze,
che noteranno molto in parvo loco.

E parranno a ciascun l'opere sozze   136
del barba e del fratel, che tanto egregia
nazione e due corone han fatte bozze.

E quel di Portogallo e di Norvegia   139
lì si conosceranno, e quel di Rascia
che male ha visto il conio di Vinegia.

O beata Ungheria, se non si lascia   142
più malmenare! e beata Navarra,
se s'armasse del monte che la fascia!

E creder de' ciascun che già, per arra   145
di questo, Niccosïa e Famagosta
per la lor bestia si lamenti e garra,

che dal fianco de l'altre non si scosta."   148

the Ethiopian will shame such Christians 109
when the two companies are separated,
the one forever rich, the other poor.

What shall the Persians, when they come to see 112
that open volume in which they shall read
the misdeeds of your rulers, say to them?

There one shall see, among the deeds of Albert, 115
that which is soon to set the pen in motion,
his making of a desert of Prague's kingdom.

There one shall see the grief inflicted on 118
the Seine by him who falsifies his coins,
one who shall die beneath a wild boar's blow.

There one shall see the thirst of arrogance 121
that drives the Scot and Englishman insane—
unable to remain within their borders.

That book will show the life of lechery 124
and ease the Spaniard led—and the Bohemian,
who never knew and never wished for valor.

That book will show the Cripple of Jerusalem— 127
his good deeds labeled with an *I* alone,
whereas his evils will be under *M*.

That book will show the greed and cowardice 130
of him who oversees the Isle of Fire,
on which Anchises ended his long life;

and to make plain his paltriness, the letters 133
that register his deeds will be contracted,
to note much pettiness in little space.

And all shall see the filthiness of both 136
his uncle and his brother, who dishonored
a family so famous—and two crowns.

And he of Portugal and he of Norway 139
shall be known in that book, and he of Rascia,
who saw—unluckily—the coin of Venice.

O happy Hungary, if she would let 142
herself be wronged no more! Happy Navarre,
if mountains that surround her served as armor!

And if Navarre needs token of her future, 145
now Nicosia and Famagosta offer—
as men must see—lament and anger over

their own beast, with his place beside the others." 148

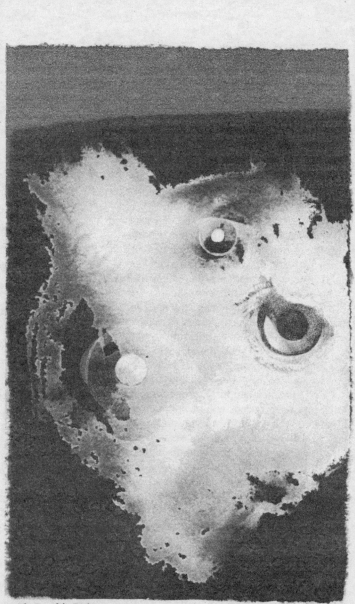

The Eye of the Eagle

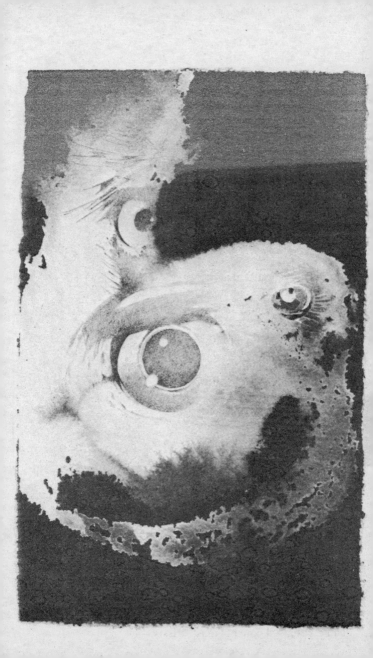

CANTO XX

Quando colui che tutto 'l mondo alluma
de l'emisperio nostro sì discende,
che 'l giorno d'ogne parte si consuma,

lo ciel, che sol di lui prima s'accende,   4
subitamente si rifà parvente
per molte luci, in che una risplende;

e questo atto del ciel mi venne a mente,   7
come 'l segno del mondo e de' suoi duci
nel benedetto rostro fu tacente;

però che tutte quelle vive luci,   10
vie più lucendo, cominciaron canti
da mia memoria labili e caduci.

O dolce amor che di riso t'ammanti,   13
quanto parevi ardente in que' flailli,
ch'avieno spirto sol di pensier santi!

Poscia che i cari e lucidi lapilli   16
ond' io vidi ingemmato il sesto lume
puoser silenzio a li angelici squilli,

udir mi parve un mormorar di fiume   19
che scende chiaro giù di pietra in pietra,
mostrando l'ubertà del suo cacume.

E come suono al collo de la cetra   22
prende sua forma, e sì com' al pertugio
de la sampogna vento che penètra,

eosì, rimosso d'aspettare indugio,   25
quel mormorar de l'aguglia salissi
su per lo collo, come fosse bugio.

Fecesi voce quivi, e quindi uscissi   28
per lo suo becco in forma di parole,
quali aspettava il core ov' io le scrissi.

W hen he who graces all the world with light
    has sunk so far below our hemisphere
that on all sides the day is spent, the sky,

    which had been lit before by him alone,   4
immediately shows itself again
with many lights reflecting one same source,

    and I remembered this celestial course   7
when, in the blessed beak, the emblem of
the world and of its guardians fell silent;

    for then all of those living lights grew more   10
resplendent, but the songs that they began
were labile—they escape my memory.

    O gentle love that wears a smile as mantle,   13
how ardent was your image in those torches
filled only with the breath of holy thoughts!

    After the precious, gleaming jewels with which   16
the sixth of Heaven's heavens was engemmed
had ended their angelic song in silence,

    I seemed to hear the murmur of a torrent   19
that, limpid, falls from rock to rock, whose flow
shows the abundance of its mountain source.

    Even as sound takes shape at the lute's neck,   22
and even as the wind that penetrates
the blow-hole of the bagpipe, so—with no

    delay—that murmur of the Eagle rose   25
straight up, directly through its neck as if
its neck were hollow; and that murmuring

    became a voice that issued from its beak,   28
taking the shape of words desired by
my heart—and that is where they were transcribed.

"La parte in me che vede e pate il sole   31
ne l'aguglie mortali," incominciommi,
"or fisamente riguardar si vole,

perché d'i fuochi ond' io figura fommi,   34
quelli onde l'occhio in testa mi scintilla,
e' di tutti lor gradi son li sommi.

Colui che luce in mezzo per pupilla,   37
fu il cantor de lo Spirito Santo,
che l'arca traslatò di villa in villa:

ora conosce il merto del suo canto,   40
in quanto effetto fu del suo consiglio,
per lo remunerar ch'è altrettanto.

Dei cinque che mi fan cerchio per ciglio,   43
colui che più al becco mi s'accosta,
la vedovella consolò del figlio:

ora conosce quanto caro costa   46
non seguir Cristo, per l'esperïenza
di questa dolce vita e de l'opposta.

E quel che segue in la circunferenza   49
di che ragiono, per l'arco superno,
morte indugiò per vera penitenza:

ora conosce che 'l giudicio etterno   52
non si trasmuta, quando degno preco
fa crastino là giù de l'odïerno.

L'altro che segue, con le leggi e meco,   55
sotto buona intenzion che fé mal frutto,
per cedere al pastor si fece greco:

ora conosce come il mal dedutto   58
dal suo bene operar non li è nocivo,
avvegna che sia 'l mondo indi distrutto.

E quel che vedi ne l'arco declivo,   61
Guiglielmo fu, cui quella terra plora
che piagne Carlo e Federigo vivo:

ora conosce come s'innamora   64
lo ciel del giusto rege, e al sembiante
del suo fulgore il fa vedere ancora.

Chi crederebbe giù nel mondo errante   67
che Rifëo Troiano in questo tondo
fosse la quinta de le luci sante?

"Now you must watch—and steadily—that part   31
of me that can, in mortal eagles, see
and suffer the sun's force," it then began

    to say to me, "because, of all the flames   34
from which I shape my form, those six with which
the eye in my head glows hold highest rank.

    He who gleams in the center, my eye's pupil—   37
he was the singer of the Holy Spirit,
who bore the ark from one town to another;

    now he has learned the merit will can earn—   40
his song had not been spurred by grace alone,
but his own will, in part, had urged him on.

    Of those five flames that, arching, form my brow,   43
he who is nearest to my beak is one
who comforted the widow for her son;

    now he has learned the price one pays for not   46
following Christ, through his experience
of this sweet life and of its opposite.

    And he whose place is next on the circumference   49
of which I speak, along the upward arc,
delayed his death through truthful penitence;

    now he has learned that the eternal judgment   52
remains unchanged, though worthy prayer below
makes what falls due today take place tomorrow.

    The next who follows—one whose good intention   55
bore evil fruit—to give place to the Shepherd,
with both the laws and me, made himself Greek;

    now he has learned that, even though the world   58
be ruined by the evil that derives
from his good act, that evil does not harm him.

    He whom you see—along the downward arc—   61
was William, and the land that mourns his death,
for living Charles and Frederick, now laments;

    now he has learned how Heaven loves the just   64
ruler, and he would show this outwardly
as well, so radiantly visible.

    Who in the erring world below would hold   67
that he who was the fifth among the lights
that formed this circle was the Trojan Ripheus?

Ora conosce assai di quel che 'l mondo   70
veder non può de la divina grazia,
ben che sua vista non discerna il fondo."

Quale allodetta che 'n aere si spazia   73
prima cantando, e poi tace contenta
de l'ultima dolcezza che la sazia,

tal mi sembiò l'imago de la 'mprenta   76
de l'etterno piacere, al cui disio
ciascuna cosa qual ell' è diventa.

E avvegna ch'io fossi al dubbiar mio   79
lì quasi vetro a lo color ch'el veste,
tempo aspettar tacendo non patio,

ma de la bocca, "Che cose son queste?"   82
mi pinse con la forza del suo peso:
per ch'io di coruscar vidi gran feste.

Poi appresso, con l'occhio più acceso,   85
lo benedetto segno mi rispuose
per non tenermi in ammirar sospeso:

"Io veggio che tu credi queste cose   88
perch' io le dico, ma non vedi come;
sì che, se son credute, sono ascose.

Fai come quei che la cosa per nome   91
apprende ben, ma la sua quiditate
veder non può se altri non la prome.

Regnum celorum vïolenza pate   94
da caldo amore e da viva speranza,
che vince la divina volontate:

non a guisa che l'omo a l'om sobranza,   97
ma vince lei perché vuole esser vinta,
e, vinta, vince con sua beninanza.

La prima vita del ciglio e la quinta   100
ti fa maravigliar, perché ne vedi
la regïon de li angeli dipinta.

D'i corpi suoi non uscir, come credi,   103
Gentili, ma Cristiani, in ferma fede
quel d'i passuri e quel d'i passi piedi.

Ché l'una de lo 'nferno, u' non si riede   106
già mai a buon voler, tornò a l'ossa;
e ciò di viva spene fu mercede:

Now he has learned much that the world cannot   70
discern of God's own grace, although his sight
cannot divine, not reach its deepest site."

As if it were a lark at large in air,   73
a lark that sings at first and then falls still,
content with final sweetness that fulfills,

such seemed to me the image of the seal   76
of that Eternal Pleasure through whose will
each thing becomes the being that it is.

And though the doubt I felt there was as plain   79
as any colored surface cloaked by glass,
it could not wait to voice itself, but with

the thrust and weight of urgency it forced   82
"Can such things be?" out from my lips, at which
I saw lights flash—a vast festivity.

And then the blessed sign—its eye grown still   85
more bright—replied, that I might not be kept
suspended in amazement: "I can see

that, since you speak of them, you do believe   88
these things but cannot see *how* they may be;
and thus, though you believe them, they are hidden.

You act as one who apprehends a thing   91
by name but cannot see its quiddity
unless another set it forth to him.

Regnum celorum suffers violence   94
from ardent love and living hope, for these
can be the conquerors of Heaven's Will;

yet not as man defeats another man: 97
the Will of God is won because It would
be won and, won, wins through benevolence.

You were amazed to see the angels' realm.   100
adorned with those who were the first and fifth
among the living souls that form my eyebrow.

When these souls left their bodies, they were not   103
Gentiles—as you believe—but Christians, one
with firm faith in the Feet that suffered, one

in Feet that were to suffer. One, from Hell,   106
where there is no returning to right will,
returned to his own bones, as the reward

di viva spene, che mise la possa   109
ne' prieghi fatti a Dio per suscitarla,
sì che potesse sua voglia esser mossa.

L'anima glorïosa onde si parla,   112
tornata ne la carne, in che fu poco,
credette in lui che potëa aiutarla;

e credendo s'accese in tanto foco   115
di vero amor, ch'a la morte seconda
fu degna di venire a questo gioco.

L'altra, per grazia che da sì profonda   118
fontana stilla, che mai creatura
non pinse l'occhio infino a la prima onda,

tutto suo amor là giù pose a drittura: 121
per che, di grazia in grazia, Dio li aperse
l'occhio a la nostra redenzion futura;

ond' ei credette in quella, e non sofferse   124
da indi il puzzo più del paganesmo;
e riprendiene le genti perverse.

Quelle tre donne li fur per battesmo   127
che tu vedesti da la destra rota,
dinanzi al battezzar più d'un millesmo.

O predestinazion, quanto remota   130
è la radice tua da quelli aspetti
che la prima cagion non veggion tota!

E voi, mortali, tenetevi stretti   133
a giudicar: ché noi, che Dio vedemo,
non conosciamo ancor tutti li eletti;

ed ènne dolce così fatto scemo,   136
perché il ben nostro in questo ben s'affina,
che quel che vole Iddio, e noi volemo."

Così da quella imagine divina,   139
per farmi chiara la mia corta vista,
data mi fu soave medicina.

E come a buon cantor buon citarista   142
fa seguitar lo guizzo de la corda,
in che più di piacer lo canto acquista,

sì, mentre ch'e' parlò, sì mi ricorda   145
ch'io vidi le due luci benedette,
pur come batter d'occhi si concorda,

con le parole mover le fiammette.   148

bestowed upon a living hope, the hope   109
that gave force to the prayers offered God
to resurrect him and convert his will.

Returning briefly to the flesh, that soul   112
in glory—he of whom I speak—believed
in Him whose power could help him and, believing,

was kindled to such fire of true love   115
that, when he died a second death, he was
worthy to join in this festivity.

The other, through the grace that surges from   118
a well so deep that no created one
has ever thrust his eye to its first source.

below, set all his love on righteousness,   121
so that, through grace on grace, God granted him
the sight of our redemption in the future;

thus he, believing that, no longer suffered   124
the stench of paganism and rebuked
those who persisted in that perverse way.

More than a thousand years before baptizing,   127
to baptize him there were the same three women
you saw along the chariot's right-hand side.

How distant, o predestination, is   130
your root from those whose vision does not see
the Primal Cause in Its entirety!

And, mortals, do take care—judge prudently: 133
for we, though we see God, do not yet know
all those whom He has chosen; but within

the incompleteness of our knowledge is   136
a sweetness, for our good is then refined
in this good, since what God wills, we too will."

So, from the image God Himself had drawn,   139
what I received was gentle medicine;
and I saw my shortsightedness plainly.

And as a lutanist accompanies—   142
expert—with trembling strings, the expert singer,
by which the song acquires sweeter savor,

so, while the Eagle spoke—I can remember—   145
I saw the pair of blessed lights together,
like eyes that wink in concord, move their flames

in ways that were at one with what he said.   148

CANTO XXI

Già eran li occhi miei rifissi al volto
de la mia donna, e l'animo con essi,
e da ogne altro intento s'era tolto.

E quella non ridea; ma "S'io ridessi," 4
mi cominciò, "tu ti faresti quale
fu Semelè quando di cener fessi:

ché la bellezza mia, che per le scale 7
de l'etterno palazzo più s'accende,
com' hai veduto, quanto più si sale,

se non si temperasse, tanto splende, 10
che 'l tuo mortal podere, al suo fulgore,
sarebbe fronda che trono scoscende.

Noi sem levati al settimo splendore, 13
che sotto 'l petto del Leone ardente
raggia mo misto giù del suo valore.

Ficca di retro a li occhi tuoi la mente, 16
e fa di quelli specchi a la figura
che 'n questo specchio ti sarà parvente."

Qual savesse qual era la pastura 19
del viso mio ne l'aspetto beato
quand' io mi trasmutai ad altra cura,

conoscerebbe quanto m'era a grato 22
ubidire a la mia celeste scorta,
contrapesando l'un con l'altro lato.

Dentro al cristallo che 'l vocabol porta, 25
cerchiando il mondo, del suo caro duce
sotto cui giacque ogne malizia morta,

di color d'oro in che raggio traluce 28
vid' io uno scaleo eretto in suso
tanto, che nol seguiva la mia luce.

B y now my eyes were set again upon
  my lady's face, and with my eyes, my mind:
from every other thought, it was withdrawn.

    She did not smile. Instead her speech to me   4
began: "Were I to smile, then you would be
like Semele when she was turned to ashes,

    because, as you have seen, my loveliness—   7
which, even as we climb the steps of this
eternal palace, blazes with more brightness—

    were it not tempered here, would be so brilliant   10
that, as it flashed, your mortal faculty
would seem a branch a lightning bolt has cracked.

    We now are in the seventh splendor; this,   13
beneath the burning Lion's breast, transmits
to earth its rays, with which his force is mixed.

    Let your mind follow where your eyes have led, 16
and let your eyes be mirrors for the figure
that will appear to you within this mirror."

    That man who knows just how my vision pastured 19
upon her blessed face, might recognize
the joy I found when my celestial guide

    had asked of me to turn my mind aside,   22
were he to weigh my joy when I obeyed
against my joy in contemplating her.

    Within the crystal that—as it revolves   25
around the earth—bears as its name the name
of that dear king whose rule undid all evil,

    I saw a ladder rising up so high   28
that it could not be followed by my sight:
its color, gold when gold is struck by sunlight.

Vidi anche per li gradi scender giuso 31
tanti splendor, ch'io pensai ch'ogne lume
che par nel ciel, quindi fosse diffuso.

E come, per lo natural costume, 34
le pòle insieme, al cominciar del giorno,
si movono a scaldar le fredde piume;

poi altre vanno via sanza ritorno, 37
altre rivolgon sé onde son mosse,
e altre roteando fan soggiorno;

tal modo parve me che quivi fosse 40
in quello sfavillar che 'nsieme venne,
sì come in certo grado si percosse.

E quel che presso più ci si ritenne, 43
si fé sì chiaro, ch'io dicea pensando:
"Io veggio ben l'amor che tu m'accenne.

Ma quella ond' io aspetto il come e 'l quando 46
del dire e del tacer, si sta; ond' io,
contra 'l disio, fo ben ch'io non dimando."

Per ch'ella, che vedëa il tacer mio 49
nel veder di colui che tutto vede,
mi disse: "Solvi il tuo caldo disio."

E io incominciai: "La mia mercede 52
non mi fa degno de la tua risposta;
ma per colei che 'l chieder mi concede,

vita beata che ti stai nascosta 55
dentro a la tua letizia, fammi nota
la cagion che sì presso mi t'ha posta;

e di perché si tace in questa rota 58
la dolce sinfonia di paradiso,
che giù per l'altre suona sì divota."

"Tu hai l'udir mortal sì come il viso," 61
rispuose a me; "onde qui non si canta
per quel che Bëatrice non ha riso.

Giù per li gradi de la scala santa 64
discesi tanto sol per farti festa
col dire e con la luce che mi ammanta;

né più amor mi fece esser più presta, 67
ché più e tanto amor quinci sù ferve,
sì come il fiammeggiar ti manifesta.

I also saw so many flames descend 31
those steps that I thought every light displayed
in heaven had been poured out from that place.

And just as jackdaws, at the break of day, 34
together rise—such is their nature's way—
to warm their feathers chilled by night; then some

fly off and never do return, and some 37
wheel back to that point where they started from,
while others, though they wheel, remain at home;

such were the ways I saw those spendors take 40
as soon as they had struck a certain step,
where they had thronged as one in radiance.

The flame that halted nearest us became 43
so bright that in my mind I said: "I see
you clearly signaling to me your love.

But she from whom I wait for word on how 46
and when to speak and to be silent, pauses;
thus, though I would, I do well not to ask."

And she who, seeing Him who sees all things, 49
had seen the reason for my silence, said
to me: "Do satisfy your burning longing."

And I began: "My merit does not make 52
me worthy of reply, but for the sake
of her who gives me leave to question you—

a blessed living soul—who hide within 55
your joy, do let me know the reason why
you drew so near to me. And tell me, too,

why the sweet symphony of Paradise 58
is silent in this heaven, while, below,
it sounds devoutly through the other spheres."

"Your hearing is as mortal as your sight; 61
thus, here there is no singing," he replied,
"and Beatrice, in like wise, did not smile.

When, down the sacred staircase, I descended, 64
I only came to welcome you with gladness—
with words and with the light that mantles me.

The love that prompted me is not supreme; 67
above, is love that equals or exceeds
my own, as spirit-flames will let you see.

   Ma l'alta carità, che ci fa serve   70
pronte al consiglio che 'l mondo governa,
sorteggia qui sì come tu osserve."

   "Io veggio ben," diss' io, "sacra lucerna,   73
come libero amore in questa corte
basta a seguir la provendenza etterna;

   ma questo è quel ch'a cerner mi par forte,   76
perché predestinata fosti sola
a questo officio tra le tue consorte."

   Né venni prima a l'ultima parola,   79
che del suo mezzo fece il lume centro,
girando sé come veloce mola;

   poi rispuose l'amor che v'era dentro: 82
"Luce divina sopra me s'appunta,
penetrando per questa in ch'io m'inventro,

   la cui virtù, col mio veder congiunta,   85
mi leva sopra me tanto, ch'i' veggio
la somma essenza de la quale è munta.

   Quinci vien l'allegrezza ond' io fiammeggio;   88
per ch'a la vista mia, quant' ella è chiara,
la chiarità de la fiamma pareggio.

   Ma quell' alma nel ciel che più si schiara,   91
quel serafin che 'n Dio più l'occhio ha fisso,
a la dimanda tua non satisfara,

   però che sì s'innoltra ne lo abisso   94
de l'etterno statuto quel che chiedi,
che da ogne creata vista è scisso.

   E al mondo mortal, quando tu riedi,   97
questo rapporta, sì che non presumma
a tanto segno più mover li piedi.

   La mente, che qui luce, in terra fumma;   100
onde riguarda come può là giùe
quel che non pote perché 'l ciel l'assumma."

   Sì mi prescrisser le parole sue,   103
ch'io lasciai la quistione e mi ritrassi
a dimandarla umilmente chi fue.

   "Tra ' due liti d'Italia surgon sassi,   106
e non molto distanti a la tua patria,
tanto che ' troni assai suonan più bassi,

But the deep charity, which makes us keen   70
to serve the Providence that rules the world,
allots our actions here, as you perceive."

"O holy lamp," I said, "I do indeed   73
see how, within this court, it is your free
love that fulfills eternal Providence;

but this seems difficult for me to grasp: 76
why you alone, of those who form these ranks,
were he who was predestined to this task."

And I had yet to reach the final word   79
when that light made a pivot of its midpoint
and spun around as would a swift millstone.

Then, from within its light, that love replied: 82
"Light from the Deity descends on me;
it penetrates the light that enwombs me;

its power, as it joins my power of sight,   85
lifts me so far beyond myself that I
see the High Source from which that light derives.

From this there comes the joy with which I am   88
aflame; I match the clearness of my light
with equal measure of my clear insight.

But even Heaven's most enlightened soul,   91
that Seraph with his eye most set on God,
could not provide the *why,* not satisfy

what you have asked; for deep in the abyss   94
of the Eternal Ordinance, it is
cut off from all created beings' vision.

And to the mortal world, when you return,   97
tell this, lest men continue to trespass
and set their steps toward such a reachless goal.

The mind, bright here, on earth is dulled and smoky. 100
Think: how, below, can mind see that which hides
even when mind is raised to Heaven's height?"

His words so curbed my query that I left   103
behind my questioning; and I drew back
and humbly asked that spirit who he was.

"Not far from your homeland, between two shores   106
of Italy, the stony ridges rise
so high that, far below them, thunder roars.

    e fanno un gibbo che si chiama Catria,   109
di sotto al quale è consecrato un ermo,
che suole esser disposto a sola latria."

    Così ricominciommi il terzo sermo;   112
e poi, continüando, disse: "Quivi
al servigio di Dio mi fe' sì fermo,

    che pur con cibi di liquor d'ulivi   115
lievemente passava caldi e geli,
contento ne' pensier contemplativi.

    Render solea quel chiostro a questi cieli   118
fertilemente; e ora è fatto vano,
sì che tosto convien che si riveli.

    In quel loco fu' io Pietro Damiano,   121
e Pietro Peccator fu' ne la casa
di Nostra Donna in sul lito adriano.

    Poca vita mortal m'era rimasa,   124
quando fui chiesto e tratto a quel cappello,
che pur di male in peggio si travasa.

    Venne Cefàs e venne il gran vasello   127
de lo Spirito Santo, magri e scalzi,
prendendo il cibo da qualunque ostello.

    Or voglion quinci e quindi chi rincalzi   130
li moderni pastori e chi li meni,
tanto son gravi, e chi di rietro li alzi.

    Cuopron d'i manti loro i palafreni,   133
sì che due bestie van sott' una pelle:
oh pazïenza che tanto sostieni!"

    A questa voce vid' io più fiammelle   136
di grado in grado scendere e girarsi,
e ogne giro le facea più belle.

    Dintorno a questa vennero e fermarsi,   139
e fero un grido di sì alto suono,
che non potrebbe qui assomigliarsi;

    né io lo 'ntesi, sì mi vinse il tuono.   142

These ridges form a hump called Catria;   109
a consecrated hermitage beneath
that peak was once devoted just to worship."

So his third speech to me began; then he   112
continued: "There, within that monastery,
in serving God, I gained tenacity:

with food that only olive juice had seasoned,   115
I could sustain with ease both heat and frost,
content within my contemplative thoughts.

That cloister used to offer souls to Heaven,   118
a fertile harvest, but it now is barren—
as Heaven's punishment will soon make plain.

There I was known as Peter Damian   121
and, on the Adriatic shore, was Peter
the Sinner when I served Our Lady's House.

Not much of mortal life was left to me   124
when I was sought for, dragged to take that hat
which always passes down from bad to worse.

Once there were Cephas and the Holy Ghost's   127
great vessel: they were barefoot, they were lean,
they took their food at any inn they found.

But now the modern pastors are so plump   130
that they have need of one to prop them up
on this side, one on that, and one in front,

and one to hoist them saddleward. Their cloaks   133
cover their steeds, two beasts beneath one skin:
o patience, you who must endure so much!"

These words, I saw, had summoned many flames,   136
descending step by step; I saw them wheel
and, at each turn, become more beautiful.

They joined around him, and they stopped, and raised   139
a cry so deep that nothing here can be
its likeness; but the words they cried I could

not understand—their thunder overcame me.   142

The Ridges of Catria

CANTO XXII

Oppresso di stupore, a la mia guida
  mi volsi, come parvol che ricorre
sempre colà dove più si confida;

  e quella, come madre che soccorre   4
sùbito al figlio palido e anelo
con la sua voce, che 'l suol ben disporre,

  mi disse: "Non sai tu che tu se' in cielo?   7
e non sai tu che 'l cielo è tutto santo,
e ciò che ci si fa vien da buon zelo?

  Come t'avrebbe trasmutato il canto,   10
e io ridendo, mo pensar lo puoi,
poscia che 'l grido t'ha mosso cotanto;

  nel qual se 'nteso avessi i prieghi suoi,   13
già ti sarebbe nota la vendetta
che tu vedrai innanzi che tu muoi.

  La spada di qua sù non taglia in fretta   16
né tardo, ma' ch'al parer di colui
che disïando o temendo l'aspetta.

  Ma rivolgiti omai inverso altrui;   19
ch'assai illustri spiriti vedrai,
se com' io dico l'aspetto redui."

  Come a lei piacque, li occhi ritornai,   22
e vidi cento sperule che 'nsieme
più s'abbellivan con mutüi rai.

  Io stava come quei che 'n sé represe   25
la punta del disio, e non s'attenta
di domandar, sì del troppo si teme;

  e la maggiore e la più luculenta   28
di quelle margherite innanzi fessi,
per far di sé la mia voglia contenta.

Still the Seventh Heaven: the Sphere of Saturn. Beatrice on the spirits'
outcry. St. Benedict and other contemplatives. Dante's desire to see the
face of St. Benedict. St. Benedict on the degeneracy of the Benedictines.
Ascent to the Eighth Heaven, the Sphere of the Fixed Stars. Invocation
to the constellation Gemini. Dante's earthward gaze.

A mazement overwhelming me, I—like
 a child who always hurries back to find
that place he trusts the most—turned to my guide;

and like a mother quick to reassure   4
her pale and panting son with the same voice
that she has often used to comfort him,

she said: "Do you not know you are in Heaven,   7
not know how holy all of Heaven is,
how righteous zeal moves every action here?

Now, since this cry has agitated you   10
so much, you can conceive how—had you seen
me smile and heard song here—you would have been

confounded; and if you had understood   13
the prayer within that cry, by now you would
know the revenge you'll see before your death.

The sword that strikes from Heaven's height is neither 16
hasty nor slow, except as it appears
to him who waits for it—who longs or fears.

But turn now toward the other spirits here;   19
for if you set your sight as I suggest,
you will see many who are notable."

As pleased my guide, I turned my eyes and saw   22
a hundred little suns; as these together
cast light, each made the other lovelier.

I stood as one who curbs within himself   25
the goad of longing and, in fear of being
too forward, does not dare to ask a question.

At this, the largest and most radiant   28
among those pearls moved forward that he might
appease my need to hear who he might be.

Poi dentro a lei udi': "Se tu vedessi   31
com' io la carità che tra noi arde,
li tuoi concetti sarebbero espressi.

Ma perché tu, aspettando, non tarde   34
a l'alto fine, io ti farò risposta
pur al pensier, da che sì ti riguarde.

Quel monte a cui Cassino è ne la costa   37
fu frequentato già in su la cima
da la gente ingannata e mal disposta;

e quel son io che sù vi portai prima   40
lo nome di colui che 'n terra addusse
la verità che tanto ci soblima;

e tanta grazia sopra me relusse,   43
ch'io ritrassi le ville circunstanti
da l'empio cólto che 'l mondo sedusse.

Questi altri fuochi tutti contemplanti   46
uomini fuoro, accesi di quel caldo
che fa nascere i fiori e ' frutti santi.

Qui è Maccario, qui è Romoaldo,   49
qui son li frati miei che dentro ai chiostri
fermar li piedi e tennero il cor saldo."

E io a lui: "L'affetto che dimostri   52
meco parlando, e la buona sembianza
ch'io veggio e noto in tutti li ardor vostri,

così m'ha dilatata mia fidanza,   55
come 'l sol fa la rosa quando aperta
tanto divien quant' ell' ha di possanza.

Però ti priego, e tu, padre, m'accerta   58
s'io posso prender tanta grazia, ch'io
ti veggia con imagine scoverta."

Ond' elli: "Frate, il tuo alto disio   61
s'adempirà in su l'ultima spera,
ove s'adempion tutti li altri e 'l mio.

Ivi è perfetta, matura e intera   64
ciascuna disianza; in quella sola
è ogne parte là ove sempr' era,

perché non è in loco e non s'impola;   67
e nostra scala infino ad essa varca,
onde così dal viso ti s'invola.

Then, in that light, I heard: "Were you to see,   31
even as I do see, the charity
that burns in us, your thoughts would have been uttered.

But lest, by waiting, you be slow to reach   34
the high goal of your seeking, I shall answer
what you were thinking when you curbed your speech.

That mountain on whose flank Cassino lies   37
was once frequented on its summit by
those who were still deluded, still awry;

and I am he who was the first to carry   40
up to that peak the name of Him who brought
to earth the truth that lifts us to the heights.

And such abundant grace had brought me light   43
that, from corrupted worship that seduced
the world, I won away the nearby sites.

These other flames were all contemplatives,   46
men who were kindled by that heat which brings
to birth the blessed flowers and blessed fruits.

Here is Macarius, here is Romualdus,   49
here are my brothers, those who stayed their steps
in cloistered walls, who kept their hearts steadfast."

I answered: "The affection that you show   52
in speech to me, and kindness that I see
and note within the flaming of your lights,

have given me so much more confidence,   55
just like the sun that makes the rose expand
and reach the fullest flowering it can.

Therefore I pray you, father—and may you   58
assure me that I can receive such grace—
to let me see, unveiled, your human face."

And he: "Brother, your high desire will be   61
fulfilled within the final sphere, as all
the other souls' and my own longing will.

There, each desire is perfect, ripe, intact;   64
and only there, within that final sphere,
is every part where it has always been.

That sphere is not in space and has no poles;   67
our ladder reaches up to it, and that
is why it now is hidden from your sight.

Infin là sù la vide il patriarca   70
Iacobbe porger la superna parte,
quando li apparve d'angeli sì carca.

Ma, per salirla, mo nessun diparte   73
da terra i piedi, e la regola mia
rimasa è per danno de le carte.

Le mura che solieno esser badia   76
fatte sono spelonche, e le cocolle
sacca son piene di farina ria.

Ma grave usura tanto non si tolle   79
contra 'l piacer di Dio, quanto quel frutto
che fa il cor de' monaci sì folle;

ché quantunque la Chiesa guarda, tutto   82
è de la gente che per Dio dimanda;
non di parenti né d'altro più brutto.

La carne d'i mortali è tanto blanda,   85
che giù non basta buon cominciamento
dal nascer de la quercia al far la ghianda.

Pier cominciò sanz' oro e sanz' argento,   88
e io con orazione e con digiuno,
e Francesco umilmente il suo convento;

e se guardi 'l principio di ciascuno,   91
poscia riguardi là dov' è trascorso,
tu vederai del bianco fatto bruno.

Veramente Iordan vòlto retrorso   94
più fu, e 'l mar fuggir, quando Dio volse,
mirabile a veder che qui 'l soccorso."

Così mi disse, e indi si raccolse   97
al suo collegio, e 'l collegio si strinse;
poi, come turbo, in sù tutto s'avvolse.

La dolce donna dietro a lor mi pinse   100
con un sol cenno su per quella scala,
sì sua virtù la mia natura vinse;

né mai qua giù dove si monta e cala   103
naturalmente, fu sì ratto moto
ch'agguagliar si potesse a la mia ala.

S'io torni mai, lettore, a quel divoto   106
trïunfo per lo quale io piango spesso
le mie peccata e 'l petto mi percuoto,

Up to that sphere, Jacob the patriarch   70
could see that ladder's topmost portion reach,
when it appeared to him so thronged with angels.

But no one now would lift his feet from earth   73
to climb that ladder, and my Rule is left
to waste the paper it was written on.

What once were abbey walls are robbers' dens;   76
what once were cowls are sacks of rotten meal.
But even heavy usury does not

offend the will of God as grievously   79
as the appropriation of that fruit
which makes the hearts of monks go mad with greed;

for all within the keeping of the Church   82
belongs to those who ask it in God's name,
and not to relatives or concubines.

The flesh of mortals yields so easily—   85
on earth a good beginning does not run
from when the oak is born until the acorn.

Peter began with neither gold nor silver,   88
and I with prayer and fasting, and when Francis
began his fellowship, he did it humbly;

if you observe the starting point of each,   91
and look again to see where it has strayed,
then you will see how white has gone to gray.

And yet, the Jordan in retreat, the sea   94
in flight when God had willed it so, were sights
more wonderful than His help here will be."

So did he speak to me, and he drew back   97
to join his company, which closed, compact;
then, like a whirlwind, upward, all were swept.

The gentle lady—simply with a sign—   100
impelled me after them and up that ladder,
so did her power overcome my nature;

and never here below, where our ascent   103
and descent follow nature's law, was there
motion as swift as mine when I took wing.

So, reader, may I once again return   106
to those triumphant ranks—an end for which
I often beat my breast, weep for my sins—

tu non avresti in tanto tratto e messo   109
nel foco il dito, in quant' io vidi 'l segno
che segue il Tauro e fui dentro da esso.

O glorïose stelle, o lume pregno   112
di gran virtù, dal quale io riconosco
tutto, qual che si sia, il mio ingegno,

con voi nasceva e s'ascondeva vosco   115
quelli ch'è padre d'ogne mortal vita,
quand' io senti' di prima l'aere tosco;

e poi, quando mi fu grazia largita   118
d'entrar ne l'alta rota che vi gira,
la vostra regïon mi fu sortita.

A voi divotamente ora sospira   121
l'anima mia, per acquistar virtute
al passo forte che a sé la tira.

"Tu se' sì presso a l'ultima salute,"   124
cominciò Bëatrice, "che tu dei
aver le luci tue chiare e acute;

e però, prima che tu più t'inlei,   127
rimira in giù, e vedi quanto mondo
sotto li piedi già esser ti fei;

sì che 'l tuo cor, quantunque può, giocondo   130
s'appresenti a la turba trïunfante
che lieta vien per questo etera tondo."

Col viso ritornai per tutte quante   133
le sette spere, e vidi questo globo
tal, ch'io sorrisi del suo vil sembiante;

e quel consiglio per migliore approbo   136
che l'ha per meno; e chi ad altro pensa
chiamar si puote veramente probo.

Vidi la figlia di Latona incensa   139
sanza quell' ombra che mi fu cagione
per che già la credetti rara e densa.

L'aspetto del tuo nato, Iperïone,   142
quivi sostenni, e vidi com' si move
circa e vicino a lui Maia e Dïone.

Quindi m'apparve il temperar di Giove   145
tra 'l padre e 'l figlio; e quindi mi fu chiaro
il varïar che fanno di lor dove;

more quickly than your finger can withdraw   109
from flame and be thrust into it, I saw,
and was within, the sign that follows Taurus.

O stars of glory, constellation steeped   112
in mighty force, all of my genius—
whatever be its worth—has you as source:

with you was born and under you was hidden   115
he who is father of all mortal lives,
when I first felt the air of Tuscany;

and then, when grace was granted me to enter   118
the high wheel that impels your revolutions,
your region was my fated point of entry.

To you my soul now sighs devotedly,   121
that it may gain the force for this attempt,
hard trial that now demands its every strength.

"You are so near the final blessedness,"   124
so Beatrice began, "that you have need
of vision clear and keen; and thus, before

you enter farther, do look downward, see   127
what I have set beneath your feet already:
much of the world is there. If you see that,

your heart may then present itself with all   130
the joy it can to the triumphant throng
that comes in gladness through this ether's rounds."

My eyes returned through all the seven spheres   133
and saw this globe in such a way that I
smiled at its scrawny image: I approve

that judgment as the best, which holds this earth   136
to be the least; and he whose thoughts are set
elsewhere, can truly be called virtuous.

I saw Latona's daughter radiant,   139
without the shadow that had made me once
believe that she contained both rare and dense.

And there, Hyperion, I could sustain   142
the vision of your son, and saw Dïone
and Maia as they circled nearby him.

The temperate Jupiter appeared to me   145
between his father and his son; and I
saw clearly how they vary their positions.

  e tutti e sette mi si dimostraro   148
quanto son grandi e quanto son veloci
e come sono in distante riparo.
  L'aiuola che ci fa tanto feroci,   151
volgendom' io con li etterni Gemelli,
tutta m'apparve da' colli a le foci;
  poscia rivolsi li occhi a li occhi belli.   154

And all the seven heavens showed to me   148
their magnitudes, their speeds, the distances
of each from each. The little threshing floor
    that so incites our savagery was all—   151
from hills to river mouths—revealed to me
while I wheeled with eternal Gemini.
    My eyes then turned again to the fair eyes.   154

CANTO XXIII

Come l'augello, intra l'amate fronde,
  posato al nido de' suoi dolci nati
la notte che le cose ci nasconde,

  che, per veder li aspetti disïati   4
e per trovar lo cibo onde li pasca,
in che gravi labor li sono aggrati,

  previene il tempo in su aperta frasca,   7
e con ardente affetto il sole aspetta,
fiso guardando pur che l'alba nasca;

  così la donna mïa stava eretta   10
e attenta, rivolta inver' la plaga
sotto la quale il sol mostra men fretta:

  sì che, veggendola io sospesa e vaga,   13
fecimi qual è quei che disïando
altro vorria, e sperando s'appaga.

  Ma poco fu tra uno e altro quando,   16
del mio attender, dico, e del vedere
lo ciel venir più e più rischiarando;

  e Bëatrice disse: "Ecco le schiere   19
del trïunfo di Cristo e tutto 'l frutto
ricolto del girar di queste spere!"

  Pariemi che 'l suo viso ardesse tutto,   22
e li occhi avea di letizia sì pieni,
che passarmen convien sanza costrutto.

  Quale ne' plenilunïi sereni   25
Trivïa ride tra le ninfe etterne
che dipingon lo ciel per tutti i seni,

  vid' i' sopra migliaia di lucerne   28
un sol che tutte quante l'accendea,
come fa 'l nostro le viste superne;

As does the bird, among beloved branches,
when, through the night that hides things from us, she
has rested near the nest of her sweet fledglings

and, on an open branch, anticipates   4
the time when she can see their longed-for faces
and find the food with which to feed them—chore

that pleases her, however hard her labors—   7
as she awaits the sun with warm affection,
steadfastly watching for the dawn to break:

so did my lady stand, erect, intent,   10
turned toward that part of heaven under which
the sun is given to less haste; so that,

as I saw her in longing and suspense,   13
I grew to be as one who, while he wants
what is not his, is satisfied with hope.

But time between one and the other *when*   16
was brief—I mean the *whens* of waiting and
of seeing heaven grow more radiant.

And Beatrice said: "There you see the troops   19
of the triumphant Christ—and all the fruits
ingathered from the turning of these spheres!"

It seemed to me her face was all aflame,   22
and there was so much gladness in her eyes—
I am compelled to leave it undescribed.

Like Trivia—at the full moon in clear skies—   25
smiling among the everlasting nymphs
who decorate all reaches of the sky,

I saw a sun above a thousand lamps;   28
it kindled all of them as does our sun
kindle the sights above us here on earth;

e per la viva luce trasparea   31
la lucente sustanza tanto chiara
nel viso mio, che non la sostenea.

Oh Bëatrice, dolce guida e cara!   34
Ella mi disse: "Quel che ti sobranza
è virtù da cui nulla si ripara.

Quivi è la sapïenza e la possanza   37
ch'aprì le strade tra 'l cielo e la terra,
onde fu già sì lunga disïanza."

Come foco di nube si diserra   40
per dilatarsi sì che non vi cape,
e fuor di sua natura in giù s'atterra,

la mente mia così, tra quelle dape   43
fatta più grande, di sé stessa uscìo,
e che si fesse rimembrar non sape.

"Apri li occhi e riguarda qual son io;   46
tu hai vedute cose, che possente
se' fatto a sostener lo riso mio."

Io era come quei che si risente   49
di visïone oblita e che s'ingegna
indarno di ridurlasi a la mente,

quand' io udi' questa proferta, degna   52
di tanto grato, che mai non si stingue
del libro che 'l preterito rassegna.

Se mo sonasser tutte quelle lingue   55
che Polimnïa con le suore fero
del latte lor dolcissimo più pingue,

per aiutarmi, al millesmo del vero   58
non si verria, cantando il santo riso
e quanto il santo aspetto facea mero;

e così, figurando il paradiso,   61
convien saltar lo sacrato poema,
come chi trova suo cammin riciso.

Ma chi pensasse il ponderoso tema   64
e l'omero mortal che se ne carca,
nol biasmerebbe se sott' esso trema:

non è pareggio da picciola barca   67
quel che fendendo va l'ardita prora,
né da nocchier ch'a sé medesmo parca.

and through its living light the glowing Substance   31
appeared to me with such intensity—
my vision lacked the power to sustain it.

O Beatrice, sweet guide and dear! She said   34
to me: "What overwhelms you is a Power
against which nothing can defend itself.

This is the Wisdom and the Potency   37
that opened roads between the earth and Heaven,
the paths for which desire had long since waited."

Even as lightning breaking from a cloud,   40
expanding so that it cannot be pent,
against its nature, down to earth, descends,

so did my mind, confronted by that feast,   43
expand; and it was carried past itself—
what it became, it cannot recollect.

"Open your eyes and see what I now am;   46
the things you witnessed will have made you strong
enough to bear the power of my smile."

I was as one who, waking from a dream   49
he has forgotten, tries in vain to bring
that vision back into his memory,

when I heard what she offered me, deserving   52
of so much gratitude that it can never
be canceled from the book that tells the past.

If all the tongues that Polyhymnia   55
together with her sisters made most rich
with sweetest milk, should come now to assist

my singing of the holy smile that lit   58
the holy face of Beatrice, the truth
would not be reached—not its one-thousandth part.

And thus, in representing Paradise,   61
the sacred poem has to leap across,
as does a man who finds his path cut off.

But he who thinks upon the weighty theme,   64
and on the mortal shoulder bearing it,
will lay no blame if, burdened so, I tremble:

this is no crossing for a little bark—   67
the sea that my audacious prow now cleaves—
nor for a helmsman who would spare himself.

"Perché la faccia mia sì t'innamora,   70
che tu non ti rivolgi al bel giardino
che sotto i raggi di Cristo s'infiora?

Quivi è la rosa in che 'l verbo divino   73
carne si fece; quivi son li gigli
al cui odor si prese il buon cammino."

Così Beatrice; e io, che a' suoi consigli   76
tutto era pronto, ancora mi rendei
a la battaglia de' debili cigli.

Come a raggio di sol, che puro mei   79
per fratta nube, già prato di fiori
vider, coverti d'ombra, li occhi miei;

vid' io così più turbe di splendori,   82
folgorate di sù da raggi ardenti,
sanza veder principio di folgóri.

O benigna vertù che sì li 'mprenti,   85
sù t'essaltasti per largirmi loco
a li occhi lì che non t'eran possenti.

Il nome del bel fior ch'io sempre invoco   88
e mane e sera, tutto mi ristrinse
l'animo ad avvisar lo maggior foco;

e come ambo le luci mi dipinse   91
il quale e il quanto de la viva stella
che là sù vince come qua giù vinse,

per entro il cielo scese una facella,   94
formata in cerchio a guisa di corona,
e cinsela e girossi intorno ad ella.

Qualunque melodia più dolce suona   97
qua giù e più a sé l'anima tira,
parrebbe nube che squarciata tona,

comparata al sonar di quella lira   100
onde si coronava il bel zaffiro
del quale il ciel più chiaro s'inzaffira.

"Io sono amore angelico, che giro   103
l'alta letizia che spira del ventre
che fu albergo del nostro disiro;

e girerommi, donna del ciel, mentre   106
che seguirai tuo figlio, e farai dia
più la spera suprema perché li entre."

"Why are you so enraptured by my face   70
as to deny your eyes the sight of that
fair garden blossoming beneath Christ's rays?

The Rose in which the Word of God became   73
flesh grows within that garden; there—the lilies
whose fragrance let men find the righteous way."

Thus Beatrice, and I—completely ready   76
to do what she might counsel—once again
took up the battle of my feeble brows.

Under a ray of sun that, limpid, streams   79
down from a broken cloud, my eyes have seen,
while shade was shielding them, a flowered meadow;

so I saw many troops of splendors here   82
lit from above by burning rays of light,
but where those rays began was not in sight.

O kindly Power that imprints them thus,   85
you rose on high to leave space for my eyes—
for where I was, they were too weak to see You!

The name of that fair flower which I always   88
invoke, at morning and at evening, drew
my mind completely to the greatest flame.

And when, on both my eye-lights, were depicted   91
the force and nature of the living star
that conquers heaven as it conquered earth,

descending through that sky there came a torch,   94
forming a ring that seemed as if a crown:
wheeling around her—a revolving garland.

Whatever melody most sweetly sounds   97
on earth, and to itself most draws the soul,
would seem a cloud that, torn by lightning, thunders,

if likened to the music of that lyre   100
which sounded from the crown of that fair sapphire,
the brightest light that has ensapphired heaven.

"I am angelic love who wheel around   103
that high gladness inspired by the womb
that was the dwelling place of our Desire;

so shall I circle, Lady of Heaven, until   106
you, following your Son, have made that sphere
supreme, still more divine by entering it."

Così la circulata melodia   109
si sigillava, e tutti li altri lumi
facean sonare il nome di Maria.

Lo real manto di tutti i volumi   112
del mondo, che più ferve e più s'avviva
ne l'alito di Dio e nei costumi,

avea sopra di noi l'interna riva   115
tanto distante, che la sua parvenza,
là dov' io era, ancor non appariva:

però non ebber li occhi miei potenza   118
di seguitar la coronata fiamma
che si levò appresso sua semenza.

E come fantolin che 'nver' la mamma   121
tende le braccia, poi che 'l latte prese,
per l'animo che 'nfin di fuor s'infiamma;

ciascun di quei candori in sù si stese   124
con la sua cima, sì che l'alto affetto
ch'elli avieno a Maria mi fu palese.

Indi rimaser lì nel mio cospetto,   127
"Regina celi" cantando sì dolce,
che mai da me non si partì 'l diletto.

Oh quanta è l'ubertà che si soffolce   130
in quelle arche ricchissime che fuoro
a seminar qua giù buone bobolce!

Quivi si vive e gode del tesoro   133
ch s'acquistò piangendo ne lo essilio
di Babillòn, ove si lasciò l'oro.

Quivi trïunfa, sotto l'alto Filio   136
di Dio e di Maria, di sua vittoria,
e con l'antico e col novo concilio,

colui che tien le chiavi di tal gloria.   139

    So did the circulating melody,   109
sealing itself, conclude; and all the other
lights then resounded with the name of Mary.

    The royal cloak of all the wheeling spheres   112
within the universe, the heaven most
intense, alive, most burning in the breath

    of God and in His laws and ordinance,   115
was far above us at its inner shore,
so distant that it still lay out of sight

    from that point where I was; and thus my eyes   118
possessed no power to follow that crowned flame,
which mounted upward, following her Son.

    And like an infant who, when it has taken   121
its milk, extends its arms out to its mother,
its feeling kindling into outward flame,

    each of those blessed splendors stretched its peak   124
upward, so that the deep affection each
possessed for Mary was made plain to me.

    Then they remained within my sight, singing   127
"Regina coeli" with such tenderness
that my delight in that has never left me.

    Oh, in those richest coffers, what abundance   130
is garnered up for those who, while below,
on earth, were faithful workers when they sowed!

    Here do they live, delighting in the treasure   133
they earned with tears in Babylonian
exile, where they had no concern for gold.

    Here, under the high Son of God and Mary,   136
together with the ancient and the new
councils, he triumphs in his victory—

    he who is keeper of the keys of glory.   139

Christ Radiant

The Virgin

CANTO XXIV

O sodalizio eletto a la gran cena
    del benedetto Agnello, il qual vi ciba
sì, che la vostra voglia è sempre piena,

    se per grazia di Dio questi preliba   4
di quel che cade de la vostra mensa,
prima che morte tempo li prescriba,

    ponete mente a l'affezione immensa   7
e roratelo alquanto: voi bevete
sempre del fonte onde vien quel ch'ei pensa."

    Così Beatrice; e quelle anime liete   10
si fero spere sopra fissi poli,
fiammando, volte, a guisa di comete.

    E come cerchi in tempra d'orïuoli   13
si giran sì, che 'l primo a chi pon mente
quïeto pare, e l'ultimo che voli;

    così quelle carole, differente-   16
mente danzando, de la sua ricchezza
mi facieno stimar, veloci e lente.

    Di quella ch'io notai di più carezza   19
vid' ïo uscire un foco sì felice,
che nullo vi lasciò di più chiarezza;

    e tre fïate intorno di Beatrice   22
si volse con un canto tanto divo,
che la mia fantasia nol mi ridice.

    Però salta la penna e non lo scrivo: 25
chè l'imagine nostra a cotai pieghe,
non che 'l parlar, è troppo color vivo.

    "O santa suora mia che sì ne prieghe   28
divota, per lo tuo ardente affetto
da quella bella spera mi disleghe."

*Still the Eighth Heaven: the Sphere of the Fixed Stars. Beatrice's request
to the spirits, and St. Peter's reply. Her asking of St. Peter to examine
Dante on Faith. Dante's preparation and his examination. The approval
and blessing of Dante by St. Peter.*

O fellowship that has been chosen for
the Blessed Lamb's great supper, where He feeds
you so as always to fulfill your need,

since by the grace of God, this man receives   4
foretaste of something fallen from your table
before death has assigned his time its limit,

direct your mind to his immense desire,   7
quench him somewhat: you who forever drink
from that Source which his thought and longing seek."

So Beatrice; and these delighted souls   10
formed companies of spheres around fixed poles,
flaming as they revolved, as comets glow.

And just as, in a clock's machinery,   13
to one who watches them, the wheels turn so
that, while the first wheel seems to rest, the last

wheel flies; so did those circling dancers—as   16
they danced to different measures, swift and slow—
make me a judge of what their riches were.

From that sphere which I noted as most precious,   19
I saw a flame come forth with so much gladness
that none it left behind had greater brightness;

and that flame whirled three times round Beatrice   22
while singing so divine a song that my
imagination cannot shape it for me.

My pen leaps over it; I do not write: 25
our fantasy and, all the more so, speech
are far too gross for painting folds so deep.

"O you who pray to us with such devotion—   28
my holy sister—with your warm affection,
you have released me from that lovely sphere."

Poscia fermato, il foco benedetto   31
a la mia donna dirizzò lo spiro,
che favellò così com' i' ho detto.

Ed ella: "O luce etterna del gran viro   34
a cui Nostro Segnor lasciò le chiavi,
ch'ei portò giù, di questo gaudio miro,

tenta costui di punti lievi e gravi,   37
come ti piace, intorno de la fede,
per la qual tu su per lo mare andavi.

S'elli ama bene e bene spera e crede,   40
non t'è occulto, perché 'l viso hai quivi
dov' ogne cosa dipinta si vede;

ma perché questo regno ha fatto civi   43
per la verace fede, a glorïarla,
di lei parlare è ben ch'a lui arrivi."

Sì come il baccialier s'arma e non parla   46
fin che 'l maestro la question propone,
per approvarla, non per terminarla,

così m'armava io d'ogne ragione   49
mentre ch'ella dicea, per esser presto
a tal querente e a tal professione.

"Dì, buon Cristiano, fatti manifesto: 52
fede che è?" Ond' io levai la fronte
in quella luce onde spirava questo;

poi mi volsi a Beatrice, ed essa pronte   55
sembianze femmi perch' ïo spandessi
l'acqua di fuor del mio interno fonte.

"La Grazia che mi dà ch'io mi confessi,"   58
comincia' io, "da l'alto primipilo,
faccia li miei concetti bene espressi."

E seguitai: "Come 'l verace stilo   61
ne scrisse, padre, del tuo caro frate
che mise teco Roma nel buon filo,

fede è sustanza di cose sperate   64
e argomento de le non parventi;
e questa pare a me sua quiditate."

Allora udi': "Dirittamente senti,   67
se bene intendi perché la ripuose
tra le sustanze, e poi tra li argomenti."

So, after he had stopped his motion, did   31
the blessed flame breathe forth unto my lady;
and what he said I have reported here.

She answered: "O eternal light of that   34
great man to whom our Lord bequeathed the keys
of this astonishing gladness—the keys

He bore to earth—do test this man concerning   37
the faith by which you walked upon the sea;
ask him points lights and grave, just as you please.

That he loves well and hopes well and has faith   40
is not concealed from you: you see that Place
where everything that happens is displayed.

But since this realm has gained its citizens   43
through the true faith, it rightly falls to him
to speak of faith, that he may glorify it."

Just as the bachelor candidate must arm   46
himself and does not speak until the master
submits the question for discussion—not

for settlement—so while she spoke I armed   49
myself with all my arguments, preparing
for such a questioner and such professing.

On hearing that light breathe, "Good Christian, speak,   52
show yourself clearly: what is faith?" I raised
my brow, then turned to Beatrice, whose glance

immediately signaled me to let   55
the waters of my inner source pour forth.
Then I: "So may the Grace that grants to me

to make confession to the Chief Centurion   58
permit my thoughts to find their fit expression";
and followed, "Father, as the truthful pen

of your dear brother wrote—that brother who,   61
with you, set Rome upon the righteous road—
faith is the substance of the things we hope for

and is the evidence of things not seen;   64
and this I take to be its quiddity."
And then I heard: "You understand precisely,

if it is fully clear to you why he   67
has first placed faith among the substances
and then defines it as an evidence."

E io appresso: "Le profonde cose   70
che mi largiscon qui la lor parvenza,
a li occhi di là giù son sì ascose,

　　che l'esser loro v'è in sola credenza,   73
sopra la qual si fonda l'alta spene;
e però di sustanza prende intenza.

E da questa credenza ci convene   76
silogizzar, sanz' avere altra vista:
però intenza d'argomento tene."

Allora udi': "Se quantunque s'acquista   79
giù per dottrina, fosse così 'nteso,
non li avria loco ingegno di sofista."

Così spirò di quello amore acceso;   82
indi soggiunse: "Assai bene è trascorsa
d'esta moneta già la lega e 'l peso;

　　ma dimmi se tu l'hai ne la tua borsa."   85
Ond' io: "Sì ho, sì lucida e sì tonda,
che nel suo conio nulla mi s'inforsa."

Appresso uscì de la luce profonda   88
che lì splendeva: "Questa cara gioia
sopra la quale ogne virtù si fonda,

　　onde ti venne?" E io: "La larga ploia   91
de lo Spirito Santo, ch'è diffusa
in su le vecchie e 'n su le nuove cuoia,

　　è silogismo che la m'ha conchiusa   94
acutamente sì, che 'nverso d'ella
ogne dimostrazion mi pare ottusa."

Io udi' poi: "L'antica e la novella   97
proposizion che così ti conchiude,
perché l'hai tu per divina favella?"

E io: "La prova che 'l ver mi dischiude,   100
son l'opere seguite, a che natura
non scalda ferro mai né batte incude."

Risposto fummi: "Dì, chi t'assicura   103
che quell' opere fosser? Quel medesmo
che vuol provarsi, non altri, il ti giura."

"Se 'l mondo si rivolse al cristianesmo,"   106
diss' io, "sanza miracoli, quest' uno
è tal, che li altri non sono il centesmo:

I next: "The deep things that on me bestow   70
their image here, are hid from sight below,
so that their being lies in faith alone,

    and on that faith the highest hope is founded;   73
and thus it is that faith is called a substance.
And it is from this faith that we must reason,

    deducing what we can from syllogisms,   76
without our being able to see more:
thus faith is also called an evidence."

    And then I heard: "If all one learns below   79
as doctrine were so understood, there would
be no place for the sophist's cleverness."

    This speech was breathed from that enkindled love.   82
He added: "Now this coin is well-examined,
and now we know its alloy and its weight.

    But tell me: do you have it in your purse?"   85
And I: "Indeed I do—so bright and round
that nothing in its stamp leads me to doubt."

    Next, from the deep light gleaming there, I heard: 88
"What is the origin of the dear gem
that comes to you, the gem on which all virtues

    are founded?" I: "The Holy Ghost's abundant   91
rain poured upon the parchments old and new;
that is the syllogism that has proved

    with such persuasiveness that faith has truth—   94
when set beside that argument, all other
demonstrations seem to me obtuse."

    I heard: "The premises of old and new   97
impelling your conclusion—why do you
hold these to be the speech of God?" And I:

    "The proof revealing truth to me relies   100
on acts that happened; for such miracles,
nature can heat no iron, beat no anvil."

    "Say, who assures you that those works were real?" 103
came the reply. "The very thing that needs
proof—no thing else—attests these works to you."

    I said: "If without miracles the world   106
was turned to Christianity, that is
so great a miracle that all the rest

ché tu intrasti povero e digiuno   109
in campo, a seminar la buona pianta
che fu già vite e ora è fatta pruno."

Finito questo, l'alta corte santa   112
risonò per le spere un "Dio laudamo"
ne la melode che là sù si canta.

E quel baron che sì di ramo in ramo,   115
essaminando, già tratto m'avea,
che a l'ultime fronde appressavamo,

ricominciò: "La Grazia, che donnea   118
con la tua mente, la bocca t'aperse
infino a qui come aprir si dovea,

sì ch'io approvo ciò che fuori emerse;   121
ma or convien espremer quel che credi,
e onde a la credenza tua s'offerse."

"O santo padre, e spirito che vedi   124
ciò che credesti sì, che tu vincesti
ver' lo sepulcro più giovani piedi,"

comincia io, "tu vuo' ch'io manifesti   127
la forma qui del pronto creder mio,
e anche la cagion di lui chiedesti.

E io rispondo: Io credo in uno Dio   130
solo ed etterno, che tutto 'l ciel move,
non moto, con amore e con disio;

e a tal creder non ho io pur prove   133
fisice e metafisice, ma dalmi
anche la verità che quinci piove

per Moïsè, per profeti e per salmi,   136
per l'Evangelio e per voi che scriveste
poi che l'ardente Spirto vi fé almi;

e credo in tre persone etterne, e queste   139
credo una essenza sì una e sì trina,
che soffera congiunto 'sono' ed 'este.'

De la profonda condizion divina   142
ch'io tocco mo, la mente mi sigilla
più volte l'evangelica dottrina.

Quest' è 'l principio, quest' è la favilla   145
che si dilata in fiamma poi vivace,
e come stella in cielo in me scintilla."

are not its hundredth part: for you were poor 109
and hungry when you found the field and sowed
the good plant—once a vine and now a thorn."

This done, the high and holy court resounded 112
throughout its spheres with *"Te Deum laudamus,"*
sung with the melody they use on high.

Then he who had examined me, that baron 115
who led me on from branch to branch so that
we now were drawing close to the last leaves,

began again: "That Grace which—lovingly— 118
directs your mind, until this point has taught
you how to find the seemly words for thought,

so that I do approve what you brought forth; 121
but now you must declare what you believe
and what gave you the faith that you receive."

"O holy father, soul who now can see 124
what you believed with such intensity
that, to His tomb, you outran younger feet,"

I then began, "you would have me tell plainly 127
the form of my unhesitating faith,
and also ask me to declare its source.

I answer: I believe in one God—sole, 130
eternal—He who, motionless, moves all
the heavens with His love and love for Him;

for this belief I have not only proofs 133
both physical and metaphysical;
I also have the truth that here rains down

through Moses and the Prophets and the Psalms 136
and through the Gospels and through you who wrote
words given to you by the Holy Ghost.

And I believe in three Eternal Persons, 139
and these I do believe to be one essence,
so single and threefold as to allow

both *is* and *are.* Of this profound condition 142
of God that I have touched on, Gospel teaching
has often set the imprint on my mind.

This is the origin, this is the spark 145
that then extends into a vivid flame
and, like a star in heaven, glows in me."

Come 'l segnor ch'ascolta quel che i piace,   148
da indi abbraccia il servo, gratulando
per la novella, tosto ch'el si tace;
    così, benedicendomi cantando,   151
tre volte cinse me, sì com' io tacqui,
l'appostolico lume al cui comando
    io avea detto: sì nel dir li piacqui!   154

Just as the lord who listens to his servant's   148
announcement, then, as soon as he is silent,
embraces him, both glad with the good news,

so did the apostolic light at whose   151
command I had replied, while blessing me
and singing, then encircle me three times:

the speech I spoke had brought him such delight.   154

CANTO XXV

Se mai continga che 'l poema sacro
al quale ha posto mano e cielo e terra,
si che m'ha fatto per molti anni macro,

vinca la crudeltà che fuor mi serra   4
del bello ovile ov' io dormi' agnello,
nimico ai lupi che li danno guerra;

con altra voce omai, con altro vello   7
ritornerò poeta, e in sul fonte
del mio battesmo prenderò 'l cappello;

però che ne la fede, che fa conte   10
l'anime a Dio, quivi intra' io, e poi
Pietro per lei sì mi girò la fronte.

Indi si mosse un lume verso noi   13
di quella spera ond' uscì la primizia
che lasciò Cristo d'i vicari suoi;

e la mia donna, piena di letizia,   16
mi disse: "Mira, mira: ecco il barone
per cui là giù si vicita Galizia."

Sì come quando il colombo si pone   19
presso al compagno, l'uno a l'altro pande,
girando e mormorando, l'affezione;

così vid' ïo l'un da l'altro grande   22
principe glorïoso essere accolto,
laudando il cibo che là sù li prande.

Ma poi che 'l gratular si fu assolto,   25
tacito *coram me* ciascun s'affisse,
ignito sì che vincëa 'l mio volto.

Ridendo allora Bëatrice disse: 28
"Inclita vita per cui la larghezza
de la nostra basilica si scrisse,

I f it should happen . . . If this sacred poem—
this work so shared by heaven and by earth
that it has made me lean through these long years—

    can ever overcome the cruelty   4
that bars me from the fair fold where I slept,
a lamb opposed to wolves that war on it,

    by then with other voice, with other fleece,   7
I shall return as poet and put on,
at my baptismal font, the laurel crown;

    for there I first found entry to that faith   10
which makes souls welcome unto God, and then,
for that faith, Peter garlanded my brow.

    Then did a light move toward us from that sphere   13
from which emerged the first—the dear, the rare—
of those whom Christ had left to be His vicars;

    and full of happiness, my lady said   16
to me: "Look, look—and see the baron whom,
below on earth, they visit in Galicia."

    As when a dove alights near its companion,   19
and each unto the other, murmuring
and circling, offers its affection, so

    did I see both those great and glorious   22
princes give greeting to each other, praising
the banquet that is offered them on high.

    But when their salutations were complete,   25
each stopped in silence *coram me,* and each
was so aflame, my vision felt defeat.

    Then Beatrice said, smiling: "Famous life   28
by whom the generosity of our
basilica has been described, do let

fa risonar la spene in questa altezza: 31
tu sai, che tante fiate la figuri,
quante Iesù ai tre fé più carezza."

"Leva la testa e fa che t'assicuri: 34
ché ciò che vien qua sù del mortal mondo,
convien ch'ai nostri raggi si maturi."

Questo conforto del foco secondo   37
mi venne; ond' io leväi li occhi a' monti
che li 'ncurvaron pria col troppo pondo.

"Poi che per grazia vuol che tu t'affronti   40
lo nostro Imperadore, anzi la morte,
ne l'aula più secreta co' suoi conti,

sì che, veduto il ver di questa corte,   43
la spene, che là giù bene innamora,
in te e in altrui di ciò conforte,

dì quel ch'ell' è, di come se ne 'nfiora   46
la mente tua, e dì onde a te venne."
Così seguì 'l secondo lume ancora.

E quella pïa che guidò le penne   49
de le mie ali a così alto volo,
a la risposta così mi prevenne:

"La Chiesa militante alcun figliuolo   52
non ha con più speranza, com' è scritto
nel Sol che raggia tutto nostro stuolo:

però li è conceduto che d'Egitto   55
vegna in Ierusalemme per vedere,
anzi che 'l militar li sia prescritto.

Li altri due punti, che non per sapere   58
son dimandati, ma perch' ei rapporti
quanto questa virtù t'è in piacere,

a lui lasc' io, ché non li saran forti   61
né di iattanza; ed elli a ciò risponda,
e la grazia di Dio ciò li comporti."

Come discente ch'a dottor seconda   64
pronto e libente in quel ch'elli è esperto,
perché la sua bontà si disasconda,

"Spene," diss' io, "è uno attender certo   67
de la gloria futura, il qual produce
grazia divina e precedente merto.

matters of hope reecho at this height;   31
you can—for every time that Jesus favored
you three above the rest, you were the figure

of hope." "Lift up your head, and be assured: 34
whatever comes here from the mortal world
has to be ripened in our radiance."

The second fire offered me this comfort;   37
at which my eyes were lifted to the mountains
whose weight of light before had kept me bent.

"Because our Emperor, out of His grace,   40
has willed that you, before your death, may face
His nobles in the inmost of His halls,

so that, when you have seen this court in truth,   43
hope—which, below, spurs love of the true good—
in you and others may be comforted,

do tell what hope is, tell how it has blossomed   46
within your mind, and from what source it came
to you"—so did the second flame continue.

And she, compassionate, who was the guide   49
who led my feathered wings to such high flight,
did thus anticipate my own reply:

"There is no child of the Church Militant   52
who has more hope than he has, as is written
within the Sun whose rays reach all our ranks:

thus it is granted him to come from Egypt   55
into Jerusalem that he have vision
of it, before his term of warring ends.

The other two points of your question, which   58
were not asked so that you may know, but that
he may report how much you prize this virtue,

I leave to him; he will not find them hard   61
or cause for arrogance; as you have asked,
let him reply, and God's grace help his task."

As a disciple answering his master,   64
prepared and willing in what he knows well,
that his proficiency may be revealed,

I said: "Hope is the certain expectation   67
of future glory; it is the result
of God's grace and of merit we have earned.

Da molte stelle mi vien questa luce;   70
ma quei la distillò nel mio cor pria
che fu sommo cantor del sommo duce.

'Sperino in te,' ne la sua tëodia   73
dice, 'color che sanno il nome tuo':
e chi nol sa, s'elli ha la fede mia?

Tu mi stillasti, con lo stillar suo,   76
ne la pistola poi; sì ch'io son pieno,
e in altrui vostra pioggia repluo."

Mentr' io diceva, dentro al vivo seno   79
di quello incendio tremolava un lampo
sùbito e spesso a guisa di baleno.

Indi spirò: "L'amore ond' ïo avvampo   82
ancor ver' la virtù che mi seguette
infin la palma e a l'uscir del campo,

vuol ch'io respiri a te che ti dilette   85
di lei; ed emmi a grato che tu diche
quello che la speranza ti 'mpromette."

E io: "Le nove e le scritture antiche   88
pongon lo segno, ed esso lo mi addita,
de l'anime che Dio s'ha fatte amiche.

Dice Isaia che ciascuna vestita   91
ne la sua terra fia di doppia vesta:
e la sua terra è questa dolce vita;

e 'l tuo fratello assai vie più digesta,   94
là dove tratta de le bianche stole,
questa revelazion ci manifesta."

E prima, appresso al fin d'este parole,   97
"Sperent in te" di sopr' a noi s'udì;
a che rispuoser tutte le carole.

Poscia tra esse un lume si schiarì   100
sì che, se 'l Cancro avesse un tal cristallo,
l'inverno avrebbe un mese d'un sol dì.

E come surge e va ed entra in ballo   103
vergine lieta, sol per fare onore
a la novizia, non per alcun fallo,

così vid' io lo schiarato splendore   106
venire a' due che si volgieno a nota
qual conveniesi al loro ardente amore.

This light has come to me from many stars;   70
but he who first instilled it in my heart
was the chief singer of the Sovereign Guide.

'May those'—he says within his theody—   73
'who know Your name, put hope in You'; and if
one has my faith, can he not know God's name?

And just as he instilled, you then instilled   76
with your Epistle, so that I am full
and rain again your rain on other souls."

While I was speaking, in the living heart   79
of that soul-flame there came a trembling flash,
sudden, repeated, just as lightning cracks.

Then it breathed forth: "The love with which I still   82
burn for the virtue that was mine until
the palm and my departure from the field,

would have me breathe again to you who take   85
such joy in hope; and I should welcome words
that tell what hope has promised unto you."

And I: "The new and ancient Scriptures set   88
the mark for souls whom God befriends; for me,
that mark means what is promised us by hope.

Isaiah says that all of the elect   91
shall wear a double garment in their land:
and their land is this sweet life of the blessed.

And where your brother treats of those white robes,   94
he has—with words direct and evident—
made clear to us Isaiah's revelation."

At first, as soon as I had finished speaking,   97
"Sperent in te" was heard above us, all
the circling garlands answering this call.

And then, among those souls, one light became   100
so bright that, if the Crab had one such crystal,
winter would have a month of one long day.

And as a happy maiden rises and   103
enters the dance to honor the new bride—
and not through vanity or other failing—

so did I see that splendor, brightening,   106
approach those two flames dancing in a ring
to music suited to their burning love.

Misesi lì nel canto e ne la rota;   109
e la mia donna in lor tenea l'aspetto,
pur come sposa tacita e immota.

"Questi è colui che giacque sopra 'l petto   112
del nostro pellicano, e questi fue
di su la croce al grande officio eletto."

La donna mia così; né però piùe   115
mosser la vista sua di stare attenta
poscia che prima le parole sue.

Qual è colui ch'adocchia e s'argomenta   118
di vedere eclissar lo sole un poco,
che, per veder, non vedente diventa;

tal mi fec' ïo a quell' ultimo foco   121
mentre che detto fu: "Perché t'abbagli
per veder cosa che qui non ha loco?

In terra è terra il mio corpo, e saragli   124
tanto con li altri, che 'l numero nostro
con l'etterno proposito s'agguagli.

Con le due stole nel beato chiostro   127
son le due luci sole che saliro;
e questo apporterai nel mondo vostro."

A questa voce l'infiammato giro   130
si quïetò con esso il dolce mischio
che si facea nel suon del trino spiro,

sì come, per cessar fatica o rischio,   133
li remi, pria ne l'acqua ripercossi,
tutti si posano al sonar d'un fischio.

Ahi quanto ne la mente mi commossi,   136
quando mi volsi per veder Beatrice,
per non poter veder, benché io fossi

presso di lei, e nel mondo felice!   139

And there it joined the singing and the circling,   109
on which my lady kept her eyes intent,
just like a bride, silent and motionless.

"This soul is he who lay upon the breast   112
of Christ our Pelican, and he was asked
from on the Cross to serve in the great task."

So spoke my lady; but her gaze was not   115
to be diverted from its steadfastness,
not after or before her words were said.

Even as he who squints and strains to see   118
the sun somewhat eclipsed and, as he tries
to see, becomes sightless, just so did I

in my attempt to watch the latest flame,   121
until these words were said: "Why do you daze
yourself to see what here can have no place?

On earth my body now is earth and shall   124
be there together with the rest until
our number equals the eternal purpose.

Only those two lights that ascended wear   127
their double garment in this blessed cloister.
And carry this report back to your world."

When he began to speak, the flaming circle   130
had stopped its dance; so, too, its song had ceased—
that gentle mingling of their threefold breath—

even as when, avoiding danger or   133
simply to rest, the oars that strike the water,
together halt when rowers hear a whistle.

Ah, how disturbed I was within my mind,   136
when I turned round to look at Beatrice,
on finding that I could not see, though I

was close to her, and in the world of gladness!   139

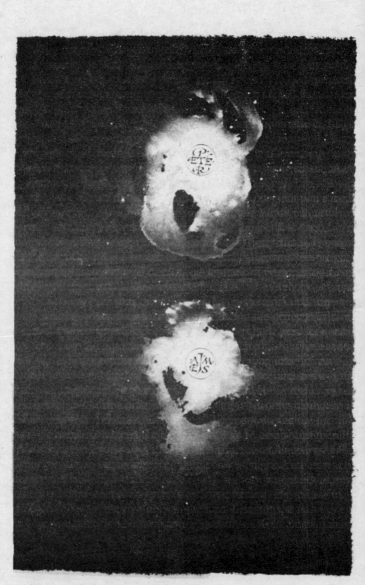

The Four Lights of Peter, James, John, and Adam

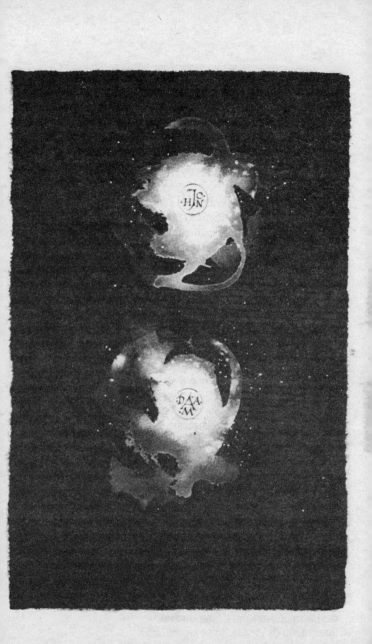

CANTO XXVI

Mentr' io dubbiava per lo viso spento,
de la fulgida fiamma che lo spense
uscì un spiro che mi fece attento,

dicendo: "Intanto che tu ti risense   4
de la vista che haï in me consunta,
ben è che ragionando la compense.

Comincia dunque; e dì ove s'appunta   7
l'anima tua, e fa ragion che sia
la vista in te smarrita e non defunta:

perché la donna che per questa dia   10
regïon ti conduce, ha ne lo sguardo
la virtù ch'ebbe la man d'Anania."

Io dissi: "Al suo piacere e tosto e tardo   13
vegna remedio a li occhi, che fuor porte
quand' ella entrò col foco ond' io sempr' ardo.

Lo ben che fa contenta questa corte,   16
Alfa e O è di quanta scrittura
mi legge Amore o lievemente o forte."

Quella medesma voce che paura   19
tolta m'avea del sùbito abbarbaglio,
di ragionare ancor mi mise in cura;

e disse: "Certo a più angusto vaglio   22
ti conviene schiarar: dicer convienti
chi drizzò l'arco tuo a tal berzaglio."

E io: "Per filosofici argomenti   25
e per autorità che quinci scende
cotale amor convien che in me si 'mprenti:

ché 'l bene, in quanto ben, come s'intende,   28
così accende amore, e tanto maggio
quanto più di bontate in sé comprende.

While I, with blinded eyes, was apprehensive,
from that bright flame which had consumed my vision,
there breathed a voice that centered my attention,

saying: "Until you have retrieved the power   4
of sight, which you consumed in me, it would
be best to compensate by colloquy.

Then do begin; declare the aim on which   7
your soul is set—and be assured of this:
your vision, though confounded, is not dead,

because the woman who conducts you through   10
this godly region has, within her gaze,
that force the hand of Ananias had."

I said: "As pleases her, may solace—sooner   13
or later—reach these eyes, her gates when she
brought me the fire with which I always burn.

The good with which this court is satisfied   16
is Alpha and Omega of all writings
that Love has—loud or low—read out to me."

It was the very voice that had dispelled   19
the fear I felt at sudden dazzlement,
that now, with further words, made me concerned

to speak again. He said: "You certainly   22
must sift with a still finer sieve, must tell
who led your bow to aim at such a target."

And I: "By philosophic arguments   25
and by authority whose source is here,
that love must be imprinted in me; for

the good, once it is understood as such,   28
enkindles love; and in accord with more
goodness comes greater love. And thus the mind

Dunque a l'essenza ov' è tanto avvantaggio,   31
che ciascun ben che fuor di lei si trova
altro non è ch'un lume di suo raggio,

più che in altra convien che si mova   34
la mente, amando, di ciascun che cerne
il vero in che si fonda questa prova.

Tal vero a l'intelletto mïo sterne   37
colui che mi dimostra il primo amore
di tutte le sustanze sempiterne.

Sternel la voce del verace autore,   40
che dice a Moïsè, di sé parlando:
'Io ti farò vedere ogne valore.'

Sternilmi tu ancora, incominciando   43
l'alto preconio che grida l'arcano
di qui là giù sovra ogne altro bando."

E io udi': "Per intelletto umano   46
e per autoritadi a lui concorde
d'i tuoi amori a Dio guarda il sovrano.

Ma dì ancor se tu senti altre corde   49
tirarti verso lui, sì che tu suone
con quanti denti questo amor ti morde."

Non fu latente la santa intenzione   52
de l'aguglia di Cristo, anzi m'accorsi
dove volea menar mia professione.

Però ricominciai: "Tutti quei morsi   55
che posson far lo cor volgere a Dio,
a la mia caritate son concorsi:

ché l'essere del mondo e l'esser mio,   58
la morte ch'el sostenne perch' io viva,
e quel che spera ogne fedel com' io,

con la predetta conoscenza viva,   61
tratto m'hanno del mar de l'amor torto,
e del diritto m'han posto a la riva.

Le fronde onde s'infronda tutto l'orto   64
de l'ortolano etterno, am' io cotanto
quanto da lui a lor di bene è porto."

Sì com io tacqui, un dolcissimo canto   67
risonò per lo cielo, e la mia donna
dicea con li altri: "Santo, santo, santo!"

of anyone who can discern the truth 31
on which this proof is founded must be moved
to love, more than it loves all else, that Essence

which is preeminent (since any good 34
that lies outside of It is nothing but
a ray reflected from Its radiance).

My mind discerns this truth, made plain by him 37
who demonstrates to me that the first love
of the eternal beings is their Maker.

The voice of the true Author states this, too, 40
where He tells Moses, speaking of Himself:
'I shall show you all goodness.' You reveal

this, too, when you begin your high Evangel, 43
which more than any other proclamation
cries out to earth the mystery of Heaven."

I heard: "Through human reasoning and through 46
authorities according with it, you
conclude: your highest love is bent on God.

But tell me, too, if you feel other cords 49
draw you toward Him, so that you voice aloud
all of the teeth by which this love grips you."

The holy intent of Christ's Eagle was 52
not hidden; I indeed was made aware
of what he would most have my words declare.

Thus I began again: "My charity 55
results from all those things whose bite can bring
the heart to turn to God; the world's existence

and mine, the death that He sustained that I 58
might live, and that which is the hope of all
believers, as it is my hope, together

with living knowledge I have spoken of— 61
these drew me from the sea of twisted love
and set me on the shore of the right love.

The leaves enleaving all the garden of 64
the Everlasting Gardener, I love
according to the good He gave to them."

As soon as I was still, a song most sweet 67
resounded through that heaven, and my lady
said with the others: "Holy, holy, holy!"

    E come a lume acuto si disonna   70
per lo spirto visivo che ricorre
a lo splendor che va di gonna in gonna,

    e lo svegliato ciò che vede aborre,   73
sì nescïa è la sùbita vigilia
fin che la stimativa non soccorre;

    così de li occhi miei ogne quisquilia   76
fugò Beatrice col raggio d'i suoi,
che rifulgea da più di mille milia:

    onde mei che dinanzi vidi poi;   79
e quasi stupefatto domandai
d'un quarto lume ch'io vidi tra noi.

    E la mia donna: "Dentro da quei rai   82
vagheggia il suo fattor l'anima prima
che la prima virtù creasse mai."

    Come la fronda che flette la cima   85
nel transito del vento, e poi si leva
per la propria virtù che la soblima,

    fec' io in tanto in quant' ella diceva,   88
stupendo, e poi mi rifece sicuro
un disio di parlare ond' ïo ardeva.

    E cominciai: "O pomo che maturo   91
solo prodotto fosti, o padre antico
a cui ciascuna sposa è figlia e nuro,

    divoto quanto posso a te supplìco   94
perché mi parli: tu vedi mia voglia,
e per udirti tosto non la dico."

    Talvolta un animal coverto broglia,   97
sì che l'affetto convien che si paia
per lo seguir che face a lui la 'nvoglia;

    e similmente l'anima primaia   100
mi facea trasparer per la coverta
quant' ella a compiacermi venìa gaia.

    Indi spirò: "Sanz' essermi proferta   103
da te, la voglia tua discerno meglio
che tu qualunque cosa t'è più certa;

    perch' io la veggio nel verace speglio   106
che fa di sé pareglio a l'altre cose,
e nulla face lui di sé pareglio.

And just as a sharp light will startle us   70
from sleep because the spirit of eyesight
races to meet the brightness that proceeds

from layer to layer in the eye, and he   73
who wakens is confused by what he sees,
awaking suddenly, and knows no thing

until his judgment helps him; even so   76
did Beatrice dispel, with her eyes' rays,
which shone more than a thousand miles, the chaff

from my eyes: I saw better than I had   79
before; and as if stupefied, I asked
about the fourth light that I saw among us.

My lady answered: "In those rays there gazes   82
with love for his Creator the first soul
ever created by the Primal Force."

As does a tree that bends its crown because   85
of winds that gust, and then springs up, raised by
its own sustaining power, so did I

while she was speaking. I, bewildered, then   88
restored to confidence by that desire
to speak with which I was inflamed, began:

"O fruit that was the only one to be   91
brought forth already ripe, o ancient father
to whom each bride is as a daughter and

daughter-in-law, devoutly as I can,   94
I do beseech you: speak with me. You see
my wish; to hear you sooner, I do not

declare it." And the primal soul—much as   97
an animal beneath a cover stirs,
so that its feelings are made evident

when what enfolds it follows all its movements—   100
showed me, through that which covered him, with what
rejoicing he was coming to delight me.

Then he breathed forth: "Though you do not declare   103
your wish, I can perceive it better than
you can perceive the things you hold most certain;

for I can see it in the Truthful Mirror   106
that perfectly reflects all else, while no
thing can reflect that Mirror perfectly.

    Tu vuogli udir quant' è che Dio mi puose   109
ne l'eccelso giardino, ove costei
a così lunga scala ti dispuose,

    e quanto fu diletto a li occhi miei,   112
e la propria cagion del gran disdegno,
e l'idïoma ch'usai e che fei.

    Or, figliuol mio, non il gustar del legno   115
fu per sé la cagion di tanto essilio,
ma solamente il trapassar del segno.

    Quindi onde mosse tua donna Virgilio,   118
quattromilia trecento e due volumi
di sol desiderai questo concilio;

    e vidi lui tornare a tutt' i lumi   121
de la sua strada novecento trenta
fïate, mentre ch'ïo in terra fu'mi.

    La lingua ch'io parlai fu tutta spenta   124
innanzi che a l'ovra inconsummabile
fosse la gente di Nembròt attenta:

    ché nullo effetto mai razïonabile,   127
per lo piacere uman che rinovella
seguendo il cielo, sempre fu durabile.

    Opera naturale è ch'uom favella;   130
ma così o così, natura lascia
poi fare a voi secondo che v'abbella.

    Pria ch'i' scendessi a l'infernale ambascia,   133
I s'appellava in terra il sommo bene
onde vien la letizia che mi fascia;

    e *El* si chiamò poi: e ciò convene,   136
ché l'uso d'i mortali è come fronda
in ramo, che sen va e altra vene.

    Nel monte che si leva più da l'onda,   139
fu' io, con vita pura e disonesta,
da la prim' ora a quella che seconda,

    come 'l sol muta quadra, l'ora sesta."   142

You wish to hear how long it is since I   109
was placed by God in that high garden where
this lady readied you to climb a stair

so long, and just how long it pleased my eyes,   112
and the true cause of the great anger, and
what idiom I used and shaped. My son,

the cause of my long exile did not lie   115
within the act of tasting of the tree,
but solely in my trespass of the boundary.

During four thousand three hundred and two   118
re-turnings of the sun, while I was in
that place from which your Lady sent you Virgil,

I longed for this assembly. While on earth,   121
I saw the sun return to all the lights
along its way, nine hundred thirty times.

The tongue I spoke was all extinct before   124
the men of Nimrod set their minds upon
the unaccomplishable task; for never

has any thing produced by human reason   127
been everlasting—following the heavens,
men seek the new, they shift their predilections.

That man should speak at all is nature's act,   130
but how you speak—in this tongue or in that—
she leaves to you and to your preference.

Before I was sent down to Hell's torments,   133
on earth, the Highest Good—from which derives
the joy that now enfolds me—was called *I;*

and then He was called *El.* Such change must be: 136
the ways that mortals take are as the leaves
upon a branch—one comes, another goes.

On that peak rising highest from the sea,   139
my life—first pure, then tainted—lasted from
the first hour to the hour that follows on

the sixth, when the sun shifts to a new quadrant."   142

CANTO XXVII

A l Padre, al Figlio, a lo Spirito Santo,"
cominciò, "gloria!" tutto 'l paradiso,
sì che m'inebrïava il dolce canto.

Ciò ch'io vedeva mi sembiava un riso   4
de l'universo; per che mia ebbrezza
intrava per l'udire e per lo viso.

Oh gioia! oh ineffabile allegrezza!   7
oh vita intègra d'amore e di pace!
oh sanza brama sicura ricchezza!

Dinanzi a li occhi miei le quattro face   10
stavano accese, e quella che pria venne
incominciò a farsi più vivace,

e tal ne la sembianza sua divenne,   13
qual diverrebbe Iove, s'elli e Marte
fossero augelli e cambiassersi penne.

La provedenza, che quivi comparte   16
vice e officio, nel beato coro
silenzio posto avea da ogne parte,

quand' ïo udi': "Se io mi trascoloro,   19
non ti maravigliar, ché, dicend' io,
vedrai trascolorar tutti costoro.

Quelli ch'usurpa in terra il luogo mio,   22
il luogo mio, il luogo mio che vaca
ne la presenza del Figliuol di Dio,

fatt' ha del cimitero mio cloaca   25
del sangue e de la puzza; onde 'l perverso
che cadde di qua sù, là giù si placa."

Di quel color che per lo sole avverso   28
nube dipigne da sera e da mane,
vid' ïo allora tutto 'l ciel cosperso.

Still the Eighth Heaven: the Sphere of the Fixed Stars. The hymn of the blessed. St. Peter's condemnation of the popes and the corrupt Church. His urging of Dante to fulfill his mission on earth. Dante's earthward gaze. Ascent to the Ninth Heaven, the Primum Mobile. Its nature explained by Beatrice. Her discourse on the present straying of the world; her prophecy of its redemption.

U nto the Father, Son, and Holy Ghost,
    glory!"—all Paradise began, so that
the sweetness of the singing held me rapt.

    What I saw seemed to me to be a smile   4
the universe had smiled; my rapture had
entered by way of hearing and of sight.

    O joy! O gladness words can never speak!   7
O life perfected by both love and peace!
O richness so assured, that knows no longing!

    Before my eyes, there stood, aflame, the four   10
torches, and that which had been first to come
began to glow with greater radiance,

    and what its image then became was like   13
what Jupiter's would be if Mars and he
were birds and had exchanged their plumages.

    After the Providence that there assigns   16
to every office its appointed time
had, to those holy choirs, on every side,

    commanded silence, I then heard: "If I   19
change color, do not be amazed, for as
I speak, you will see change in all these flames.

    He who on earth usurps my place, my place,   22
my place that in the sight of God's own Son
is vacant now, has made my burial ground

    a sewer of blood, a sewer of stench, so that   25
the perverse one who fell from Heaven, here
above, can find contentment there below."

    Then I saw all the heaven colored by   28
the hue that paints the clouds at morning and
at evening, with the sun confronting them.

E come donna onesta che permane   31
di sé sicura, e per l'altrui fallanza,
pur ascoltando, timida si fane,

   così Beatrice trasmutò sembianza;   34
e tale eclissi credo che 'n ciel fue
quando patì la suprema possanza.

Poi procedetter le parole sue   37
con voce tanto da sé trasmutata,
che la sembianza non si mutò piùe:

   "Non fu la sposa di Cristo allevata   40
del sangue mio, di Lin, di quel di Cleto,
per essere ad acquisto d'oro usata;

   ma per acquisto d'esto viver lieto   43
e Sisto e Pïo e Calisto e Urbano
sparser lo sangue dopo molto fleto.

Non fu nostra intenzion ch'a destra mano   46
d'i nostri successor parte sedesse,
parte da l'altra del popol cristiano;

   né che le chiavi che mi fuor concesse,   49
divenisser signaculo in vessillo
che contra battezzati combattesse;

   né ch'io fossi figura di sigillo   52
a privilegi venduti e mendaci,
ond' io sovente arrosso e disfavillo.

In vesta di pastor lupi rapaci   55
si veggion di qua sù per tutti i paschi:
o difesa di Dio, perché pur giaci?

Del sangue nostro Caorsini e Guaschi   58
s'apparecchian di bere: o buon principio,
a che vil fine convien che tu caschi!

Ma l'alta provedenza, che con Scipio   61
difese a Roma la gloria del mondo,
soccorrà tosto, sì com' io concipio;

   e tu, figliuol, che per lo mortal pondo   64
ancor giù tornerai, apri la bocca,
e non asconder quel ch'io non ascondo."

Sì come di vapor gelati fiocca   67
in giuso l'aere nostro, quando 'l corno
de la capra del ciel col sol si tocca,

And like a woman who, although secure   31
in her own honesty, will pale on even
hearing about another woman's failing,

just so did Beatrice change in appearance;   34
and I believe that such eclipse was in
the sky when He, the Highest Power, suffered.

Then his words followed with a voice so altered   37
from what it was before—even his likeness
did not display a greater change than that.

"The Bride of Christ was never nurtured by   40
my blood, and blood of Linus and of Cletus,
to be employed in gaining greater riches;

but to acquire this life of joyousness,   43
Sixtus and Pius, Urban and Calixtus,
after much lamentation, shed their blood.

We did not want one portion of Christ's people   46
to sit at the right side of our successors,
while, on the left, the other portion sat,

nor did we want the keys that were consigned   49
to me, to serve as an escutcheon on
a banner that waged war against the baptized;

nor did we want my form upon a seal   52
for trafficking in lying privileges—
for which I often blush and flash with anger.

From here on high one sees rapacious wolves   55
clothed in the cloaks of shepherds. You, the vengeance
of God, oh, why do you still lie concealed?

The Gascons and the Cahorsines—they both   58
prepare to drink our blood: o good beginning,
to what a miserable end you fall!

But that high Providence which once preserved,   61
with Scipio, the glory of the world
for Rome, will soon bring help, as I conceive;

and you, my son, who through your mortal weight   64
will yet return below, speak plainly there,
and do not hide that which I do not hide."

As, when the horn of heaven's Goat abuts   67
the sun, our sky flakes frozen vapors downward,
so did I see that ether there adorned;

in sù vid' io così l'etera addorno   70
farsi e fioccar di vapor trïunfanti
che fatto avien con noi quivi soggiorno.

Lo viso mio seguiva i suoi sembianti,   73
e seguì fin che 'l mezzo, per lo molto,
li tolse il trapassar del più avanti.

Onde la donna, che mi vide assolto   76
de l'attendere in sù, mi disse: "Adima
il viso e guarda come tu se' vòlto."

Da l'ora ch'ïo avea guardato prima   79
i' vidi mosso me per tutto l'arco
che fa dal mezzo al fine il primo clima;

sì ch'io vedea di là da Gade il varco   82
folle d'Ulisse, e di qua presso il lito
nel qual si fece Europa dolce carco.

E più mi fora discoverto il sito   85
di questa aiuola; ma 'l sol procedea
sotto i mie' piedi un segno e più partito.

La mente innamorata, che donnea   88
con la mia donna sempre, di ridure
ad essa li occhi più che mai ardea;

e se natura o arte fé pasture   91
da pigliare occhi, per aver la mente,
in carne umana o ne le sue pitture,

tutte adunate, parrebber nïente   94
ver' lo piacer divin che mi refulse,
quando mi volsi al suo viso ridente.

E la virtù che lo sguardo m'indulse,   97
del bel nido di Leda mi divelse
e nel ciel velocissimo m'impulse.

Le parti sue vivissime ed eccelse   100
sì uniforme son, ch'i' non so dire
qual Bëatrice per loco mi scelse.

Ma ella, che vedëa 'l mio disire,   103
incominciò, ridéndo tanto lieta,
che Dio parea nel suo volto gioire:

"La natura del mondo, che quïeta   106
il mezzo e tutto l'altro intorno move,
quinci comincia come da sua meta;

for from that sphere, triumphant vapors now   70
were flaking up to the Empyrean—
returning after dwelling here with us.

My sight was following their semblances—   73
until the space between us grew so great
as to deny my eyes all farther reach.

At this, my lady, seeing me set free   76
from gazing upward, told me: "Let your eyes
look down and see how far you have revolved."

I saw that, from the time when I looked down   79
before, I had traversed all of the arc
of the first clime, from its midpoint to end,

so that, beyond Cadiz, I saw Ulysses'   82
mad course and, to the east, could almost see
that shoreline where Europa was sweet burden.

I should have seen more of this threshing floor   85
but for the motion of the sun beneath
my feet: it was a sign and more away.

My mind, enraptured, always longing for   88
my lady gallantly, was burning more
than ever for my eyes' return to her;

and if—by means of human flesh or portraits—   91
nature or art has fashioned lures to draw
the eye so as to grip the mind, all these

would seem nothing if set beside the godly   94
beauty that shone upon me when I turned
to see the smiling face of Beatrice.

The powers that her gaze now granted me   97
drew me out of the lovely nest of Leda
and thrust me into heaven's swiftest sphere.

Its parts were all so equally alive   100
and excellent, that I cannot say which
place Beatrice selected for my entry.

But she, who saw what my desire was—   103
her smile had so much gladness that within
her face there seemed to be God's joy—began:

"The nature of the universe, which holds   106
the center still and moves all else around it,
begins here as if from its turning-post.

e questo cielo non ha altro dove   109
che la mente divina, in che s'accende
l'amor che 'l volge e la virtù ch'ei piove.

Luce e amor d'un cerchio lui comprende,   112
sì come questo li altri; e quel precinto
colui che 'l cinge solamente intende.

Non è suo moto per altro distinto,   115
ma li altri son mensurati da questo,
sì come diece da mezzo e da quinto;

e come il tempo tegna in cotal testo   118
le sue radici e ne li altri le fronde,
omai a te può esser manifesto.

Oh cupidigia, che i mortali affonde   121
sì sotto te, che nessuno ha podere
di trarre li occhi fuor de le tue onde!

Ben fiorisce ne li uomini il volere;   124
ma la pioggia continüa converte
in bozzacchioni le sosine vere.

Fede e innocenza son reperte   127
solo ne' parvoletti; poi ciascuna
pria fugge che le guance sian coperte.

Tale, balbuzïendo ancor, digiuna,   130
che poi divora, con la lingua sciolta,
qualunque cibo per qualunque luna;

e tal, balbuzïendo, ama e ascolta   133
la madre sua, che, con loquela intera,
disïa poi di vederla sepolta.

Così si fa la pelle bianca nera   136
nel primo aspetto de la bella figlia
di quel ch'apporta mane e lascia sera.

Tu, perché non ti facci maraviglia,   139
pensa che 'n terra non è chi governi;
onde si svïa l'umana famiglia.

Ma prima che gennaio tutto si sverni   142
per la centesma ch'è là giù negletta,
raggeran sì questi cerchi superni,

che la fortuna che tanto s'aspetta,   145
le poppe volgerà u' son le prore,
sì che la classe correrà diretta;

e vero frutto verrà dopo 'l fiore."   148

This heaven has no other *where* than this: 109
the mind of God, in which are kindled both
the love that turns it and the force it rains.

As in a circle, light and love enclose it,   112
as it surrounds the rest—and that enclosing,
only He who encloses understands.

No other heaven measures this sphere's motion,   115
but it serves as the measure for the rest,
even as half and fifth determine ten;

and now it can be evident to you   118
how time has roots within this vessel and,
within the other vessels, has its leaves.

O greediness, you who—within your depths—   121
cause mortals to sink so, that none is left
able to lift his eyes above your waves!

The will has a good blossoming in men;   124
but then the never-ending downpours turn
the sound plums into rotten, empty skins.

For innocence and trust are to be found   127
only in little children; then they flee
even before a full beard cloaks the cheeks.

One, for as long as he still lisps, will fast,   130
but when his tongue is free at last, he gorges,
devouring any food through any month;

and one, while he still lisps, will love and heed   133
his mother, but when he acquires speech
more fully, he will long to see her buried.

Just so, white skin turns black when it is struck   136
by direct light—the lovely daughter of
the one who brings us dawn and leaves us evening.

That you not be amazed at what I say,   139
consider this: on earth no king holds sway;
therefore, the family of humans strays.

But well before a thousand years have passed   142
(and January is unwintered by
day's hundredth part, which they neglect below),

this high sphere shall shine so, that Providence,   145
long waited for, will turn the sterns to where
the prows now are, so that the fleet runs straight;

and then fine fruit shall follow on the flower."   148

Mediterranean

CANTO XXVIII

Poscia che 'ncontro a la vita presente
  d'i miseri mortali aperse 'l vero
quella che 'mparadisa la mia mente,
    come in lo specchio fiamma di doppiero   4
vede colui che se n'alluma retro,
prima che l'abbia in vista o in pensiero,
    e sé rivolge per veder se 'l vetro   7
li dice il vero, e vede ch'el s'accorda
con esso come nota con suo metro;
    così la mia memoria si ricorda   10
ch'io feci riguardando ne' belli occhi
onde a pigliarmi fece Amor la corda.
    E com' io mi rivolsi e furon tocchi   13
li miei da ciò che pare in quel volume,
quandunque nel suo giro ben s'adocchi,
    un punto vidi che raggiava lume   16
acuto sì, che 'l viso ch'elli affoca
chiuder conviensi per lo forte acume;
    e quale stella par quinci più poca,   19
parrebbe luna, locata con esso
come stella con stella si collòca.
    Forse cotanto quanto pare appresso   22
alo cigner la luce che 'l dipigne
quando 'l vapor che 'l porta più è spesso,
    distante intorno al punto un cerchio d'igne   25
si girava sì ratto, ch'avria vinto
quel moto che più tosto il mondo cigne;
    e questo era d'un altro circumcinto,   28
e quel dal terzo, e 'l terzo poi dal quarto,
dal quinto il quarto, e poi dal sesto il quinto.

After the lady who imparadises
my mind disclosed the truth that is unlike
the present life of miserable mortals,

    then, just as one who sees a mirrored flame—   4
its double candle stands behind his back—
even before he thought of it or gazed

    directly at it, and he turns to gauge   7
if that glass tells the truth to him, and sees
that it accords, like voice and instrument,

    so—does my memory recall—I did   10
after I looked into the lovely eyes
of which Love made the noose that holds me tight.

    And when I turned and my own eyes were met   13
by what appears within that sphere whenever
one looks intently at its revolution,

    I saw a point that sent forth so acute   16
a light, that anyone who faced the force
with which it blazed would have to shut his eyes,

    and any star that, seen from earth, would seem   19
to be the smallest, set beside that point,
as star conjoined with star, would seem a moon.

    Around that point a ring of fire wheeled,   22
a ring perhaps as far from that point as
a halo from the star that colors it

    when mist that forms the halo is most thick.   25
It wheeled so quickly that it would outstrip
the motion that most swiftly girds the world.

    That ring was circled by a second ring,   28
the second by a third, third by a fourth,
fourth by a fifth, and fifth ring by a sixth.

Sopra seguiva il settimo sì sparto   31
già di larghezza, che 'l messo di Iuno
intero a contenerlo sarebbe arto.

Così l'ottavo e 'l nono; e ciascheduno   34
più tardo si movea, secondo ch'era
in numero distante più da l'uno;

e quello avea la fiamma più sincera   37
cui men distava la favilla pura,
credo, però che più di lei s'invera.

La donna mia, che mi vedëa in cura   40
forte sospeso, disse: "Da quel punto
depende il cielo e tutta la natura.

Mira quel cerchio che più li è congiunto;   43
e sappi che 'l suo muovere è sì tosto
per l'affocato amore ond' elli è punto."

E io a lei: "Se 'l mondo fosse posto   46
con l'ordine ch'io veggio in quelle rote,
sazio m'avrebbe ciò che m'è proposto;

ma nel mondo sensibile si puote   49
veder le volte tanto più divine,
quant' elle son dal centro più remote.

Onde, se 'l mio disir dee aver fine   52
in questo miro e angelico templo
che solo amore e luce ha per confine,

udir convienmi ancor come l'essemplo   55
e l'essemplare non vanno d'un modo,
ché io per me indarno a ciò contemplo."

"Se li tuoi diti non sono a tal nodo   58
sufficïenti, non è maraviglia:
tanto, per non tentare, è fatto sodo!"

Così la donna mia; poi disse: "Piglia   61
quel ch'io ti dicerò, se vuo' saziarti;
e intorno da esso t'assottiglia.

Li cerchi corporai sono ampi e arti   64
secondo il più e 'l men de la virtute
che si distende per tutte lor parti.

Maggior bontà vuol far maggior salute;   67
maggior salute maggior corpo cape,
s'elli ha le parti igualmente compiute.

Beyond, the seventh ring, which followed, was   31
so wide that all of Juno's messenger
would be too narrow to contain that circle.

The eighth and ninth were wider still; and each,   34
even as greater distance lay between
it and the first ring, moved with lesser speed;

and, I believe, the ring with clearest flame   37
was that which lay least far from the pure spark
because it shares most deeply that point's truth.

My lady, who saw my perplexity—   40
I was in such suspense—said: "On that Point
depend the heavens and the whole of nature.

Look at the circle that is nearest It,   43
and know: its revolutions are so swift
because of burning love that urges it."

And I to her: "If earth and the nine spheres   46
were ordered like those rings, then I would be
content with what you have set out before me,

but in the world of sense, what one can see   49
are spheres becoming ever more divine
as they are set more distant from the center.

Thus, if my longing is to gain its end   52
in this amazing and angelic temple
that has, as boundaries, only love and light,

then I still have to hear just how the model   55
and copy do not share in one same plan—
for by myself I think on this in vain."

"You need not wonder if your fingers are   58
unable to undo that knot: no one
has tried, and so that knot is tightened, taut!"

my lady said, and then continued: "If   61
you would be satisfied, take what I tell you—
and let your mind be sharp as I explain.

The size of spheres of matter—large or small—   64
depends upon the power—more and less—
that spreads throughout their parts. More excellence

yields greater blessedness; more blessedness   67
must comprehend a greater body when
that body's parts are equally complete.

Dunque costui che tutto quanto rape   70
l'altro universo seco, corrisponde
al cerchio che più ama e che più sape:

per che, se tu a la virtù circonde   73
la tua misura, non a la parvenza
de le sustanze che t'appaion tonde,

tu vederai mirabil consequenza   76
di maggio a più e di minore a meno,
in ciascun cielo, a süa intelligenza."

Come rimane splendido e sereno   79
l'emisperio de l'aere, quando soffia
Borea da quella guancia ond' è più leno,

per che si purga e risolve la roffia   82
che pria turbava, sì che 'l ciel ne ride
con le bellezze d'ogne sua paroffia;

così fec'ïo, poi che mi provide   85
la donna mia del suo risponder chiaro,
e come stella in cielo il ver si vide.

E poi che le parole sue restaro,   88
non altrimenti ferro disfavilla
che bolle, come i cerchi sfavillaro.

L'incendio suo seguiva ogne scintilla;   91
ed eran tante, che 'l numero loro
più che 'l doppiar de li scacchi s'inmilla.

Io sentiva osannar di coro in coro   94
al punto fisso che li tiene a li *ubi,*
e terrà sempre, ne' quai sempre fuoro.

E quella che vedëa i pensier dubi   97
ne la mia mente, disse: "I cerchi primi
t'hanno mostrato Serafi e Cherubi.

Così veloci seguono i suoi vimi,   100
per somigliarsi al punto quanto ponno;
e posson quanto a veder son soblimi.

Quelli altri amori che 'ntorno li vonno,   103
si chiaman Troni del divino aspetto,
per che 'l primo ternaro terminonno;

e dei saper che tutti hanno diletto   106
quanto la sua veduta si profonda
nel vero in che si queta ogne intelletto.

And thus this sphere, which sweeps along with it   70
the rest of all the universe, must match
the circle that loves most and knows the most,

so that, if you but draw your measure round   73
the power within—and not the semblance of—
the angels that appear to you as circles,

you will discern a wonderful accord   76
between each sphere and its Intelligence:
greater accords with more, smaller with less."

Just as the hemisphere of air remains   79
splendid, serene, when from his gentler cheek
Boreas blows and clears the scoriae,

dissolves the mist that had defaced the sky,   82
so that the heavens smile with loveliness
in all their regions; even so did I

become after my lady had supplied   85
her clear response to me, and—like a star
in heaven—truth was seen. And when her words

were done, even as incandescent iron   88
will shower sparks, so did those circles sparkle;
and each spark circled with its flaming ring—

sparks that were more in number than the sum   91
one reaches doubling in succession each
square of a chessboard, one to sixty-four.

I heard *"Hosanna"* sung, from choir to choir   94
to that fixed Point which holds and always shall
hold them to where they have forever been.

And she who saw my mind's perplexities   97
said: "The first circles have displayed to you
the Seraphim and Cherubim. They follow

the ties of love with such rapidity   100
because they are as like the Point as creatures
can be, a power dependent on their vision.

Those other loves that circle round them are   103
called Thrones of the divine aspect, because
they terminated the first group of three;

and know that all delight to the degree   106
to which their vision sees—more or less deeply—
that truth in which all intellects find rest.

Quinci si può veder come si fonda   109
l'esser beato ne l'atto che vede,
non in quel ch'ama, che poscia seconda;

e del vedere è misura mercede,   112
che grazia partorisce e buona voglia:
così di grado in grado si procede.

L'altro ternaro, che così germoglia   115
in questa primavera sempiterna
che notturno Arïete non dispoglia,

perpetüalemente 'Osanna' sberna   118
con tre melode, che suonano in tree
ordini di letizia onde s'interna.

In essa gerarcia son l'altre dee: 121
prima Dominazioni, e poi Virtudi;
l'ordine terzo di Podestadi èe.

Poscia ne' due penultimi tripudi   124
Principati e Arcangeli si girano;
l'ultimo è tutto d'Angelici ludi.

Questi ordini di sù tutti s'ammirano,   127
e di giù vincon sì, che verso Dio
tutti tirati sono e tutti tirano.

E Dïonisio con tanto disio   130
a contemplar questi ordini si mise,
che li nomò e distinse com'io.

Ma Gregorio da lui poi si divise;   133
onde, sì tosto come li occhi aperse
in questo ciel, di sé medesmo rise.

E se tanto secreto ver proferse   136
mortale in terra, non voglio ch'ammiri:
ché chi 'l vide qua sù gliel discoperse

con altro assai del ver di questi giri."   139

From this you see that blessedness depends   109
upon the act of vision, not upon
the act of love—which is a consequence;

    the measure of their vision lies in merit,   112
produced by grace and then by will to goodness:
and this is the progression, step by step.

    The second triad—blossoming in this   115
eternal springtime that the nightly Ram
does not despoil—perpetually sings

    'Hosanna' with three melodies that sound   118
in the three ranks of bliss that form this triad;
within this hierarchy there are three

    kinds of divinities: first, the Dominions,   121
and then the Virtues; and the final order
contains the Powers. The two penultimate

    groups of rejoicing ones within the next   124
triad are wheeling Principalities
and the Archangels; last, the playful Angels.

    These orders all direct—ecstatically—   127
their eyes on high; and downward, they exert
such force that all are drawn and draw to God.

    And Dionysius, with much longing, set   130
himself to contemplate these orders: he
named and distinguished them just as I do.

    Though, later, Gregory disputed him,   133
when Gregory came here—when he could see
with opened eyes—he smiled at his mistake.

    You need not wonder if a mortal told   136
such secret truth on earth: it was disclosed
to him by one who saw it here above—

    both that and other truths about these circles." 139

CANTO XXIX

Quando ambedue li figli di Latona
   coperti del Montone e de la Libra,
fanno de l'orizzonte insieme zona,

   quant' è dal punto che 'l cenìt inlibra   4
infin che l'uno e l'altro da quel cinto,
cambiando l'emisperio, si dilibra,

   tanto, col volto di riso dipinto,   7
si tacque Bëatrice, riguardando
fiso nel punto che m'avëa vinto.

   Poi cominciò: "Io dico, e non dimando,   10
quel che tu vuoli udir, perch' io l'ho visto
là 've s'appunta ogne *ubi* e ogne *quando*.

   Non per aver a sé di bene acquisto,   13
ch'esser non può, ma perché suo splendore
potesse, risplendendo, dir *'Subsisto,'*

   in sua etternità di tempo fore,   16
fuor d'ogne altro comprender, come i piacque,
s'aperse in nuovi amor l'etterno amore.

   Né prima quasi torpente si giacque;   19
ché né prima né poscia procedette
lo discorrer di Dio sovra quest' acque.

   Forma e materia, congiunte e purette,   22
usciro ad esser che non avia fallo,
come d'arco tricordo tre saette.

   E come in vetro, in ambra o in cristallo   25
raggio resplende sì, che dal venire
a l'esser tutto non è intervallo,

   così 'l triforme effetto del suo sire   28
ne l'esser suo raggiò insieme tutto
sanza distinzïone in essordire.

A s long as both Latona's children take
   (when, covered by the Ram and Scales, they make
their belt of the horizon at the same

   moment) to pass from equilibrium—   4
the zenith held in balance—to that state
where, changing hemispheres, each leaves that belt,

   so long did Beatrice, a smile upon   7
her face, keep silent, even as she gazed
intently at the Point that overwhelmed me.

   Then she began: "I tell—not ask—what you   10
now want to hear, for I have seen it there
where, in one point, all *whens* and *ubis* end.

   Not to acquire new goodness for Himself—   13
which cannot be—but that his splendor might,
as it shines back to Him, declare *'Subsisto,'*

   in His eternity outside of time,   16
beyond all other borders, as pleased Him,
Eternal Love opened into new loves.

   Nor did he lie, before this, as if languid;   19
there was no *after,* no *before*—they were
not there until God moved upon these waters.

   Then form and matter, either separately   22
or in mixed state, emerged as flawless being,
as from a three-stringed bow, three arrows spring.

   And as a ray shines into amber, crystal,   25
or glass, so that there is no interval
between its coming and its lighting all,

   so did the three—form, matter, and their union—   28
flash into being from the Lord with no
distinction in beginning: all at once.

Concreato fu ordine e costrutto   31
a le sustanze; e quelle furon cima
nel mondo in che puro atto fu produtto;

pura potenza tenne la parte ima;   34
nel mezzo strinse potenza con atto
tal vime, che già mai non si divima.

Ieronimo vi scrisse lungo tratto   37
di secoli de li angeli creati
anzi che l'altro mondo fosse fatto;

ma questo vero è scritto in molti lati   40
da li scrittor de lo Spirito Santo,
e tu te n'avvedrai se bene agguati;

e anche la ragione il vede alquanto,   43
che non concederebbe che' motori
sanza sua perfezion fosser cotanto.

Or sai tu dove e quando questi amori   46
furon creati e come: sì che spenti
nel tuo disïo già son tre ardori.

Né giugneriesi, numerando, al venti   49
sì tosto, come de li angeli parte
turbò il suggetto d'i vostri alimenti.

L'altra rimase, e cominciò quest' arte   52
che tu discerni, con tanto diletto,
che mai da circüir non si diparte.

Principio del cader fu il maladetto   55
superbir di colui che tu vedesti
da tutti i pesi del mondo costretto.

Quelli che vedi qui furon modesti   58
a riconoscer sé da la bontate
che li avea fatti a tanto intender presti:

per che le viste lor furo essaltate   61
con grazia illuminante e con lor merto,
sì c'hanno ferma e piena volontate;

e non voglio che dubbi, ma sia certo,   64
che ricever la grazia è meritorio
secondo che l'affetto l'è aperto.

Omai dintorno a questo consistorio   67
puoi contemplare assai, se le parole
mie son ricolte, sanz' altro aiutorio.

   Created with the substances were order   31
and pattern; at the summit of the world
were those in whom pure act had been produced;

   and pure potentiality possessed   34
the lowest part; and in the middle, act
so joined potentiality that they

   never disjoin. For you, Jerome has written   37
that the creation of the angels came
long centuries before all else was made;

   but this, the truth I speak, is written by   40
scribes of the Holy Ghost—as you can find
if you look carefully—on many pages;

   and reason, too, can see in part this truth,   43
for it would not admit that those who move
the heavens could, for so long, be without

   their perfect task. Now you know where and when   46
and how these loving spirits were created:
with this, three flames of your desire are quenched.

   Then, sooner than it takes to count to twenty,   49
a portion of the angels violently
disturbed the lowest of your elements.

   The rest remained; and they, with such rejoicing,   52
began the office you can see, that they
never desert their circling contemplation.

   The fall had its beginning in the cursed   55
pride of the one you saw, held in constraint
by all of the world's weights. Those whom you see

   in Heaven here were modestly aware   58
that they were ready for intelligence
so vast, because of that Good which had made them:

   through this, their vision was exalted with   61
illuminating grace and with their merit,
so that their will is constant and intact.

   I would not have you doubt, but have you know   64
surely that there is merit in receiving
grace, measured by the longing to receive it.

   By now, if you have taken in my words,   67
you need no other aid to contemplate
much in regard to this consistory.

Ma perché 'n terra per le vostre scole   70
si legge che l'angelica natura
è tal, che 'ntende e si ricorda e vole,

ancor dirò, perché tu veggi pura   73
la verità che là giù si confonde,
equivocando in sì fatta lettura.

Queste sustanze, poi che fur gioconde   76
de la faccia di Dio, non volser viso
da essa, da cui nulla si nasconde:

però non hanno vedere interciso   79
da novo obietto, e però non bisogna
rememorar per concetto diviso;

sì che là giù, non dormendo, si sogna,   82
credendo e non credendo dicer vero;
ma ne l'uno è più colpa e più vergogna.

Voi non andate giù per un sentiero   85
filosofando: tanto vi trasporta
l'amor de l'apparenza e 'l suo pensiero!

E ancor questo qua sù si comporta   88
con men disdegno che quando è posposta
la divina Scrittura o quando è torta.

Non vi si pensa quanto sangue costa   91
seminarla nel mondo e quanto piace
chi umilmente con essa s'accosta.

Per apparer ciascun s'ingegna e face   94
sue invenzioni; e quelle son trascorse
da' predicanti e 'l Vangelio si tace.

Un dice che la luna si ritorse   97
ne la passion di Cristo e s'interpuose,
per che 'l lume del sol giù non si porse;

e mente, ché la luce si nascose   100
da sé: però a li Spani e a l'Indi
come a' Giudei tale eclissi rispuose.

Non ha Fiorenza tanti Lapi e Bindi   103
quante sì fatte favole per anno
in pergamo si gridan quinci e quindi:

sì che le pecorelle, che non sanno,   106
tornan del pasco pasciute di vento,
e non le scusa non veder lo danno.

But since on earth, throughout your schools, they teach   70
that it is in the nature of the angels
to understand, to recollect, to will,

I shall say more, so that you may see clearly   73
the truth that, there below, has been confused
by teaching that is so ambiguous.

These beings, since they first were gladdened by   76
the face of God, from which no thing is hidden,
have never turned their vision from that face,

so that their sight is never intercepted   79
by a new object, and they have no need
to recollect an interrupted concept.

So that, below, though not asleep, men dream,   82
speaking in good faith or in bad—the last,
however, merits greater blame and shame.

Below, you do not follow one sole path   85
as you philosophize—your love of show
and thought of it so carry you astray!

Yet even love of show is suffered here   88
with less disdain than the subordination
or the perversion of the Holy Scripture.

There, they devote no thought to how much blood   91
it costs to sow it in the world, to how
pleasing is he who—humbly—holds it fast.

Each one strives for display, elaborates   94
his own inventions; preachers speak at length
of these—meanwhile the Gospels do not speak.

One says that, to prevent the sun from reaching   97
below, the moon—when Christ was crucified—
moved back along the zodiac, so as

to interpose itself; who says so, lies—   100
for sunlight hid itself; not only Jews,
but Spaniards, Indians, too, saw that eclipse.

Such fables, shouted through the year from pulpits—   103
some here, some there—outnumber even all
the Lapos and the Bindos Florence has;

so that the wretched sheep, in ignorance,   106
return from pasture, having fed on wind—
but to be blind to harm does not excuse them.

Non disse Cristo al suo primo convento: 109
'Andate, e predicate al mondo ciance';
ma diede lor verace fondamento;

e quel tanto sonò ne le sue guance,   112
sì ch'a pugnar per accender la fede
de l'Evangelio fero scudo e lance.

Ora si va con motti e con iscede   115
a predicare, e pur che ben si rida,
gonfia il cappuccio e più non si richiede.

Ma tale uccel nel becchetto s'annida,   118
che se 'l vulgo il vedesse, vederebbe
la perdonanza di ch'el si confida:

per cui tanta stoltezza in terra crebbe,   121
che, sanza prova d'alcun testimonio,
ad ogne promession si correrebbe.

Di questo ingrassa il porco sant'Antonio,   124
e altri assai che sono ancor più porci,
pagando di moneta sanza conio.

Ma perché siam digressi assai, ritorci   127
li occhi oramai verso la dritta strada,
sì che la via col tempo si raccorci.

Questa natura sì oltre s'ingrada   130
in numero, che mai non fu loquela
né concetto mortal che tanto vada;

e se tu guardi quel che si revela   133
per Danïel, vedrai che 'n sue migliaia
determinato numero si cela.

La prima luce, che tutta la raia,   136
per tanti modi in essa si recepe,
quanti son li splendori a chi s'appaia.

Onde, però che a l'atto che concepe   139
segue l'affetto, d'amar la dolcezza
diversamente in essa ferve e tepe.

Vedi l'eccelso omai e la larghezza   142
de l'etterno valor, poscia che tanti
speculi fatti s'ha in che si spezza,

uno manendo in sé come davanti."   145

Christ did not say to his first company: 109
'Go, and preach idle stories to the world';
but he gave them the teaching that is truth,

   and truth alone was sounded when they spoke;   112
and thus, to battle to enkindle faith,
the Gospels served them as both shield and lance.

   But now men go to preach with jests and jeers,   115
and just as long as they can raise a laugh,
the cowl puffs up, and nothing more is asked.

   But such a bird nests in that cowl, that if   118
the people saw it, they would recognize
as lies the pardons in which they confide—

   pardons through which the world's credulity   121
increases so, that people throng to every
indulgence backed by no authority;

   and this allows the Antonines to fatten   124
their pigs, and others, too, more piggish still,
who pay with counterfeit, illegal tender.

   But since we have digressed enough, turn back   127
your eyes now to the way that is direct;
our time is short—so, too, must be our path.

   The number of these angels is so great   130
that there has never been a mortal speech
or mortal thought that named a sum so steep;

   and if you look at that which is revealed   133
by Daniel, you will see that, while he mentions
thousands, he gives no number with precision.

   The First Light reaches them in ways as many   136
as are the angels to which It conjoins
Itself, as It illumines all of them;

   and this is why (because affection follows   139
the act of knowledge) the intensity
of love's sweetness appears unequally.

   By now you see the height, you see the breadth,   142
of the Eternal Goodness: It has made
so many mirrors, which divide Its light,

   but, as before, Its own Self still is One."   145

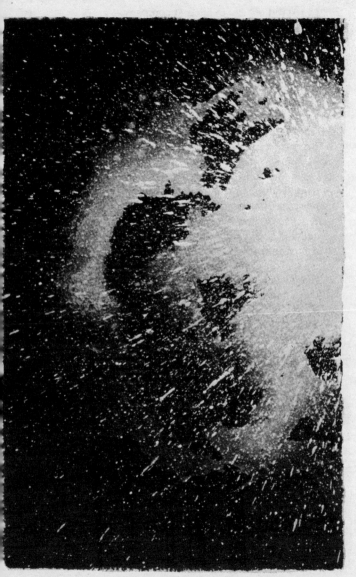

The Celestial Rose

CANTO XXX

Forse semilia miglia di lontano
  ci ferve l'ora sesta, e questo mondo
china già l'ombra quasi al letto piano,

  quando 'l mezzo del cielo, a noi profondo,   4
comincia a farsi tal, ch'alcuna stella
perde il parere infino a questo fondo;

  e come vien la chiarissima ancella   7
del sol più oltre, così 'l ciel si chiude
di vista in vista infino a la più bella.

  Non altrimenti il trïunfo che lude   10
sempre dintorno al punto che mi vinse,
parendo inchiuso da quel ch'elli 'nchiude,

  a poco a poco al mio veder si stinse: 13
per che tornar con li occhi a Bëatrice
nulla vedere e amor mi costrinse.

  Se quanto infino a qui di lei si dice   16
fosse conchiuso tutto in una loda,
poca sarebbe a fornir questa vice.

  La bellezza ch'io vidi si trasmoda   19
non pur di là da noi, ma certo io credo
che solo il suo fattor tutta la goda.

  Da questo passo vinto mi concedo   22
più che già mai da punto di suo tema
soprato fosse comico o tragedo:

  ché, come sole in viso che più trema,   25
così lo rimembrar del dolce riso
la mente mia da me medesmo scema.

  Dal primo giorno ch'i' vidi il suo viso   28
in questa vita, infino a questa vista,
non m'è il seguire al mio cantar preciso;

Perhaps six thousand miles away from us,
the sixth hour burns, and now our world inclines
its shadow to an almost level bed,

so that the span of heaven high above   4
begins to alter so, that some stars are
no longer to be seen from our deep earth;

and as the brightest handmaid of the sun   7
advances, heaven shuts off, one by one,
its lights, until the loveliest is gone.

So did the triumph that forever plays   10
around the Point that overcame me (Point
that seems enclosed by that which It encloses)

fade gradually from my sight, so that   13
my seeing nothing else—and love—compelled
my eyes to turn again to Beatrice.

If that which has been said of her so far   16
were all contained within a single praise,
it would be much too scant to serve me now.

The loveliness I saw surpassed not only   19
our human measure—and I think that, surely,
only its Maker can enjoy it fully.

I yield: I am defeated at this passage   22
more than a comic or a tragic poet
has ever been by a barrier in his theme;

for like the sun that strikes the frailest eyes,   25
so does the memory of her sweet smile
deprive me of the use of my own mind.

From that first day when, in this life, I saw   28
her face, until I had this vision, no
thing ever cut the sequence of my song,

    ma or convien che mio seguir desista   31
più dietro a sua bellezza, poetando,
come a l'ultimo suo ciascuno artista.

    Cotal qual io la lascio a maggior bando   34
che quel de la mia tuba, che deduce
l'ardüa sua matera terminando,

    con atto e voce di spedito duce   37
ricominciò: "Noi siamo usciti fore
del maggior corpo al ciel ch'è pura luce:

    luce intellettüal, piena d'amore;   40
amor di vero ben, pien di letizia;
letizia che trascende ogne dolzore.

    Qui vederai l'una e l'altra milizia   43
di paradiso, e l'una in quelli aspetti
che tu vedrai a l'ultima giustizia."

    Come sùbito lampo che discetti   46
li spiriti visivi, sì che priva
da l'atto l'occhio di più forti obietti,

    così mi circunfulse luce viva,   49
e lasciommi fasciato di tal velo
del suo fulgor, che nulla m'appariva.

    "Sempre l'amor che queta questo cielo   52
accoglie in sé con sì fatta salute,
per far disposto a sua fiamma il candelo."

    Non fur più tosto dentro a me venute   55
queste parole brievi, ch'io compresi
me sormontar di sopr' a mia virtute;

    e di novella vista mi raccesi   58
tale, che nulla luce è tanto mera,
che li occhi miei non si fosser difesi;

    e vidi lume in forma di rivera   61
fulvido di fulgore, intra due rive
dipinte di mirabil primavera.

    Di tal fiumana uscian faville vive,   64
e d'ogne parte si mettien ne' fiori,
quasi rubin che oro circunscrive;

    poi, come inebrïate da li odori,   67
riprofondavan sé nel miro gurge,
e s'una intrava, un'altra n'uscia fori.

but now I must desist from this pursuit,   31
in verses, of her loveliness, just as
each artist who has reached his limit must.

So she, in beauty (as I leave her to   34
a herald that is greater than my trumpet,
which nears the end of its hard theme), with voice

and bearing of a guide whose work is done,   37
began again: "From matter's largest sphere,
we now have reached the heaven of pure light,

light of the intellect, light filled with love,   40
love of true good, love filled with happiness,
a happiness surpassing every sweetness.

Here you will see both ranks of Paradise   43
and see one of them wearing that same aspect
which you will see again at Judgment Day."

Like sudden lightning scattering the spirits   46
of sight so that the eye is then too weak
to act on other things it would perceive,

such was the living light encircling me,   49
leaving me so enveloped by its veil
of radiance that I could see no thing.

"The Love that calms this heaven always welcomes   52
into Itself with such a salutation,
to make the candle ready for its flame."

No sooner had these few words entered me   55
than I became aware that I was rising
beyond the power that was mine; and such

new vision kindled me again, that even   58
the purest light would not have been so bright
as to defeat my eyes, deny my sight;

and I saw light that took a river's form—   61
light flashing, reddish-gold, between two banks
painted with wonderful spring flowerings.

Out of that stream there issued living sparks,   64
which settled on the flowers on all sides,
like rubies set in gold; and then, as if

intoxicated with the odors, they   67
again plunged into the amazing flood:
as one spark sank, another spark emerged.

"L'alto disio che mo t'infiamma e urge,   70
d'aver notizia di ciò che tu vei,
tanto mi piace più quanto più turge;

    ma di quest' acqua convien che tu bei   73
prima che tanta sete in te si sazi";
così mi disse il sol de li occhi miei.

    Anche soggiunse: "Il fiume e li topazi   76
ch'entrano ed escono e 'l rider de l'erbe
son di lor vero umbriferi prefazi.

    Non che da sé sian queste cose acerbe;   79
ma è difetto da la parte tua,
che non hai viste ancor tanto superbe."

    Non è fantin che sì sùbito rua   82
col volto verso il latte, se si svegli
molto tardato da l'usanza sua,

    come fec' io, per far migliori spegli   85
ancor de li occhi, chinandomi a l'onda
che si deriva perché vi s'immegli;

    e sì come di lei bevve la gronda   88
de le palpebre mie, così mi parve
di sua lunghezza divenuta tonda.

    Poi, come gente stata sotto larve,   91
che pare altro che prima, se si sveste
la sembianza non süa in che disparve,

    così mi si cambiaro in maggior feste   94
li fiori e le faville, sì ch'io vidi
ambo le corti del ciel manifeste.

    O isplendor di Dio, per cu' io vidi   97
l'alto trïunfo del regno verace,
dammi virtù a dir com' ïo il vidi!

    Lume è là sù che visibile face   100
lo creatore a quella creatura
che solo in lui vedere ha la sua pace.

    E' si distende in circular figura,   103
in tanto che la sua circunferenza
sarebbe al sol troppo larga cintura.

    Fassi di raggio tutta sua parvenza   106
reflesso al sommo del mobile primo,
che prende quindi vivere e potenza.

"The high desire that now inflames, incites, 70
you to grasp mentally the things you see,
pleases me more as it swells more; but first,

that you may satisfy your mighty thirst, 73
you must drink of these waters." So did she
who is the sun of my eyes speak to me.

She added this: "The river and the gems 76
of topaz entering and leaving, and
the grasses' laughter—these are shadowy

prefaces of their truth; not that these things 79
are lacking in themselves; the defect lies
in you, whose sight is not yet that sublime."

No infant who awakes long after his 82
usual hour would turn his face toward milk
as quickly as I hurried toward that stream;

to make still finer mirrors of my eyes, 85
I bent down toward the waters which flow there
that we, in them, may find our betterment.

But as my eyelids' eaves drank of that wave, 88
it seemed to me that it had changed its shape:
no longer straight, that flow now formed a round.

Then, just as maskers, when they set aside 91
the borrowed likenesses in which they hide,
seem to be other than they were before,

so were the flowers and the sparks transformed, 94
changing to such festivity before me
that I saw—clearly—both of Heaven's courts.

O radiance of God, through which I saw 97
the noble triumph of the true realm, give
to me the power to speak of what I saw!

Above, on high, there is a light that makes 100
apparent the Creator to the creature
whose only peace lies in his seeing Him.

The shape which that light takes as it expands 103
is circular, and its circumference
would be too great a girdle for the sun.

All that one sees of it derives from one 106
light-ray reflected from the summit of
the Primum Mobile, which from it draws

E come clivo in acqua di suo imo   109
si specchia, quasi per vedersi addorno,
quando è nel verde e ne' fioretti opimo,

sì, soprastando al lume intorno intorno,   112
vidi specchiarsi in più di mille soglie
quanto di noi là sù fatto ha ritorno.

E se l'infimo grado in sé raccoglie   115
sì grande lume, quanta è la larghezza
di questa rosa ne l'estreme foglie!

La vista mia ne l'ampio e ne l'altezza   118
non si smarriva, ma tutto prendeva
il quanto e 'l quale di quella allegrezza.

Presso e lontano, lì, né pon né leva: 121
ché dove Dio sanza mezzo governa,
la legge natural nulla rileva.

Nel giallo de la rosa sempiterna,   124
che si digrada e dilata e redole
odor di lode al sol che sempre verna,

qual è colui che tace e dicer vole,   127
mi trasse Bëatrice, e disse: "Mira
quanto è 'l convento de le bianche stole!

Vedi nostra città quant' ella gira;   130
vedi li nostri scanni sì ripieni,
che poca gente più ci si disira.

E 'n quel gran seggio a che tu li occhi tieni   133
per la corona che già v'è sù posta,
prima che tu a queste nozze ceni,

sederà l'alma, che fia giù agosta,   136
de l'alto Arrigo, ch'a drizzare Italia
verrà in prima ch'ella sia disposta.

La cieca cupidigia che v'ammalia   139
simili fatti v'ha al fantolino
che muor per fame e caccia via la balia.

E fia prefetto nel foro divino   142
allora tal, che palese e coverto
non anderà con lui per un cammino.

Ma poco poi sarà da Dio sofferto   145
nel santo officio: ch'el sarà detruso
là dove Simon mago è per suo merto,

e farà quel d'Alagna intrar più giuso."   148

    power and life. And as a hill is mirrored   109
in waters at its base, as if to see
itself—when rich with grass and flowers—graced,

    so, in a thousand tiers that towered above   112
the light, encircling it, I saw, mirrored,
all of us who have won return above.

    And if the lowest rank ingathers such   115
vast light, then what must be the measure of
this Rose where it has reached its highest leaves!

    Within that breadth and height I did not find   118
my vision gone astray, for it took in
that joy in all its quality and kind.

    There, near and far do not subtract or add;   121
for where God governs with no mediator,
no thing depends upon the laws of nature.

    Into the yellow of the eternal Rose   124
that slopes and stretches and diffuses fragrance
of praise unto the Sun of endless spring,

    now Beatrice drew me as one who, though   127
he would speak out, is silent. And she said:
"See how great is this council of white robes!

    See how much space our city's circuit spans!   130
See how our seated ranks are now so full
that little room is left for any more!

    And in that seat on which your eyes are fixed   133
because a crown already waits above it,
before you join this wedding feast, shall sit

    the soul of noble Henry, he who is,   136
on earth, to be imperial; he shall
show Italy the righteous way—but when

    she is unready. The blind greediness   139
bewitching you, has made you like the child
who dies of hunger and drives off his nurse.

    And in the holy forum such shall be   142
the Prefect then, that either openly
or secretly he will not walk with Henry.

    But God will not endure him long within   145
the holy ministry: he shall be cast
down there, where Simon Magus pays; he shall

    force the Anagnine deeper in his hole."   148

CANTO XXXI

In forma dunque di candida rosa
mi si mostrava la milizia santa
che nel suo sangue Cristo fece sposa;

   ma l'altra, che volando vede e canta   4
la gloria di colui che la 'nnamora
e la bontà che la fece cotanta,

   sì come schiera d'ape che s'infiora   7
una fïata e una si ritorna
là dove suo laboro s'insapora,

   nel gran fior discendeva che s'addorna   10
di tante foglie, e quindi risaliva
là dove 'l süo amor sempre soggiorna.

   Le facce tutte avean di fiamma viva   13
e l'ali d'oro, e l'altro tanto bianco,
che nulla neve a quel termine arriva.

   Quando scendean nel fior, di banco in banco   16
porgevan de la pace e de l'ardore
ch'elli acquistavan ventilando il fianco.

   Né l'interporsi tra 'l disopra e 'l fiore   19
di tanta moltitudine volante
impediva la vista e lo splendore:

   ché la luce divina è penetrante   22
per l'universo secondo ch'è degno,
sì che nulla le puote essere ostante.

   Questo sicuro e gaudïoso regno,   25
frequente in gente antica e in novella,
viso e amore avea tutto ad un segno.

   Oh trina luce che 'n unica stella   28
scintillando a lor vista, sì li appaga!
guarda qua giuso a la nostra procella!

So, in the shape of that white Rose, the holy
legion was shown to me—the host that Christ,
with His own blood, had taken as His bride.

The other host, which, flying, sees and sings   4
the glory of the One who draws its love,
and that goodness which granted it such glory,

just like a swarm of bees that, at one moment,   7
enters the flowers and, at another, turns
back to that labor which yields such sweet savor,

descended into that vast flower graced   10
with many petals, then again rose up
to the eternal dwelling of its love.

Their faces were all living flame; their wings   13
were gold; and for the rest, their white was so
intense, no snow can match the white they showed.

When they climbed down into that flowering Rose,   16
from rank to rank, they shared that peace and ardor
which they had gained, with wings that fanned their sides.

Nor did so vast a throng in flight, although   19
it interposed between the candid Rose
and light above, obstruct the sight or splendor,

because the light of God so penetrates   22
the universe according to the worth
of every part, that no thing can impede it.

This confident and joyous kingdom, thronged   25
with people of both new and ancient times,
turned all its sight and ardor to one mark.

O threefold Light that, in a single star   28
sparkling into their eyes, contents them so,
look down and see our tempest here below!

Se i barbari, venendo da tal plaga   31
che ciascun giorno d'Elice si cuopra,
rotante col suo figlio ond' ella è vaga,

veggendo Roma e l'ardüa sua opra,   34
stupefaciensi, quando Laterano
a le cose mortali andò di sopra;

ïo, che al divino da l'umano,   37
a l'etterno dal tempo era venuto,
e di Fiorenza in popol giusto e sano,

di che stupor dovea esser compiuto!   40
Certo tra esso e 'l gaudio mi facea
libito non udire e starmi muto.

E quasi peregrin che si ricrea   43
nel tempio del suo voto riguardando,
e spera già ridir com' ello stea,

su per la viva luce passeggiando,   46
menava ïo li occhi per li gradi,
mo sù, mo giù e mo recirculando.

Vedëa visi a carità süadi,   49
d'altrui lume fregiati e di suo riso,
e atti ornati di tutte onestadi.

La forma general di paradiso   52
già tutta mïo sguardo avea compresa,
in nulla parte ancor fermato fiso;

e volgeami con voglia rïaccesa   55
per domandar la mia donna di cose
di che la mente mia era sospesa.

Uno intendëa, e altro mi rispuose: 58
credea veder Beatrice e vidi un sene
vestito con le genti glorïose.

Diffuso era per li occhi e per le gene   61
di benigna letizia, in atto pio
quale a tenero padre si convene.

E "Ov' è ella?" sùbito diss' io.   64
Ond' elli: "A terminar lo tuo disiro
mosse Beatrice me del loco mio;

e se riguardi sù nel terzo giro   67
dal sommo grado, tu la rivedrai
nel trono che suoi merti le sortiro."

   If the Barbarians, when they came from   31
a region that is covered every day
by Helice, who wheels with her loved son,
      were, seeing Rome and her vast works, struck dumb   34
(when, of all mortal things, the Lateran
was the most eminent), then what amazement
      must have filled me when I to the divine   37
came from the human, to eternity
from time, and to a people just and sane
      from Florence came! And certainly, between   40
the wonder and the joy, it must have been
welcome to me to hear and speak nothing.
      And as a pilgrim, in the temple he   43
had vowed to reach, renews himself—he looks
and hopes he can describe what it was like—
      so did I journey through the living light,   46
guiding my eyes, from rank to rank, along
a path now up, now down, now circling round.
      There I saw faces given up to love—   49
graced with Another's light and their own smile—
and movements graced with every dignity.
      By now my gaze had taken in the whole   52
of Paradise—its form in general—
but without looking hard at any part;
      and I, my will rekindled, turning toward   55
my lady, was prepared to ask about
those matters that inclined my mind to doubt.
      Where I expected her, another answered: 58
I thought I should see Beatrice, and saw
an elder dressed like those who are in glory.
      His gracious gladness filled his eyes, suffused   61
his cheeks; his manner had that kindliness
which suits a tender father. "Where is she?"
      I asked him instantly. And he replied: 64
"That all your longings may be satisfied,
Beatrice urged me from my place. If you
      look up and to the circle that is third   67
from that rank which is highest, you will see
her on the throne her merits have assigned her."

Sanza risponder, li occhi sù levai,   70
e vidi lei che si facea corona
reflettendo da sé li etterni rai.

Da quella regïon che più sù tona   73
occhio mortale alcun tanto non dista,
qualunque in mare più giù s'abbandona,

quanto lì da Beatrice la mia vista;   76
ma nulla mi facea, ché süa effige
non discendëa a me per mezzo mista.

"O donna in cui la mia speranza vige,   79
e che soffristi per la mia salute
in inferno lasciar le tue vestige,

di tante cose quant' i' ho vedute,   82
dal tuo podere e da la tua bontate
riconosco la grazia e la virtute.

Tu m'hai di servo tratto a libertate   85
per tutte quelle vie, per tutt' i modi
che di ciò fare avei la potestate.

La tua magnificenza in me custodi,   88
sì che l'anima mia, che fatt' hai sana,
piacente a te dal corpo si disnodi."

Così orai; e quella, sì lontana   91
come parea, sorrise e riguardommi;
poi si tornò a l'etterna fontana.

E 'l santo sene: "Acciò che tu assommi   94
perfettamente," disse, "il tuo cammino,
a che priego e amor santo mandommi,

vola con li occhi per questo giardino;   97
ché veder lui t'acconcerà lo sguardo
più al montar per lo raggio divino.

E la regina del cielo, ond' ïo ardo   100
tutto d'amor, ne farà ogne grazia,
però ch'i' sono il suo fedel Bernardo."

Qual è colui che forse di Croazia   103
viene a veder la Veronica nostra,
che per l'antica fame non sen sazia,

ma dice nel pensier, fin che si mostra: 106
"Segnor mio Iesù Cristo, Dio verace,
or fu sì fatta la sembianza vostra?";

I, without answering, then looked on high   70
and saw that round her now a crown took shape
as she reflected the eternal rays.

No mortal eye, not even one that plunged   73
into deep seas, would be so distant from
that region where the highest thunder forms,

as—there—my sight was far from Beatrice;   76
but distance was no hindrance, for her semblance
reached me—undimmed by any thing between.

"O lady, you in whom my hope gains strength,   79
you who, for my salvation, have allowed
your footsteps to be left in Hell, in all

the things that I have seen, I recognize   82
the grace and benefit that I, depending
upon your power and goodness, have received.

You drew me out from slavery to freedom   85
by all those paths, by all those means that were
within your power. Do, in me, preserve

your generosity, so that my soul,   88
which you have healed, when it is set loose from
my body, be a soul that you will welcome."

So did I pray. And she, however far   91
away she seemed, smiled, and she looked at me.
Then she turned back to the eternal fountain.

And he, the holy elder, said: "That you   94
may consummate your journey perfectly—
for this, both prayer and holy love have sent me

to help you—let your sight fly round this garden;   97
by gazing so, your vision will be made
more ready to ascend through God's own ray.

The Queen of Heaven, for whom I am all   100
aflame with love, will grant us every grace:
I am her faithful Bernard." Just as one

who, from Croatia perhaps, has come   103
to visit our Veronica—one whose
old hunger is not sated, who, as long

as it is shown, repeats these words in thought: 106
"O my Lord Jesus Christ, true God, was then
Your image like the image I see now?"—

    tal era io mirando la vivace   109
carità di colui che 'n questo mondo,
contemplando, gustò di quella pace.

    "Figliuol di grazia, quest' esser giocondo,"   112
cominciò elli, "non ti sarà noto,
tenendo li occhi pur qua giù al fondo;

    ma guarda i cerchi infino al più remoto,   115
tanto che veggi seder la regina
cui questo regno è suddito e devoto."

    Io levai li occhi; e come da mattina   118
la parte orïental de l'orizzonte
soverchia quella dove 'l sol declina,

    così, quasi di valle andando a monte   121
con li occhi, vidi parte ne lo stremo
vincer di lume tutta l'altra fronte.

    E come quivi ove s'aspetta il temo   124
che mal guidò Fetonte, più s'infiamma,
e quinci e quindi il lume si fa scemo,

    così quella pacifica oriafiamma   127
nel mezzo s'avvivava, e d'ogne parte
per igual modo allentava la fiamma;

    e a quel mezzo, con le penne sparte,   130
vid' io più di mille angeli festanti,
ciascun distinto di fulgore e d'arte.

    Vidi a lor giochi quivi e a lor canti   133
ridere una bellezza, che letizia
era ne li occhi a tutti li altri santi;

    e s'io avessi in dir tanta divizia   136
quanta ad imaginar, non ardirei
lo minimo tentar di sua delizia.

    Bernardo, come vide li occhi miei   139
nel caldo suo caler fissi e attenti,
li suoi con tanto affetto volse a lei,

    che' miei di rimirar fé più ardenti.   142

      such was I as I watched the living love   109
of him who, in this world, in contemplation,
tasted that peace. And he said: "Son of grace,

      you will not come to know this joyous state   112
if your eyes only look down at the base;
but look upon the circles, look at those

      that sit in a position more remote,   115
until you see upon her seat the Queen
to whom this realm is subject and devoted."

      I lifted up my eyes; and as, at morning,   118
the eastern side of the horizon shows
more splendor than the side where the sun sets,

      so, as if climbing with my eyes from valley   121
to summit, I saw one part of the farthest
rank of the Rose more bright than all the rest.

      And as, on earth, the point where we await   124
the shaft that Phaethon had misguided glows
brightest, while, to each side, the light shades off,

      so did the peaceful oriflamme appear   127
brightest at its midpoint, so did its flame,
on each side, taper off at equal pace.

      I saw, around that midpoint, festive angels—   130
more than a thousand—with their wings outspread;
each was distinct in splendor and in skill.

      And there I saw a loveliness that when   133
it smiled at the angelic songs and games
made glad the eyes of all the other saints.

      And even if my speech were rich as my   136
imagination is, I should not try
to tell the very least of her delights.

      Bernard—when he had seen my eyes intent,   139
fixed on the object of his burning fervor—
turned his own eyes to her with such affection

      that he made mine gaze still more ardently.   142

CANTO XXXII

Affetto al suo piacer, quel contemplante
libero officio di dottore assunse,
e cominciò queste parole sante:

"La piaga che Maria richiuse e unse,   4
quella ch'è tanto bella da' suoi piedi
è colei che l'aperse e che la punse.

Ne l'ordine che fanno i terzi sedi,   7
siede Rachel di sotto da costei
con Bëatrice, sì come tu vedi.

Sarra e Rebecca, Iudìt e colei   10
che fu bisava al cantor che per doglia
del fallo disse *'Miserere mei,'*

puoi tu veder così di soglia in soglia   13
giù digradar, com' io ch'a proprio nome
vo per la rosa giù di foglia in foglia.

E dal settimo grado in giù, sì come   16
infino ad esso, succedono Ebree,
dirimendo del fior tutte le chiome;

perché, secondo lo sguardo che fée   19
la fede in Cristo, queste sono il muro
a che si parton le sacre scalee.

Da questa parte onde 'l fiore è maturo   22
di tutte le sue foglie, sono assisi
quei che credettero in Cristo venturo;

da l'altra parte onde sono intercisi   25
di vòti i semicirculi, si stanno
quei ch'a Cristo venuto ebber li visi.

E come quinci il glorïoso scanno   28
de la donna del cielo e li altri scanni
di sotto lui cotanta cerna fanno,

Still the Tenth Heaven: the Empyrean. The placement of the blessed in the Rose. Predestination and the blessed infants. Mary. The angel Gabriel. The great patricians of the Empyrean. Bernard's urging of Dante to beseech Mary.

Though he had been absorbed in his delight,
    that contemplator freely undertook
the task of teaching; and his holy words

        began: "The wound that Mary closed and then   4
anointed was the wound that Eve—so lovely
at Mary's feet—had opened and had pierced.

        Below her, in the seats of the third rank,   7
Rachel and Beatrice, as you see, sit.
Sarah, Rebecca, Judith, and the one

        who was the great-grandmother of the singer   10
who, as he sorrowed for his sinfulness,
cried, *'Miserere mei'*—these you can see

        from rank to rank as I, in moving through   13
the Rose, from petal unto petal, give
to each her name. And from the seventh rank,

        just as they did within the ranks above,   16
the Hebrew women follow—ranging downward—
dividing all the tresses of the Rose.

        They are the wall by which the sacred stairs   19
divide, depending on the view of Christ
with which their faith aligned. Upon one side,

        there where the Rose is ripe, with all its petals, 22
are those whose faith was in the Christ to come;
and on the other side—that semicircle

        whose space is broken up by vacant places—   25
sit those whose sight was set upon the Christ
who had already come. And just as on

        this side, to serve as such a great partition,   28
there is the throne in glory of the Lady
of Heaven and the seats that range below it,

    così di contra quel del gran Giovanni,   31
che sempre santo 'l diserto e 'l martiro
sofferse, e poi l'inferno da due anni;

    e sotto lui così cerner sortiro   34
Francesco, Benedetto e Augustino
e altri fin qua giù di giro in giro.

    Or mira l'alto proveder divino: 37
ché l'uno e l'altro aspetto de la fede
igualmente empierà questo giardino.

    E sappi che dal grado in giù che fiede   40
a mezzo il tratto le due discrezioni,
per nullo proprio merito si siede,

    ma per l'altrui, con certe condizioni: 43
ché tutti questi son spiriti ascolti
prima ch'avesser vere elezïoni.

    Ben te ne puoi accorger per li volti   46
e anche per le voci püerili,
se tu li guardi bene e se li ascolti.

    Or dubbi tu e dubitando sili;   49
ma io discioglierò 'l forte legame
in che ti stringon li pensier sottili.

    Dentro a l'ampiezza di questo reame   52
casüal punto non puote aver sito,
se non come tristizia o sete o fame:

    ché per etterna legge è stabilito   55
quantunque vedi, sì che giustamente
ci si risponde da l'anello al dito;

    e però questa festinata gente   58
a vera vita non è *sine causa*
intra sé qui più e meno eccellente.

    Lo rege per cui questo regno pausa   61
in tanto amore e in tanto diletto,
che nulla volontà è di più ausa,

    le menti tutte nel suo lieto aspetto   64
creando, a suo piacer di grazia dota
diversamente; e qui basti l'effetto.

    E ciò espresso e chiaro vi si nota   67
ne la Scrittura santa in quei gemelli
che ne la madre ebber l'ira commota.

so, opposite, the seat of the great John—   31
who, always saintly, suffered both the desert
and martyrdom, and then two years of Hell—

serves to divide; below him sit, assigned   34
to this partition, Francis, Benedict,
and Augustine, and others, rank on rank,

down to this center of the Rose. Now see   37
how deep is God's foresight: both aspects of
the faith shall fill this garden equally.

And know that there, below the transverse row   40
that cuts across the two divisions, sit
souls who are there for merits not their own,

but—with certain conditions—others' merits;   43
for all of these are souls who left their bodies
before they had the power of true choice.

Indeed, you may perceive this by yourself—   46
their faces, childlike voices, are enough,
if you look well at them and hear them sing.

But now you doubt and, doubting, do not speak;   49
yet I shall loose that knot; I can release
you from the bonds of subtle reasoning.

Within the ample breadth of this domain,   52
no point can find its place by chance, just as
there is no place for sorrow, thirst, or hunger;

whatever you may see has been ordained   55
by everlasting law, so that the fit
of ring and finger here must be exact;

and thus these souls who have, precociously,   58
reached the true life do not, among themselves,
find places high or low without some cause.

The King through whom this kingdom finds content   61
in so much love and so much joyousness
that no desire would dare to ask for more,

creating every mind in His glad sight,   64
bestows His grace diversely, at His pleasure—
and here the fact alone must be enough.

And this is clearly and expressly noted   67
for you in Holy Scripture, in those twins
who, in their mother's womb, were moved to anger.

Però, secondo il color d'i capelli,   70
di cotal grazia l'altissimo lume
degnamente convien che s'incappelli.

Dunque, sanza mercé di lor costume,   73
locati son per gradi differenti,
sol differendo nel primiero acume.

Bastavasi ne' secoli recenti   76
con l'innocenza, per aver salute,
solamente la fede d'i parenti;

poi che le prime etadi fuor compiute,   79
convenne ai maschi a l'innocenti penne
per circuncidere acquistar virtute;

ma poi che 'l tempo de la grazia venne,   82
sanza battesmo perfetto di Cristo
tale innocenza là giù si ritenne.

Riguarda omai ne la faccia che a Cristo   85
più si somiglia, ché la sua chiarezza
sola ti può disporre a veder Cristo."

Io vidi sopra lei tanta allegrezza   88
piover, portata ne le menti sante
create a trasvolar per quella altezza,

che quantunque io avea visto davante,   91
di tanta ammirazion non mi sospese,
né mi mostrò di Dio tanto sembiante;

e quello amor che primo lì discese,   94
cantando *"Ave, Maria, gratïa plena,"*
dinanzi a lei le sue ali distese.

Rispuose a la divina cantilena   97
da tutte parti la beata corte,
sì ch'ogne vista sen fé più serena.

"O santo padre, che per me comporte   100
l'esser qua giù, lasciando il dolce loco
nel qual tu siedi per etterna sorte,

qual è quell' angel che con tanto gioco   103
guarda ne li occhi la nostra regina,
innamorato sì che par di foco?"

Così ricorsi ancora a la dottrina   106
di colui ch'abbelliva di Maria,
come del sole stella mattutina.

Thus, it is just for the celestial light   70
to grace their heads with a becoming crown,
according to the color of their hair.

Without, then, any merit in their works,   73
these infants are assigned to different ranks—
proclivity at birth, the only difference.

In early centuries, their parents' faith   76
alone, and their own innocence, sufficed
for the salvation of the children; when

those early times had reached completion, then   79
each male child had to find, through circumcision,
the power needed by his innocent

member; but then the age of grace arrived,   82
and without perfect baptism in Christ,
such innocence was kept below, in Limbo.

Look now upon the face that is most like   85
the face of Christ, for only through its brightness
can you prepare your vision to see Him."

I saw such joy rain down upon her, joy   88
carried by holy intellects created
to fly at such a height, that all which I

had seen before did not transfix me with   91
amazement so intense, nor show to me
a semblance that was so akin to God.

And the angelic love who had descended   94
earlier, now spread his wings before her,
singing *"Ave Maria, gratïa plena."*

On every side, the blessed court replied,   97
singing responses to his godly song,
so that each spirit there grew more serene.

"O holy father—who, for me, endure   100
your being here below, leaving the sweet
place where eternal lot assigns your seat—

who is that angel who with such delight   103
looks into our Queen's eyes—he who is so
enraptured that he seems to be a flame?"

So, once again, I called upon the teaching   106
of him who drew from Mary beauty, as
the morning star draws beauty from the sun.

Ed elli a me: "Baldezza e leggiadria   109
quant' esser puote in angelo e in alma,
tutta è in lui; e sì volem che sia,

perch' elli è quelli che portò la palma   112
giuso a Maria, quando 'l Figliuol di Dio
carcar si volse de la nostra salma.

Ma vieni omai con li occhi sì com' io   115
andrò parlando, e nota i gran patrici
di questo imperio giustissimo e pio.

Quei due che seggon là sù più felici   118
per esser propinquissimi ad Agusta,
son d'esta rosa quasi due radici:

colui che da sinistra le s'aggiusta   121
è 'l padre per lo cui ardito gusto
l'umana specie tanto amaro gusta;

dal destro vedi quel padre vetusto   124
di Santa Chiesa a cui Cristo le chiavi
raccomandò di questo fior venusto.

E quei che vide tutti i tempi gravi,   127
pria che morisse, de la bella sposa
che s'acquistò con la lancia e coi clavi,

siede lungh' esso, e lungo l'altro posa   130
quel duca sotto cui visse di manna
la gente ingrata, mobile e retrosa.

Di contr' a Pietro vedi sedere Anna,   133
tanto contenta di mirar sua figlia,
che non move occhio per cantare osanna;

e contro al maggior padre di famiglia   136
siede Lucia, che mosse la tua donna
quando chinavi, a rovinar, le ciglia.

Ma perché 'l tempo fugge che t'assonna,   139
qui farem punto, come buon sartore
che com' elli ha del panno fa la gonna;

e drizzeremo li occhi al primo amore,   142
sì che, guardando verso lui, penètri
quant' è possibil per lo suo fulgore.

Veramente, ne forse tu t'arretri   145
movendo l'ali tue, credendo oltrarti,
orando grazia conven che s'impetri

And he to me: "All of the gallantry   109
and confidence that there can be in angel
or blessed soul are found in him, and we
    would have it so, for it was he who carried   112
the palm below to Mary, when God's Son
wanted to bear our flesh as His own burden.
    But follow with your eyes even as I   115
proceed to speak, and note the great patricians
of this most just and merciful empire.
    Those two who, there above, are seated, most   118
happy to be so near the Empress, may
be likened to the two roots of this Rose:
    the one who, on her left, sits closest, is   121
the father whose presumptuous tasting
caused humankind to taste such bitterness;
    and on the right, you see that ancient father   124
of Holy Church, into whose care the keys
of this fair flower were consigned by Christ.
    And he who saw, before he died, all of   127
the troubled era of the lovely Bride—
whom lance and nails had won—sits at his side;
    and at the side of Adam sits that guide   130
under whose rule the people, thankless, fickle,
and stubborn, lived on manna. Facing Peter,
    Anna is seated, so content to see   133
her daughter that, as Anna sings hosannas,
she does not move her eyes. And opposite
    the greatest father of a family,   136
Lucia sits, she who urged on your lady
when you bent your brows downward, to your ruin.
    But time, which brings you sleep, takes flight, and now   139
we shall stop here—even as a good tailor
who cuts the garment as his cloth allows—
    and turn our vision to the Primal Love,   142
that, gazing at Him, you may penetrate—
as far as that can be—His radiance.
    But lest you now fall back when, even as   145
you move your wings, you think that you advance,
imploring grace, through prayer you must beseech

grazia da quella che puote aiutarti;   148
e tu mi seguirai con l'affezione,
sì che dal dicer mio lo cor non parti."
    E cominciò questa santa orazione: 151

grace from that one who has the power to help you;   148
and do you follow me with your affection—
so may my words and your heart share one way."

And he began this holy supplication: 151

CANTO XXXIII

Vergine Madre, figlia del tuo figlio,
umile e alta più che creatura,
termine fisso d'etterno consiglio,

tu se' colei che l'umana natura   4
nobilitasti sì, che 'l suo fattore
non disdegnò di farsi sua fattura.

Nel ventre tuo si raccese l'amore,   7
per lo cui caldo ne l'etterna pace
così è germinato questo fiore.

Qui se' a noi meridïana face   10
di caritate, e giuso, intra' mortali,
se' di speranza fontana vivace.

Donna, se' tanto grande e tanto vali,   13
che qual vuol grazia e a te non ricorre,
sua disïanza vuol volar sanz' ali.

La tua benignità non pur soccorre   16
a chi domanda, ma molte fïate
liberamente al dimandar precorre.

In te misericordia, in te pietate,   19
in te magnificenza, in te s'aduna
quantunque in creatura è di bontate.

Or questi, che da l'infima lacuna   22
de l'universo infin qui ha vedute
le vite spiritali ad una ad una,

supplica a te, per grazia, di virtute   25
tanto, che possa con li occhi levarsi
più alto verso l'ultima salute.

E io, che mai per mio veder non arsi   28
più ch'i' fo per lo suo, tutti miei preghi
ti porgo, e priego che non sieno scarsi,

Virgin mother, daughter of your Son,
more humble and sublime than any creature,
fixed goal decreed from all eternity,

you are the one who gave to human nature   4
so much nobility that its Creator
did not disdain His being made its creature.

That love whose warmth allowed this flower to bloom   7
within the everlasting peace—was love
rekindled in your womb; for us above,

you are the noonday torch of charity,   10
and there below, on earth, among the mortals,
you are a living spring of hope. Lady,

you are so high, you can so intercede,   13
that he who would have grace but does not seek
your aid, may long to fly but has no wings.

Your loving-kindness does not only answer   16
the one who asks, but it is often ready
to answer freely long before the asking.

In you compassion is, in you is pity,   19
in you is generosity, in you
is every goodness found in any creature.

This man—who from the deepest hollow in   22
the universe, up to this height, has seen
the lives of spirits, one by one—now pleads

with you, through grace, to grant him so much virtue   25
that he may lift his vision higher still—
may lift it toward the ultimate salvation.

And I, who never burned for my own vision   28
more than I burn for his, do offer you
all of my prayers—and pray that they may not

perché tu ogne nube li disleghi   31
di sua mortalità co' prieghi tuoi,
sì che 'l sommo piacer li si dispieghi.

Ancor ti priego, regina, che puoi   34
ciò che tu vuoli, che conservi sani,
dopo tanto veder, li affetti suoi.

Vinca tua guardia i movimenti umani: 37
vedi Beatrice con quanti beati
per li miei prieghi ti chiudon le mani!"

Li occhi da Dio diletti e venerati,   40
fissi ne l'orator, ne dimostraro
quanto i devoti prieghi le son grati;

indi a l'etterno lume s'addrizzaro,   43
nel qual non si dee creder che s'invii
per creatura l'occhio tanto chiaro.

E io ch'al fine di tutt' i disii   46
appropinquava, sì com' io dovea,
l'ardor del desiderio in me finii.

Bernardo m'accennava, e sorridea,   49
perch' io guardassi suso; ma io era
già per me stesso tal qual ei volea:

ché la mia vista, venendo sincera,   52
e più e più intrava per lo raggio
de l'alta luce che da sé è vera.

Da quinci innanzi il mio veder fu maggio   55
che 'l parlar mostra, ch'a tal vista cede,
e cede la memoria a tanto oltraggio.

Qual è colüi che sognando vede,   58
che dopo 'l sogno la passione impressa
rimane, e l'altro a la mente non riede,

cotal son io, ché quasi tutta cessa   61
mia visïone, e ancor mi distilla
nel core il dolce che nacque da essa.

Così la neve al sol si disigilla;   64
così al vento ne le foglie levi
si perdea la sentenza di Sibilla.

O somma luce che tanto ti levi   67
da' concetti mortali, a la mia mente
ripresta un poco di quel che parevi,

fall short—that, with your prayers, you may disperse   31
all of the clouds of his mortality
so that the Highest Joy be his to see.

This, too, o Queen, who can do what you would,   34
I ask of you: that after such a vision,
his sentiments preserve their perseverance.

May your protection curb his mortal passions.   37
See Beatrice—how many saints with her!
They join my prayers! They clasp their hands to you!"

The eyes that are revered and loved by God,   40
now fixed upon the supplicant, showed us
how welcome such devotions are to her;

then her eyes turned to the Eternal Light—   43
there, do not think that any creature's eye
can find its way as clearly as her sight.

And I, who now was nearing Him who is   46
the end of all desires, as I ought,
lifted my longing to its ardent limit.

Bernard was signaling—he smiled—to me   49
to turn my eyes on high; but I, already
was doing what he wanted me to do,

because my sight, becoming pure, was able   52
to penetrate the ray of Light more deeply—
that Light, sublime, which in Itself is true.

From that point on, what I could see was greater   55
than speech can show: at such a sight, it fails—
and memory fails when faced with such excess.

As one who sees within a dream, and, later,   58
the passion that had been imprinted stays,
but nothing of the rest returns to mind,

such am I, for my vision almost fades   61
completely, yet it still distills within
my heart the sweetness that was born of it.

So is the snow, beneath the sun, unsealed;   64
and so, on the light leaves, beneath the wind,
the oracles the Sibyl wrote were lost.

O Highest Light, You, raised so far above   67
the minds of mortals, to my memory
give back something of Your epiphany,

    e fa la lingua mia tanto possente,   70
ch'una favilla sol de la tua gloria
possa lasciare a la futura gente;
    ché, per tornare alquanto a mia memoria   73
e per sonare un poco in questi versi,
più si conceperà di tua vittoria.
    Io credo, per l'acume ch'io soffersi   76
del vivo raggio, ch'i' sarei smarrito,
se li occhi miei da lui fossero aversi.
    E' mi ricorda ch'io fui più ardito   79
per questo a sostener, tanto ch'i' giunsi
l'aspetto mio col valore infinito.
    Oh abbondante grazia ond' io presunsi   82
ficcar lo viso per la luce etterna,
tanto che la veduta vi consunsi!
    Nel suo profondo vidi che s'interna,   85
legato con amore in un volume,
ciò che per l'universo si squaderna:
    sustanze e accidenti e lor costume   88
quasi conflati insieme, per tal modo
che ciò ch'i' dico è un semplice lume.
    La forma universal di questo nodo   91
credo ch'i' vidi, perché più di largo,
dicendo questo, mi sento ch'i' godo.
    Un punto solo m'è maggior letargo   94
che venticinque secoli a la 'mpresa
che fé Nettuno ammirar l'ombra d'Argo.
    Così la mente mia, tutta sospesa,   97
mirava fissa, immobile e attenta,
e sempre di mirar faceasi accesa.
    A quella luce cotal si diventa,   100
che volgersi da lei per altro aspetto
è impossibil che mai si consenta;
    però che 'l ben, ch'è del volere obietto,   103
tutto s'accoglie in lei, e fuor di quella
è defettivo ciò ch'è li perfetto.
    Omai sarà più corta mia favella,   106
pur a quel ch'io ricordo, che d'un fante
che bagni ancor la lingua a la mammella.

and make my tongue so powerful that I   70
may leave to people of the future one
gleam of the glory that is Yours, for by

returning somewhat to my memory   73
and echoing awhile within these lines,
Your victory will be more understood.

The living ray that I endured was so   76
acute that I believe I should have gone
astray had my eyes turned away from it.

I can recall that I, because of this,   79
was bolder in sustaining it until
my vision reached the Infinite Goodness.

O grace abounding, through which I presumed   82
to set my eyes on the Eternal Light
so long that I spent all my sight on it!

In its profundity I saw—ingathered   85
and bound by love into one single volume—
what, in the universe, seems separate, scattered:

substances, accidents, and dispositions   88
as if conjoined—in such a way that what
I tell is only rudimentary.

I think I saw the universal shape   91
which that knot takes; for, speaking this, I feel
a joy that is more ample. That one moment

brings more forgetfulness to me than twenty-five   94
centuries have brought to the endeavor
that startled Neptune with the *Argo*'s shadow!

So was my mind—completely rapt, intent,   97
steadfast, and motionless—gazing; and it
grew ever more enkindled as it watched.

Whoever sees that Light is soon made such   100
that it would be impossible for him
to set that Light aside for other sight;

because the good, the object of the will,   103
is fully gathered in that Light; outside
that Light, what there is perfect is defective.

What little I recall is to be told,   106
from this point on, in words more weak than those
of one whose infant tongue still bathes at the breast.

Non perché più ch'un semplice sembiante   109
fosse nel vivo lume ch'io mirava,
che tal è sempre qual s'era davante;

   ma per la vista che s'avvalorava   112
in me guardando, una sola parvenza,
mutandom' io, a me si travagliava.

   Ne la profonda e chiara sussistenza   115
de l'alto lume parvermi tre giri
di tre colori e d'una contenenza;

   e l'un da l'altro come iri da iri   118
parea reflesso, e 'l terzo parea foco
che quinci e quindi igualmente si spiri.

   Oh quanto è corto il dire e come fioco   121
al mio concetto! e questo, a quel ch'i' vidi,
è tanto, che non basta a dicer "poco."

   O luce etterna che sola in te sidi,   124
sola t'intendi, e da te intelletta
e intendente te ami e arridi!

   Quella circulazion che sì concetta   127
pareva in te come lume reflesso,
da li occhi miei alquanto circunspetta,

   dentro da sé, del suo colore stesso,   130
mi parve pinta de la nostra effige:
per che 'l mio viso in lei tutto era messo.

   Qual è 'l geomètra che tutto s'affige   133
per misurar lo cerchio, e non ritrova,
pensando, quel principio ond' elli indige,

   tal era io a quella vista nova: 136
veder voleva come si convenne
l'imago al cerchio e come vi s'indova;

   ma non eran da ciò le proprie penne: 139
se non che la mia mente fu percossa
da un fulgore in che sua voglia venne.

   A l'alta fantasia qui mancò possa;   142
ma già volgeva il mio disio e 'l *velle,*
sì come rota ch'igualmente è mossa,

   l'amor che move il sole e l'altre stelle.   145

And not because more than one simple semblance   109
was in the Living Light at which I gazed—
for It is always what It was before—

but through my sight, which as I gazed grew stronger,   112
that sole appearance, even as I altered,
seemed to be changing. In the deep and bright

essence of that exalted Light, three circles   115
appeared to me; they had three different colors,
but all of them were of the same dimension;

one circle seemed reflected by the second,   118
as rainbow is by rainbow, and the third
seemed fire breathed equally by those two circles.

How incomplete is speech, how weak, when set   121
against my thought! And this, to what I saw
is such—to call it little is too much.

Eternal Light, You only dwell within   124
Yourself, and only You know You; Self-knowing,
Self-known, You love and smile upon Yourself!

That circle—which, begotten so, appeared   127
in You as light reflected—when my eyes
had watched it with attention for some time,

within itself and colored like itself,   130
to me seemed painted with our effigy,
so that my sight was set on it completely.

As the geometer intently seeks   133
to square the circle, but he cannot reach,
through thought on thought, the principle he needs,

so I searched that strange sight: I wished to see   136
the way in which our human effigy
suited the circle and found place in it—

and my own wings were far too weak for that.   139
But then my mind was struck by light that flashed
and, with this light, received what it had asked.

Here force failed my high fantasy; but my   142
desire and will were moved already—like
a wheel revolving uniformly—by

the Love that moves the sun and the other stars.   145

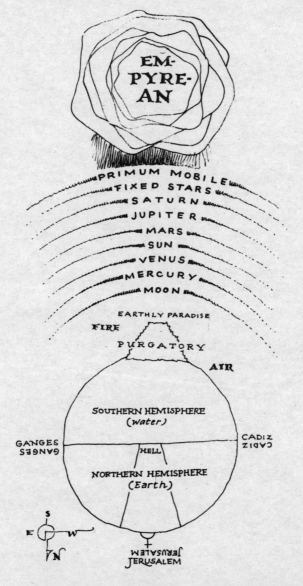

EM-PYRE-AN

PRIMUM MOBILE
FIXED STARS
SATURN
JUPITER
MARS
SUN
VENUS
MERCURY
MOON

EARTHLY PARADISE

FIRE

PURGATORY

AIR

SOUTHERN HEMISPHERE
(water)

GANGES

CADIZ

HELL

NORTHERN HEMISPHERE
(Earth)

S
E — W
N

JERUSALEM

THE UNIVERSE OF DANTE

NOTES

The following annotations are meant to serve as a very basic apparatus; they do not substitute for the three volumes-in-progress, one devoted to each *cantica* of the *Comedy,* of the California Lectura Dantis. From its own century until today, the *Comedy* has given rise to many commentaries. Chronologies of Dante's life and works and interpretations of vexed points in the *Comedy* are various and, at times, more conflicting than complementary. Much that is said bears the implicit qualifications, "possibly," "probably," and "perhaps." But some assertions do have more cogency than others, and this modest guide has garnered reasonable, helpful opinion in addition to a fair sum of certainties.

The notes are supplemented by a drawing-diagram by Barry Moser, showing the spatial organization of Dante's cosmos.

The quotations from the Scriptures are from the Jerusalem Bible (1966).

In the following notes, the *Aeneid* is cited with the English line numbers of the Bantam Classics edition (that edition carries Latin line numbers at the top of each page). Other works by Virgil carry the Latin line numbers of the Loeb Classical Library editions, as do all works of Ovid, Lucan, and Statius. Ovid's *Metamorphoses* is abbreviated as *Met.;* Lucan's *Pharsalia* as *Phars.;* and the *Thebaid* of Statius as *Theb.*

The *Summa theologica* of St. Thomas Aquinas is abbreviated as *Summa theol.* These notes use the standard mode of referring to the *Summa.* The Roman numeral I refers to Part I of the work; I–II refers to the *Prima Secundae,* or first portion of Part II; and II–II refers to the *Secunda Secundae,* or second portion of Part II. The Roman numeral is followed by the Arabic numeral of the question ("q.") considered and then by the Arabic numeral of the article ("a.") under that question.

A.M.

CANTO I

1–12 In these opening lines, glossed at length in his dedicatory Letter to Cangrande della Scala (*Epistole,* XIII), the poet states "the matter of [his] song": his intention, in this third and final canticle, is to describe as much of his vision of the "holy kingdom" of Paradise as his memory has been able to retain. The first great difficulty he will encounter, then, is re-membering. (The second, as we shall immediately see, will be putting what he remembers into words, given the inadequacy of human language to speak of things divine.) The events of *Paradiso* are different in kind from all others, even from those of *Inferno* and *Purgatorio,* far surpass-ing all human capacity. In order to experience the bliss of Heaven, Dante must pass "beyond the human" (70). The powers of his soul—his mem-ory, his intellect or understanding, and his will—must be immeasurably increased. But this enhancement of his faculties is a privilege granted only for the duration of his vision: in order to return among men, to ful-fill his mission of speaking of what was revealed, he must be restored to his earthly humanity. There is, between the almost infinite receptivity of his imparadised soul and the renewed limits of his all-too-human mem-ory, an incalculable disparity, which the reader is never allowed to forget. To paraphrase St. Paul (an insistent, if implicit, presence behind these opening lines), what Dante saw face-to-face on his heavenly journey, he now can remember only, as it were, through a glass, darkly (cf. 2 Cor. 12:2–4).

1–3 God, who created the universe, and (like the Aristotelian "First Cause" or "Unmoved Mover") maintains it in motion, is conceived by Dante in terms of light and radiance, "glory." His light—intellectual il-lumination, understanding, revealed knowledge—is everywhere present in His Creation. As a consequence, however, of factors that are part of the order that He has willed (of which more later, in lines 103–142), this light is more or less apparent in each creature, depending on its nearness to Him. The identity of light ("glory") and love are, incidentally, con-firmed by the perfect circularity of *Paradiso,* whose last line, "the Love that moves the sun and the other stars" (XXXIII, 145), brings us back to its first.

4–5 God's glory is most effulgent in the outermost sphere of the heav-ens, the Empyrean, in which He dwells. Dante's basically Ptolemaic model of the universe is geocentric, or earth-centered. The earth is sur-rounded by ten concentric heavenly spheres, the first nine revolving, each in its particular orbit, with a velocity that increases the farther the sphere is from the earth; the last, the Empyrean, the heaven of pure "'light and love'" (XXVII, 112), is motionless. Nonmaterial, beyond space and time, it is the dwelling place of Light and Love—of God— where all desire, whose unfulfillment is the source of motion, is fulfilled. The contained spheres turn ever faster the closer they are to the

Empyrean because they perceive more directly and immediately, as it were, the object of their (and our) desire, and their desire is thereby quickened. The lower spheres—the first seven, which contain the moving stars or planets (the Moon, Mercury, Venus, the Sun, Mars, Jupiter, and Saturn, in that order); the eighth, which contains the Fixed Stars; and the ninth, the crystalline Primum Mobile—are all composed of matter, however diaphanous and refined, and thus fall short of complete perfection.

The fact that Dante, claiming special divine concession, encounters the spirits of certain of the blessed throughout the lower heavens, even though the true seats of all the blessed are in the Empyrean, is a brilliant literary strategem. By this method, the poet overcomes the reticence of the true visionary (cf. St. Paul, 2 Cor. 12, an important cryptic subtext), as well as the static quality that often characterizes visionary narrative. Dante adapts what could have been a nondynamic revelation (and the contents of his theological encyclopedia [cf. the didactic scholasticism of his Letter to Cangrande]) to the needs of suspenseful narrative and step-by-step dialectical exposition.

7 The "desired end" of the intellect is God, in whom is perfect knowledge.

13–36 "both crests": i.e., the inspiration of Apollo as well as the Muses. The reader will recall that *Purgatorio* also opened with an invocation—a briefer one—of the nine Muses, who, for Dante, had their seat on "one of Parnassus' peaks" (16). The second crest, Cyrrha, was sacred to Apollo himself, the sun god and the god of music and poetry, lover of the nymph Daphne, the daughter of the river god Peneus (whence the adjective "Peneian" [31]). According to Ovid, Daphne was transformed by her father into a laurel tree to save her from the god's embrace. Thereafter, Apollo's love was transferred to the laurel itself, which became his sacred plant; its leaves were used to weave the triumphant crowns of the emperor and the poet "laureate."

21 Ovid recounts (*Met.* VI, 383–391) how the satyr Marsyas was foolhardy enough to challenge Apollo to a musical duel. After Marsyas' inevitable defeat, he was tied to a tree and flayed alive by the victorious god, who drew him like a sword from the scabbard of his limbs. This allusion to the awesome power of Apollo (cf. *Purg.* I, 9–12, for a similar allusion to the power of the Muses), far from being a gruesome and gratuitous embellishment, is yet another oblique reminder of the tragic consequences of human presumption and of the need for humility and submission to the Divine Will. One is reminded again of the warning implicit in the episode of Ulysses in *Inferno* XXVI.

31 "Peneian": See 13–36, note.

33 Apollo is the "Delphic deity," since his chief shrine was located at Delphi, on the slopes of Mount Parnassus.

34–36 After expressing his regrets—and, in essence, apologizing to "Cyrrha's god," Apollo—for the pusillanimity of his fellow men, for their lack of epic and imperial ambition (28–33). Dante dares to hope, with fitting humility, that the "small spark" of his *Commedia* may lead to a "great fire" of emulators.

37–42   The actual narrative of events begins here (or rather, continues, since the events of *Paradiso* begin where *Purgatorio* left off). Throughout the year, the sun ("the lantern of the world") rises at different points on the horizon. The most favorable point (and the point from which, as we shall see, it now rises) is reached at the vernal equinox, when four astronomical circles—the equator, the ecliptic, the equinoctial colure, and the horizon itself—meet, forming among themselves three crosses. (The four and three allude on the allegorical level to the cardinal and theological virtues.) At this point the sun is joined to the constellation of Aries. It is spring, and the "world's wax" is most disposed to receive the seal or imprint of the sun (that is, nature is most ready to respond to his fecundating warmth and stir herself from the suspended animation of winter).

43–48   The sun had earlier risen over the horizon of Purgatory, bringing morning with it. Consequently, at the antipodes, in the inhabited hemisphere of land, which has its pole at Jerusalem, night had fallen. The exact time in Eden, where Dante is, must in fact be shortly after noon, since he arrived at the twin source of the Lethe and Eunoe rivers, accompanied by Beatrice, Matilda, Statius, and the seven women, at precisely that hour (cf. *Purg.* XXXIII, 104). The passage through Inferno began as night was falling, the ascent of the mountain of Purgatory at dawn. Appropriately, after his direct appeal to the sun god Apollo, Dante's journey to Paradise begins at midday. Turning left, from their position facing eastward, where we left them at the end of *Purgatorio,* Beatrice turns north, and it is into the noonday sun, in all its dazzling brightness, that she stares so fixedly. The eagle was reputed to have the unique ability to look unflinchingly at the sun, just as, of all birds, it soared closest to it.

49–57   Dante, seeing Beatrice staring at the sun, is led automatically to do the same. He finds, here in Eden, where God first placed Adam—father and representative of all mankind—that though he cannot contemplate the sun with the same fixity as Beatrice, he can nevertheless bear its brightness for longer than he ever could before. The simile of the reflected ray stresses Dante's continuing dependence on Beatrice as intermediary between himself and God.

50   The Italian term *pelegrin,* besides meaning "pilgrim" (with all the nostalgic lyrical connotations of *peregrin* in *Purg.* II, 63, and VIII, 4), may also indicate the peregrine falcon, a bird that shares the same characteristics as the eagle, though, like Dante with respect to Beatrice at this moment, it possesses them to a lesser degree.

62   "The One who can": God, to whom all things are possible.

65   "The eternal circles": the heavenly spheres.

67–72   Ovid recounts (in *Met.* XIII, 898–968) how Glaucus, a fisherman of Boeotia, surprised to see his catch of fish, which he had set down on the grass ("herb"), regain vigor and jump back into the sea after eating some of the herb, decided to taste it himself and was immediately filled with an uncontrollable longing to plunge into the sea. Diving from the cliff, he was transformed into a sea god by Oceanus and Tethys. Glaucus' change of nature from human to divine parallels the qualitative change Dante feels within himself as he gazes upon Beatrice.

73–75 Though he is not yet aware of it, Dante has already begun his upward journey (Beatrice will reveal this to him in lines 91–93). Like Saint Paul (in 2 Cor. 12:3), he cannot in retrospect say whether at this point he was pure soul ("the part of me / that You created last," [see the account of the soul's creation in *Purg.* XXV, 71–75]) or soul and body combined. The passage in Paul had given rise to considerable theological debate, and the poet may leave the question in suspense for reasons of doctrinal prudence. In any case, there are various clues in the subsequent text that suggest that Dante imagined his journey to have been made not merely in the spirit but also in the flesh, albeit a flesh without weight, purged and purified by his passage through Purgatory and by the rituals of Earthly Paradise.

76–78 It is the heavens' longing for God, who dwells ideally, as we have seen, in the outermost Empyrean, that imparts to them their eternal wheeling motion. The farther they are from the earth, and the more space they encompass, the swifter their gyre. Their different speeds and motions produce different musical notes, which, Pythagoras and Plato imagined, combined to make the divinely ordered harmony of the music of the spheres. Aristotle and his Scholastic followers rejected the latter idea. The artist in Dante recovered the concept from Book VI of Cicero's *De re publica,* which was widely known in the Middle Ages through the commentary of Macrobius, called the *Somnium Scipionis* (Scipio's Dream).

79–81 Dante may be rising through the so-called Sphere of Fire, which medieval science placed just below the circle of the moon. Alternatively, his perception of the sun (whose brightness was already seen as redoubled in lines 61–63) may simply be becoming more complete.

82–93 Beatrice (who, gazing upon the Mind of God, where all things are reflected, has even less difficulty than did Virgil, Dante's former guide, in perceiving Dante's thoughts) now reveals to him that they have left the earth and the Earthly Paradise behind and are speeding, swifter than lightning, toward their heavenly home, toward the Empyrean. Beatrice draws her simile from the phenomenon of lightning. Medieval science held that all fire—and lightning is a kind of fire—naturally strove upward to reach its proper abode in the Sphere of Fire. The descent of lightning to the earth, proverbial for its swiftness, was therefore an unnatural phenomenon in violation of this generally valid scientific axiom. But Beatrice's simile, though paradoxical, is quite felicitous here; and by implicitly invoking the general principle that everything seeks its true place in the universe, including the human soul, whose true place is in Heaven, Beatrice prepares the way for the answer to Dante's second perplexity.

94–99 Dante's free-fall upward into space appears to him as a violation of the natural laws of gravity. How can he transcend " 'these lighter bodies,' " the spheres of air and fire? Beatrice's reply, which will occupy the remainder of the canto, essentially points out that there is a metaphysical order superior to the so-called laws of physics.

103–141 More than a dry scholastic argument, Beatrice's discourse, with the exhilarating rhythm and cadenced incisiveness of its tercets and the spontaneous and apposite flow of its imagery, is, like so many of the doctrinal excursuses of *Paradiso,* an enthusiastic hymn in praise of the providential order of the cosmos.

103–114 The perfect order of Creation is a reflection of Divine Perfection. It is visible only to the " 'higher beings,' " to angels and to man, whose intellect enables them to discern the divine " 'pattern' "— the image of the Supreme Good imprinted on the world—and therefore to seek God as their goal. Within this universal order, however, there is a hierarchy of natures, each moving toward its decreed end, according to its innate tendency.

115–126 This is the divinely implanted instinct that carries the element of fire up toward the Sphere of Fire, governs the behavior of the lower " 'mortal creatures' " (i.e., those lacking an immortal soul), and causes the earth to gravitate toward its center. The same principle is also operative in those "higher beings" possessed of a soul. The same divine impetus shoots them like arrows toward their true goal. Divine Providence, which has predisposed things thus, has its true dwelling beyond the fastest spinning of the heavens, the Primum Mobile, in the Empyrean, " 'the heaven of pure light' " (XXX, 39). That is where the bow of God's infallible design is now propelling us.

127–141 Every artist knows that what is created does not always correspond perfectly to its creator's intentions. One reason for this is the resistance offered by the raw materials. (Cf. XIII, 77–78.) Like the recalcitrance of the artist's materials, the gift of free will, wrongly used, can lead the rational creature away from its predestined end, toward some lesser good, just as a lightning bolt may fall, against its nature, down from the sky.

139–141 Dante, " 'no longer hindered' " by the obstacles that his soul was cleansed of by his passage through Purgatory, should no more wonder at his upward flight than he would at the natural phenomena of a waterfall that falls or a flame that rises.

CANTO II

1–18 Before beginning the account of his journey upward through the heavens, Dante exhorts his readers to consider well whether they are adequately prepared to continue following his ship, his poem (taking up again the nautical metaphor with which *Purgatorio* opened), as it "crosses to deep seas" (3), that is, to the profound treatment and experience of theological and philosophical problems that will in large measure constitute the subject matter of this third *cantica*. Dante warns his readers that he will be crossing waves that "were never sailed before" (7), for although the journey to Paradise by a living man was completed before Dante by St. Paul (see 2 Cor. 12:2–4), Dante's *poetic* voyage is indeed unprecedented—if not in the mere fact of his description of Paradise (for earlier such descriptions did exist), certainly unprecedented in the elaborateness of that description, and in its theological and philosophical scope.

The "bread of angels" (11) is Divine Wisdom, upon which the angels feed (see Ps. 78 [77 in the Vulgate]:25 and Wisdom 16:20, and cf. the opening to Dante's *Convivio* [I, i, 7]: "Oh blessed those few who sit at that table where the bread of angels is served"). And only those few who have "turned [their] minds in time / unto the bread of angels" (10–11), that is, only those who, through the prolonged study of speculative theology and philosophy, have devoted themselves to acquiring wisdom, dare undertake to follow the poet on his voyage. The arduousness of this journey is such that it will require that even the well-prepared, dependent on the poet's guidance, keep their course "within / his wake," behind which "waves smooth again," traceless. The ill- or un-prepared, Dante insists, had better return to the safety of familiar shores, lest in the midst of "deep seas," they find themselves unprepared to continue and unable to return.

8 Minerva, the goddess of wisdom, "breathes" (*spira*), filling the sails of Dante's "ship" (3); while Apollo, the god of poetry and poetic inspiration (invoked by Dante in Canto I, 13–33), acts as pilot and guide—a reversal, perhaps, of the roles one might expect for these deities, that aptly expresses the interrelatedness, the inseparability, of the doctrinal and poetical aspects of the poem.

9 "The nine Muses," overseers of all the arts (invoked by Dante in *Inf.* II, 7–9, and *Purg.* I, 7–12, and XXIX, 40–42), point out to Dante the Big and Little Bears—the constellations of Ursa Major and Ursa Minor. The former contains the Big Dipper, and the latter is identical with the Little Dipper, whose tail star is the North Star, or polestar, used by sailors in navigation (and usually located by following the line formed by the outer stars of the Big Dipper's bowl).

11–12 "the bread of angels": see 1–18, note. The inherent limits of the human intellect prevent it, in this life, from comprehending the Truth completely. Thus man's hunger for the bread of angels remains "unsatisfied." Only the beatific vision granted to the blessed in Paradise, and to the angels, can satisfy this hunger (cf. IV, 124–126).

16–18 "Those men of glory" were the Argonauts, who "crossed to Colchis" with Jason in quest of the Golden Fleece. Jason was encountered, and his exploits described, in *Inferno* XVIII, 82–96, and Dante will refer to his voyage again here, in *Canto* XXXIII, 93–96. The first of three trials that the king of Colchis imposed on Jason was that of taming a pair of fire-breathing oxen with sharp horns of iron and using them to plow a field. The story is told by Ovid (*Met.* VII, 100–148), but while in Ovid's account it is the men of Colchis who are amazed. Dante's version is more incisive in its likening Dante's "followers" to Jason's. The former, Dante says, will be more amazed than were the latter at Jason's exploit, when they see Dante mastering such formidable problems in theology and philosophy.

19–20 The "thirst for the godly realm" is "innate," created together with the intellective soul, and "everlasting," because, in life, insatiable. (Cf. VII, 142–144.) Dante, with Beatrice, is borne naturally upward toward "the godly realm" by his desire for it (see I, 139–141).

21 "as swiftly as the heavens that you see": i.e., "as swiftly as the heavens rotate about the earth," or perhaps more likely, "as quickly as you see the heavens," i.e., in the time it takes to scan their expanse, the mere wink of an eye. (Cf. X, 37–39.)

23–24 The events in the flight of a shaft or arrow shot from a crossbow are presented here in reverse order (a rhetorical figure called *hysteron proteron*), so that the arrow's flight is viewed beginning from the end, suggesting a teleological view, in which the aim or end is viewed as a cause. The effect reinforces the idea that Dante is being carried "as toward a destined place" (I, 124) (ultimately, the Empyrean, but first the moon). The *hysteron proteron*—which actually accords with experience, in that an arrow's flight, too quick to be perceived, is reconstructed by the mind in retrospect upon seeing the arrow strike—seems also to convey again tremendous velocity (cf. line 21).

30 "'the first star'": the moon, in the First Heaven (see Intro., p. xii, and diagram, p. 305). The term *star,* for Dante, includes the sun, the moon, and the planets, as well as the fixed stars.

31 The "brilliant, solid, dense, and stainless cloud" is the material of the moon itself, as conceived by Dante. In his *Monarchia* (*Monarchy,* III and IV, 17–18) Dante argues that the moon has a certain luminosity of its own, "as is evident in a lunar eclipse."

35–36 Dante (with Beatrice) is received into the body of the moon without its undergoing any displacement (as would, for example, a cloud)—a miraculous phenomenon anticipated by Dante's reference to the moon's solidity and density (32). (See 37–42, note.)

37–42 Presumably Dante did conceive his journey to Paradise as also corporeal (cf. I, 73–75 and note), so that his entering the body of the moon without its undergoing any displacement can only have been miraculous. (The fundamental scientific principle that two bodies cannot occupy the same space at the same time, is superable, according to St. Thomas, but only through divine miracle *[Summa theol. Suppl.,* q. 83, a. 3].) And this miracle should inflame still more our longing "to see that

Essence"—Jesus Christ—in whom divine nature and human nature were united, in the Incarnation.

43–45 "What we hold here by faith" is the miracle of the Incarnation; in Paradise it will be "directly known," as self-evident as the "first," or a priori, "truth."

49 " 'the dark marks' ": Having entered the very body of the moon, Dante wonders as to the nature of the lunar spots visible from the earth. Before answering Dante's question, Beatrice will elicit and then rigorously confute his own opinion. But her subsequent explanation of the true principle involved will far transcend the relatively minor problem of the lunar spots and comprise an explanation of the manner in which, from the timeless and spaceless Empyrean (" 'the heaven of the godly peace' " [112]), the power of God descends downward through the various heavens (" 'these organs of the universe' " [121]) and is shed as spiritual and material light upon the earth and upon the plurality of beings. This explanation, which complements that of Canto I on the tendency of all beings to move toward God (I, 98–141), will complete the grand preliminary overview given by Beatrice of the material and spiritual structure and operation of the universe.

51 " 'the tale of Cain' ": A popular belief in Dante's time held that the spots on the moon resulted from Cain's being confined there, condemned for all eternity to carry a bundle of thorns on his shoulders as punishment for slaying his brother Abel (cf. *Inf.* XX, 124).

52–57 Beatrice begins her response in a metaphorical mode characteristic of the highest medieval rhetorical style and appropriate to the elevated character of her discourse. Since reason cannot progress very far toward the truth even when considering physical phenomena—in which sense perception, "from which our knowledge begins" (*Convivio* II, iv, 17), provides material for the intellect—then Dante should not be amazed that where spiritual matters are concerned—in which the senses do not provide adequate (or any) material for the intellect—mortals' opinions fall into error.

59–60 Dante is expressing the opinion he had held when he wrote the *Convivio* (see II, xiii, 9)—an opinion derived perhaps from Averroës, but one that Dante had rejected by the time he was writing the *Paradiso*—namely, that the dark spots appearing on the surface of the moon result from the presence of materially rarer portions within the body of the moon that fail to reflect the sun's rays to the same degree as the denser parts. Beatrice will now refute (in lines 64–105) Dante the poet's former opinion, which was dependent upon physical causality, and advance the principles underlying his revised opinion (106–148), dependent instead upon spiritual causality.

64–66 The fixed stars, in the Eighth Heaven, differ in the quality and quantity of their light. Note that Beatrice begins her refutation by discussing differences in appearance between the fixed stars rather than between parts of the moon, the implication being that the underlying principle is the same.

67–73 Fundamental to Beatrice's argument is the medieval presupposition that the different stars are endowed with different " 'powers' " *("virtù"),* which they exert, by means of the light they shed, on the sublunar world. Beatrice argues that if the formal principle of rarity and density *alone* determined the essential nature and power of the stars, (and so, the differences in their appearance), then there would be only one power in all the stars, because *different* powers can arise only from *different* formal principles. Since different powers do exist, so must different formal principles.

73–78 Furthermore, " 'were rarity / the cause' " of the lunar spots, then either the rarity would extend through the entire thickness of the moon, or else rare and dense portions (" 'lean / and fat' ") would alternate in strata.

79–82 If the first of these hypotheses were true, then during a solar eclipse, when the moon is between the sun and the earth, the sun would be visible through the rare portions of the moon, as through any rare (" 'slender' ") matter. But " 'this is not so.' "

85–90 If the second hypothesis were true, then where rare matter ended and dense began, the sun's rays would be reflected, just as they are from the dense portions of the moon's surface.

89 " 'glass that hides lead at its back' ": a mirror.

91–93 Beatrice anticipates the possible objection, on Dante's part, that if the second of the two hypotheses were true, that might yet account for the lunar spots, since a ray reflected from within the body of the moon, rather than from its surface, will appear dimmer. But Beatrice proposes an experiment to rebut this objection.

95–96 " 'the source / of your arts' course springs from experiment' ": This idea, already present in Aristotle (see, e.g., *Metaphysics* I, 1), was familiar to the Scholastics as the basis for the "argument *per experimentum.*"

103–105 Although the image of the light reflected in the mirror placed farther back will be smaller than the images reflected in the two closer mirrors, it will be of the same brightness *per unit of size;* its quality of light will be the same.

106–108 The " 'sub-matter of the snow' " is water. Beneath the " 'warm rays' " of the sun, the water is stripped of the accidental (as opposed to essential) qualities of whiteness and cold that it had as snow.

112 " 'the heaven of the godly peace' ": the Empyrean, the heaven purely of " 'light and love' " (XXVII, 112). Beatrice begins here her exposition of the true principle underlying the phenomenon of the lunar spots.

113–114 The " 'body in whose power lies / the being of all things that it enfolds'" is the Primum Mobile, the Ninth or Crystalline Heaven, surrounded by the Empyrean and revolving within it with an "almost incomprehensible" swiftness (*Convivio* II, iii, 9). From the Empyrean a power is transmitted to the Primum Mobile, which, being uniform itself, transmits that power without differentiation to "'the sphere that follows'" (115).

115–117 "'The sphere...where so much is shown'" is the Heaven of the Fixed Stars, the Eighth Heaven, which receives the undifferentiated power transmitted by the Primum Mobile, and begins the process of differentiation, by distributing ("'bestow[ing]'") that power to its different stars.

118–123 The seven heavens below that of the fixed stars modify and further differentiate the powers transmitted downward to them so that they can properly exercise their influences over earthly things.

124–126 "'cross the ford alone'": i.e., apply the true principle behind the differences in appearance between stars, which Beatrice will reveal, to the question concerning the lunar spots ("'the truth you want'").

127–129 Just as the smith himself is the efficient cause of the "'hammer's art'" (e.g., in the forging of a tool)—the hammer being merely the instrument (or instrumental cause)—so "'the force and motion of the holy spheres'"—i.e., the entire process outlined by Beatrice (112–123)—has its efficient cause in (is "'inspired by'") the "'blessed movers,'" i.e., the Celestial Intelligences. As Dante writes in the *Convivio* (II, iv, 2), "the movers of those heavens are substances separate from matter, that is, Intelligences, which the common people call angels." (For the angelic orders, see XXVIII, 97–129.)

130–132 Beatrice now applies this principle of spiritual causality to the Heaven of the Fixed Stars, with which she began her argument (64). The "'deep Mind that makes it wheel'" is the Intelligence, or angelic order, presiding over the Heaven of the Fixed Stars, the Cherubim. The heaven is stamped (like wax with a "'seal'") with the knowledge and purposes of the Cherubim. And the "'force and motion'" (127) of the heaven are the means by which those purposes are effected.

133 "'your dust'": the human body. (See Gen. 3:19: "For dust you are and to dust you shall return.")

135 "'a different potency'": i.e., the particular function to which each of the "'different organs'" (134) is adapted.

139–141 Each "'different power'" imparted by the Intelligence is combined with a different star ("'dear body'"), which it "'quickens,'" or vivifies, much as the soul, bound to the human body, vivifies it; and each particular combination of power and celestial body forms a different "'compound,'" with properties particular to it.

142–148 "'Because of the glad nature of its source,'" i.e., the gladness of the Angelic Intelligences, which derives from the gladness of God (cf. *Purg.* XVI, 89), the power manifests itself as radiant light, shin-

ing (like gladness in the human eye) from the sphere with which it is
" 'mingled.' " But each " 'different compound' " has properties particular to it and therefore shines with a particular quantity and quality of
light.

145–148 The " 'differences from light to light' " (from star to star) derive from the diverse shining of different compounds. It follows, then
(though Beatrice has left it up to Dante to draw this conclusion
[124–126]), that the lunar spots result from the diverse shining of the
different compounds formed by the different parts of the moon mingled
with the power that " 'quickens' " (139) the moon—the parts of lesser
" 'worth' " shining less brightly.

CANTO III

1 Readers of the *Vita nuova* and of the *Purgatorio* will recall that
Dante was first visited by the warmth of love at the age of nine ("when I
had not yet left / my boyhood" [*Purg.* XXX, 41–42], when he first set eyes
on Beatrice, "the glorious lady of my mind" (*Vita nuova* II, 1).

2 "Confuting, proving": Beatrice's argumentative technique, as we
have had occasion to observe in the previous two cantos, is that typical
of medieval Scholasticism. The *questio* is first raised, false opinions are
refuted, then the true solution is proved. Dante uses and defends the
technique in his *Convivio* IV, ii, 16: "And this was the method followed
by the master of human reason, Aristotle, who always combatted the ad-
versaries of the truth first, and then, when they had been discomfited,
demonstrated the truth."

10–22 Dante is able to distinguish faintly the faces of the blessed in
the First Heaven, the Heaven of the Moon. In contrast, however, to the
spirits he had met in the previous two *cantiche,* whose appearance had
been so real as to lead him upon occasion to do as Statius had done—to
" '[treat] the shades as . . . solid things' " (*Purg.* XXI, 136)—the vision he
has of them is extremely attenuated and evanescent. Their contours are
no more marked than would be those of white pearls strung, as was then
the fashion, upon a woman's white forehead, to invite favorable comparison with her complexion. They appear to be faces reflected on an unsil-
vered pane of glass (rather than in a mirror), or on water too shallow to
give back a clear image. Dante is deceived into thinking that what he
sees are reflections, and he instinctively turns around, believing the actual faces to be behind him.

17–18 Ovid is once again Dante's probable source for the Narcissus
story. Narcissus, "the man [who] love[d] the fountain," seeing his own
face reflected in the pool, took it for the face of another (see *Met.* III,
407–510). Dante's contrary mistake is to believe the reality of the spirits—their "true substances" (29)—to be "merely mirrorings" (20).

30 Because of its monthly fluctuations, the moon has always been associated with mutability and inconstancy. In this, the lowest of the heav-

ens, Dante encounters the souls of those compelled by the violence of others to fall short of the vows they had made to God. In like manner, the souls he meets in the other planetary spheres—the glory-seeking souls in Mercury, the loving in Venus, the wisdom-seeking in the Sun, the war-like in Mars, the just in Jupiter, the meditative in Saturn—will illustrate the characteristic influence of the star.

43–45 That is, "Our charitable love cannot deny any just request, any more than God's love can." The entire canto is an enthusiastic celebra-tion of *caritas* (charity), or spiritual love.

46–51 Piccarda Donati was the sister of both Forese Donati—the friend of Dante's youth with whom he was reunited, among the glutton-ous, on the next to the last cornice of Purgatory—and the violent Corso Donati—the leader of the Black Guelphs (the faction opposed to Dante's party, the Whites), whose coming damnation Forese had prophesied (*Purg.* XXIV, 82–87). Forese had also assured Dante, who was related to the family through his wife, Gemma Donati, that Forese's lovely and good sister Piccarda was in Heaven (*Purg.* XXIV, 13–15).

50–54 Though they appear in the lowest and slowest sphere, the beati-tude of Piccarda and her companions is complete. They delight in what-ever place they are privileged to fill in the Divine Order. " 'The flame / that is the pleasure of the Holy Ghost' " is the flame of charity or spiri-tual love.

51 The Sphere of the Moon, being the smallest in diameter and closest to the center (the earth), moves more slowly in its revolutions than the outer spheres. (Cf. I, 76–78, note.)

69 Most commentators interpret "love's first flame" as referring to Divine Love, the love of the Holy Spirit, the "Primal Love" of *Inferno* III, 6. It could also point back, however, to the allusion to a first human love, Dante's love for Beatrice, with which the present canto began. The lan-guage of the canto, indeed, recalls at times the tender sweetness of the *Vita nuova* and the "sweet new style," a tone that characterized much of the language of *Purgatorio*.

70 Singleton points out that the vocative " 'Brother,' " used by the Apostles in their Epistles, is often used by the speakers in the poem to take the sting out of a lesson or correction.

70–72 Elsewhere, Dante explains in a similar fashion the paradox of an equal hierarchy among the blessed: "And this is another reason why the saints have no envy of one another, for every one attains the end of his desire, a desire commensurate with the excellence of his nature" (*Convivio* III, XV, 10).

85 Cf. St. Paul, Ephesians 2:14: *"Ipse enim est pax nostra"* ("For he is our peace") and St. Augustine's *Confessions,* XIII, 9: "In thy good will is our peace." " 'That sea / to which all beings move' " recalls " 'the mighty sea of being' " of Canto I, 113. This conjunction of love and of flowing toward peace suggests that the circumlocution used by Francesca da

Rimini in *Inferno* V, 97–99, to designate her birthplace ("'that shore / to which the Po . . . / descends to final rest'" [the Italian text has *"pace,"* "peace"]) was not casual. The love Francesca professed could never bring her to this peace.

95–96 For Singleton, the unfinished web, the cloth whose weaving had been interrupted, is Piccarda's account of herself, interrupted by Dante's question in line 58. For most other modern commentators, the metaphor refers to her broken vow.

98 The "'woman'" is the founder of the order of the Poor Clares, St. Clare of Assisi (1194–1253), a follower of St. Francis. We learn here that her soul is in a higher heaven, though Dante never actually meets her.

100–101 At the moment of her final vows, the nun enters into a mystical marriage as the bride of Christ.

102 "'All vows'" that are inspired by true charity and therefore in conformity with His will.

106–108 Piccarda was snatched violently from her convent by her brother Corso, who forced her to marry his henchman Rossellino della Tosa. Here Piccarda's charitable reticence resorts to a generic locution, "'men more used to malice than to good,'" avoiding the mention of her brother Corso's name.

118 The brightest of the souls in the Heaven of the Moon is Constance (1154–1198), daughter of Roger of Hauteville and last heir of the Norman rulers of Sicily. Dynastic pressures forced her to leave her monastery and marry the emperor Henry VI (1165–1197), the "'Swabian's second gust,'" son of Frederick Barbarossa. Their son, the emperor Frederick II, was the Swabian's "'third and final power.'" With him the Swabian (or Hohenstaufen) dynasty ended.

123 As the spirits, when they first appeared, had seemed to be reflected on water, so it is as if into water that they depart, presumably to return to their seats in the Empyrean.

CANTO IV

1–12 Piccarda's words in the previous canto have raised two doubts in Dante's mind, both of which are equally compelling. Thus, like Perseus (see *Met.* V, 164), Dante is uncertain and remains silent.

13–18 Daniel, inspired by God, interpreted Nebuchadnezzar's dream (Dan. 2:1–46), thus saving the lives of the wise men of Babylon, whom the king, enraged by their inability to interpret his dream, had ordered put to death. Similarly Beatrice, through divine inspiration, discovers and resolves Dante's doubts.

19–27 The first of Dante's doubts is: If the will to good remains constant, why should one's merit diminish before God because of another's violence? (See III, 106–108 and 115–117.) His second doubt, springing from the appearance within the moon of the souls of Piccarda and

Costanza, is whether Plato might not be justified in his assertion in the *Timaeus* that the creator of the universe had assigned the souls to stars, and that upon the body's death the soul returned to the particular star from which it came. This Platonic idea, in possibly suggesting an over-powering influence of the stars on human actions, threatens the crucial idea of the freedom of the will and although Marco Lombardo already explained that free will is not constrained by the stars' influence (*Purg.* XVI, 67–81 [cf. also *Purg.* XVIII, 46–75]), the importance of this idea is such that any doubt that threatens it is still "'insidious'" (27). Thus Beatrice treats Dante's second question first.

28–48 "'nor either John'": i.e., neither the Baptist nor the Evangelist. In truth, all the blessed souls, says Beatrice, reside in the Empyrean; they appear to Dante in the different spheres only to show him, a mortal, the degrees of their beatitude. Since all human knowledge begins from sense perception (see II, 52–57, note), "'such signs'" (40) are necessary for Dante if he is to grasp this purely spiritual truth. For this same reason the Scriptures ascribe to God feet and hands, and the Church represents in human figures the three Archangels, Gabriel, Michael, and Raphael ("'the angel / who healed the eyes of Tobit'" [see Tobit 3:16–17, and 11:1–15]). (Cf. *Summa theol.* I, q. 84, a. 1, 6; I, q. 3, a. 1, ad 3.)

49–63 Dante in these verses is reluctant to dismiss altogether Plato's theory of the souls returning to their stars. He suggests that Plato's words might have been intended figuratively, as meaning that what "'returns'" to the stars is the "'honor and blame'" (59) for their influence upon the human soul (an influence Dante of course admitted [see e.g., *Canto* XXII, 112–123, and *Purg.* XVI, 73]). It may be, therefore, that Plato's opinion is "'one to be derided'" (57).

73–87 Regarding Dante's first doubt (19–21), Beatrice explains that while Piccarda and Costanza were forced by violence, they did not op-pose that violence with an absolute will, that is, a will unconditioned by any external forces. Such a will, unremitting, is like a flame, which by its natural impulse shoots upward, "'though force—a thousand times—tries to compel'" (78) it otherwise. Thus, had Piccarda and Costanza ex-ercised an absolute will, they would "'have fled back to their holy shelter'" (81). In not doing so, their wills yielded somewhat and "'abet-ted [the] force'" (80) used against them.

Beatrice mentions two exemplary instances of "'whole'" (82), "'in-tact'" (87), unbending, absolute will, one drawn from Christian history and one from Roman pagan history: St. Lawrence, a deacon of the Church in Rome, was martyred in A.D. 258 by the emperor Valerian, who ordered him grilled alive on an iron grate. St. Lawrence is said to have mocked his persecutors by suggesting that they turn him so that he might be properly roasted. Caius Mucius Scaevola, a Roman citizen, failed in his attempt to kill Lars Porsena of Clusium, who was besieging Rome. Ordered by Porsena to be burnt alive, Mucius thrust his right hand into a nearby fire already lit for sacrifices and held it there unflinchingly as he explained to Porsena that one after another the Romans would try to kill

Porsena until they succeeded. In admiration for his fortitude and the Romans' determination, Porsena spared Mucius' life and ended his siege.

88–90 The " 'argument / that would have troubled [Dante] again,' " the argument concerning the apparent injustice of God (19–21), is thus quashed, " 'eliminate[d]' " (89).

91–99 " 'Another obstacle' " obstructs Dante's understanding of the truth that Beatrice has set forth concerning the will. Earlier, she made it quite clear to Dante that " 'souls in blessedness can never lie, / since they are always near the Primal Truth' " (see III, 31–33). Yet Piccarda has said that " 'the veil upon [Costanza's] heart was never loosed' " (III. 117). That assertion " 'seems to contradict' " Beatrice's words (82–87). And if Beatrice is right, Piccarda has spoken untruth. Beatrice will dissolve this " 'obstacle' " by explaining the distinction between the absolute will and the relative, or contingent, will.

100–105 Alcmaeon was the son of Amphiaraus, one of the seven kings who warred against Thebes. Amphiaraus foresaw his death in the war and tried to avert it by hiding from battle, but his wife Eriphyle betrayed him to his enemies (see *Purg.* XII, 50–51 and note). Before dying, he enjoined Alcmaeon to revenge his death by slaying his mother Eriphyle, and in order not to be remiss in filial devotion, Alcmaeon did so (see Statius, *Theb.* II. 265–305). As with Alcmaeon, " 'it has often happened' " that to avoid an evil considered greater, men have unwillingly committed evil acts. (Cf. Aristotle, *Nicomachean Ethics* III. 1.)

106–114 Absolute will is completely unyielding to evil, but " 'contingent,' " or relative, will consents, or yields, to evil out of fear that resisting evil " 'might bring greater harm.' " Thus, in failing to flee " 'back to their holy shelter' " (81), Piccarda and Costanza yielded somewhat to the violent force that took them from the cloister. Therefore, " 'no excuse can pardon' " them for not having fulfilled their vows. When Piccarda said that " 'the veil upon [Costanza's] heart was never loosed' " (III, 117), she was referring to Costanza's absolute will, while Beatrice is speaking of Costanza's relative will, without the consent of which, Costanza would not have remained away from the cloister. Thus there is no contradiction between Piccarda's and Beatrice's words.

115–117 Beatrice's divinely inspired explanation is "the holy stream / issuing from the fountain from which springs / all truth," i.e., from God, the " 'First / Lover' " (118–119).

126–138 The " 'truth beyond whose boundary no truth lies' " is the Truth of Divine Wisdom. In seeking the Truth, doubting is a natural process, spurring us on from truth to greater truth to Truth. Dante's understanding of the vital importance of doubting encourages him to voice a further question. He wants to know whether one can compensate for unfulfilled vows by the performance of other " 'good works,' " meritorious deeds.

CANTO V

1–3 " 'the fire of love' ": i.e., the ardor of Divine Love. The narrative here continues directly from the end of Canto IV.

5–6 " 'perfected vision' ": i.e., a vision partaking in Divine Wisdom, so that as the intellect apprehends the good, the will, perfected, moves immediately toward it. Nearing the good, the soul increases in love and so increases in its splendor (cf. XXVI, 28–36); thus Beatrice, flaming with Divine Love, " 'overcome[s Dante's] vision's force' " (3).

8 The " 'never-ending light' " is the light of Truth, of Divine Wisdom.

10–12 On the love of a " 'lesser thing' " see *Purgatorio* XVI, 85–93, and XVII, 91–102, and corresponding notes (cf. *Convivio,* IV, XII, 13–19, on the progress of the soul from the desire of lesser objects to ever greater objects and, finally, to the desire of the "highest object of desire, which is God").

13–15 " 'a promise unfulfilled' ": i.e., an unfulfilled vow. Beatrice is restating the question asked by Dante in Canto IV, 136–138.

19–22 In order to answer Dante's question, Beatrice will first explain the nature and significance of a vow (19–30). On the freedom of the will, see *Purgatorio* XVI, 67–81, and XVIII, 46–75.

23 " 'those beings that have intellect' ": humans and angels.

25–30 Not all vows are acceptable to God, for according to St. Thomas, since "God welcomes only virtuous actions... it is clear that one must not make a vow to perform any illicit or indifferent act, but only virtuous acts" (*Summa theol.* II–II, q. 88, a. 2). But the making of a vow accepted by God constitutes " 'a pact... drawn between a man / and God' " in which " 'a man gives up... his free will,' " that is, gives up his freedom to behave in any manner other than that prescribed by his vow, and does so " 'through free will,' " for a vow is "a voluntary promise" made to God (*Summa theol.,* ibid.).

32 To use that free will again would mean to violate one's vow.

35 " 'since the Holy Church gives dispensations' ": It is in the power of the Church to grant a release from the fulfillment of a vow.

37–39 The same metaphor of wisdom, or teaching, as food, opens Dante's *Convivio* (quoted in II, 1–18, note).

44 The " 'matter of the pledge' " is the particular obligation imposed by the vow.

45 " 'the formal compact' ": As Beatrice says (47–48), " 'it is of this' " that she has spoken " 'so precisely' " (in lines 25–30).

49–51 Under the Mosaic law (see Lev. 27), the Hebrews were obliged to make ritual sacrifices, but under certain circumstances " 'some of their offerings might be altered.' "

55–57 One must not substitute some "'other matter'" (54) for the original matter of one's vow "'through his own judgment,'" without ecclesiastical sanction. (For "'the white and yellow keys,'" symbols of priestly science, or wisdom, and priestly authority, see *Purg.* IX, 115–129 and notes.) According to St. Thomas, the Church, as the representative of God's authority, has the power to grant total dispensation from a vow, if it is judged that such a dispensation would serve some greater good (*Summa theol.* II–II, q. 88, a. 10). But Dante, reacting against abuses of the power of dispensation, dissents here, upholding the view that only the *commutation* of a vow is permissible, that is, a change in the matter of a vow.

58–60 The original obligation entailed by a vow must be clearly exceeded by the new obligation substituted for it.

61–63 "'when the matter of a vow...tips every scale, / no other weight can serve as substitute'": since none could constitute a clearly greater obligation. Beatrice is probably referring to the specific "'matter of a vow'" involved in the cases of Piccarda and Costanza (see III, 34–120), the vow of chastity, which, as St. Thomas concludes, is not subject to dispensation (*Summa theol.* II–II, q. 88, a. 11). (For Dante's figure of the scale, cf. Ecclesiasticus 26:20: "a chaste character cannot be weighed on scales.")

65–66 Jephthah was a judge of Israel who, during a war against the Ammonites, made a vow to Yahweh that in return for victory he would sacrifice the first person to greet him at the door of his house upon his return. This turned out to be his only daughter ("'his first gift'"). (See Judg. 11:29–40.)

67–68 "'by keeping faith'": i.e., by actually sacrificing his daughter, in fulfillment of his vow. According to St. Thomas, when a person has taken a vow to do something "which in the majority of cases is a good," but which in some particular case turns out to be "simply evil, or useless, or an obstacle to some greater good...it is necessary, in such a case, to decide that the vow is not to be observed" (*Summa theol.* II–II, q. 88. a. 10).

69–72 The "'Greeks' chief,'" Agamemnon, had once made a vow to the goddess Artemis that he would sacrifice to her the most beautiful thing born in his realm that year. But this turned out to be his own daughter Iphigenia, and he refused to sacrifice her. Years later, when the Greek fleet at Aulis was prepared to sail against Troy, persistent calm and unfavorable winds prevented the fleet's departure. The other Greek leaders placed the blame for this on Agamemnon's not having kept his vow and convinced him that the wrath of Artemis must be appeased by the fulfillment of that vow. Agamemnon relented, and "her fair face made Iphigenia grieve." Varying accounts of the episode appear in Ovid (*Met.* XII, 24–34) and Virgil (*Aen.* II, 164–166), but Dante's source for the version involving a vow that in a particular case turns out to be evil was probably Cicero (*De officiis* III, 25, 95).

71 "'the wise and . . . the foolish'": an expression still used in certain Italian dialects, meaning, simply, everyone.

73–74 That is, "Proceed with greater seriousness and consideration in the making of vows; do not be frivolous and easily moved to make ill-considered vows that are soon regretted."

75 That is, "Do not think that the making of vows is sufficient to wash away your sins," the way baptismal water washes away original sin, and holy water venial sin; or perhaps, "Do not think that you can be easily released from the fulfillment of your vows, and by merely any priest." The dispensation or commutation of certain vows requires the authority of a bishop, while only the pope can dispense from the most important of the dispensable vows (see *Summa theol.* II–II, q. 88, a. 12).

77 The "'shepherd of the Church'" is the pope.

80 "'like sheep gone mad'": turning this way and that in religious matters, following one another mindlessly.

81 "'so that / the Jew,'" regulating his behavior strictly by the Law, "'not deride you'" for capriciousness, not only in the making of vows, but in religious matters generally.

82–84 That is, "Do not abandon the spiritual nourishment of the Old and New Testaments and the guidance of the Church and its 'shepherd,' the pope, for in doing so, you 'war against' and 'harm' yourself spiritually." (Cf. XI, 124–131, where the "'sheep, remote and vagabond'" are Dominicans who have strayed from St. Dominic's rule.)

87 "to where the world is more alive with light": toward the higher, surrounding heavens and beyond, toward the Empyrean, the heaven of "'light and love'" (XXVII, 112).

93 "the second realm": the Second Heaven, that of Mercury.

96–97 In response to Beatrice's joy, even the planet—the immutable planet!—"grew more bright" and "changed and smiled."

105 In answering Dante's questions and helping him resolve his doubts, these souls will increase in their charity, in their love. And as Virgil explained to Dante in Purgatory, "'where there are more souls above who love, / there's more to love well there, and they love more'" (*Purg.* XV, 73–74).

106 "each shade": Here in the Second Heaven, the image of a corporeal figure is still just barely discernible within the "bright radiance" (107) issuing from and surrounding these souls.

115 "'O you born unto gladness'": cf. *Purgatorio* V, 59–60.

116–117 "'the thrones of the eternal / triumph'": the seats of the blessed, triumphing eternally in the Empyrean (see IV, 28–39.)

117 "'your war of life'": i.e., man's life on earth. Cf. Job 7:1: "Is not man's life on earth nothing more than pressed service [i.e., forced military service]." Those still fighting the war of life are contrasted with the triumphant blessed in Paradise. (Cf. XXV, 57.)

118–119 The "'light.../ which spreads through all of heaven'" is the light of divine love, or charity. Cf. the opening to *Paradiso* (I, 1–3).

123 "'trust them as you trust gods'": cf. III, 31–33.

124–126 "'how you have nested in / your own light'": i.e., how the soul surrounds itself with its effulgence, which issues "'from [its] eyes,'" and "glistens" more brightly as the soul smiles with gladness. Cf. Dante's words in the *Convivio* (III, VIII, 12): "Ah, marvelous smile of my lady, of which I speak, that never was felt, if not from her eyes!"

128 "'your rank'": i.e., the soul's assigned position in Paradise. But this position is only *apparent,* as Beatrice explained in IV, 28–39.

128–129 In the *Convivio* (II, XIII, 11), Dante notes that Mercury "is veiled by the rays of the sun more than is any other star." (Recall that Dante applies the term *star* to planets too [see II, 30, note]; and *planet* here refers to the sun.)

136–138 The image of a corporeal figure (see 106, note) is now "concealed," rendered invisible through the increased splendor of this soul, resulting from its increased gladness (cf. line 126).

CANTO VI

1–9 In A.D. 324, the emperor Constantine the Great transferred the seat of the Roman Empire from Rome to Byzantium (renamed Constantinople in A.D. 330). In doing so he "'turned the Eagle,'" emblem of the Empire, "'counter to heaven's course,'" that is, carried it from west to east, opposite to "'the course it took / behind'" Aeneas ("'the ancient one who wed Lavinia'") when Aeneas brought it from Troy ("'the peaks from which it first emerged'") to Italy. The seat of the Empire had remained in Constantinople ("'near Europe's borders'") for over two hundred years (from A.D. 324 to 527 [though according to the chronology of Brunetto Latini's *Trésor,* probably followed by Dante, the span was from 333 to 539]) when Justinian became emperor and reestablished the seat of the Empire in Italy, at Ravenna.

The imagery here—"'counter to heaven's course'"—expresses Dante's conviction that the so-called Donation of Constantine (a document now known to be inauthentic), by which Constantine had supposedly granted temporal power in the Western Empire to the pope, was the source of many of the evils of Dante's own time. (See *Inf.* XIX, 115–117 and note, and see "Dante in His Age," Bantam Classics *Inferno,* pp. 326–328.)

10–12 "'Caesar I was and am Justinian'": The contrast here makes clear that, as is true of every soul, Justinian's beatitude is according to his virtue, his individual merit, and not to the power or dignity that was his on earth. Justinian's most enduring accomplishment was the Codex Justinianus, a codification of the vast accumulated corpus of Roman law, from which, through the inspiration of the Holy Spirit, Justinian deleted all that was contradictory, superfluous, or simply no longer applicable in the context of the 6th-century Christian empire.

12–24 Justinian states that he was a follower of the Eutychian or Monophysite heresy, which attributed to Christ only the divine nature and not the human. He was converted to " 'that faith which has truth and purity,' " that is, to faith in the dual nature of Christ, by Agapetus (pope from A.D. 533 to 536); the truth of that faith is made all the more striking here by Justinian's expression which can be paraphrased as: "I see Christ's nature was both divine and human at the very same time, as clearly as you see that 'A' and 'not A' can *not* both be true at the same time." After Justinian's conversion, God " 'inspired [his] high task,' " the production of the Codex.

25–27 The famous general Belisarius (c500–565) was entrusted by the emperor Justinian with complete control of the army. Belisarius overthrew the Vandal kingdom in Africa and defeated the Goths in Italy, which enabled the foundation of the exarchate of Ravenna. Dante, casting Justinian and Belisarius as paradigmatic emperor and general, may have been unaware of Belisarius's having been unjustly accused of conspiracy against Justinian by jealous members of Justinian's court. According to popular tradition Justinian had Belisarius blinded and confiscated his property, but in fact, Belisarius was simply confined to his own palace until Justinian discovered the falsity of the accusation.

28–33 " 'with how much reason' ": Justinian's ironic words anticipate his explicit reproach (100–111) of both the Ghibellines (who had appropriated the eagle as emblem for their own banner) and the Guelphs (who opposed the imperial eagle). (See "Dante in His Age," Bantam Classics *Inferno,* pp. 322–323.) Justinian will proceed to a sweeping narration of the illustrious history of the Empire and the " 'great virtue' " (34) that " 'made that Eagle worthy / of reverence' " (34–35), the virtue of the men who founded, governed, and fought for it, from Aeneas to Charlemagne. Fundamental throughout is the idea that the Roman Empire had been divinely appointed to prepare the world for the advent of Christianity.

36 Pallas, son of the Latin king Evander, died in battle against Turnus while fighting for Aeneas, who in revenge killed Turnus (see *Aen.* X, 657–675, and XII, 1225–1270).

37–39 The kingdom of Aeneas was transferred by his son Ascanius from Lavinium (where it was founded) to Alba Longa. There it remained for three hundred years, until the three Roman Horatii defeated the Alban Curatii (" 'three . . . fought three' "). Thus Alba fell to Rome, though Dante, following Virgil, notes that the Albans and the Romans were both descended from the Trojans who came to Italy with Aeneas (see *Mon.* II, ix, 15).

40–42 During the era of the Roman monarchy (" 'under seven kings' "), the Eagle " 'conquered / its neighbors,' " steadily extending its dominion. The first Roman king, Romulus, in order to provide his people with wives, ordered the rape of the Sabine women, who had come to attend the public games. The seventh and last king, Tarquin the Proud, was driven out in 510 B.C. by the people, who were outraged by his rape of Lucrece, famous for her steadfast goodness and driven to suicide in her grief.

43–54 With the abolition of the monarchy, the period of the Roman Republic began. The Republic's continued and successful struggle against various enemies is now outlined by Justinian with the impetus of a swooping eagle. Lucius Quinctius Cincinnatus (whose name, *cincinnatus,* means "curly," rather than "disheveled locks," as was believed), a farmer called to the dictatorship, defeated the Aequians in 458 B.C. Brennus, leader of the Senonian Gauls who besieged the Capitol, was defeated in 390 B.C. by Torquatus (45) and one of the Fabii (48), a renowned Roman family. In 280 B.C. a member of another family, the Decii (47), defeated the Greek Pyrrhus, who had come to Italy to help the Tarentines in their fight against the Romans. The greatest of the Fabii, Quinctius Fabius Maximus, employed his famous delaying tactics to save Rome from Hannibal and the Carthaginians, who had crossed the Alps (from which the river Po descends) and successfully invaded Italy in 218 B.C. (Dante anachronistically refers to the Carthaginians as "Arabs," for in Dante's time the latter occupied what had been the Carthaginian territory.) Scipio Africanus the Elder, who as a boy of seventeen won fame by saving his father's life at the battle of Ticinus (218 B.C.), at age thirty-three forced Hannibal to withdraw from Italy through his counter invasion of Africa and then defeated Hannibal at Zama. Leaping ahead more than a century to 81 B.C., Justinian mentions the first triumph of Pompey, at age twenty-five, against the faction led by Marius. Next, " 'that standard,' " the eagle, " 'seemed most harsh' " to Fiesole, a hill town overlooking Florence (" 'that hill beneath / which you were born' "). According to legend, the Romans destroyed Fiesole when Catiline had taken refuge there.

55–57 Near the time ordained by God for the birth of Jesus Christ, so that through him man might be reconciled with God, Caesar came to power (" 'took up that standard' "). The idea of a single ruler was essential to Dante's conception of political harmony and order, and Dante, sharing a popular misconception of the Middle Ages, believed Caesar to have been the first Roman emperor.

58–60 Caesar's campaigns in Gaul are referred to with the names of five of the region's principal rivers and mention of " 'all / the valley-floors' " through which run tributaries that " 'feed the Rhone,' " another of Gaul's rivers.

61–63 In leaving Ravenna and crossing the Rubicon River (the border between Cisalpine Gaul and Italy) without permission of the Senate, Caesar exceeded the limits of his jurisdiction, thus provoking the civil war against Pompey (49 B.C.). The civil war, "even if deplorable, was necessary for the final success of the Empire" (Bosco-Reggio). (In *Inferno* [XXVIII, 96–102] Dante encountered Caius Curio, who "quenched the doubt in Caesar" about crossing the Rubicon.)

64–66 Caesar overcame Pompey's legates in Spain and followed Pompey to Durazzo (the modern Durrës, on the Dalmatian coast) in Thessaly. At Pharsalia, in Thessaly, Caesar decisively defeated Pompey's troops (in 48 B.C.). Pompey escaped to Egypt (where " 'the warm Nile' " runs) to the court of Ptolemy, who, hoping to win favor with Caesar, treacherously slew him (see 69).

67–68 Pursuing Pompey after the battle of Pharsalia, Caesar (bearing the eagle, still the subject of Justinian's discourse) detoured to the Troad in Asia Minor, to see the ruins of Troy (" 'where Hector lies' ") and the town of Antandros (near the river Simois) from which, after the Trojan War, Aeneas first set forth. (See Lucan, *Phars.* IX, 950–999, and Virgil, *Aen.* III, 7–10.)

69 Ptolemy XII, king of Egypt from 51 to 47 B.C., ruled jointly with his sister Cleopatra for three years, afterward expelling her. Cleopatra enlisted Caesar's help, and Caesar successfully invaded Egypt, granting Ptolemy's kingdom to Cleopatra. Ptolemy drowned while escaping from Caesar.

70–72 Caesar, bearing the eagle, next defeated Juba, king of the Numidians, who had been an ally of Pompey. Then Caesar returned to Spain where, at the battle of Munda in 45 B.C., Caesar defeated the sons and last followers of Pompey.

73–81 Augustus, the nephew of Caesar, " 'bore [the Eagle] next.' " Augustus defeated Mark Antony at Modena (43 B.C.) and Mark Antony's brother Lucius at Perugia (41 B.C.). In 42 B.C., with Antony as his ally at the battle of Philippi, Augustus defeated Brutus and Cassius (who had assassinated Caesar in 44 B.C.). Brutus and Cassius then both committed suicide (cf. *Inf.* XXXIV, 64–67 and note). Augustus finally defeated Mark Antony in 31 B.C. at Actium, after which Antony took his own life. Antony's lover, Cleopatra, rather than be taken to Rome as a captive, inflicted on herself the fatal bite of an asp (cf. *Inf.* V, 63). Having thus conquered Egypt for the Roman Empire (" 'reached / the Red Sea shore' "), Augustus was sole master of the entire Roman Empire, and under his rule universal peace prevailed, in token of which for only the third time in Rome's history, the gates of the temple of Janus, always kept open during wartime (since the god was presumed to be away with the army), were shut. This universal peace having been achieved, the world was at last prepared for the advent of Christ.

82–90 The third Caesar was Tiberius, under whose reign Christ was crucified, thus reconciling man with God, " 'avenging [God's] own wrath' " for Adam's original sin. In Dante's view, this is the solemnest recognition of the legitimacy and providentiality of Imperial Rome (see *Monarchy* II, xii–xiii). And all the deeds of the Roman emperors, all the power and conquests of Rome "'seem faint and insignificant'" compared to this event of man's redemption through Christ's Passion.

91–93 The destruction of Jerusalem by Titus in A.D. 70 and the subsequent diaspora of the Jews were considered by many to have been God's vengeance against the Jews for their part in Christ's crucifixion.

94–96 Charlemagne "'brought help'" to the Church when Desiderius, king of the Lombards, occupied papal territory in A.D. 773. Dante's leap from Titus to Charlemagne is significant in suggesting the continuity and the direct derivation of the legitimacy of the Holy Roman Empire (dating from Charlemagne) from the ancient Roman Empire.

97–102 "'Those [Justinian] condemned above'" (see 31–33) are the Guelphs and the Ghibellines. The Guelphs opposed the imperial eagle ("'the universal emblem'") with yellow (or golden) lilies, the emblem of the royal house of France, and the Ghibellines appropriated the eagle as the emblem of their own political faction. (See "Dante in His Age," Bantam Classics *Inferno,* pp. 322–323).

106 "'This new Charles'" is Charles II of Anjou, king of Naples from 1285 to 1309 and leader of the Guelph party in Italy. The "'claws that stripped / a more courageous lion of its hide'" are the claws of the imperial eagle.

109 "'The sons have often wept for a father's fault'": cf. Exodus 20:5 and Lamentations 5:7.

112–117 "'This little planet'": i.e., Mercury, in the Second Heaven. Here appear souls of those who acted righteously, but more for the sake of "'honor and . . . fame'" than from love of God ("'the true love'").

128–142 Romeo (or Romieu) of Villeneuve (1170–1250) was a minister and chamberlain to Raymond Berenger IV, count of Provence. The legend circulated in Dante's time, that Romeo had been a poor and humble pilgrim, who, on returning from his pilgrimage, stopped at the court of Count Raymond. The count quickly appreciated Romeo's virtue and wisdom, and before long appointed him minister. With prudence and sagacity Romeo succeeded in making each of Raymond Berenger's four daughters a queen, arranging their marriages to Louis IX (St. Louis) of France, Henry III of England, Henry's brother Richard of Cornwall, king elect of the Romans, and Charles of Anjou, brother to St. Louis. Certain barons of Provence, jealous of Romeo's influence with the count, accused him of maladministration of the count's treasure and incited Count Raymond to ask Romeo for an accounting. Seeing the count's ungratefulness, Romeo renounced his service, returned to him all but the few poor possessions with which he had come, and, in spite of the count's regretful protestations, departed, to no one knows where. A particular sympathy for the figure of Romeo is evident in Dante, himself a faithful servant of his city, who "'met ungratefulness.'"

CANTO VII

1–3 "Hosanna, holy God of hosts, superabundantly illuminating with your brightness the happy fires of these kingdoms!" This hymn sung by the soul of Justinian ("that substance" [5]), though Dante's invention and not an actual church hymn, recalls liturgical language (in particular, the *Sanctus* from the liturgy of the Mass: *"Sanctus Dominus Deus sabaòth... Hosanna in excelsis")* in mingling with its Latin three Hebrew terms: *Hosanna,* a shout of acclaim originally meaning "O save" (the cry with which the multitude greeted Christ as he entered Jerusalem on the occasion commemorated on Palm Sunday [see Matt. 21:9]); *sabaòth,* "hosts"; and *malacòth* (properly, *mamlacòth),* "kingdoms."

6 These "double lights" probably signify the twin ornaments of arms and laws, with which, according to the prologue of Justinian's *Institutiones,* imperial majesty must be adorned. They may, however, represent Justinian's imperial majesty and his beatitude or, simply, the lights common to all the blessed, the illumination of divine grace and the soul's own effulgence.

14 *"Be* and *ice":* the first and last parts of the name of Beatrice.

19–21 For the first of three times in this canto, Beatrice reads Dante's thoughts reflected in the Mind of God (cf. 52 and 124)—hence her " 'never-erring judgment' " (cf. IX, 19–21, 73–75, XI, 19–21, and XV, 61–63). In each case she voices Dante's doubts and questions and immediately instructs him in their resolution. The " 'question that perplexes' " Dante here is this: If Christ's crucifixion represented " 'just vengeance' " for man's original sin (as Justinian asserted in his discourse on the history and destiny of the imperial eagle [VI, 88–90]), how can that crucifixion " 'deserve just punishment,' " i.e., the destruction of Jerusalem by Titus and the subsequent diaspora of the Jews as punishment for their part in that crucifixion? (See VI, 91–93.) In other words, it would seem that if Christ's crucifixion was just, the punishment of the Jews must have been unjust.

25–27 Adam, " 'the man who was not born' " (having been created directly by God), " 'could not endure the helpful curb / on his willpower,' " that is, the injunction given him by God that "of the Tree of the Knowledge of Good and Evil you are not to eat, for on the day you eat of it you shall most surely die" (Gen. 2:17). (Cf. XXVI, 115–117.) As a result, not only Adam himself, but " 'all his progeny' "—all people—were damned.

30–33 " 'until the Word of God willed to descend' ": i.e., until the Incarnation, in which human nature, " 'sundered from / its Maker' " by original sin, was united with divine nature in the person of Christ, " 'the Word of God.' " (See John I.) " 'Where the nature... was united to His person' ": in the womb of Mary, where "the Word was made flesh" (John 1:14). This union of divine and human nature "came about *in the person, not in the nature*" (*Summa theol.* III, q. 2, a. 2). In other words, divine and human natures were both present in the unity of Christ's person, yet those natures themselves remained distinct.

35–39 Human nature, thus united to God in the person of Christ, " 'was good and pure,' " as Adam had been before the Fall. But human nature " 'in itself' "—i.e., by its own doing, through its own fault— " 'had been banished / from paradise, because' " in committing original sin it " 'turned aside / from its own path, from truth, from its own life' "—from God. Cf. John 14:6: "Jesus said: 'I am the Way, the Truth and the Life.' "

40–45 " 'measured by the nature He assumed,' " that is, insofar as He was *human,* Christ's crucifixion was a *just* punishment of mankind for original sin, yet insofar as He was *divine* (" 'if we regard the Person made to suffer' "), " 'none was ever done so great a wrong.' "

47 " 'God and the Jews were pleased by one same death' "—God, because that death (Christ's upon the Cross) atoned for man's original sin, and the Jews, because that death appeased their resentment and envy of Jesus. For that death "earth trembled" (see Matt. 27:51) from God's wrath at " 'so great a wrong' " (43), and at the same time " 'Heaven opened' " (48) to man, reconciled with God through Christ's Passion.

57 " 'this pathway' ": i.e., the Incarnation and Passion of Christ. (This question [56–57] is the subject of St. Anselm's *Cur Deus homo?*—which was probably an important source for the substance of Beatrice's answer [64–120].)

64–66 The Goodness of God is free of every passion opposed to Its own perfect Love, from the ardor of which springs creation, giving visible form to God's "eternal beauties." (Cf. XXIX, 13–18, and cf. Boethius, *Consolatione philosophiae* III, IX, $\overline{4}$–6: "No external causes impelled You to make this work from chaotic matter. Rather it was the form of the highest good, existing within You without envy.")

67–72 Those things created directly by God, without any intermediary causes (" 'immediately' ") are "everlasting" (for the image of the " 'seal' " and " 'imprint,' " cf. II, 130–132) and " 'fully free,' " not constrained by the influence of the heavens or any other natural causes. Beatrice will elaborate when she returns " 'to explain one point' " (121–148), to free Dante of an uncertainty turning on just this question.

76–77 " 'The human being / has all these gifts' ": namely, immortality (his soul having been created directly by God) and liberty (for though influenced by the heavens, he is " 'not constrained' " [71] by that influence [this crucial point was explained to Dante by Marco Lombardo in Purgatory (see *Purg.* XVI, 67–84)]).

79–81 As St. Thomas explains, "by sinning man forsakes the order of reason, and consequently falls away from human dignity, which consists in being free and in existing for himself, and he degenerates, in a way, into the slavish state of the beasts" (*Summa theol.* II–II, q. 64, a. 2). Sin makes man " 'unlike the Highest Good,' " so that " 'the Sacred Ardor' " (74) gleams less brightly in him.

83–84 The image of filling a void aptly expresses the critical point here, that the atonement for a sin must be commensurate with the gravity of that sin.

85–93 Man's dignities of immortality and liberty were lost when Adam (man's " 'seed' ") "sinned so totally." These " 'could never be regained' " without there taking place one of two things: God's pardoning man " 'through nothing other than His mercy' " (without requiring that justice be carried out), or man's proffering " 'payment for his folly,' " that is, making suitable and just atonement, commensurate with the gravity of his sin.

97–102 Adam and Eve had been assured by the serpent, "the day you eat it [the fruit of the Tree of the Knowledge of Good and Evil] your eyes will be opened and you will be like gods, knowing good and evil" (Gen. 3:5). Adequate atonement was thus impossible for man, because " 'no obedience, no humility / . . . could have been so deep' " that it could compensate for man's infinite presumptuousness in aspiring to the level of God.

103–120 God's " 'own ways' " are mercy and justice (cf. 91–93). But to restore to man the fullness of life lost in the Fall, it pleased God to proceed not by one only but by both His ways, thereby more greatly manifesting His Goodness. The pathway "God willed . . . for our redemption" (56–57), the Incarnation and Passion of Christ, satisfied at once the greatest liberalities of mercy and the strictest demands of justice—the former, in that God gave " 'His own self' " (116), in the Person of Christ, for the accomplishment of an atonement " 'man lacked the power / to offer . . . by himself' " (101–102), and the latter, justice, in that " 'the penalty the Cross inflicted' " (40) upon Christ justly punished man for original sin. Indeed, " 'every other means fell short of justice' " (118), since only the act of infinite humility whereby Christ became incarnate and suffered the Passion, could compensate for the infinite presumptuousness of man in committing original sin.

124–129 Beatrice perceives and voices an objection on Dante's part, that in spite of " ' "what has been said above," ' " i.e., that " 'all that derives directly from [the Godly] Goodness / is everlasting' " (67–68), it is yet apparent that the four elements, earth, water, air, and fire, although created by God, are not everlasting, but rather, together with all things made from them, " ' "come to corruption." ' " Beatrice's response and resolution of this objection fills the remainder of the canto.

130–138 The angels and the heavens and heavenly bodies were indeed created directly by God in the entirety of their being. But this is not true of the elements, for although their material had been created directly by God (matter in the absence of form being conceived of as the *potential* to receive form), they actually " 'receive their form from a created power,' " namely, from the heavenly bodies. These bodies, presided over by the Angelic Intelligences (see II, 112–138), " 'wheel about them [the elements],' " and have the " 'power to give form' " to the elements. Thus the elements do not derive, in the entirety of their being, " 'directly from [the Godly] Goodness' " (67). They are, therefore, neither everlasting nor free of the continued " 'influence of other things' " (72).

139–144 Shining downward as they " 'wheel about' " (137), and so exercising their influences—their " 'power to give form' " (138)—on the sublunar world, the stars and other heavenly bodies (" 'the holy lights' ") " 'draw forth' " the vegetative and sensitive souls of plants and animals (for plants the former only, for animals both) from appropriate mixtures of the elements. The human soul, however, is " 'breathed forth' " directly by God into the human fetus. (See Statius' explanation in *Purg.* XXV, 52–75 and notes.)

143–144 " 'who so enamors it / of His own Self that it desires Him always' ": cv. *Convivio* III, ii, 7, 9 (quoted in XXVI, 37–39, note) and *Convivio* IV, xii, 14: "the greatest desire of each thing, and the first given it by nature, is to return to its origin. And since God is the origin of our souls, who made them similar to Himself (as it is written: 'Let us make man in our image and likeness'), that soul most greatly desires to return to Him."

145–148 Not only the human *soul,* but human flesh as well, was created directly by God, when Adam and Eve were created (see Gen. 2:7, 21–22). Thus, since " 'all that derives directly from [the Godly] Goodness / is everlasting,' " (67–68), the human body and the human soul are both immortal. Man's physical death must, therefore, be followed, ultimately, by his resurrection.

CANTO VIII

1–3 In pagan times, when the world, as yet unredeemed by Christ, was "still in peril," it was believed that sensual or "frenzied love" was "sent down" by "Cyprian / the fair," i.e., Venus (who was believed to have arisen from the sea near the island of Cyprus), as Venus wheeled in the third epicycle (see note below). (Both the goddess and the planet are intended here, since it was believed that the influence of the former was communicated by the latter; in Dante's conception too, of course, "the rays of each heaven are the means by which their power descends to things here below" [*Convivio* II, vi, 9].)

2 In addition to the overall east to west movement of the heavens and the orbital movement of each planet around the earth, the Ptolemaic system postulated an epicycle, a small rotation of each planet around a point of its circumference, thus eliminating a discrepancy between the calculated and observed positions of the planets.

8–9 Virgil narrates how Cupid, taking the form of Ascanius, son of

Aeneas, was sent by Venus to Dido, who upon embracing him was wounded with a fatal love for Aeneas (see *Aen.* I, 946–962).

11–12 Venus is both a morning and an evening star (see *Convivio* II, xii, 13–14), rising above the horizon shortly before the sun does and setting on the horizon after sunset.

13–15 Beatrice, as we have seen, grows more beautiful the higher she ascends toward the Empyrean. (Cf. V, 94–96.)

17–18 "plainsong": i.e., medieval polyphonic song, in which, as long as the voices sound in unison, one is not readily distinguished from another; but when most of the voices stay fixed, while one sings melody ("comes and goes"), then that voice is heard clearly among the others.

22–30 "the heaven of the high Seraphim": the Primum Mobile, presided over by the Seraphim, the highest order of angels. "A *'Hosanna'* sounded": see VII, 1–3, note.

34–38 These souls, revolving in the Third Heaven, the Heaven of Venus (presided over by the third lowest order of Angelic Intelligence, the Principalities [" 'the celestial / Princes' "]), move in perfect harmony, united in their path (" 'one circle' "), their dance (" 'one circling' "), and their love and desire for God (" 'one thirst' "). In the opening line of his first canzone in Book II of the *Convivio,* Dante invoked the Angelic Intelligence that moves Venus (which, however, Dante believed at that time to be the Thrones, adhering to an ordering of the Angelic Intelligences proposed by St. Gregory [see XXVIII, esp. 97–102, note]).

49–57 The soul speaking to Dante is that of Charles Martel (born c1271), grandson of Charles I of Anjou. According to G. Villani (*Cronica* VIII, 13), Charles Martel spent about twenty days in Florence in 1294, while awaiting his parents' return from Provence. It was probably then that Dante and Charles formed the friendship expressed by Charles's words (in lines 55–57) and by his recitation of the opening line of Dante's canzone (37–38), which he had probably heard and admired at the time of their meeting. Charles Martel died only one year later, in 1295, at the age of twenty-four, and here says that had he lived longer, " 'much evil that will be, would not have been,' " referring to the misrule by the house of Anjou that led to the uprising called the Sicilian Vespers (see 67–75 and note), and to the "ill-rule" (76) by his own brother Robert (see 75–84 and notes).

58–63 To the west, or left, of the Rhone, below its confluence with the Sorgue, is the region of Provence. Had he lived, Charles Martel would have inherited Provence, which had been the dowry of Raymond Berenger's daughter Beatrice when she married Charles of Anjou, Charles Martel's grandfather (cf. *Canto* VI, 128–142, note, and *Purg.* XX, 61 and note).

Ausonia was an ancient name for Italy. " 'Ausonia's horn' " indicates the southern portion of Italy, specifically, the kingdom of Naples and Apulia, which lies to the south of the Tronto and Verde rivers (the latter is now called the Liri for three-fourths of its course and the Garigliano for its final reach to the Tyrrhenian Sea). The kingdom is designated here by three towns, Catona, Bari, and Gaeta, situated near its southern, eastern, and western borders, respectively.

64–66 In 1292 Charles Martel's mother, Mary of Hungary, had granted him the kingdom of Hungary, when the former king, Charles Martel's uncle Ladislaus, died without issue. Charles never actually reigned in Hungary, however, for his cousin Andrew seized the throne.

67–75 Trinacria is the ancient name for Sicily. Sicily, says Charles, would have been ruled by the descendants of Charles of Anjou and Rudolf of Hapsburg (Charles Martel's grandfather and father-in-law respectively), which is to say, his own descendants, if misrule by Charles I of Anjou had not provoked the popular uprising in Palermo in 1282, called the Sicilian Vespers, in which Charles I and the supporters of the house of Anjou were driven out, the crown passing to Peter III of Aragon.

75–81 Charles Martel's younger brother Robert (b1278) served as a hostage of the Aragonese in Catalonia from 1288 to 1295, in return for the release of his father, Charles II, taken prisoner in a naval battle near Naples. It was then that Robert first became acquainted with the Catalan noblemen who would later serve as his ministers and officers when he succeeded to the throne of Naples in 1309 and whose notorious avarice chroniclers of the period reported Robert to have adopted. Out of metaphor, Robert's " 'loaded boat' " is, presumably, the weight of responsibility of the kingship of Naples (already promised to him in 1300, the poem's supposed present).

82–84 Robert's avarice contrasts with the generous nature of his father Charles II (who was known for his liberality toward his subjects, notwithstanding his ancestor Hugh Capet's condemnation of his having "[sold] his daughter" for a large dowry [see *Purg.* XX, 79–81]; it may be, however, that the generous nature referred to here is that of Charles I). Charles Martel criticizes here Robert's use of mercenary soldiers, who aggravated the consequences of Robert's illiberality by concerning themselves primarily with " 'filling up their coffers.' "

91–93 Charles Martel's words (in lines 82–83) have given rise in Dante's mind to the question of how a good, or "gentle," seed can yield bad, or "harsh," fruit, in apparent contradiction to Jesus' words in Matthew 7:17–18: "A sound tree produces good fruit but a rotten tree bad fruit. A sound tree cannot bear bad fruit, nor a rotten tree bear good fruit."

97–99 The process outlined by Beatrice, in Canto II, of the " 'stage by stage' " (II, 122) transmission downward through the various celestial spheres (" 'these great heavens' bodies' ") of the power emanating from the Empyrean is the means by which God enacts His Providence in the world.

100–111 God provides not only for " 'the natures of His creatures,' " but also for their well-being, giving to each creature "the disposition to fulfill [its] place in the universal order" (Sapegno). Without this ordering and orchestration by God, the effects of the heavens' influences would be fragmentary and chaotic, not contributing toward a harmonious whole. But " 'that cannot be,' " for it would imply a defect in the Celestial Intelligences, and an imperfection in God, who created them.

113–114 " 'it is impossible / for nature to fall short' ": The term *nature,* here, includes both creating and created nature, that is, God and "natural" nature. Dante's formulation of this principle fundamental to Scholastic philosophy echoes Aristotle: "Nature never falls short in what is necessary" (*De anima* III, 14). (Cf. *Convivio* IV, xxiv, 10, and *Monarchy* I, x, 1.)

115–120 Society is a good for man, contributing to his welfare and happiness. Cf. Dante's " 'master' " (120), Aristotle: "Man is by nature a social animal" (*Politics* I, I, 2). Society depends upon the cooperative co-existence of people of different natures and " 'diverse duties' "—for "man has need of many things which no one is able to provide by himself" (*Convivio* IV, iv, 1).

122–126 Since society requires that people have diverse duties and tasks, their natures must be providentially ordained by God to predispose them toward those diverse tasks. Thus, one is meant to be a legislator, like Solon; another a warrior, like Xerxes; one a priest, like Melchizedek (Gen. 14:18); another an inventor, like Daedalus (" 'he who flew through the air and lost his son' " [see *Inf.* XVII, 109–111, note]).

127–132 The celestial bodies, as they revolve, exert their influences upon human natures and predispositions, thereby effecting God's Providence. But those influences (and so, human natures and predispositions) do not correspond to distinctions of family (" 'house' "). Thus it was that Isaac and Rebekah's twin sons Esau and Jacob were of two such different natures (see Gen. 25:22–28); and Quirinus, or Romulus, one of the founders of Rome, was of such humble origin that the Romans afterward claimed that his father had been the god Mars.

133–135 If Divine Providence did not " 'intervene' " to influence human natures, children's natures (" 'engendered natures' ") would always be like those of their fathers (" 'those who had engendered them' ").

136 Cf. 95–96.

139–141 In unfavorable circumstances (" 'discrepant fortune' ") natural dispositions cannot yield the results they should—just as a " 'seed outside its proper region' " will die, or at best grow poorly.

142–148 If the world would pay more heed to the natural dispositions of people, those dispositions would yield the proper results, and the world " 'would have its people worthy.' " The early commentators saw in Dante's examples of the failure to follow natural dispositions an allusion to Charles Martel's brothers Louis and Robert. Louis joined the

Franciscan Friars Minor and later became bishop of Toulouse. Robert, king of Naples after 1309, concerned himself with problems of theology and composed and recited at court a great number of sermons. Louis's being " 'more fit to gird a sword,' " may imply not that he was a born warrior, but that he would have made a better king (the sword being "almost an iconographic attribute" of kingship [Bosco-Reggio]) than his brother Robert, whom Dante condemned, through Charles Martel's words, in lines 75–84.

CANTO IX

1 There has been continuing disagreement, from the earliest commentators to the present, as to whether, in invoking "fair Clemence," Dante had in mind Charles's late wife, Clemence, who died in 1295, at only twenty-seven years of age, in the same epidemic as her husband, or his daughter, Clemence, married by the time of Dante's otherworld journey, to Louis X of France. A persuasive argument in favor of the wife is the use in the Italian text of the first name with the intimate possessive, *"Carlo tuo,"* rendered in the translation as "your dear Charles." Charles has of course "enlightened" Dante by explaining " 'how from a gentle seed, harsh fruit derives' " (VIII, 93).

2 Charles's "seed," his son and Clemence's, is Charles Robert (known in Italy as Caroberto), king of Hungary from 1308 to 1342. According to Dante, he was defrauded as rightful heir to the kingdom of Naples by his uncle Robert of Anjou, who succeeded to the throne in 1309, with the approval of the reigning pope, Clement V. (At the same time, the pope approved Charles Robert's Hungarian succession.) Dante thought Robert an ineffective ruler, but, as the eldest surviving son, he had in fact been designated as successor as early as 1296, by his father Charles II, Charles Robert's grandfather. Pope Boniface VIII, though unnamed, is once again the target of Dante's disapproval, since he supported the candidacy of Robert of Anjou.

3–6 Dante claims to have been sworn to secrecy by the soul of Charles Martel. This is why he cannot be specific regarding the "wrongs" that threaten Charles's family or about the "vengeance well-deserved" that will redress them.

25–30 In northeast Italy, between "Rialto," i.e., Venice (designated by the name of the largest of her islands), and the Alps (where the Brenta and the Piave rivers have their origin), lies the hill of Romano, where the family of Ezzelino III da Romano (1194–1259) had its stronghold. From there, the "firebrand" Ezzelino himself descended to conquer and lay waste the surrounding countryside. Popular legend attributed to the infamous Ezzelino's mother a dream in which she dreamt she would give birth to a flaming torch that would destroy the entire March of Treviso. (In *Canto* XII, 58–60, the poet will allude to a similar prophetic vision granted St. Dominic's mother.) Ezzelino (or Azzolino) was condemned among the Violent against their Neighbors in *Inferno* XII, 109–110.

31–33 Cunizza da Romano (c1198–c1279) was Ezzelino's sister, saved, like Piccarda Donati, while her brother was damned. Married for political reasons to Rizzardo di San Bonifacio, lord of Verona, she was abducted by the Italian troubadour Sordello (see *Purg.* VI, 58, *et seq.*), with whom she lived for several years. She subsequently eloped with Enrico da Bovio of Treviso, traveling far and wide in considerable style before returning to Treviso, where Enrico met with a violent death. Freed to marry again by the demise of her husband, Cunizza this time wed a Count Almerio (or Neimerio) di Braganza. The Paduan chronicler Rolandino, on whom we rely for the details of her life, speaks of a subsequent marriage of the widowed Cunizza to a Veronese nobleman, after the death of her disapproving brother Ezzelino in 1259. She would have been about sixty at the time. Whether or not Rolandino was gilding the lily, it is clear that Cunizza was very much under the influence of the planet Venus. Jacopo della Lana, the author of one of the earliest commentaries on the *Comedy* (published 1324–8), remarks: "She was a woman in love in all her ages, and so generous in her love she would have counted it great villainy to refuse it to any man who sought it courteously."

34–36 Cunizza pardons in herself her abundantly amorous disposition, which, although it made her a figure of scandal in her early life, was directed in later life toward God and earned her a seat in Heaven. Like the other blessed souls, she is perfectly content with the place alotted to her and does not grieve. Vulgar and censorious minds find the salvation of so exuberant and impetuous a lover hard to fathom. The 14th-century commentator Benvenuto da Imola (d1387), however, stressed the compatibility of sacred and profane love and the positive, charitable side of Cunizza's temperament: "a true daughter of Venus, she was always amorous and desiring . . . and at the same time she was full of pity, kind, merciful, and compassionate toward the poor wretches whom her brother so cruelly afflicted."

37 The " 'precious jewel' " is another blessed soul, that of Folco (or Folquet) of Marseilles (d1231), a famous Provençal love poet who later became a Cistercian monk and ended his life as bishop of Toulouse.

39–40 Folco's earthly fame will last another five hundred years from the present centennial year 1300. The expression is not intended to be restrictive and implies simply that he will be famous for centuries.

41–42 Folco is an example of how by seeking excellence in this world a man can live on, as it were, after his physical death, through the fame he leaves behind. It has been objected that this concern for earthly fame is not entirely appropriate for a soul in Heaven (especially after Oderisi's strictures on temporal fame in *Purgatorio* XI, 82–117), for whom eternal salvation should be the touchstone of all actions. Dante's present concern, however, is with rebuking the corrupt inhabitants of the March of Treviso (which lay between the Adige and the Tagliamento rivers), a " 'rabble' " (43) who never aspired to nobility or fame.

46–48 Cunizza's prophecy most likely alludes to the bloody punishment that fell upon the Paduan Guelphs, who obstinately refused to recognize the authority of the emperor Henry VII. They were routed in 1314 by the imperial vicar Cangrande della Scala (to whom the *Paradiso* is dedicated), allied with the Ghibellines of Vicenza. The Bacchiglione River runs through Vicenza before it reaches Padua.

49–51 The Sile and the Cagnano rivers meet at Treviso. Rizzardo da Camino, arrogant despot of Treviso from 1306 until his death, was attacked from behind and killed in 1312, as he was playing chess, by a peasant with a billhook, no doubt the agent of his noble rivals.

52–54 Alessandro Novello, bishop of Feltre from 1298 to 1320, treacherously handed over to Pino della Tosa, representative of King Robert and the pope, in Ferrara, a group of conspiratorial refugees from Ferrara who had placed themselves under Novello's protection. Along with their associates, the Ferrarese victims, thirty in all, were publicly beheaded.

61–63 That is, "We who are blessed feel ourselves authorized to speak of God's judgments in this way because we are privileged to behold His justice reflected in the angelic order of the Thrones."

71 "down below": i.e., in Hell.

77–78 The "'pious fires'" are the highest of the angelic orders, the Seraphim (in Hebrew, "ardent," "burning"), who are associated with charity or love, as the Cherubim are with wisdom. The Bible pictures them with six wings, with which they cover themselves as with a hooded cowl: "Above him stood seraphs, each one with six wings: two to cover its face, two to cover its feet, and two for flying" (Isa. 6:2).

82–87 The "'widest valley'" of water, the largest sea in the hemisphere of land, is the Mediterranean, the *Mare Magnum,* spread between the "'discrepant shores'" of Africa and Europe. (The other hemisphere contains "'the sea that girds the world,'" with the island mountain of Purgatory at its center.) Curiously, medieval geography saw the Mediterranean as extending eastward for a full ninety degrees, ending under the meridian of Jerusalem, from which point the zenith of the Strait of Gibraltar (where the sea began) lay on the horizon. The first part of this speech made by Folco of Marseilles, a poet praised by Dante in his *De vulgari eloquentia* for his mastery of rhetorical construction, is appropriately composed of solemn and learned circumlocutions and is reminiscent, for instance, of the elaborate diction of the chancellor poet Pier della Vigna in *Inferno* XIII.

88–90 It is as if Folco, from his heavenly vantage point, were gradually zeroing in on Marseilles, his birthplace. This second step toward locating his native city places it on the northernmost of the Mediterranean's "'discrepant shores,'" somewhere between Spain (where we find the river Ebro) and Italy (where the Magra formed the boundary line between the territories of Genoa and Tuscany).

91–93 Another of the coordinates, Bougie, in North Africa, lies on the same meridian as Marseilles. The place of Folco's birth is finally designated by an historical allusion, usually taken to refer to Brutus' naval siege of the rebel city in 49 B.C. (Cf. Lucan, *Phars.* III, 572–573.)

97–102 Three examples of extreme love: Belus' daughter was Dido, whose fatal love for Aeneas was an offense to the memory of both her dead husband Sychaeus (to whose ashes she had vowed fidelity), as well as Aeneas' late wife Creusa (cf. *Inf.* V. 61–62 and note). The Thracian princess Phyllis, believing that her lover Demophoön, son of Theseus and Phaedra, had deserted her, hanged herself and was changed into an almond tree. She is called *"Rhodopeia Phyllis"* by Ovid (*Heroides* II, 2), after the Rhodope Mountain range where she lived. Heracles (or Hercules), grandson of Alcaeus (whence the Greek patronymic Alcides), carried off Iole from her home in Thessaly. To win back his love, Hercules' wife, Deianeira, sent him the tunic of Nessus, which instead caused his death (see *Inf.* XII, 67–69, note).

103–105 These souls died repentant and made reparation for their sins in Purgatory. Immersion in the river Lethe, in the Earthly Paradise, canceled all recollection of their faults. Now they rejoice in God, who predisposed them for salvation.

115 The harlot Rahab hid in her house the two messengers from Shittim sent by Joshua to spy out the land of Canaan and the city of Jericho. Because she helped them escape, she and her family alone were spared when the Israelites took and destroyed the city and its inhabitants (see Josh. 2:1–21 and 6:17). For St. Paul, Rahab was an example of salvation by faith: "It was by faith that Rahab the prostitute welcomed the spies and so was not killed with the unbelievers" (Heb. 11:31); while for St. James she illustrates salvation by good works (see James 2:25).

117–120 Rahab, the brightest light and "'highest rank[ing]'" soul in this order of beatitude, was the first of the souls of the pre-Christian elect to be taken up into the Heaven of Venus, when they were liberated from Limbo at the time of Christ's Harrowing of Hell (see *Inf.* IV, 52–61 and note). According to the astronomers Ptolemy and Alfraganus, the Earth casts a cone-shaped shadow on the three lower heavens. The tip of that shadow reaches as far as the Heaven of Venus. Dante interprets this supposed shadow in a moral and spiritual dimension, as indicating that the blessed in the first three heavens were too much influenced by earthly considerations.

126 That is, "Pope Boniface VIII appears to have no further thought for the liberation of the Holy Land," which had been usurped by the Saracens. This rebuke recalls the invective of *Inferno* XXVII, 85–93, and introduces a further attack on the corruption of the Church.

127–129 Dante's native city of Florence, he insinuates, sprang from a seed planted by Lucifer (or Satan) the emperor of Hell, who, out of envy for Adam and Eve, led the revolt of the rebellious angels against their Maker.

130   The coin of Florence, the florin, bore on one of its faces the imprint of a flower, the Florentine lily.

133–135   The spiritual message of the Gospels and the great theological writings of the early Christian Fathers are neglected in favor of the Decretals, the collections of decrees and decisions issued by the popes and the Church councils. The extensive annotations in the margins of these latter texts (along with the lack of such annotations in the former) attest to their regrettable popularity. The Decretals formed the basis for the Church's claims to temporal dominion, as well as for the privileges enjoyed by the Church hierarchy—both abuses virulently opposed by Dante.

136–142   The pope and his cardinals neglect the lesson of humility implicit in the New Testament scene of the Annunciation at Nazareth, where the Archangel Gabriel bowed his head with wings outstretched in adoration before the future mother of Christ. But soon, Folco prophesies, the Vatican hill, where St. Peter was crucified and buried, and the rest of Rome, sacred to the memory of the early Christian martyrs, will be rid at last of the simoniacal adultery of these evil shepherds. In the final line of the canto, the Italian word for " 'adultery' " is " 'avoltero,' " recalling the *"avolterate"* of *Inferno* (XIX, 4), in the canto of the Simonists.

CANTO X

1–6   Cf. St. Thomas: "To create belongs to God according to His being, that is. His essence, which is common to the three Persons. Hence to create is not proper to any one Person, but is common to the whole Trinity" (*Summa theol.* I, q. 45, a.6). God the Father ("the Power—first and inexpressible"), gazing upon His Son (His Word, or Wisdom) with the Love that is the Holy Spirit, made all creation—the spiritual and the material—in such perfect harmony and order that he who contemplates creation cannot but admire its Creator. In emphasizing that the Holy Spirit emanates from both the Father and the Son, Dante adheres to the Roman Catholic position in the controversy that had led to the severing of the Greek and Latin churches in the Great Schism of 1054.

7–21   Dante, drawing the reader to contemplate the divine perfection of the universal order, invites him or her to "gaze directly" at the constellation Aries, in which the point of the spring equinox lies. This is one of the two points (the other is the point of the autumn equinox) where the celestial equator (the plane of revolution of the heaven's diurnal east to west motion) and the ecliptic (the plane of revolution of the heaven's annual west to east motion) intersect ("where the one motion strikes against the other"). There one readily sees the obliquity of the path of the zodiac—the band eighteen degrees in width, within which are contained the orbits of the sun and all the planets—as it forms an angle of twenty-three and a half degrees with the celestial equator at their point of intersection ("cross-point"). Without this obliquity there would be no seasonal variation (consider, for example, how the lower position of the sun in the sky during winter results in shorter days and lower temperatures), and the generative cycle of plants could not take place; furthermore, the powers ("virtue[s]") of the stars and planets, dependent, for their effect, upon the heavenly bodies' properly varying positions, would be largely wasted. On the precise path of the stars and planets depends "earth's harmony," the perfect regulation of the seasons, which "would be defective" if the zodiac were more or less oblique.

23–27   "that of which you have foretaste": namely, Divine Wisdom and the harmony of Creation. For the metaphor of wisdom as food, cf. Cantos II, 1–18, note and XXIV, 4–5, note.

28–33   "The greatest minister of nature" is the sun, which, of all the celestial bodies, exercises the greatest influence upon the earth and, with its diurnal movement, determines day and night and "provides the measurement for time." Since the sun was in Aries, the time of year of Dante's journey was, as we know, spring, when the sun rises earlier each day, and farther northward, thus tracing a spiral path from day to day.

34–39   "I was with him": i.e., in the Fourth Heaven, the Sphere of the Sun.

40–42   Dante perceives these soul-lights not because their color is different from that of the sun, but because they are brighter than the sun!

49–51   God's "fourth family," the spirits who appear within the Fourth Heaven, the Sphere of the Sun (cf. IV, 28–39), are the spirits of the wise. These souls' desire for wisdom is at last fully satisfied, for to them God grants an understanding of the greatest mystery of the Christian faith, that of the Trinity.

53   " 'The angels' Sun' ": i.e., God. In the *Convivio* (III, xii, 7) Dante writes: "No object of sense in all the universe is more worthy to serve as a symbol of God than the sun, which, with sensible light, illuminates first itself, and then all the celestial and elemental bodies; and just so, God illuminates, with intellectual light, first Himself, and then the celestial and other intelligible creatures."

62–63   Dante's love for God, causes the "splendor of [Beatrice's] smiling eyes" to become more dazzling still, catching some part of Dante's attention, so that his mind is "divided . . . between two objects."

67–69   "Latona's daughter" (and Jove's) is Diana (see *Purg.* XX, 130, note), who is identified with the moon. The "crown" (65) of lights is likened to a halo that sometimes forms around the moon in misty air.

70–7   In Paradise there are many things of such beauty and sublimity that they cannot be re-presented by description here on earth. (Cf. I, 4–7.)

74–75   He who does not live in a manner that earns him a place in Paradise, where he may hear the song of those splendors himself, should not expect to have even the least idea of its indescribable and inconceivable beauty. For the image of "tak[ing] wings," cf. Isaiah 40:31.

77   "three times," in celebration of the Trinity.

83   " 'true love' ": i.e., the love of God.

86–87   Since " 'none / descends who will not climb that stair again,' " this soul is implying that Dante's salvation is assured. (Cf. *Purg.* XXXII, 101–103 and note.)

88–90   Charity is as natural to the souls of the blessed as flowing downward is natural to water. Thus these souls are no freer to refuse to quench Dante's thirst for knowledge, than water would be to " 'not flow toward the sea.' "

94–99   The soul addressing Dante identifies himself as a member of the Dominican order. (His words—" 'the path where one / may fatten well if one does not stray off' "—will be amply explained in Canto XI, in response to Dante's uncertainty.) A student of his fellow Dominican (" 'my brother' ") Albert of Cologne (see 98–99, note), he is none other than Thomas Aquinas, the most famous of the Scholastic theologians and philosophers, known as the Angelic Doctor. Born in 1225 at Roccasecca near Aquino in northwest Campania, the son of the count of Aquino and kin to several of the royal houses of Europe, Thomas Aquinas was educated first at the nearby Benedictine monastery of Monte Cassino and then, till the age of sixteen, at the University of Naples. In 1243 he joined the Dominican order and went to Cologne to study under Albertus Magnus. In 1257 he became a doctor of theology at the Sorbonne in Paris, and from 1261 to 1264 served in Rome as papal theologian for Urban IV. In 1269 he again taught in Paris, where he opposed Siger de Brabant (see 136–138 and note), and in 1272 taught at the University of Naples. Summoned by Pope Gregory X in 1274 to participate in the Council of Lyons (intended to reconcile the Greek and Latin churches), Thomas Aquinas undertook the journey but died of illness along the way, having stopped at the Cistercian monastery of Fossanova. (He was unjustly rumored to have been poisoned at the behest of Charles of Anjou [see *Purg.* XX, 68–69].) He was canonized in 1323 (two years after Dante's death).

St. Thomas's great reconciliation of Christian and Aristotelian thought was accomplished in his *Summa theologica.* He wrote, in addition, the *Summa contra gentiles,* as well as commentaries on most of the works of Aristotle, and on the works of other theologians.

98–99   Albert of Cologne, St. Albertus Magnus, was born of noble parents in Lauingen, in Swabia (c1193). He joined the Dominican order in 1223 and studied in Paris, Padua, and Bologna, afterward teaching in Cologne, Hildesheim, Freiburg, Ratisbon, Strasbourg, and Paris. In 1254 he was elected provincial of the Dominican order at Worms and was appointed bishop of Ratisbon in 1260. He died in Cologne in 1280, at the age of eighty-seven. Albertus was among the first to seek to reconcile Aristotelian thought with Christianity. A voluminous writer, his works include commentaries on Aristotle, the Scriptures, Dionysius the Areopagite (see 115–117 and note), the *Sentences* of Peter Lombard (see 106–108 and note), as well as his *Summa theologica,* a *Summa de creaturis,* a treatise on the Virgin, and various scientific works, one of which is on alchemy.

103–105 St. Thomas now introduces the other soul-lights making up the "'holy wreath'" (102). Next to Albertus Magnus is Gratian (Franciscus Gratianus). Born in Tuscany near the end of the 11th century, Gratian, a Benedictine monk, wrote the *Concordia discordantium canonum*, known as the *Decretum Gratiani*, in which (drawing on the canons of the Apostles and the councils, the Decretals of the popes, Scripture, and the patristic writings) he reconciled the ecclesiastical and secular laws and firmly established the basis of canon law.

106–108 Peter Lombard was born near Novara, circa 1095, and studied in Bologna and Paris, where he was sent with a letter from Bernard of Clairvaux, and where he later taught theology at the school of the cathedral. Appointed bishop of Paris in 1159, he died either in 1160 or 1164. His greatest work, the *Libri sententiarum quatuor* (*Sentences*), principally an organized collection of the sayings of the Church Fathers, became the standard textbook in schools of theology and was widely commented upon.

In his preface to the *Sentences,* Peter Lombard likens his work to the offering of the poor widow: "As [Jesus] looked up he saw rich people putting their offerings into the treasury; then he happened to notice a poverty-stricken widow putting in two small coins, and he said, 'I tell you truly, this poor widow has put in more than any of them; for these have all contributed money they had over, but she from the little she had has put in all she had to live on' " (Luke 21:1–4).

109–114 "'The fifth . . . and . . . fairest light'" is the soul of Solomon, son of David and king of Israel, who "'breathes forth such love'"—the love that went into composing his Song of Songs, interpreted allegorically by Christian exegetical tradition as an expression of the mutual love between Christ and His Church. "'All the world below / hungers for tidings'" of Solomon, since theologians were divided on the question of his damnation or salvation. In Solomon "'such profound / wisdom was placed'"—Proverbs, Ecclesiastes, and the Book of Wisdom were all attributed to him—that, Thomas says, "'no other ever rose with so much vision.'" In Canto XIII Thomas will amply elucidate these words in response to a doubt they raise in Dante's mind.

115–117 He who "'beheld most deeply / the angels' nature and their ministry'" is Dionysius the Areopagite, an Athenian converted to Christianity by St. Paul (see Acts 17:34). The *De coelestia Hierarchia* (*On the Celestial Hierarchy*) was erroneously attributed to him in the Middle Ages (see XXVIII, 97–102, note). (He will later be referred to as Pseudo-Dionysius in these notes.)

118–120 "'That champion of the Christian centuries'" is probably

Paulus Orosius the historian. A Spanish priest, born in the late 4th century, Orosius was the author of a universal history, the *Historiarum adversus paganos,* in which he countered the pagan charge that the world had deteriorated under Christianity. Orosius was encouraged in his work by St. Augustine, who saw in Orosius's *History* confirmation of the ideas in his own *De civitate Dei (The City of God).*

123–129 Within the eighth light is the "'blessed soul'" of Boethius (Anicius Manlius Severinus Boethius), Roman statesman and philosopher, born circa A.D. 480. Famed for his virtue and wisdom and honored and entrusted with high offices by Theodoric, king of the Ostrogoths (then in control of Italy), in 525 Boethius was unjustly accused by jealous enemies of plotting against Theodoric, who had Boethius imprisoned and later cruelly put to death. The writings of Boethius were of tremendous importance for the transmission of late classical learning and culture in the Middle Ages. His last and most famous work, composed while he was in prison, the *De consolatione philosophiae (On the Consolation of Philosophy),* was of particular importance to Dante after the death of Beatrice (see *Convivio* II, xii, 2). In that work Philosophy, personified as a gracious and beautiful woman, argues that only virtue is secure and "'makes the world's deceit / most plain.'" In the Middle Ages, Boethius came to be regarded as a martyr for the Christian faith and, though never canonized, is revered as St. Severinus. His tomb is in the basilica of San Pietro in Ciel d'Oro (Cieldauro) in Pavia.

131 St. Isidore of Seville (c560–630), archbishop of Seville in 600, was the author of a vast and extremely influential encyclopedia of medieval learning, the *Etymologiarum sive Originum libri XX,* as well as the *De ecclesiasticis officiis (On the Ecclesiastical Offices)* and the *Libri sententiarum,* on dogmatic theology and ethics.

The Venerable Bede (674–735), an Anglo-Saxon monk born at Monkwearmouth in county Durham, wrote—among many other works—the *Historia ecclesiastica gentis Anglorum (Ecclesiastical History of England)* and is considered to be the father of English history.

131–132 Richard of St. Victor, probably a native of Scotland, was among the greatest of the 12th-century mystics. From 1162 till his death in 1173 he was prior of the famed Augustinian monastery of St. Victor in Paris. A fierce opponent of rationalism, his writings (several of which are dedicated to his friend Bernard of Clairvaux) include commentaries on portions of the Old Testament, the Epistles of Paul, and the Book of Revelation, and works on theology and on mystical contemplation. The latter earned him the title Magnus Contemplator, reflected in Dante's words, "'he / whose meditation made him more than man.'"

136–138 Siger de Brabant (c1225–c1283), a professor in the Faculty of Arts at the University of Paris (located in "'the Street of Straw'" [Rue du Fouarre, today called Rue Dante]), was a leading proponent of the Averroist interpretation of Aristotle (see *Purg.* XXV, 61–66, note) and became a central figure in the fierce controversy that arose concerning the teaching of Aristotle and Averroës. In 1269 St. Thomas (here placed next to Siger) was sent to Paris to combat the Averroist doctrines of Siger and others, and in 1270 Siger's teaching was officially condemned by the archbishop of Paris, Etienne Tempier. Anathematized again in 1277 and summoned before the inquisitor Simon du Val, Siger fled to Rome to appeal to the pope (probably without success). According to tradition, Siger was stabbed to death by a demented servant in about 1283 at Orvieto.

139–142 The "Bride of God" is the Church, which, at dawn, sings matins to "her Bridegroom," Christ, "encouraging / His love."

CANTO XI

1–12 From the height of the Heaven of the Sun, too far away to be affected, as were the three lower heavens, by the shadow cast by the earth (see IX, 117–120, note), Dante views with superior detachment the bustle of human activity and the error of those whose lives (virtuous or vicious as they may be by earthly standards) are directed toward merely practical ends. Here, at the center of the crown of lights formed by the great thinkers of the near and distant past, the contemplative delights of pure intellectual speculation are seen to transcend by far, not only the despicable rewards of violence, fraud, sensuality, and indolence (6–9), but also the goals of an acceptable professional career (law, medicine, the priesthood, politics [4–6]). Dante's condemnation of "syllogistic reasonings" is not, of course, an outright condemnation; indeed, Aquinas and the other medieval followers of Aristotle (to say nothing of the poet himself, principally in the *Convivio* and the *Paradiso)* made almost exclusive use of this quintessentially Scholastic form of argument. Nor is Dante's recognition of the unsatisfactory nature of an exclusively earthbound existence tantamount to a total repudiation of the active life. It is fitting, however, that a canto almost wholly devoted to the eloquent celebration of the mystic faith of St. Francis of Assisi should begin by pointing out the dangers of an excessive reliance on human reason. (Cf. 40–42, note.)

22–27 St. Thomas Aquinas, reading Dante's perplexity, will offer two corollaries or explanatory footnotes to his discourse in the previous canto. The first will make explicit his implied reservation concerning the present corrupt tendencies of the Dominican order (cf. X, 94–96), the second, for which we will have to wait until Canto XIII, will quash possible objections to the declared preeminence of Solomon (X, 109–114).

28–36 Divine Providence sent two "'princes'" to hearten and guide His medieval Church. The Church (the sum of all the faithful) is the metaphorical Bride of Christ. Christ wedded the Church through the covenant of His precious blood, shed for mankind in His Passion. Christ's death was accompanied, according to three of the Evangelists, by "'loud cries'" (see, e.g., Mark 15:37).

37–39 The prince "'seraphic in his ardor'" was St. Francis of Assisi (1182–1226), founder of the Franciscan, or Minorite, religious order;

the other, who "'possessed / the splendor of cherubic light,'" was St.
Dominic, founder of the Order of Preachers, or Dominicans. The
Seraphim and the Cherubim, the two highest angelic orders, symbolize,
respectively, ardent love and knowledge.

40–42   There had been considerable discordance throughout the 13th
century between the Franciscan and Dominican orders, the Franciscans
retaining a basically Augustinian perspective, which viewed rational reflection as posterior to, and an explication of, faith—a perspective felt to
be threatened by the rise of the Aristotelianism (propagated, most no-
tably, by the Dominican Thomas Aquinas) according to which reason
might formulate the premises of theology (see Tullio Gregory, "Filosofia
e Teologia Nella Crisi del XIII Secolo," *Belfagor* XXI, Jan. 1964, pp.
1–16). A spirit of grand conciliation, then, underlies Dante's envisioning
of the amicable praise by St. Thomas, a Dominican, for St. Francis,
which will be reciprocated (in Canto XII) by the Franciscan St.
Bonaventure's praise of St. Dominic.

43–48   The site of Assisi, where Francis was born, lies on the hillside
below the "'high peak'" of Mount Subasio, between the Topino River,
which empties into the Tiber, and the Chiascio (a tributary of the
Topino), which flows down from the hill chosen by the saintly Ubaldo
(bishop of Gubbio, 1129–1160) as the site of his remote hermitage.
From this eastern quarter, Perugia, across the valley, receives its most intense summer heat and bitterest winter cold (on the side of the city
where the gate known as Porta Sole [Sun Gate] was situated). Assisi itself lies in the lee of the mountains, unlike the nearby hill towns of
Nocera and Gualdo, which lie over the crest exposed to the "'hard
yoke'" of the prevailing winds. The solemn allusive eloquence, modeled
on classical geographical circumlocutions, recalls the self-presentations
of Charles Martel (VIII, 58–70), Cunizza (IX, 25–30), and Folco of
Marseilles (IX, 82–93). It will find an exact parallel in the rhetorical des-
ignation of St. Dominic's birthplace in Canto XII, 46–54.

49–51   St. Francis, the author of a "Hymn to Our Brother the Sun," is
often compared to a spiritual sun in Franciscan devotional literature. The
real sun (referred to as "'this sun'" because Dante is within its sphere)
is at its most resplendent "'when it is climbing from the Ganges,'" i.e.,
from the point on the horizon that in Dante's cosmology marks true east.
It rises there at the vernal equinox.

52–54   A lofty pun on the place-name *Assisi,* usually written *Ascesi* in
Dante's Tuscan Italian. The past perfect of the verb *ascendere, ascesi,*
means "I rose," or "I ascended." By a kind of folk etymology, Dante
reads the name as prophetic of an ascent, or rising, to take place there.
But considering the importance to the Christian world of the "sun" who
dawned there, it would be more appropriate, Dante says, to rename it as
the absolute "'Orient.'"

55–59   Francis was still a youth when, in 1206, he gave the first signs of
his vocation, turning from the world into which, as the son of a well-to-

do merchant, he had been born, to embrace an ascetic life of loving self-sacrifice.

58–63 The " 'lady unto whom, just as to death, / none willingly unlocks the door' " is (as is made explicit in line 74) the allegorical figure of Lady Poverty. In repudiating his former wealth, Francis contracted a symbolic marriage with Poverty. Francis's father, Pietro Bernardone, perturbed by his son's rash donations to the poor, took him before the episcopal court of Assisi to compel him to renounce his claim to his inheritance. Not only did Francis gladly do so, but he went so far as to strip off the clothes he was wearing, before the court and *" 'coram patre' "* ("in his father's presence"), and don a sackcloth garment, in uncompromising obedience to the evangelical precept of poverty. And Francis "said to his father: 'Until now I have called you father here on earth, but now I can say without reservation, Our Father who art in heaven [Matt. 6:9] since I have placed all my treasure and all my hope in him' " (St. Bonaventure, *The Life of St. Francis [Legenda Maior]*, II, 4).

64 Poverty's " 'first husband' " was Jesus Christ.

67–69 The reference is to Lucan's account (*Phars.* V, 515–531) of the meeting of Caesar (" 'he / who made earth tremble' ") and the fisherman Amyclas, whose extreme poverty made him unafraid of Caesar's foraging and plundering legions. Lucan's moralizing reflections on the advantages of indigence (echoed in line 82) are quoted at length in *Convivio* IV, xiii, 11–12. Not even the security from thieves and predators that she confers has sufficed to make men choose Poverty.

70–72 Neither did the constancy with which Lady Poverty stood by her " 'first husband,' " Christ (who died on the cross stripped of all He had, including His garments), win her many followers.

78 The first of Francis's disciples (all of whom went discalced, or barefoot, in imitation of Christ's Apostles) was the wealthy and influential merchant Bernard of Quintavalle, who sold all he owned to follow the saint, donating the proceeds to the needy.

83 Egidius of Assisi (known in English as the Blessed Giles) and Sylvester were two other early followers of Francis and of the rule of poverty.

85–87 In late 1209 or early 1210 Francis and his monks left Assisi for Rome to seek papal approval of his order. Dressed in coarse sackcloth, they girded their loins with a plain rope, a symbol of their rejection of earthly finery.

93 Innocent III's verbal approval of the new order (1210) and his granting of permission to preach on moral (but not dogmatic) issues, constituted the first "seal," or confirmation, of three granted to the order.

98 The second " 'seal' " (or " 'crown' ") came with Honorius III's solemn recognition of the Franciscan order by papal bull in 1223.

100–105 In 1219 Francis, with twelve of his followers, accompanied the army of the Fifth Crusade to Egypt, where he attempted to convert the sultan al-Malik al-Kámil to Christianity. The sultan, " 'too unripe / to be converted,' " nevertheless granted Francis and his followers safe passage back.

107   The " 'final seal' " was conferred, not by the Vicar of Christ, but by Christ Himself. In 1224, on the " 'naked crag' " (106) of Mount Verna in the Tuscan Apennines, St. Francis was visited with the Stigmata, the five wounds of Christ's Passion (the wounds of the nails in His hands and feet, and the wound of the centurion's lance in His side), bleeding wounds that St. Francis bore for the remaining two years of his life.

117   Like Christ, faithful to his "bride" till the very last, as death approached, Francis asked to be taken to the remote church of the Porziuncola, where, at his request, his disciples stripped him and laid him naked on the bare earth to die.

118–139   After the eloquent "digression" in praise of St. Francis, St. Thomas Aquinas returns to speak of his own order and to elaborate on the first of the two points from his previous discourse that called for clarification—the phrase " ' "They fatten well" ' " (25).

118–119   The " 'colleague / worthy of Francis' " is St. Dominic (see 28–39, notes). The " 'bark [or boat] of Peter' " is the Church.

125   The " 'new nourishment' " sought by the erring members of the order has been variously interpreted to mean the pursuit of ecclesiastical benefices or that of profane studies.

137   The " 'splinters on the plant' " refer metaphorically to the corruption of the Dominican order.

CANTO XII

1   "the blessed flame": the soul of Thomas Aquinas.

2–3   "the millstone / of holy lights": the souls of the twelve great thinkers introduced in Canto X.

7–9   The song of the souls surpasses in sweetness—as a direct light surpasses in brightness its reflection—even the songs of the Muses (the nine sister divinities who presided over the arts) and the songs of the Sirens (mythological creatures, half woman, half bird, who, from the rocky islands where they dwelt, lured sailors to destruction with the enchanting sweetness of their song).

10–13   Juno's "handmaid" is Iris, goddess of the rainbow. (Cf. *Aen.* IV, 964–966.) The secondary rainbow sometimes seen outside, or surrounding, a primary rainbow was believed in Dante's time to be a reflection or "echo" of that primary inner rainbow.

14–15   The "wandering nymph" is Echo, daughter of Earth and Air, who was consumed by her love for Narcissus, till only her voice remained (see *Met.* III, 339–510).

16–18 "the pact God made with Noah": God set the rainbow in the clouds as a sign of the Covenant He established with Noah: "There shall be no flood to destroy the earth again." (See Gen. 9:8–17.)

32–33 The soul speaking to Dante is that of St. Bonaventure, a Franciscan mystic and one of St. Francis's foremost hagiographers (see 127–129, note), who will eulogize " 'the other leader,' " St. Dominic, just as St. Thomas, a Dominican, did St. Francis (XI, 43–117), for " 'in praising either prince one praises both' " (XI, 41). (See XI, 40–42, note.)

37 " 'Christ's army,' " humanity, which had lost its defense against evil when Adam and Eve succumbed to Lucifer's temptation, was rearmed at so dear a cost—Christ's sacrifice upon the cross.

39 "its ensign": the Cross.

39–41 God " 'helped his ranks in danger' " of damnation, by giving His Son to accomplish man's atonement (cf. VII, 28–33). And this God did " 'only out of His grace and not [man's] merits' " (cf. VII, 97–120).

42–45 " 'as was said, . . .' " in XI, 28–39.

46–51 " 'gentle zephyr' ": Zephyrus, the west wind, which was believed to bring with it the spring. St. Bonaventure's circumlocution designates Spain, at the western extreme of Europe. In spring, the sun (as seen from Italy) appears to set behind the western coast of Spain.

52–54 Calaroga, or Caleruega, in old Castile in Spain, was the birthplace of St. Dominic (c1170). The coat of arms of the king of Castile bore on one side a lion above a castle, and on the other, a castle above a lion. Thus the lion " 'loses and prevails.' "

55 " 'the loving vassal / of Christian faith' ": St. Dominic. The "holy athlete": i.e., a champion of the faith. St. Bonaventure uses the same term to describe St. Francis, in his *Legenda maior* (II, 2).

58–60 It is recounted that before St. Dominic's birth his mother dreamed that she gave birth to a black-and-white dog holding a torch in its mouth, with which it set the world on fire. Black and white became the colors of the Dominican habit; the torch symbolized the zeal of Dominic's preaching.

61–63 Through baptism (" 'at the sacred font' "), Dominic wedded Faith (just as Francis had wed Poverty [XI, 61–63]), receiving salvation from that Faith, and destined to bring salvation to it.

64–66 St. Dominic's godmother had a dream in which Dominic appeared with a bright star on his forehead, symbolizing the great work that he and " 'his heirs,' " the Dominicans, would do in guiding and illuminating the world.

67–71 Through divine inspiration his parents gave him the name Dominicus (the possessive of *Dominus*), meaning "of the Lord."

71–72 Christ's " 'garden' " is the Church.

71–75 Note, in the Italian, that Dante will rhyme the name *Christ* only with itself (see XIV, 104–108, XIX, 104–108, and XXXII, 83–87, in the Italian).

73–75 The " 'first injunction Christ had given' ": This may refer to the First Beatitude of the Sermon on the Mount: "How happy are the poor in spirit; theirs is the kingdom of heaven" (Matt. 5:3); or perhaps to Christ's words in Matthew 6:25–34 (with which the description of Dominic in lines 76–78 accords); or (with " 'first' " understood as "first in importance") to Christ's words to the rich young man: "If you wish to be perfect, go and sell what you own and give the money to the poor, and you will have treasure in heaven; then come, follow me" (see Matt. 19:16–22). St. Dominic's early biographers relate that during a famine he sold his clothes and books to help feed the poor.

79 Dominic's father's name, Felice, means "happy." His mother's name, Giovanna, is from the Hebrew *Johana,* meaning "the grace of God," or "full of grace," as Dante would have found " 'asserted' " (81) in the medieval lexicons. Thus, as the parents of Dominic, both are appropriately named.

83 " 'Taddeo's way or Ostian's' ": The former is probably Taddeo d'Alderotto (c1215–1295), founder of a famed school of medicine in Bologna and author of numerous works, including philosophical commentaries on Hippocrates and Galen. The latter is Enrico Bartolomei (da Susa) (c1200–1271), cardinal bishop of Ostia from 1261 until his death and the author of a famous commentary on the Decretals that became a standard text in the medieval schools of law. Those who " 'travail / along . . . Ostian's [way]' " are those who neglect the study of Scripture and the patristic writings, studying instead the Decretals (worthy of reverence in themselves, but no substitute for the former). In the *Monarchia,* Dante especially condemns those who, "ignorant in every kind of theology and philosophy," base on the Decretals their support of the Church's claims to temporal power. (Cf. XI, 4–5.)

84 " 'the true manna' ": i.e., spiritual knowledge, Divine Wisdom. (Cf. *Purg.* XI, 13.)

86–87 Dominic began to oversee the Church (" 'the vineyard' "), caring for it and nourishing it with true doctrine. (Cf. Jer. 2:21.)

88–90 The " 'seat that once was kinder to / the righteous poor' " is the papacy. Dante draws a sharp distinction between the papacy as an institution (as sacred as ever) and the degeneracy of the pope (Boniface VIII), under whom it has " 'gone astray.' "

91–96 Dominic, in Rome in 1205, did not ask the pope for permission to retain for himself part of the money intended for the poor (" 'to offer two or three / for six' "), nor did he ask for the first fat benefice that fell available, nor for the right to apply the tithe that belongs to God's poor (*" 'decimas, quae sunt pauperum Dei' "*) to his own purposes. Rather, he pleaded for the right to preach against heresy—in particular, against the Albigenses (members of a Manichaean sect in southern France), whom he strove to convert to the true faith, " 'the seed from which / there grew' " the twenty-four men of wisdom whose souls, in two rings, surround Beatrice and Dante.

97–102 " 'where the thickets of the heretics / offered the most resistance' ": Provence, in southern France, where the Albigensian heresy was most widely diffused. Dominic's " 'force' " (100), however, was confined to his zealous and learned preaching; he neither took personal part in nor advocated the violent persecutions of the Albigenses.

103 " 'the streams' ": i.e., the followers of St. Dominic.

106–111 The " 'one wheel' " is St. Dominic, " 'the other wheel' " is St. Francis. The imagery in these lines seems perhaps more appropriate to St. Dominic, though as Nardi points out, Francis, too, through his example, battled corrupt and avaricious prelates.

112–117 Just as Thomas, following his praise of St. Francis, reproached the members of his own order, the Dominicans, for straying from the right path, so Bonaventure here, his praise of St. Dominic complete, rebukes the Franciscans for falling into corruption and for abandoning or retrogressing on the path St. Francis established.

118–120 That is, "Those Franciscans who have deviated from Francis's true path will soon weep to find themselves denied a place in the kingdom of heaven." Cf. Matthew 13:30: "Let them both grow till the harvest; and at harvest time I shall say to the reapers: First collect the darnel and tie it in bundles to be burnt, then gather the wheat into my barn."

121–126 " 'our volume' ": i.e., the Franciscan order, whose members are the volume's leaves or pages. Matteo d'Acquasparta was general of the Franciscan order from 1287 until his death in 1302. Made a cardinal by Pope Nicholas IV in 1288, he was sent by Pope Boniface VIII to Florence in 1300, ostensibly to make peace between the White and the Black political factions, but covertly to strengthen Papal influence in Florence (see "Dante in His Age," Bantam Classics *Inferno,* p. 324). As general of the Franciscans, he advocated certain relaxations of the Rule prescribed by Francis. These relaxations were vehemently opposed by Ubertino da Casale, leader of the Franciscan Spirituals. Under Pope Clement V the Spirituals prevailed, and it was then, in 1305, that Ubertino wrote his *Arbor vitae crucifixae Iesu,* a work undoubtedly known to Dante. In 1317, with the condemnation of the Spirituals by Pope John XXII, Ubertino transferred to the Benedictine order. Nevertheless accused of heresy (in 1325), Ubertino fled, and of his life afterward, nothing is known.

127–129 Only now does Bonaventure identify himself. Born Giovanni di Fidanza in 1221 at Bagnorea (Bagnoregio) near Orvieto, he joined the Franciscans in 1243 (or 1238) and in 1257 became general of the order. He declined the archbishopric of York in 1265 but in 1273 was appointed cardinal and in 1274 bishop of Albano. He died later that year at the second Council of Lyons. "'In high offices,'" Bonaventure says, he always gave priority to spiritual matters over temporal matters ("'left-hand interests'"). ("Wisdom, like other spiritual goods, belongs to the right hand, while temporal nourishment belongs to the left, according to Proverbs 3:16: 'In her left hand are riches and glory'" [St. Thomas, *Summa theol.* I–II, q. 102, a. 4, ad 6].) The greatest of St. Bonaventure's mystical-philosophical works, the *Itinerarium mentis in Deum (The Journey of the Mind to God),* was well known by Dante, and his numerous other writings include a famous life of St. Francis. Canonized in 1482 by Pope Sixtus IV, he was given the title Doctor Seraphicus by Sixtus V.

130–132 Bonaventure now identifies the other eleven soul-lights forming the outer ring. Illuminato da Rieti and Augustine of Assisi were two of St. Francis's earliest followers. Illuminato accompanied Francis to Egypt when he preached before "'the haughty Sultan'" (XI, 101); Augustine became head of the Franciscan order at Terra di Lavoro in 1216.

133 Hugh of St. Victor (c1097–1141) was among the great mystical theologians of the 12th century. Born near Ypres in Flanders, in 1115 he entered the monastery of St. Victor in Paris, of which he was appointed prior in 1133, and where, from 1130 until his death, he taught theology. Among his numerous works, much admired by St. Thomas, are the *Didascalicon* (an encyclopedia of the sciences, seen from a theological standpoint) and the theological treatise *On the Sacraments of the Christian Faith (De sacramentis Christianae fidei).*

134–135 Peter of Spain (Petrus Juliani), born in Lisbon (c1226), pursued his father's profession, medicine, before being ordained a priest. Appointed archbishop of Braga in 1273 and cardinal bishop of Frascati in 1274, he was elected pope in 1276, taking the name of John XXI. He died at Viterbo in 1277 when a ceiling in the papal palace collapsed. His *Summulae logicales* (a treatise on logic, in "'twelve books'"), notable for its treatment of certain issues in logic from a grammatical point of view, became widely popular in medieval schools.

135 Peter Book-Devourer (Petrus Comestor), an omnivorous reader, was born at the beginning of the 12th century in Troyes. In 1164 he became chancellor of the University of Paris and canon of the monastery of St. Victor, where he died in 1179. Of his many works, the most famous is the *Historia scholastica,* a history of the world up until the time of the Apostles, drawn principally from the Bible.

136 Nathan the prophet was sent by God to rebuke David for arranging the death of Uriah the Hittite so that he might take Uriah's wife Bathsheba for his own. (See II Sam. 12:1–15.) Anselm, one of the greatest theologians and philosophers of the Middle Ages, was born at Aosta in Piedmont in 1033. In 1060 he joined the Benedictine order and became abbot of the monastery of Bec in Normandy in 1078. In 1093 he was appointed archbishop of Canterbury, where he died in 1109. The most famous of his many works is the *Cur Deus homo?* on the necessity of the Incarnation (see VII, 57, note).

136–137 St. John Chrysostom (from the Greek, meaning "golden-mouthed"), so named for the great eloquence of his preaching, is one of the foremost fathers of the Greek Church. He was born at Antioch (c345) and became metropolitan (primate) of Constantinople in 398. Exiled for his public criticism of the empress Eudoxia (403) but immediately recalled in response to the ensuing revolt of the people, he was then (in 404) exiled again and died in 407.

137–138 Aelius Donatus, famed Roman scholar and grammarian of the 4th century, was the teacher of St. Jerome. His *Ars grammatica* became the standard textbook of Latin grammar ("'that art which comes first'" in the medieval trivium, followed by rhetoric and logic).

139 Rabanus Maurus, born at Mainz in 776, was educated at the Benedictine monastery at Fulda, of which he was later abbot from 822 to 842. From 847 till his death in 856, he was archbishop of Mainz. Renowned for his learning, he left numerous works of biblical exegesis and theology.

140–141 Joachim of Flora was born c1145 at Celico in Calabria. A Cistercian monk, in 1177 he reluctantly accepted the abbacy of the monastery of Corazzo in Calabria and in 1189 founded a new monastery, San Giovanni in Fiore, in the forest of Sila in the Calabrian Mountains. Joachim greatly influenced the Franciscan Spirituals with his doctrine, derived from mystical interpretation of the Bible, that the dispensation of the Father (the Old Testament) and that of the Son (the New Testament and the Church) would be followed by a dispensation of the Holy Spirit, corresponding to a coming period of perfection and freedom. A number of Joachim's ideas were condemned by the Church in 1215 and again in 1245, and Dante's placing him among the blessed demonstrates "both the independence of his judgment, and his desire for the renewal of the Church that Joachim had preached" (Casini-Barbi). Among the critics of Joachim's ideas and of the Franciscan Spirituals influenced by him was Bonaventure, whose praise of him here (like Thomas's of Siger, in Canto X, 133–138) springs from Dante's spirit of grand conciliation (cf. XI, 40–42, note).

142 "'such a paladin'": i.e., St. Dominic, the "'holy athlete'" (56).

143–144 "'the glowing courtesy and the discerning / language of Thomas,'" in praising St. Francis (in XI, 43–117).

CANTO XIII

1–21 So that he may form some idea, however inadequate, of the "double dance" (20) of the souls encircling Dante and Beatrice at this point, the reader is invited to imagine the twenty-four brightest stars of the firmament brought together into two concentric but oppositely wheeling circles of twelve stars each. The twenty-four stars comprise: all fifteen of the stars classified as stars of the first magnitude by Ptolemy and Alfraganus, so radiant they are able to penetrate any perturbation of our atmosphere (4–6); the seven stars that make up the constellation of Ursa Major, always visible in the northern hemisphere (7–9); and the two brightest stars of Ursa Minor (10–12). The shape formed by the latter constellation is interpreted as representing a horn of plenty, with the North Star, or polestar, as its tip and the two stars referred to by Dante at its mouth. The last nine stars, incidentally, are placed in the second order of magnitude by Dante's sources. The North Star forms the axis around which the "first wheel" (12) of the heavens, the Primum Mobile, revolves.

14–15 The daughter of Minos and Pasiphae, Ariadne, was not herself transformed into a constellation. According to Ovid (*Met.* VIII, 174–182), it was her floral crown that Bacchus immortalized among the stars.

22–24 The same proportion exists between heavenly truth and our ability to grasp it as between the slowest moving of rivers, the Chiana, little more than a stagnant swamp in Dante's time, and the Primum Mobile, the swiftest moving of the heavens.

25–27 The hymn that accompanied the celestial dance was no pagan Bacchic chorus, no paean to Apollo, but a sacred hymn in praise of the Holy Trinity and the hypostatic union of the two natures ("the divine and human") in Jesus Christ.

32 "the very light": St. Thomas.

34–36 The stalk already threshed (the problem discussed) is Thomas's first corollary (see XI, 22–27 and note), on the seeds of corruption within the Dominican order. The stalk yet to be threshed concerns Thomas's assertion, in Canto X, that " 'no other' " (X, 114) ever had wisdom as great as Solomon's.

37–39 The objection Thomas attributes to Dante could be stated syllogistically as follows: All " 'light' " (wisdom) is directly infused into His creatures by God (" 'that Force' "). But God created directly only Adam and Christ. Therefore, Adam and Christ were the wisest of men. Solomon must therefore have been less wise than they were.

40–45 Adam, Eve, and Christ are designated by a series of synecdoches and circumlocutions that refer to the two central events of Christian history, the Fall and the Redemption. (See Gen. 2:21–3:24, and John 19:31–37.)

49–51 That is, "What I am about to say will prove we are both right."

52–87 The first part of Thomas's reply actually does no more than put into words the line of reasoning that led to Dante's perplexity in the first place. The lean rigor of its concatenated tercets, however, provides a fine example of Dante's poeticizing of theology, of the stupendous symbiosis between philosophical stringency and poetic technique that is one of the chief triumphs of the *Paradiso*. The argument is as follows: All of creation—both what is incorruptible ("'that which never dies'"), because created by God directly (this category includes the angels, the heavens, primal matter, and the human soul), and what is corruptible ("'that which dies'"), because created indirectly, through secondary causes—is a reflection of the Divine Idea, the "Highest Wisdom" of *Inferno* III, 6, the archetype of all created things. The Idea, the Logos, or the Word ("In the beginning was the Word: the Word was with God and the Word was God" [John 1:1]) is the Son, the Second Person of the Holy Trinity, "begotten" by the act of Divine self-contemplation and self-understanding, existing from all eternity and indistinguishable from God Himself, as is the Third Person, the Holy Spirit, "the Love intrined with them" (57), God's Love for Himself as Supreme Good. (Cf. x, 1–6.)

59   The "'nine essences'" are the nine angelic orders.

62   In Scholastic philosophy the technical term *potentiality* designates what might be but as yet does not exist because it has not received its form. The "'last potentialities'" are those of the sublunar material world.

66   "'with or without seed'": i.e., organic (animal and vegetable) and inorganic.

67–75   For the metaphor of the created world as "'wax'" and the form imposed by the Creator as "'seal,'" cf. Canto I, 42.

76   "'Nature'" is the sum of the secondary causes by means of which God shapes His Creation.

82–84   The two cases of such complete human perfection are: Adam, who was placed on earth directly by God, and Christ, placed by God in the womb of the Virgin Mary.

91–108   Thomas will now add a *distinguo,* between absolute and specific wisdom, which will allow both him and Dante to be right. So that the obscure can be made even plainer, the reader would do well to recall the biblical account of 1 Kings 3:5–12: "At Gibeon Yahweh appeared in a dream to Solomon during the night. God said, 'Ask what you would like me to give you.' Solomon replied '... Give your servant a heart to understand how to discern between good and evil, for who could govern this people of yours that is so great?' It pleased Yahweh that Solomon should have asked for this. 'Since you have asked for this' Yahweh said 'and not asked for long life for yourself or riches or the lives of your enemies, but have asked for a discerning judgment for yourself, here and now I do what you ask. I give you a heart wise and shrewd as none before you has had and none will have after you.'"

97–102   For the practical hypothetical requests of the biblical narrative (long life, riches, the life of his enemies), Thomas substitutes a sampling of the intellectual conundrums that exercised the medieval mind: the exact number of the angels (incalculable), whether an absolute (or necessary) premise followed by a contingent (or conditional) premise can produce an absolute conclusion (Aristotle said no), whether motion is possible without an efficient cause *(" 'si est dare,' "* etc.), whether it is possible to inscribe within a semicircle a non-right-angled triangle.

111   Adam is the " 'first father' " of mankind; Jesus Christ is " 'our Beloved.' "

124   Parmenides, Melissus, and Bryson were three ancient Greek philosophers whose methods were impugned by Aristotle. The first two are also cited by Dante in his *Monarchia* (III, iv, 4): "Since the error may be in the matter and in the form of the argument, it is possible to err in two ways: either by basing one's case on false assumptions, or by reasoning incorrectly—two faults that the Philosopher [Aristotle] imputed to Parmenides and Melissus, saying: They take false things for good and do not know how to construct an argument." Aristotle criticized Bryson's ideas on the squaring of the circle. It is possible, since the same three examples occur in Albertus Magnus's *Physica,* that that work, rather than the original texts of Aristotle, is Dante's direct source.

127   Sabellius was a 3rd-century heretic who denied the received doctrine of the Trinity; Arius, a heterodox thinker of the early 4th century for whom the popular Arian heresy (which denied the divine nature of Christ) is named.

139   Grandgent remarks that Dame Bertha and Master Martin were equivalent to our "Tom, Dick, and Harry."

142   In the course of his journey Dante has already encountered a number of souls whose eternal fate contrasted with common opinion concerning them. Setting aside the members of the Church hierarchy, against whom he is particularly ferocious, we may mention the examples of the Franciscan monk Guido da Montefeltro, whom Dante found in Hell (*Inf.* XXVII); Manfred, the excommunicated son of the emperor Frederick II, who was about to enter Purgatory (*Purg.* III, 112–145); and, among the saved in Paradise, Siger of Brabant, condemned by the bishop of Paris, Etienne Tempier, as an Averroistic heretic in 1277 (x, 133–138).

CANTO XIV

1–9   As Thomas, in the first circle of surrounding soul-lights, concludes his speech and Beatrice, at the center of the circles, begins hers, Dante is struck by the similitude of a round vessel filled with water, in which, according as it is struck on the vessel itself or struck in the center of the water, concentric waves will move from the rim to the center or from the center out to the rim.

10–18   Beatrice, anticipating a question on Dante's part—a question that he has not yet clearly formulated to himself—asks these souls to tell Dante whether the effulgence surrounding them will remain even after they are reunited with their bodies at the Resurrection of the Flesh at the end of time, and if so, how their corporeal eyes will be able to withstand a splendor so intense. Dante's treatment of the question in this canto is based on St. Thomas's (in *Summa theol.,* Suppl., q. 85, a. 1–3).

25–27 "eternal showers": the grace of God, which rains upon the souls of the blessed "on high," in Paradise.

28–33 Again the souls sing in celebration of the Trinity (cf. XIII, 25–27 and note, 52–87, note, and X, 1–3), "not circumscribed and circumscribing all" (cf. *Purg.* XI, 1–2).

34–35 "the smaller circle's / divinest light," surrounding the soul of Solomon (see X, 109).

36 "the angel's voice in speech to Mary": the Archangel Gabriel's voice at the Annunciation. (See Luke 1:26–38.)

37–39 " 'such a garment' ": the effulgence surrounding the souls of the blessed, which, like Paradise, is everlasting. (Cf. *Purg.* I, 75.)

40–47 Solomon explains first the cause of the different degrees of brightness surrounding the blessed souls: according to the grace that God bestows upon each soul (a gift so great that it exceeds all possible merit), that soul's vision of God is more or less profound, and the more profound the soul's vision of God, the greater the ardor, or love, with which it burns. In accord with that ardor, then, the soul will be more or less bright. Love springs from vision, and brightness from love.

Underlying the next part of Solomon's explanation (43–45) is the Scholastic doctrine, derived from Aristotle, that the perfection of the soul and the body lies in their unity (cf. *Inf.* VI, 106–108 and note, and see *Summa theol.* I, q. 90, a .4). Thus, Solomon continues, at the Resurrection of the Flesh, when the souls are joined to their " 'glorified and sanctified' " bodies, the two together (" 'our persons' "), " 'in being all complete' " shall be more perfect, more like God, and so more pleasing to Him (cf. *Summa theol.* Suppl., q. 93, a. 1). The grace (beyond merit) that God grants to each of the blessed will, therefore, increase; their vision will increase, which in turn will cause their ardor and " 'the brightness born of ardor' " to increase. After the Resurrection of the Flesh the brightness of the blessed within their effulgence will outshine even that effulgence itself, like an intensely glowing coal visible within its own flame. (Cf. XXVIII, 106–114.)

58–60 Solomon replies to the second part of the question (16–18). When the bodies of the blessed are " 'glorified and sanctified' " (43) in the Resurrection of the Flesh, the " 'body's organs' " will be fortified, every physical obstacle to spiritual delight eliminated. (Cf. *Summa theol.* Suppl., q. 85, a. 2, ad 2.)

61 "One and the other choir": the two circles of soul-lights.

67–75 "an added luster.../ even as a horizon brightening": A horizon brightens only on one side, around the point where the sun is about to rise, but this "added luster" rose in every direction, and within it (with a sudden shift of simile to "the approach of evening") new soul-lights appear, like faintly visible stars in a dimming sky, "forming a ring" around the two "blessed circles" (23) of the soul-lights of the wise.

76–78 The "true sparkling of the Holy Ghost" is the radiance of Love.

79–8 "the visions that take flight from memory": cf. I, 4–9, and 1–12, note.

82–87 "From this my eyes regained the strength to look . . . / to higher blessedness": cf. X, 92–93. Dante is translated to the Fifth Heaven, the Sphere of Mars. In his *Convivio* (II, xiii, 21) Dante writes that "Mars dries and burns things, because its heat is like that of fire; this is why he appears enkindled in color, sometimes more and sometimes less, according to the thickness or rarity of the vapors that follow him. Mars, here, is even redder than usual, enkindled with joy at Beatrice's arrival (cf. V, 94–96).

88–89 "that language which / is one for all": the innermost, unspoken language of the heart and soul.

90 "my holocaust": The word, originally meaning "a sacrificial victim burnt entirely," reinforces Dante's affirmation that his ardent thanks to God, for the "new grace" (89) of being raised into a higher heaven, are rendered "with all [his] heart" (88).

96 Dante uses the name *Helios* here for God. Greek for "sun," the word was fused in medieval etymologies with *Ely*, linked to the Hebrew *El*, "God." (Cf. IX, 8–9, and X, 53 and note.)

101–102 "The venerable sign / a circle's quadrants form where they are joined": i.e., a cross (specifically, a Greek cross, its two axes equal).

104–108 Note, in the Italian, that Dante will rhyme the name *Christ* only with itself (see XII, 71–75, XIX, 104–108, and XXXII, 83–87, in the Italian).

106–108 See Matthew 16:24: "Then Jesus said to his disciples, 'If anyone wants to be a follower of mine, let him renounce himself and take up his cross and follow me.'" Those who do so will readily pardon Dante's inability to describe "Christ's flaming from that cross" (104) when they behold the indescribable vision themselves in Paradise.

109 "from horn to horn": i.e., from arm to arm of the cross.

121–126 Hearing the hymn sung by these soul-lights, Dante discerns only the words "Rise" and "Conquer"—enough to tell him that it "sang high praise" of God for Christ's Resurrection and victory over death.

131–139 "the lovely eyes": Beatrice's, which increase in beauty as she ascends in Paradise. It is not, Dante says, that he deemed them less lovely than the hymn sung by the soul-lights, but simply that he "had not yet turned to them" in the Heaven of Mars, to which Beatrice and Dante have ascended. Thus he "speak[s] truly" (138) in lines 127–129.

CANTO XV

1–6 The will of the blessed souls who make up the fiery Greek cross, being in harmony with God's will and directed toward righteousness, is, as a consequence, generous and not selfish. Their eagerness to assist

Dante by responding to his prayers causes the soul-lights to be still and their music to fall silent, inviting him to speak.

4 The simile of Canto XIV, 118–120 ("And just as harp and viol..."), here becomes a metaphor: the configuration of melodious lights is a lyre whose strings are plucked by God's hand; the souls are perfectly attuned to His will.

7–9 Dante's experience confirms in passing the doctrine according to which the saints may intercede with God on behalf of the living.

13–18 The simile of the shooting star (meteor) expands a simile of Ovid's used to describe the fall of Phaethon, the son of Apollo and Clymene, whose foolish insistence that he be allowed to drive the chariot of the sun almost set the heavens and earth on fire and led Zeus to step in and strike down the unskilled charioteer with a thunderbolt: "As sometimes from the clear heavens a star, though it falls not, yet seems to fall..." (*Met.* II, 321–322).

19–24 From the right arm ("horn") of the cross, whose moving lights were now still, a single light left its place, sped to the center, then traveled down the vertical axis, coursing to meet Dante. While the other lights are still, the welcoming light, in movement, does not, as it were, break ranks, but continues to observe the conformation imposed on the souls by their perfect conformity with the Divine Will. The singular "gem" will soon reveal itself to be the light that clothes the soul of Dante's ancestor Cacciaguida.

25–27 Dante's meeting with his great-great-grandfather is one of the focal events of the *Paradiso*. It occupies, in fact, three of the central cantos of the *Cantica*—XV, XVI, and XVII. Even before Cacciaguida begins to speak, the reference to the encounter of Aeneas with the shade of his dead father Anchises, recounted at the structural and moral center of the *Aeneid*, alerts us to the importance of the episode. "Our greatest muse" is of course Virgil ("our greatest poet" [*Convivio* IV, xxvi, 8]), the singer of the historic destiny of Rome. See *Aeneid* VI, 905–910: "And when he saw Aeneas cross the meadow, / he stretched out both hands eagerly, the tears / ran down his cheeks, these words fell from his lips: / 'And have you come at last, and has the pious / love that your father waited for defeated / the difficulty of the journey?'" As we shall immediately see, the explicit reference to the classical epic hero will be followed, in Cacciaguida's first words, by an implicit allusion to the Christian apostle Paul—a combination of paradigms that reaffirms the parallels suggested by the modest disclaimer of *Inferno* II, 32: "'For I am not Aeneas, am not Paul.'"

28–30 This tercet, Cacciaguida's first utterance, is rendered even more solemn in Dante's original text by the fact that it is in Latin, not Italian. The initial exclamation, "'O blood of mine,'" is adapted from Anchises' speech to Aeneas foretelling the future greatness of Rome. There, this same salutation was applied to no less a personage than Julius Caesar, the founder of the Roman Empire. The only other person to whom

Heaven's gate was opened twice was St. Paul, who, like Dante, was a recipient of "'celestial grace / bestowed beyond all measure,'" when he "was caught up into paradise and heard things which must not and cannot be put into human language" (2 Cor. 12:4).

32–33 The pilgrim is stupefied on one side by the words of the spirit (who has not yet identified himself), and on the other by the intensity of the joy that irradiates Beatrice's smile. This is the first time in the Heaven of Mars that Dante has glimpsed her smile, which is continually enhanced as they ascend from heaven to heaven.

49–54 Just as Anchises had anticipated and longed for Aeneas' coming, so Cacciaguida has hungered for Dante's, having read of it in the metaphorical "'volume'" of the eternally immutable decrees of Divine Providence.

55–69 Cacciaguida realizes that Dante does not question him because he is aware by now that the blessed souls are able to read his thoughts directly in the Mind of God, the source of all thought, as unity is the source of the value of all the derivative numbers. Nevertheless, in order that his ardent desire for charitable communication find seemly fulfillment, he urges Dante to an almost ritual formulation of his wishes.

88 After the direct reference to Aeneas and the oblique allusions to St. Paul and Caesar, this is an even more exalted paradigm. Behind the words with which Cacciaguida—who has already called Dante "'blood of mine'" (28), "'my seed'" (48), and "'son'" (51)—formally declares the nature of his paternity, we hear an echo of no less a model than the Gospels themselves and the voice from heaven that was heard at the baptism of Christ: "This is my Son, the Beloved; my favor rests on him." The Italian text recalls more closely than the English the words of the Latin Vulgate: *"Hic est Filius meus dilectus, in quo mihi complacui."* (Cf. *Matt.* 3:17; Mark 1:11; Luke 3:22.)

91–94 The man who gave Dante's family its name was Alighiero I, son of Cacciaguida and father of Bellincione, Dante's grandfather. Though modern archival research has turned up a document dated August 14, 1201, showing that Alighiero I was still alive at that date, the context suggests Dante was under the impression he had died before 1200. Otherwise, since we are in the year 1300, he could not have spent over a century among the Prideful on the first ledge of the mountain of Purgatory.

97–99 Florence in those days was still contained within her first and smallest circle of walls, whose construction legend attributed to the time of Charlemagne. Those walls followed the course, more or less, of the ancient Roman walls. As the city expanded, a second circle was built in 1173, and a third was begun in Dante's lifetime in 1284. The Alighieri house was located at the heart of the city, within the ancient circle, as was the Badia (the Benedictine convent of St. Mary), whose bells were officially recognized as telling the correct time of day. The canonical hours of "'tierce'" (nine in the morning) and "'nones'" (three in the afternoon) marked the beginning and the end of the artisan's normal working day. (See *Purg.* XV, 6, note.)

103–105   In those days girls married when they were ripe for marriage and dowries were not ruinously exorbitant. Implicit in Cacciaguida's praise of the good old days is, of course, Dante's criticism of the Florence of his time, which had all the defects Cacciaguida's Florence did not have. The reader will do well to recall Forese Donati's diatribe against the shameless women of modern Florence (*Purg.* XXIII, 94–111).

107   Sardanapalus, king of Assyria (667–626 B.C.), was a legendary example of indolence, lust, and luxury.

109–111   The Uccellatoio is a hill outside Florence that commands a fine view of the city, just as the height of Monte Mario is an excellent vantage point from which to view Rome. What is meant is that since Cacciaguida's time the rise of Florence has been swifter than the rise of Rome. Swifter, too, says Cacciaguida, will be her decline and fall.

112–117   Bellincione Berti, head of one of the most famous families of 12th-century Florence, was the father of " 'the good Gualdrada' " (*Inf.* XVI, 37), herself the grandmother of Guido Guerra. Jacopo di Ugolino dei Nerli (another prominent family of the Guelph nobility) was consul of Florence in 1204. Precisely whom Dante had in mind in mentioning " 'del Vecchio' " is uncertain. In any case, the point is clear. All of these couples—as well as the domestic genre scenes that follow (121–126)—exemplify the sober idyllic simplicity of the past as opposed to the corruption of the present.

118–120   Each wife was confident she would be buried with her husband in the local cemetery. In other words, the deplorable party struggles that would force so many families into exile were as yet unknown. Equally unknown was the early capitalist avidity for commercial profit (repeatedly censured by the poet), which led so many of Dante's contemporary Florentines to leave their native city for France and other foreign parts, abandoning their wives and children.

125–126   Cf. *Inferno* XV, 61–78 and note.

127–129   Two singularly unedifying representatives of present-day Florence—Lapo Salterello, a dishonest and conniving politician, condemned in 1302, along with Dante himself, by the victorious Black Guelphs, and Cianghella della Tosa, a female contemporary of the poet's, who seems to have been given to boasting openly about her life of unbridled self-indulgence—are opposed to two proverbial examples of public and private Roman virtue: Lucius Quinctius Cincinnatus, the famous dictator who willingly surrendered his position of power and returned to his plough, after successfully leading the Republic against the Aequians (cf. VI, 46–47, and 43–54, note), and Cornelia, mother of the Gracchi (cf. *Inf.* IV, 128).

134–135   Dante, too, was baptized a Christian in the Baptistery of San Giovanni in Florence (cf. Canto XXV, 8–9, and *Inf.* XIX, 17).

136 Cacciaguida's brother or brothers are unknown to history. The line as it stands may in fact refer to two brothers, one named Moronto and one Eliseo, or to a single brother, Moronto, who unlike Cacciaguida and his descendants, kept the family name of Eliseo or Elisei. A further genealogical complication is added by the fact that some manuscripts read " 'father' " instead of " 'brother.' "

137–138 The Po Valley lies to the north of Florence on the far side of the Apennine chain. Precisely where Cacciaguida's wife was from is uncertain, though most commentators opt for Ferrara.

139–147 Conrad III of Swabia, emperor from 1138 till his death in 1152, took part, along with Louis VII of France, in the disastrous Second Crusade (1147–1149). In that campaign against the Saracen usurpers of the Holy Land (cf. IX, 125–126), Cacciaguida met his death.

148 In Canto X, 129, an almost identical line seals epigrammatically the fate of the philosopher Boethius. There, as here, the Italian text places the word that designates heavenly " 'peace,' " " *'pace,'* " in rhyme with its polar opposite, " *'mondo fallace,'* " "the erring [or deceitful] world."

CANTO XVI

1–6 Greeted so warmly by such a noble ancestor, Dante cannot help but feel pride, and he feels that pride in Heaven, where the paltry foolishness of all values other than individual virtue ought to be constantly before our eyes. Little surprise, then, that on earth men set such store by their lineage!

7–9 For Dante, nobility is a dynamic concept, a value to be constantly and determinedly pursued. We do not patch the cloak by resting on our laurels, still less on the laurels of our ancestors. The idea that true nobility is nobility of the mind, which cannot be inherited but must be won, is frequent in his works: "Wherever there is virtue, there is nobility" (*Convivio* IV, xix, 3); "Their lineage does not make individuals noble, rather individuals make noble their lineage" (*Convivio* IV, xx, 5). It is a common theme in the works of Dante's immediate predecessors and contemporaries, where it often has an anti-aristocratic political thrust. Here the topos has lost its polemical edge and appears in an elegiac form, not as the aggressive protest of the new classes against the proud man's contumely, but as aristocratic regret for the inevitable decline of the good and the true, a lament over the triumph of violence and vulgarity.

9 Like all earthly things, nobility and reputation are vulnerable to circling time, the great destroyer. The temper of Dante's meeting with Cacciaguida foreshadows Petrarch in discerning in earthly life the triumph of time, mutability, and the inevitable corruption of sublunar things. Through the words of Cacciaguida, the poet mourns the decline and death of families, cities, nobility, virtue. The echoing litanies of family names are litanies for the dead and dying. Even the place-names on Cacciaguida's lips have nostalgic resonance—their geography is that of another time.

10 The *you* the pilgrim is about to use to Cacciaguida is the second person plural *you*—in the Italian text, *voi*—the pronoun of deference, reserved for persons deserving of the greatest respect. This *voi*—in its nominative or possessive form—has previously been used in speaking to only seven people: Farinata (*Inf.* X, 51), Cavalcante (*Inf.* X, 63), Brunetto Latini (*Inf.* XV, 30), Currado Malaspina (*Purg.* VIII, 121), Pope Hadrian V (*Purg.* XIX, 131), Guido Guinizzelli (*Purg.* XXVI, 112), and Beatrice. Moreover, in Canto XV, before knowing who he was, Dante had used the more normal *tu,* even with Cacciaguida. This is one of those moments when one may appreciate the poet's psychological detachment from the pilgrim and see the latter for the constructed character that he is. Certainly Cacciaguida is a venerable ancient, and on earth he had been a knight; on the other hand, Dante has encountered and will encounter personages far more venerable and exalted. What makes Dante so ceremonious at this point, rather than Cacciaguida's distance, is his very closeness. Beatrice's cough and her smile, along with the canto's opening considerations on the vanity of pride in blood—Cacciaguida had in fact saluted Dante as his " 'blood' " (XV, 28)—suggest that there may be some irony here at Dante's own expense, as the pilgrim, with his pompous allocution, perhaps basks in a little reflected glory.

11 It was believed, on the authority of a misreading of Lucan, that the first individual to be addressed with the plural *you* had been Julius Caesar, on his triumphant return to Rome.

12 Today, Dante says, when the custom of the respectful *voi* has spread to all Italy, it is remarkable that it is precisely the people of Rome and Latium who seem most reluctant to use it. This linguistic "democracy" of the Romans of Dante's time is mentioned in other contemporary sources.

13–15 In the medieval French *Lancelot,* the Lady of Malehaut, herself secretly in love with Sir Lancelot, on overhearing an indiscreet conversation between the knight and Queen Guinevere, coughed to let them know someone was there. Beatrice's smile is a comment on Dante's choice of pronouns. It reminds us of Dante's smile at Statius' effusions over Virgil in Virgil's presence (cf. *Purg.* XXI, 109). These moments of delicate humor are certainly rare and certainly welcome.

16–18 The *voi* is repeated three times! " 'You raise me so that I am more than I' ": surely Beatrice's ironically knowing smile must have broadened at this affirmation!

25 The " 'sheepfold of St. John' ": Florence, whose patron saint was John the Baptist.

28–29 Cf. Ovid, *Metamorphoses* VII, 79–81.

33 While most commentators assume that Cacciaguida spoke in archaic

Florentine, it has been suggested that since his first words were in Latin (xv, 28–30) he spoke in that language throughout. (It is not clear however, why this would have been the case.) In any event, the words attributed to him are in fact translated by the poet into "modern speech."

34–39 Cacciaguida first tells Dante the year of his birth—1091. The "'day when *Ave* was pronounced'" is the feast of the Annunciation, March 25, which in the Florentine calendar counted as the beginning of the new year. (According to this reckoning, the Christian era began with the conception, not the birth, of Christ). In the space of time since the Annunciation, the planet Mars (in whose sphere we now find ourselves) had returned 580 times to the constellation of Leo ("'its Lion'"). According to Ptolemy and Alfraganus, Mars completes its revolution around the earth in 687 days. When 580 is multiplied by 687 and then divided by 365 (the number of days in the year), the result is 1091. Red Mars, the warrior planet, is rekindled under "'the burning Lion's breast'" (xxi, 14), because of the affinity of their fiery influences.

40–42 That is, "My ancestors and I were born within the first circle of walls [cf. xv, 97–99 and note] at the spot where a runner in the annual horse race first enters the ward of Porta San Pietro." The discreet periphrasis nevertheless declares that the family was among the oldest in Florence and came from the original "'sacred seed'" of Roman stock (cf. *Inf.* xv, 76).

46–48 The adult male population of Florence (and by inference the population as a whole) was a fifth of what it had become by Dante's time—less was better. The Baptistery of San Giovanni and the statue believed to be of Mars on the Ponte Vecchio were at the opposite ends of the city.

49–51 Campi, Certaldo, and Figline are neighboring localities several miles outside Florence from which there had been mass immigration into the city.

54 Galuzzo and Trespiano; towns close by Florence, on the roads to Siena and Bologna respectively. The Florentine state should have stayed within these boundaries.

56 "'Aguglione's wretch and Signa's wretch'": two descendants of families that immigrated to Florence from places in the surrounding countryside—identified as Baldo d'Aguglione and Bonifazio dei Morubaldini. Both were contemporary politicians and, whatever else they may have done, were in part responsible for Dante's continuing exile. Dante accuses them of barratry (political corruption).

58–60 "'Those who in the world go most astray'" are the leaders of the Church, who, instead of living in affectionate peace with the emperor ("Caesar"), like two people of the same flesh and blood, have played the role of the envious grasping stepmother. If not for the interference of the Church, and the consequent rivalry between the pro-Papal Guelphs and the pro-Imperial Ghibellines, Florence would have remained in her primitive state of innocence.

63–66 Semifonte, Montemurlo, and Acone are other castles or villages near Florence. The "'Counts'" are the Conti Guidi, who sold their castles to Florence and moved into town. The Cerchi were an enriched family who became leaders of the White faction.

70–72 Proverbial sayings to the effect that size and numbers are no advantage.

73–75 Luni, Urbisaglia, Sinigaglia, Chiusi: cities once important, now in ruins or on their way to ruin.

82–84 Just as the moon causes the tides to ebb and flow, uncovering and covering the shore, so the goddess Fortune (cf. *Inf.* VII, 61–96) keeps Florence in constant fluctuation.

88–93 All of these families are formerly important dynasties, now fallen upon evil days. This celebration of the fabulous innocence of an earlier time is also fraught with a pervasive sense of earthly mutability.

94–99 The noble Ravignani clan lived near the gate of Porta San Pietro, where the ignoble Cerchis live now (see "Dante in His Age," Bantam Classics *Inferno*, p. 323). Count Guido Guerra "'was a grandson of the good Gualdrada'" (*Inf.* XVI, 37–38), whose father was Bellincione Berti (cf. XV, 112–114).

100–111 Another roll call of resounding aristocratic names, which would have meant a great deal to contemporary Florentine readers of the *Comedy*.

103 The Pigli family arms had a vertical stripe of vair (a heraldic representation of fur) on a red ground.

105–106 "'those who / blush for the bushel'": the Chiaramontesi, who were still ashamed of one member of their family who had gone wrong by falsifying the measure of salt when distributing their rations to the citizenry.

109–110 Those "'whom pride laid low'": the Uberti, the family of Farinata (cf. *Inf.* X). The arms of the Lamberti displayed golden balls on a field of azure.

112–114 The Visdomini and Tosinghi families had an interest in keeping the bishopric of Florence vacant, since they administered the revenues in the absence of an incumbent.

115–121 The "'stock / so mean'" is the malignant, fawning, covetous clan of the Adimari. When Bellincione Berti, one of whose daughters had married a son of Ubertin Donato, wed the other to an Adimari, Donato objected to their kinship.

121–124 Caponsacco, Giuda, Infangato: once-prominent Ghibelline families, since decayed.

125–126 One possible explanation for Dante's wonder at Cacciaguida's statement is that a family so insignificant by Dante's time had been sufficiently prominent in Cacciaguida's to lend their name to one of the city gates.

127–132 All the families that incorporate into their escutcheons the arms of Hugh the Great, marquis of Tuscany (d 1001)—the anniversary of whose death is celebrated on December 21, St. Thomas's Day—received knighthood from him. Giano della Bella, the chief author of the 1293 *Ordinamenti di giustizia,* is the renegade who went over to the people's side against the magnates. His family's coat of arms had added a gold fringe to Hugh the Great's ensign.

133–135 The Gualterotti and Importuni lived peacefully in Borgo Santi Apostoli, outside the old walls, until the arrival of the troublemaking Buondelmonti.

140–144 Buondelmonte dei Buondelmonti, betrothed to a daughter of the Amidei, broke off the engagement at the last moment, at the instigation of Gualdrada Donati, in order to marry one of her daughters. Members of the Amidei clan promptly avenged the affront by killing him. This feud was commonly blamed for the origin of civil strife in Florence. It would have been better for everyone if Buondelmonte had drowned in the river Ema, which lay between his castle of origin and Florence.

145–147 Buondelmonte was killed at the foot of the ancient and mutilated statue, supposedly of Mars, at the end of the Ponte Vecchio, on Easter, 1216.

152–154 The ensign of Florence, a white lily on a red field, was never dragged upside down over the battlefield by victors as a sign of the city's humiliation. Nor were its colors yet reversed, to a red lily on a white field, as they were in 1251 by the Guelphs, victorious against the Ghibellines in the war of Pistoia. The line suggests that the crimson lily is red with the blood of a divided Florence or with shame for the changes time has wrought.

CANTO XVII

1–4 Cacciaguida's final words in Canto XVI referred to the " 'factious hatred' " destined by Dante's time to divide the city of Florence against itself. Several times on his journey the pilgrim has heard (from Farinata degli Uberti, Brunetto Latini, and Vanni Fucci in Hell ["the dead world" (21)], and from Corrado Malaspina and Oderisi da Gubbio, in Purgatory, "the mountain that heals souls" [20]) more or less veiled prophecies or "insinuations" concerning the consequences for his own future of such a tense and vindictive political climate. The moment for clarification has finally arrived, and Dante turns to his new-found "father," just as the boy Phaethon turned to his mother Clymene for reassurance, when his jealous companion Epaphus taunted him for believing that he was the offspring of the sun-god Phoebus Apollo (see XV, 13–18, note, and cf. Ovid, *Met.* I, 748–761). That the clarification should come from Cacciaguida may in fact be something of a surprise for the attentive reader who has been led by Virgil's words on more than one occasion to expect it to come from Beatrice (cf., for example, his recommendation in the Circle of the Heretics: " 'Remember / the words that have been spoken here against you . . . when you shall stand before the gentle splendor / of one whose gracious eyes see everything, / then you shall learn—from her— your lifetime's journey' " [*Inf.* x, 127–132]). The change of informants can hardly be an oversight, since in the Italian text the precise words used by Virgil after this first troubling encounter with Farinata (*" 'quel ch'udito hai contra te' "* [*Inf.* x, 127–128]) seem to be deliberately echoed here in line 2 (*"ciò ch'avëa incontro a sé udito"*). To say that the poet must have changed his mind as he went along is not a very satisfactory explanation.

23–24 The image of the firmly planted cube impervious to the blows of chance recalls Dante's earlier reply in the same vein to Brunetto Latini: " 'So long as I am not rebuked by conscience, / I stand prepared for Fortune, come what may. / . . . therefore, let Fortune turn her wheel as she / may please, and let the peasant turn his mattock' " (*Inf.* xv, 92–96).

31–36 Cacciaguida speaks his predictions clearly, not in the ambiguous and riddling terms of the ancient pre-Christian oracles.

36–42 The whole course of contingent events—the events of the material world—is present in its eternity in the Mind of God. The fact that He knows what will happen does not, however, mean that He *causes* all things to happen in a predetermined way. Man still has the free will to choose between different actions. (See *Summa theol.* I, q. 14, a. 13, and I, q. 22, a. 4.)

46 Hippolytus, the son of Theseus and Hippolyta, was the object of his stepmother Phaedra's quasi-incestuous desire. When he repulsed her, she falsely accused him to his father of attempting to seduce her. As a result, Hippolytus was forced to flee Athens, just as Dante, falsely accused of political corruption, will be exiled from Florence (in January 1302), never again to return there (see "Dante in His Age," Bantam Classics *Inferno,* pp. 324–325).

48–51 Pope Boniface VIII is the plotter of the events that will ultimately lead to Dante's exile (in the company of the others in the White Guelph party); the venal Papal Curia is the place where Christ is daily bought and sold. Boniface's policy of influence peddling and covert intervention in the internal politics of Florence was constantly denounced by Dante during his term of office as prior and in his diplomatic missions. In 1300 Boniface was already negotiating with Corso Donati and other prominent Blacks to unseat the ruling Whites; in November 1301 the papal legate, Charles of Valois, sent ostensibly as peacemaker between the rival groups, presided over a Black coup d'état. (See "Dante in His Age," Bantam Classics *Inferno,* pp. 324–325.)

52–54 Because history is written by the winners, the shortsighted judgment of contemporaries will blame the losing Whites. The vengeance of divine justice, however, will fall on the true culprits. Dante may be thinking of the violent death of Corso Donati (see *Purg.* XXIV, 82–87, and 82–90, note) and the humiliation of Boniface VIII by Philip the Fair at Anagni (see *Purg.* XX, 86–87 and note).

61–69 The " 'scheming, senseless company' " are Dante's White companions in exile. Between 1302 and 1306 they made several inconclusive attempts to return to Florence by force of arms. Dante appears to have at first played a prominent role in the organization of these campaigns, but if, as seems likely, he was already a guest of Bartolommeo della Scala (the " 'great Lombard' " [71]) before Bartolommeo died in March 1304, he must have very quickly become disgusted with their insanity, profanity, and ungratefulness and have dissociated himself from them. Their final defeat—the occasion on which their brows would be red with shame or with blood, after which the Blacks would continue to rule unchallenged—would come in 1306. Thereafter, the White faction would wither away, and its surviving adherents would be compelled, as Dante was, to turn for support and sympathy to the Ghibelline princes of northern Italy.

70–74 There is disagreement among commentators as to which member of the Della Scala family (the lords of Verona) is meant. The most likely candidate is the one indicated by Dante's son Pietro—Bartolommeo della Scala, who ruled from 1301 to 1304. It is quite possible, if we consider the lack of enthusiasm for at least one member of the Della Scala family shown in *Purgatorio* XVIII, 121–126 (lines written before Dante came under the protection and patronage of Cangrande), that this "first inn" and refuge was not quite as welcoming as he makes it sound, and that his sincere admiration for and gratitude toward Bartolommeo's younger brother, ruler from 1312 to 1329, have been allowed to color the poet's recollection of his earlier stay.

72 To the ladder (*scala*) that was the traditional blazon of the Della Scala family, the imperial eagle ("the sacred bird") was added in the early 14th century.

76–81 Beside Bartolommeo, Dante would see for the first time Bartolommeo's younger brother, Cangrande, born in 1291 and therefore only nine years old in 1300, but destined by the influence of the planet Mars for a glorious military career.

82–84 The Gascon is Pope Clement V, who initially favored what Dante had saluted in a well-known epistle—the triumphal descent into Italy of the emperor Henry VII in 1312—only to perform a last minute about-face, stirring up the Italian Guelphs against Henry. By that time Cangrande would already have given evidence of his indifference to the hardships of military life and his munificence.

93 "things beyond belief": Though Dante's regard for Cangrande is genuine, it seems unlikely that he saw him as the potential savior of Italy, the " 'Greyhound' " of *Inferno* I, 101–111.

121 The "treasure" within the light is the spirit of Cacciaguida. The light itself grows brighter, as do the other lights of Paradise, with the joy of reassuring and enlightening the pilgrim. In this latter part of the canto, the forecast of Dante's misfortunes is offset by the heavenly seal given to his divinely appointed poetic mission. His poem is destined to provide "living nourishment" (132) that will earn him the lasting gratitude of the just.

CANTO XVIII

1–2 The "blessed mirror" is Cacciaguida, in whom God's light is reflected. His "inner words" are his thoughts (cf. Thomas Aquinas, *Summa theol.* I, q. 34, a. 1: "Wherefore the exterior vocal sound is called a word from the fact that it signifies the interior concept of the mind. Therefore it follows that, first and chiefly, the interior concept of the mind is called a word.").

2–3 Dante, too, is occupied with his own thoughts, mulling over the bitter and the sweet aspects of the predictions made by Cacciaguida in the previous canto: on the one hand, his exile and subsequent alienation from his fellow Whites, on the other, the promised protection of Cangrande and the punishment of his persecutors.

11–12 Not only are words inadequate to describe the Love reflected in the lovely eyes of Beatrice, without supernatural assistance human memory is too weak and limited to summon again so profound a vision. The same notion is expressed elsewhere: see, e.g., Canto I, 5–9.

28–30 Unlike our earthly trees, the metaphorical tree of Paradise, ever green and ever fruitful of souls, grows downward from its crown, in the sense that it receives life and sustenance, not from below, but from God, who dwells in the outermost Empyrean. "This fifth resting place" in Dante's ascent is the Fifth Heaven, the Sphere of Mars.

34 Cacciaguida will name other warrior spirits—an ideal continuity of champions of Israel from the Old Testament and Christian defenders of the faith—who manifest themselves in this heaven. As he names them their individual lights flash like lightning along the "horns," or axes, of the cross formed by all the spirits together.

37 Joshua, for whom the sixth book of the Old Testament is named, was the successor of Moses and led the Hebrews in their conquest of the Promised Land.

40 Judas Maccabaeus, the great Hebrew warrior, freed the Jews from the tyranny of Antiochus Epiphanes, king of Syria. (See 1 Maccabees.)

43 Charlemagne (742–814) is remembered as the restorer of the Holy Roman Empire and the defender of Christendom against the incursions of the Saracens in Spain. Significantly, his name is linked here with that of his nephew and most famous paladin, Roland, about whom history is practically silent, was the hero of the great medieval epic *Song of Roland,* which narrates how he saved Charlemagne and his army from a treacherous attack from behind. The moment of Roland's death is evoked in *Inferno* XXXI, 16–18, where once again the names of the two heroes are linked.

46–48 Like Roland and Charlemagne, Renouard and William of Orange are the heroes of a medieval French epic cycle. Like his contemporary Charlemagne, William was an actual historical figure, a military leader who ended his life in a monastery, whereas the exploits of Renouard—a Saracen giant of fabulous strength, converted to Christianity by William—are legendary. Godfrey of Bouillon, duke of Lorraine (1058–1100), led the victorious First Crusade to recover the Holy Land and became the first Christian king of Jerusalem. Robert Guiscard (1015–1085), a Norman, defended Pope Gregory VII against the emperor Henry IV, drove the Byzantines from southern Italy, and was created duke of Calabria and Apulia by the pope in 1059.

52–63 Turning back to Beatrice for prompting, now that Cacciaguida has departed, Dante finds that she is even more joyously radiant than she was a short time ago, the last time he looked at her in the Fifth Heaven. He realizes that this increase in brilliance comes from their having passed into the Sixth Heaven, or Sphere of Jupiter, whose "arc," or circumference, contains that of Mars and is obviously greater.

64–69 Just as one may see a woman's face return to its natural paleness after the blush of modesty has left it, so Dante became aware that the red cast of Mars had given way to the silvery whiteness of the Heaven of Jupiter. The color of Jupiter—the whitest of the stars—and its "temperate complexion, halfway between the coldness of Saturn and the heat of Mars" are stressed in *Convivio* II, xiii, 25.

72 "the signs we speak": the letters of the alphabet, which represent our speech.

73–75 It is generally agreed that the birds Dante has in mind are cranes, which fly in a wedge- or V-shaped formation. The source of Dante's simile is probably a simile of Lucan's, who says of the cranes: "As they take flight they form fortuitously various figures. Soon, however, when the south wind blowing more strongly strikes their wings, confused and without order, they crowd together in formless circles, and the letter they formed vanishes, disturbed by the scattering of their feathers" (*Phars.* V, 712–716).

76–81 Though the illustration on pp. 156–157 shows the entire biblical quotation spelled out at once, the usual interpretation is that the souls formed one letter at a time, pausing briefly in the form of each successive letter before going on to the next.

82–87 The fabulous winged horse Pegasus, with a blow of his hoof, caused the fountain Hippocrene to spring up on Mount Helicon. It became the favorite haunt of the Muses. Here, to stress the solemnity of the moment and the extraordinary nature of what he is about to witness,

Dante invokes the poetic aid of one or all of the Muses who frequent the Pegasean spring. (See *Purg.* XXIX, 37–42, note.)

88–89 The total number of vowels and consonants, thirty-five, happens to be the age of Christ at the time of his death.

91–93 "DILIGITE JUSTITIAM.../ QUI IUDICATIS TERRAM" ("Love justice, you who judge the earth") is the first sentence of the Book of Wisdom in the Latin Vulgate. The Heaven of Jupiter is the seat of God's Justice (cf. lines 116–117 and 115–123, note). Here Dante will encounter the souls of the just and merciful rulers of the earth.

94–96 When they reach the last letter of the last word of the sentence, the *m* of "TERRAM," the spirits pause. The enormous Gothic letter shows as if embossed in gold against the silver of the Heaven of Jupiter. The reader must envision a Gothic capital *M,* rounded in the shape of a horseshoe and divided down the middle by a vertical stroke. By modifying their positions, the blessed souls gradually transform the letter *M*— which, in addition to being the final letter of *terram,* is also the initial letter of *monarchia* ("monarchy") and alludes to the need for a supreme temporal authority, independent of and equal to the spiritual authority (the pope), as argued by Dante in his treatise *Monarchia*—into the shape of an heraldic eagle, the symbol of Divine Justice and the emblem of the Universal Empire, appointed by God, in Dante's view, to ensure the achievement of justice on earth. (See "Dante in His Age," Bantam Classics *Inferno,* pp. 326–328.)

97–99 The first step toward forming the image of the imperial eagle is for a group of spirits to settle on the apex or tip of the Gothic *M.* This is later referred to as "form[ing] a lily on the *M"* (113). It is usually interpreted to mean that the resulting figure looked like the heraldic fleur-de-lis, though there is considerable dispute about whether this phase of the transformation has its separate symbolism and, if so, what it means. Parodi, for instance, saw the lily as an unlikely allusion to the ambitions of the French monarchy. (But cf. Sarolli in *Atti del congresso internazionale di studi danteschi,* II, Firenze, 1966, pp. 237–254.)

109–111 The painter who guides the souls through their various transformations is God. The inborn, instinctual shaping force that pervades the universe and teaches, for example, the birds how to build their nests, comes from Him.

115–123 Dante now calls on the Heaven of Jupiter, whence our earthly justice proceeds, and on the Mind of God, the source of Jupiter's just influence, and archetype of True Justice, to look down in righteous anger on the erring Rome of the popes. Rome is the place that has produced the smoke that dims the rays of the light of the planet Jupiter. And Dante also calls for the punishment of those responsible for leading the Church astray from its evangelical beginnings—away from the spiritual into the temporal sphere.

127–129 Once, war was waged with legitimate means, but now the popes are content to excommunicate and to deny the sacraments to those who oppose their illegitimate worldly ambitions, using spiritual arms to fight temporal battles.

130–132 The final scathing apostrophe is addressed to the current pope, John XXII (1316–1334), whom Dante viewed as prepared to make or unmake any of his edicts for a financial consideration ("you who only write to then erase"): he should not forget that the eyes of the Apostles Peter and Paul are upon him.

133–136 The reply that Dante sarcastically attributes to Pope John XXII stresses Dante's devotion to another figure from the Gospels, Saint John the Baptist. John the Baptist ("the voice of one crying in the wilderness") chose the solitary life of the hermit and "lived out in the wilderness until the day he appeared openly to Israel" (Luke 1:80). Salome, the daughter of Herodias, requested and obtained John's head on a dish as a reward for pleasing Herod with her dancing (see Matt. 14:3–12). The sting is in the fact that the saint's image was engraved on one side of the Florentine coin, the florin. It is filthy lucre that is the object of the pope's longing.

CANTO XIX

7–12 Marvelous to relate, the Eagle that embodies Divine Justice and is at the same time a symbol of the Universal Empire, though made up of many individual souls, moved its beak and spoke for all of them collectively with one voice, using the first person singular. The souls that make up the Eagle are the souls of these earthly rulers whose justice and mercy most closely approximated the infinite justice and mercy of God Himself.

28–30 The perfection of Divine Justice is mirrored in "another realm," i.e., in the angelic order of the Thrones, where it is contemplated directly by all the blessed. (Cf. IX, 61–63.)

33 Dante's unformulated doubt, which will be voiced by the Eagle itself in lines 73–78, ventures to question the justice according to which a pagan, who has lived a life of exemplary virtue and who was precluded by a mere accident of birth from knowing the true religion—either because he lived in a remote part of the world, or because he lived before Christ's advent—is nevertheless excluded eternally from salvation.

40 The image of God as the Artificer of Creation is frequent in the Bible: "You fixed the boundaries of the world" (Ps. 74 [73 in the Vulgate]:17); cf. Proverbs 8:27–31: "When he fixed the heavens firm, I was there" (echoed in Job 38:4–39:30). The Eagle's speech, which will end only with the end of the canto, opens with a solemn reaffirmation of the inscrutability of Divine purpose. The necessity for faith in those things that transcend our understanding was previously—and poignantly—affirmed by Virgil, Dante's former guide ("Confine yourselves, o humans, to the *quia*" [see *Purg.* III, 34–45]), one of those virtuous pagans whose condemnation it has been so difficult for Dante to accept.

43–48 God being infinite, His Word, or Idea, must surpass infinitely the comprehension of the finite beings He created. The most perfect of creatures are the angels—man is considerably less perfect—and among them, the highest of all was the Archangel Lucifer, the prideful chief of the angels that fell. Medieval theologians held that, after He had created the angels, God had assigned them a brief period of probation, before bestowing upon them the full ripeness of the light of glory. It was during this period that Lucifer and his followers rebelled, claiming autonomy, failing to recognize the limits of their nature as creatures, their dependence on the Almighty, and the fact that true freedom consists in obedience to His will. For further discussion of the fall of the rebellious angels, see Canto XXIX, 55–63.

63 Cf. Psalm 36 (35 in the Vulgate): 6: "Your judgments [are] like the mighty deep."

64–66 Cf. John 1:5: "a light that shines in the dark, a light that darkness could not overpower." Only the light of God's grace can overcome the obfuscation of the faculties of the soul by the body (the " 'shadow of the flesh' ") or the dark contagion of sin (" 'fleshly poison' ").

67 If the Eagle has laid open the hiding place of living Justice, it has not really explained anything. Divine Justice still remains beyond our human ability to fathom it, and the justness of God's decisions, a point of faith. Beatrice's earlier injunction has lost none of its validity: " 'To mortal eyes our justice seems unjust; / that this is so, should serve as evidence / for faith—not heresy's depravity' " (IV, 67–69), as is explicitly confirmed in lines 97–99.

70–72 Cf. Romans 10:14: "But they will not ask his help unless they believe in him, and they will not believe in him unless they have heard of him, and they will not hear of him unless they get a preacher." The question, the concern of Dante's that the Eagle puts into words for him, is indeed a disturbing one, a mystery of faith that has always given pause to theologians. Despite its apparent technicality, however, the Eagle's discourse, more than an intellectually satisfactory theological demonstration, is a sermon, Pauline in its intonation, against human presumption and on the need for faith in Divine Revelation.

79–81 The reprimand has a biblical ring: "But what right have you, a human being, to cross-examine God?" (Rom. 9:20).

82–84 Cf. *Monarchia* II, vii, 4–5: "There are some divine judgments to which human reason, though it cannot arrive through its own means, can nevertheless rise with the help of faith in what we have been told in Holy Scripture; such as this, for instance: that no one, however perfect in moral and intellectual virtues, by habitual disposition or in action, can be saved without faith, even if he has never heard of Christ. For human reason by itself cannot understand the justice of this, but with the aid of faith it can. In fact it is written in the Epistle to the Hebrews: 'But without faith it is impossible to please him.' "

100–102 The "Holy Ghost's bright flames" are the individual lights that make up the shape of the Eagle. It was the imperial eagle that made the Romans revered throughout the world (cf. Canto VI).

103–111 Only the souls of those who believed in Christ—in the Old Dispensation, before His Incarnation, or, after it, in the New—can hope to be saved.

106–108 Cf. Matthew 7:21: "It is not those who say to me, 'Lord, Lord,' who will enter the kingdom of heaven, but the person who does the will of my Father in heaven"; and cf. Matthew 8:11–12: "And I tell you that many will come from east and west to take their places with Abraham and Isaac and Jacob at the feast in the kingdom of heaven; but the subjects of the kingdom will be cast out into the dark, where there will be weeping and grinding of teeth."

Note again that in the Italian text the name of *Christ* is allowed to rhyme only with itself (see XII, 71–75, XIV, 104–108, and XXXII, 83–87, in the Italian).

109 The Ethiopian, like the Indian of lines 70–71 and the Persian of line 112, indicates any non-Christian.

110–111 The " 'two companies' " are the company of the saved (" 'forever rich' ") and that of the damned (" '[forever] poor' ").

112–114 Cf. Revelation 20:12: "I saw the dead, both great and small, standing in front of his throne, while the book of life was opened, and other books opened which were the record of what they had done in their lives, by which the dead were judged."

115–141 Each of the following three groups of three tercets is built on the rhetorical figure of anaphora—the regular repetition of the same word or words at the beginning of successive phrases. The first three tercets all begin " 'There one shall see' "; the second three tercets, " 'That book' "; the third three with the reiterated conjunction " 'and.' " The English text is able to reproduce the device of anaphora, but not the acrostic that the first letters of these lines form in the Italian original. Together, the first initial letters—*L, V(= U), E*—spell out the word *lue,* which means "plague" or "pestilence." In a similar fashion, in *Purgatorio* XII, 25–63 (see note), the initial letters of the tercets—*V(= U), O, M*—spelled out *uom,* "man."

115–117 The catalog of unjust and irresponsible princes, which confirms and complements Sordello's negative asides in his presentation of the negligent princes awaiting admission to Purgatory (*Purg.* VII, 85–136), begins at the top with the emperor himself, Albert of Austria (1248–1308), whose conduct of the empire has already been deplored at length in *Purgatorio* VI, 97–117. The present allusion is to Albert's imminent invasion and devastation—destined to occur in 1304—of the kingdom of Bohemia, held till then by his brother-in-law, Wenceslaus IV (the " 'Bohemian' " of line 125, also condemned in *Purg.* VII, 101–102). This action of the emperor's violated the rights of one of his vassals, a crime that for Dante was as grave as the refusal of a subaltern government to recognize imperial authority.

118–120 Philip the Fair of France (cf. *Purg.* VII, 109) died in 1314 in a boar-hunting accident. The rumor that he financed his military campaigns by minting debased coins whose real value was inferior to their face value has not been borne out by historians.

121–123 At the beginning of the 14th century, successive English kings made war against the kings of Scotland.

124–126 The " 'Spaniard' " is Ferdinando IV of Castile (1295–1312) and the " 'Bohemian' " is Wenceslaus IV (1270–1305), the emperor Albert's brother-in-law, accused of lust and indolence in *Purgatorio* VII, 102–103.

127–129 One of the honorary titles of Charles II of Anjou (Charles the Lame) was king of Jerusalem. Charles's good deeds are outweighed a thousandfold by his bad. They merit respectively the Roman numerals I (1) and M (1000). *I* and *M* are also, incidentally, the first and the last letters of *Ierusalem.* For additional condemnation of Charles's actions, cf. *Canto* XX, 63, and *Purgatorio* VII, 127–129, and XX, 79–81.

130–135 The ruler of Sicily (" 'the Isle of Fire' "), where Anchises, father of Aeneas, died (*Aen.* III, 915–921), was Frederick II of Aragon (1272–1337). His misdeeds will be noted in shorthand—to save space (because there are so many) and to show his paltry importance. Frederick is mentioned also in *Purgatorio* VII, 119.

136–138 Frederick's uncle was James, king of Majorca from 1262 to 1311; his brother, James II, was king of Sicily before Frederick, and subsequently king of Aragon. (Cf. *Purg.* VII, 115–120, and see 119–120, note.)

139–141 Dionysius (or Diniz), king of Portugal from 1279 to 1325, and Haakon V, king of Norway from 1299 to 1319, do not seem to deserve Dante's opprobrium. Stephen Urosh II of Serbia (1275–1321) is remembered in the annals of Venice as a counterfeiter of Venetian currency. His kingdom, known as Rascia from the name of its capital, corresponded more or less to present-day Yugoslavia.

142–143 Before the succession in 1301 of Caroberto, the son of Charles Martel (cf. IX, 1–3), in whom Dante placed great hopes, Hungary had been governed by a series of incompetent and evil rulers.

143–148 The kingdom of Navarre on the Spanish side of the Pyrenees, was threatened by the expansionism of the French crown. In fact, by the time Dante wrote the *Paradiso,* Navarre had been annexed to France. In 1300, at the time of the fictive journey, Navarre could take warning from the example of Cyprus (whose principal cities are Nicosia and Famagosta), which was already under the bestial rule of a prince of French descent, Henry II of Lusignan. The catalog of anathemas, pronounced by the souls of the just and merciful rulers forming the Eagle, began with the deplorable example set by the emperor himself. It closes with the abuses of a petty tyrant. For Dante, the absence of a supreme regulating head (a righteous emperor) is the cause of the degeneration of the members.

CANTO XX

1–12 This canto, like many others, begins with a description of celestial phenomena. Here, however, Dante is less the technical astronomer than is his wont, more the lay observer. When the beak of the Eagle, which had previously spoken for all of the souls with one voice, falls silent, the intensification of the single lights composing it, which accompanies their ineffable singing, reminds Dante of the bright multitude of stars that appear in the night sky after the sun has set. (In Dante's time it was believed that the stars shone with the reflected light of the sun [cf. XXIII, 28–30]). Canto XXX will begin with a description of the contrary phenomenon, the disappearance of the stars with the advance of dawn.

29–30 The Eagle reads the unspoken desire in Dante's heart to know more, and Dante transcribes in his heart the Eagle's answer.

31–33 The Eagle (which is seen in profile) draws Dante's attention to its one visible eye. The medieval belief in the ability of the eagle to stare directly into the sun was also alluded to in Canto I, 47–48.

37–38 The "'singer of the Holy Spirit'" is the psalmist David. Anointed king over Israel, he had the Ark of the Covenant transported from the house of Abinadab at Gibeah to the house of Obededom of Gath and eventually into Jerusalem, the city of David (see 2 Sam. 6).

40–42 David was not merely a passive instrument of the grace of God when he composed the Psalms. Free to accept or reject the inspiration of the Holy Spirit, he chose to accept it. It was this act of will on his part that earned him his present reward. On earth David was not fully aware of the merit of his choice; now, in Heaven he has learned what rewards await those whose will works together with the will of God.

The reader will note that, for each of the six souls that make up the eye and brow of the Eagle, the same anaphoric formula "'now he has learned'" is repeated, stressing the gulf that separates our shortsighted earthly understanding from the inscrutable judgment of God. He will also recall that a similar device was used in the previous canto in the catalog of reprehensible princes (XIX, 115–141). Thus, Dante creates a contrastive link with the present catalog of just rulers.

45 The medieval legend of the merciful justice of the emperor Trajan (A.D. 98–117), who delayed his journey to punish an injustice done a poor widow, is treated at greater length in *Purgatorio* X, 73–93 (and see note), where it forms the subject of one of the reliefs illustrating famous acts of humility sculpted on the wall of the Terrace of the Prideful. King

David is remembered in the same sculptural sequence, for the same episode for which he is remembered here.

46–48 Trajan died a pagan. Later in the canto the Eagle will explain to the surprised Dante why the Roman emperor is here in the " 'sweet life' " of Paradise. For the moment, we learn that Trajan has also experienced " 'its opposite,' " that is, he had been in Hell.

49 The third just ruler is Hezekiah, son of Ahaz, king of Judah. About Hezekiah's justness there is no question: "He put his trust in the God of Israel. No king of Judah after him could be compared with him—nor any of those before him. He was devoted to Yahweh, never turning from him, but keeping the commandments that Yahweh had laid down for Moses" (2 Kings 18:5–6). Some critics are perplexed by Dante's reference to Hezekiah's penitence, for which, it seems, he had no need. When the prophet Isaiah had come to him, however, to tell him he would have to die, he had turned his face to the wall and prayed to the Lord, "And Hezekiah shed many tears" (2 Kings 20:1–6). God heard his prayer and granted him an additional fifteen years of life. One presumes that Dante interpreted his tears as tears of repentance.

52–54 Now that he is in Heaven, Hezekiah has learned that if his death was delayed when it fell due, it was not because his prayers, however worthy, altered the immutable judgment of God. Rather his prayers themselves, and the consequent delay, were written from all eternity.

55–57 The fourth just ruler, who occupies the brightest place at the top of the brow, is Constantine the Great (274–337), the first Christian emperor, who transferred the seat of the imperial government and the emblem of the empire, " 'the laws and me' " (i.e., the imperial eagle), from Rome to Byzantium (or Constantinople) in A.D. 330 (" 'made himself Greek' "). At the time of this so-called *translatio Imperii,* Constantine was supposed to have ceded the territory of Rome to Pope Sylvester (" 'the Shepherd' "). The deplorable consequences of the Donation of Constantine were lamented in *Inferno* XIX, 115–117 (see note; and cf. *Par.* VI, 1–9, note). They were not the fault of Constantine, however, since he could not have foreseen how his gift would be abused: "If the consequences of an action follow by accident and seldom, then they did not increase the goodness or malice of the action: because we do not judge of a thing according to that which belongs to it by accident, but only according to that which belongs to it of itself" (*Summa theol.* I–II, q. 20, a. 5).

61–63 "William": William II of Hauteville, known as William the Good, the Norman king of southern Italy and Sicily from 1166 to 1189. The lands he ruled so well are now ruled by Charles II of Anjou, " 'the Cripple of Jerusalem,' " and Frederick II of Aragon (" 'who oversees the Isle of Fire' "), both of whom were cruelly rebuked by the Eagle in the previous canto (XIX, 127–135).

69 The Trojan Ripheus is not a historical figure but a minor character mentioned three times in Book II of Virgil's *Aeneid,* where Aeneas recalls his death in battle, saying, "he was first / among the Teucrians for justice and / observing right" (*Aen.* II, 573–575). Remembering these lines, Dante decided to place him in Paradise, to illustrate once more the inscrutability of the Divine Plan. Like the other souls in Paradise, Ripheus is able to penetrate more deeply now the mysteries of God's grace. Nevertheless, even the blessed cannot plumb its depths completely. What Ripheus has learned is a concise restatement of the Eagle's affirmations in Canto XIX, 52–63. Cf. *Summa theol.* I, q. 12, a. 8: "No created intellect can know what God does or can do."

73–75 The lark's song reflects the ecstasy of its flight. It soars and sings until, overcome by the sweetness of its soaring, it falls silent. The image recalls lines from a poem of the Provençal troubadour Bernart de Ventadorn: "when I see the lark beat / with joy her wings toward the rays [of the sun] / till she forgets herself and lets herself fall / for the sweetness that goes to her heart."

76–78 The Eagle is the image of Divine Justice. The "seal," or influence, of the Sphere of Jupiter is to foster justice on earth.

79–83 Dante's amazement at what he has been told is such that, though he knows that the blessed can read his thoughts, he cannot restrain a rhetorical question.

92 "'quiddity'": a technical term of Scholastic philosophy, meaning "essence." To recognize a thing by its name calls only for an imperfect, or exterior, knowledge, what St. Thomas calls "sensitive knowledge." Knowledge of its essence is "intellective" knowledge.

94 "'Regnum celorum'": "the kingdom of heaven." Cf. Matthew 11:12: "Since John the Baptist came, up to this present time, the kingdom of heaven has been subjected to violence and the violent are taking it by storm."

101–106 The first and the fifth souls were Trajan and Ripheus respectively, whom the pilgrim Dante mistakenly believed had died as "'Gentiles,'" that is, pagans. But in fact both Trajan, who died after Christ's passion (after His "'Feet'" had suffered the wounds of the nails of the Crucifixion), and Ripheus, who died before Christ was born (when His "'Feet'" had still to suffer), died with firm faith in Christ. The problem of the possible salvation of certain pagans is discussed by, among others, St. Thomas: "If, however, some were saved without receiving any revelation, they were not saved without faith in a Mediator, for, though they did not believe in Him explicitly, they did, nevertheless, have implicit faith through believing in Divine Providence, since they believed that God would deliver mankind in whatever way was pleasing to Him, and according to the revelation of the Spirit to those who knew the truth" (*Summa theol.* II–II, q. 2, a. 7 ad 3).

106–116 When Trajan died, he joined the other virtuous pagans in Limbo, where conversion and repentance are no longer possible. Supposedly the prayers of St. Gregory the Great, however, recalled him briefly to life in order that he might be converted to Christianity (see *Purg.* x, 73–93, note). The legend enjoyed wide currency throughout the Middle Ages, and the theological implications of Trajan's salvation were discussed, for instance, by Thomas Aquinas (cf. *Summa theol.* Suppl., q. 71, a. 5).

118–129   Though in Trajan's case there existed a flourishing tradition for his conversion, the salvation of Ripheus is Dante's own idea. It constitutes, however, a specific illustration of the general principle argued by Thomas Aquinas (see 101–106, note).

127–129   The chariot in which Beatrice rode in triumph in the Earthly Paradise was accompanied on its right side by three women who symbolized the three Theological Virtues—Faith, Hope, and Charity— which are sufficient for salvation.

130–138   The Eagle concludes with yet another warning not to judge hastily one's fellow men. Not even the blessed in Heaven know which of those still on earth belong to God's elect. Yet, this imperfect knowledge is, like their greater or lesser nearness to God, no impediment to their happiness, since, as Piccarda Donati declared: " 'in His will there is our peace' " (III, 85).

134   For the first time, the Eagle uses the plural pronoun *we*. This is not an oversight but occurs because the Eagle's affirmation applies, not merely to the souls that compose its shape, but to all the souls of Paradise.

CANTO XXI

6   Semele, daughter of Cadmus, king of Thebes, was pregnant with Bacchus by Jupiter. Juno, Jupiter's sister and wife (the most jealous wife in mythology), appeared to Semele in the guise of Semele's old nurse and suggested that Semele had been taken in, that her lover was not in fact a god at all. Following Juno's advice, Semele insisted that Jupiter come to her in all his godly splendor, whereupon, unable to withstand his effulgence, she was reduced to ashes (Bacchus was saved by Jupiter). (See Ovid, *Met.* III, 253–315.) Dante alluded to the myth of Semele in *Inferno* xxx, 1–3.

13–15   Dante and Beatrice have reached the Seventh Heaven, the sphere of the planet Saturn, where they will encounter the spirits of the contemplative. The rays and influence of Saturn are cold, like those of the moon. The influence of the fixed constellation of Leo (" 'the burning Lion' "), on the other hand, is hot and dry like fire. In March and April 1300, the two were in conjunction, their forces mixed, one influence tempering the other. Dante's ideal contemplatives are those who combined the meditative and mystical temperament with the zeal of the reformer.

18   The " 'mirror' " (like the "crystal" of line 25) is the transparent and lucid body of the planet.

19–24   That is, "Anyone who could understand the delight I took in gazing at Beatrice would recognize from my willingness to take my eyes off her that obeying her was an even greater joy."

25–27   The Sphere of Saturn is indicated by a circumlocution. The mythical golden age of the ancient poets, the age of perpetual spring and the innocence of mankind (which Matilda had connected with the Earthly Paradise in *Purg.* XXVIII, 139–144), was also known as the reign of Saturn. Appropriately, the ladder Dante sees here is golden.

28   The ladder of perfection is a common symbol in hagiographic and mystic texts. The most famous precedent is of course Jacob's ladder, to which Dante refers explicitly in Canto XXII, 70–72. "He had a dream: a ladder was there, standing on the ground with its top reaching to heaven; and there were angels of God going up it and coming down" (Gen. 28:12). The Rule of St. Benedict—whom Dante will meet in Canto XXII, following his encounter with a famous Benedictine in the present canto—contains the clause: "Through our actions we must raise that ladder which appeared in a dream to Jacob."

34–42   Some commentators see the extended simile of the flock of jackdaws as Dante's typically realistic expansion of the Bible's laconic "going up" and "coming down." Others, more speculatively, read particular significance into each of the various movements described, applying them to various approaches to the contemplative life (cf. Richard of St. Victor, *De gratia contemplationis* I, 5).

61–63   Just as the smile of Beatrice, in this the highest of the planetary heavens, would prove too much for Dante's all too human sight to bear, so, too, the exquisite celestial harmony of this sphere would vanquish his mortal hearing. Silence is of course conducive to contemplation.

64–72   That is, "The fact that it was I, and not another spirit, who descended lovingly to greet you is not a sign of my greater share of charity, but simply of my obedience to the perfect charity of Divine Providence, which willed it."

73–78   Dante has grasped the fundamental principle that true freedom consists in submission to God's will. What he cannot grasp is why this particular soul should have been predestined from all eternity by God to greet him now.

79–81   The swiftness of the soul's spinning upon itself, like its glowing brighter, is an outward sign of the intensity of its joy.

87   " 'the High Source' ": the Mind of God.

88–90   That is, "The degree of my joy (and consequently of the light I burn with) corresponds to the degree of my understanding of what God purposes" (cf. XIV, 40–42, and XXVIII, 106–114).

91–96   That is, "But, though I can see *what* God wills, I cannot understand *why*. Not even the angelic Seraphim, closest to God among created beings [cf. IV, 28], are able to penetrate that mystery." (Cf. XIX, 40–66.)

105 In response to the pilgrim's request, the speaker will identify himself as St. Peter Damian (1007–1072), an outstanding exemplar of the Benedictine motto *ora et labora* ("pray and work"), a devout and learned monk who accepted the cardinalship out of a sense of duty, but who returned to his cloister at the earliest opportunity. In his many writings, which earned him the title of doctor of the church, he is alternately the apologist of an uncompromisingly rigorous version of monasticism and the scourge of the privileges and abuses of the Church hierarchy. His views on the separate and complementary spheres of influence of the empire and the papacy were no doubt of particular interest to the Dante of the *Monarchia*.

106–108 The " 'stony ridges' " of the Apennine mountains (which cut through the middle of the peninsula not far from Florence, between Italy's eastern Adriatic shore and her western shore on the Tyrrhenian Sea) rise so high that their peaks are above the clouds, where thunder is formed.

109–111 Mount Catria, which dominates the site of the Camaldolese Benedictine monastery of Santa Croce di Fonte Avellana, lies sixty-five miles or so to the south of Florence, in the stretch of the Apennines that separates Umbria from the Marches of Ancona.

112–117 Attracted by monastic life, in 1035 Peter Damian gave up a brilliant career as a lawyer and teacher to enter the convent of Santa Croce, where he would distinguish himself for his sacred learning and the severity of his asceticism, becoming its abbot in 1043. The diet prescribed by the monastery's rule was one of the strictest, consisting for the most part of bread and water, with vegetables seasoned with olive oil permitted on alternate days.

120 What precise punishment Dante had in mind is not known.

121–123 The translation silently resolves a much debated double problem: first textual, then interpretational. The Italian text followed here had already taken care of the textual problem, reading *fu'* (the elided form of *fui,* "I was") in both lines 121 and 122. Some editors favor *fu,* "he was," as the second reading, arguing that the speaker is distinguishing himself from another monk also named Peter, with whom he was often confused. The sense, according to these critics, would therefore be: "Peter the Sinner was the other one, the one who served in Our Lady's House," etc. It is a fact that the monastery of Santa Maria del Porto in Ravenna on the Adriatic shore ("Our Lady's House") was not founded until 1096, a score or more years after Peter Damian's death, by Pietro (or Peter) degli Onesti, who, according to the epitaph preserved in the church, affected the name "Peter the Sinner." There was, however, a local tradition that attributed its founding to the more famous Peter Damian. It is also true that the majority of the latter's epistles and tracts are in fact signed with the same—not uncommon—formula of humility. All in all, it seems more likely that Dante, rather than attempting to correct it, is a victim of the same misapprehension as many of his contemporaries and believed the abbot of Santa Croce and the founder of Our Lady's House to have been one and the same person. As we have seen before, and shall see again in line 125, the poet was not above an occasional anachronism.

124–126 St. Peter Damian was exalted to the cardinalate, a dignity he had not sought, in 1057, at the age of fifty, fifteen years before his death in 1072. His humility and his impatience with ceremony were such that he later prevailed upon the pope to divest him of the honor in order to return to the isolation of his monastic cell and a life of contemplation and prayer. Commentators point out that in designating the office of cardinal by the red hat conferred upon the cardinal at his investiture, Dante is guilty of an anachronism, since the hat came into use only with Pope Innocent IV in 1252, two hundred years later. The example of Peter's humility and austerity prepares the way for yet another attack on the vanity and self-indulgence of the hierarchy.

127–129 At one time the Church was led by dedicated men like St. Peter and St. Paul, who abandoned all else to follow Christ and preach his word. The Hebrew name *Cephas* is the equivalent of the Latin *Petrus*. (Cf. John 1:42: "Jesus looked hard at him and said, 'You are Simon son of John; you are to be called Cephas'—meaning Rock.") The " 'Holy Ghost's / great vessel' " (cf. *Inf.* II, 28) is Paul. (Cf. Acts 9:15: "The Lord replied, 'You must go all the same, because this man is my chosen instrument to bring my name before pagans and pagan kings and before the people of Israel.' ") The Apostles' way of life reflected Jesus' instructions to those who would follow him: "Carry no purse, no haversack, no sandals. . . . Whatever house you go into, let your first words be, 'Peace to this house!' . . . Stay in the same house, taking what food and drink they have to offer, for the laborer deserves his wages" (Luke 10:4–7).

135 Cf. St. Paul: "Or else imagine that although God is ready to show his anger and display his power, yet he patiently puts up with the people who make him angry, however much they deserve to be destroyed" (Rom. 9:22).

139–142 The thunderous outcry of the righteously incensed souls, which breaks the silence of the Heaven of Saturn, overwhelming Dante with amazement, will be explained by Beatrice in Canto XXII.

CANTO XXII

11–12 At the beginning of the previous canto, on their arrival in the Seventh Heaven, Beatrice had been compelled, in order not to confound Dante's senses, to withhold her smile (XXI, 4–12). In like manner, and for the same reason, the blessed souls have suspended their singing (XXI, 57–63).

13–15 The wrathful outcry of the spirits, which climaxed Peter Damian's indictment of the shameful self-indulgence of "modern pastors" at the close of Canto XXI, contained an appeal to God for vengeance. The precise nature of the vengeance invoked, which will come in Dante's lifetime—for some critics, the humiliation of Boniface VIII at Anagni and his death in 1303, for others, the death of the Gascon pope Clement V in 1314—is, as is often the case with Dante's prophecies, left deliberately obscure.

37–39 The town of Cassino lies on the flank of Mount Cassino in the Apennines between Rome and Naples. The summit of the mountain was the site of an ancient temple of Apollo, frequented by pagans stubbornly reluctant to abandon their false beliefs. The topographical description, like the account of the life of the founder of the monastery of Montecassino that follows, is closely based on St. Gregory the Great's *Dialogues.*

40–45 The speaker is St. Benedict (480–543), founder of the Benedictine order, the first religious order in the West. Born at Norcia in Umbria of noble parents, he was sent to Rome to study. Disgusted by the corruption he found there, at the age of fourteen he went to live as a hermit in a cave near Subiaco, in the mountains east of Rome. As his reputation for sanctity grew he acquired a large number of disciples, whom he organized into monastic communities. In southern Italy he destroyed many places of pagan worship and, in about 529, founded the monastery of Montecassino, which became the cradle of the spread of his Rule and remained an important center of learning long after his death there in 543.

47–48 The heat of ardent charity, the love of God and one's neighbor, is the sun that nurtures the flowers of holy sentiments and the fruits of good works.

49 There is more than one saint called Macarius. It is possible that Dante, like the author of the *Golden Legend,* did not distinguish very rigorously between them. St. Macarius the Elder of Egypt (c300–391) spent sixty years in the Libyan desert in solitary prayer and manual labor. St. Macarius the Younger of Alexandria, his contemporary, is credited with being the father of Eastern monasticism. Both were disciples of St. Anthony of Egypt. It was no doubt Dante's intention to balance the name of Romualdus, a Western hermit, with that of a cenobite from the East, where the monastic life had a considerably longer history. Romualdus (Romualdo degli Onesti) was born at Ravenna circa 956. He founded the Camaldolese order of reformed Benedictines at Camaldoli in Tuscany in 1018 and died in 1027. St. Peter Damian wrote his biography.

61–63 The final sphere, where Dante will at last see the assembly of the blessed face to face, is the Empyrean.

64–66 There, every desire is perfectly satisfied. There, all movement, which is generated by unfulfilled longing for God (like that of the nine material heavens), is wholly quieted.

67 The Empyrean is beyond space (the outer limit of our space is the Primum Mobile). It has no poles because, unlike the heavens it contains, it does not revolve. The Empyrean "is not in any place, but was formed only in the First Mind" (*Convivio* II, iii, 11).

70–72 Cf. note to Canto XXI, 28.

73–75 The Rule of St. Benedict—which has gone by the board, says Dante, in the midst of today's general decadence—laid down strict rules for the life of the religious community, organizing the monks' spiritual exercises, and imposing upon them the duties of manual labor, study, and teaching. It created the foundations of monastic life: stable ties to a single monastic community *(stabilitas loci),* irreproachable moral character *(conversatio morum),* and absolute obedience to the abbot (from *abbas,* "father"), the representative of Christ. The Benedictine Rule, often summed up in the phrase *"ora et labora"* ("pray and work"), was eventually adopted in a more or less modified form by all religious orders.

76 Cf. Matthew 21:13: " 'According to scripture' he said 'my house will be called a house of prayer; but you are turning it into a robbers' den.' " The gospel episode of the expulsion of the dealers from the temple is referred to in a similar context in Canto XVIII, 121–123.

78–84 Even usury (which so " 'offends / divine goodness' " [*Inf.* XI, 95–96]) is not so grave as the embezzlement by the monks of monastic revenues—the fruit originally destined, like all the other monies within the keeping of the Church, not to fatten priests and their relatives and mistresses, but to alleviate the misery of the poor. In Canto XII, 93, Dante quoted approvingly the dictum *" 'decimas, quae sunt pauperum Dei' "* ("tithes, which belong to God's poor"), and in *De Monarchia* III, x, 17, he stated that what the Church holds it holds "not as possessor, but as dispenser of the fruit in favor of God's poor."

88 Cf. Acts 3:6: "but Peter said, I have neither silver nor gold."

89 The eulogy of St. Francis of Assisi was pronounced by Thomas Aquinas in Canto XI.

94–96 The sense is that God has performed greater miracles than the one needed to right the Church's wrongs. Examples of such miracles are the staying of the river's flow to permit the passage of Joshua and the Israelites over the Jordan to Jericho (Josh. 3), and the opening of the Red Sea to the children of Israel led by Moses (Exod. 14). Dante's reference to these events echoes the language of Psalm 114 (113A in the Vulgate):3: "The sea fled at the sight, the Jordon stopped flowing."

111–114 The sign that follows Taurus in the zodiac, Dante's fated point of entry into the Heaven of the Fixed Stars, is the constellation of Gemini, under which he was born, between May 21 and June 21, 1265. Its influence was held to be favorable to the pursuit of arts and letters, and hence to the achievement of humanistic glory, which Brunetto Latini had prophesied for Dante in *Inferno* XV, 55–56.

115–117 The sun, the "father of all mortal lives," rose ("was born") and set ("was hidden") in Gemini at the time of the poet's birth in Tuscany.

139 "Latona's daughter" is the moon. Dante's erroneous view regarding the spots on the moon was corrected by Beatrice in Canto II. The spots are on the side of the moon that can be seen from the earth.

142–144 The son of Hyperion is Helios, the sun. At this point in his journey, Dante's vision has become so enhanced that he has no trouble looking directly at the sun, which at the outset, in Canto I, had seemed to him so unbearably bright. Diöne was the mother of Venus; Maia, of Mercury. Their names stand for those of their children.

145–146 For the temperateness of Jupiter, see Canto XVIII, 64–69 and note. Jupiter's father was Saturn, his son Mars.

150 The smallest and most distant object of Dante's vision is the earth, scornfully labeled, here and elsewhere "the little threshing floor" (cf. Canto XXVII, 85, and *De Monarchia* III, XV, 11), whose possession is the worthless bone of contention of all our petty squabbles. Boethius, too, describes the earth as an *"angustissima area,"* "a narrow plot of land," in comparison with the vastness of the universe (cf. *De consolatione philosophiae* II, 7).

CANTO XXIII

1–9 This simile, which compares Beatrice's rapt, expectant gaze toward the Zenith with that of a mother bird eagerly scanning the eastern sky for the first signs of dawn, is no less affecting for being a mosaic of classical reminiscences. In addition to identifying the matrix of the simile in Lactantius' *De Ave Phoenice (On the Phoenix),* 39–42, Daniele Mattalia cites no less than six references to Virgil's *Georgics,* five to the *Aeneid,* and one to Statius' *Achilleid.* The note of intensity with which the canto suspensefully opens will be sustained throughout.

2 To cite but one of the classical allusions contained in these lines, "the night that hides things from us" is a recurrent topos in Virgil. Cf., for instance, *Aeneid* VI, 361–362: "When Jupiter has wrapped the sky in shadows / and black night steals the color from all things."

11–12 Since the Heaven of the Sun is actually far below them, Dante means to indicate the highest point of the Heaven of the Fixed Stars, the point corresponding to the position of the noonday sun in our sky.

19–21 " 'The troops / of the triumphant Christ' " are the souls of all those who faithfully anticipated His Coming or believed in Him after His Incarnation ("the ancient and the new councils" of lines 137–138) and were redeemed by His sacrifice. Their salvation is also the fruit of the sum of the favorable influences exerted by the divinely appointed movements of the heavens. (For the nature and limits of the influence of the stars, cf. *Purg.* XVI, 67–81.)

25–27 Trivia is another name for Diana, the chaste huntress, goddess

of the moon. The everlasting stars are the nymphs that form her en-
tourage. The play of the vowels and consonants in the Italian is exquisite; the passage from Horace usually cited as a parallel is flat by
comparison: "It was night and in a clear sky the moon was shining
among lesser stars" (*Epodes* XV, 1–2).

28–30 The sun of the triumphant Christ's light kindled the "thousand"
(i.e., innumerable) accompanying lights as our sun kindles the stars of
our firmament. The medieval notion that the sun is the source of the light
of all the heavenly bodies is repeated more than once in Dante's
Convivio (see *Convivio* III, xii, 7 [quoted in X, 53, note] and cf. *Convivio*
II, xiii, 15).

31–33 Within the transcendent "living light" that Christ radiates is discernible an even brighter light, too intense for Dante's mortal eyes,
which emanates from the "glowing Substance" of His glorified resur-
rected body. (Cf. XIV, 37–60.)

37 Cf. 1 Corinthians 1:24: "Christ who is the power and the wisdom of
God."

40–42 In Dante's time, lightning was thought to result from dry vapor
pent within a cloud. Supposedly, when the dry vapor caught fire, it expanded, the cloud exploded in thunder, and the escaping fiery vapor descended to earth as lightning. Cf. I, 82–93, note. On the natural tendency
of fire to rise, see Canto I, 115 and note.

46–48 For his own good, Dante was denied Beatrice's smile in the
Heaven of Saturn (cf. XXI, 4–12). But after witnessing Christ's triumph,
his eyes are now able "to bear the power of [her] smile."

54 The "book that tells the past" is the metaphorical book of memory.
The reader will recall that the *Vita nuova*, too, was wholly transcribed
from that book (cf. *Vita nuova* I).

55–60 That is, "Even if I were to be joined in my attempt to describe
Beatrice's smile by all the greatest poets who ever existed [all the
tongues that Polyhymnia and her sister Muses most nourished with their
milk], our combined efforts would fall a thousand times short of the
mark."

61–63 This is one of those moments when the matter to be described,
the suprahuman experience of Paradise, is too much for any poet's art,
and Dante must, as it were, leap over the obstacle and continue on the
other side.

67–69 Dante, again speaking directly to the reader, reiterates briefly
the concepts and images, one might almost say the "boast," of Canto II,
1–15. Rather than statements of personal inadequacy, these recurrent re-
minders of the objective ineffability of this world of supreme bliss draw
attention to the extent of the poet's achievement in evoking that bliss.

72–75 The court of Heaven is the garden, Christ its life-giving sun.
The proximity of the rose and the lilies no doubt derives from the Song

of Solomon 2:1: "I am the rose of Sharon, the lily of the valleys." One of the liturgical names used in the litanies in praise of Mary, the Virgin Mother of God, is Mystical Rose. The fragrant "'lilies'" are the Apostles, whose preaching led men to the true way. Cf. 2 Corinthians 2:14: "Thanks be to God who, wherever he goes, makes us, in Christ, partners of his triumph, and through us is spreading the knowledge of himself, like a sweet smell, everywhere."

76–78   That is, "Thus spoke Beatrice, and I, always ready to do her bidding, raised my feeble eyes again, strengthened by my contemplation of her smile, to do battle with the brightness that had previously [in line 33] overwhelmed them."

85–87   Christ Himself has ascended to the Empyrean (where Dante will later contemplate Him in the mystery of the Trinity) in order that the pilgrim may better distinguish the lesser splendors.

88–90   Beatrice has pronounced the name of Mary, the Mystical Rose. Now Dante devoutly infers that hers is the second brightest flame visible in the Eighth Heaven.

91–96   As Dante fixes his eyes on the light of Mary, the "living star"—another of her liturgical titles, "star of morning," "star of the sea"—whose brightness in Heaven conquers that of all other creatures, as did her virtue on earth, a torch descends and forms a moving crown, a "circulating melody" (109), around her. In all probability, the "torch," which will identify itself in line 103 as "'angelic love,'" represents the Archangel Gabriel, the angel of the Annunciation, who will return to praise Mary in Canto XXXII, 94–114.

107–108   The "'sphere supreme'" is the Empyrean, to which Christ has already ascended and where Mary will soon join Him.

112–120   The "inner shore" or concave inner surface of the Primum Mobile—"the royal cloak of all the wheeling spheres," which encases the eight lower spheres circling within it and, out of yearning for the divine Empyrean, revolves most swiftly (see *Convivio,* II, iii, 9 [quoted in XXVIII, 43–45, note])—was so far above Dante that his eyes lacked the power to follow the crowned flame of the Blessed Virgin Mary as she rose up through it.

128   The *Regina Coeli* is an Easter hymn to the Mother of Christ: "Hail, Queen of Heaven, rejoice, alleluia, / For He whom thou didst merit to bear, alleluia, / Hath risen, as He said, alleluia."

132   Cf. Galatians 6:7: "Where a man sows, there he reaps."

133–135   Our mortal life is a "vale of tears," a "Babylonian exile." (Cf. Psalm 137 [136 in the Vulgate]:1: "Beside the streams of Babylon we sat and wept at the memory of Zion.")

"they had no concern for gold": see Matthew 19:21: "Jesus said, 'If you wish to be perfect, go and sell what you own and give the money to the poor, and you will have treasure in heaven; then come, follow me.'"

137–138 The "ancient and the new / councils" are the souls of the true believers, the saved from the Old and the New Covenants.

139 The keeper of the keys of Heaven, the realm of glory, is St. Peter. Cf. Matthew 16:19: "I will give you the keys of the kingdom of heaven."

CANTO XXIV

1–2 For Jesus as the " 'Blessed Lamb,' " see John 1:29: "The next day, seeing Jesus coming toward him, John said, 'Look, there is the Lamb of God that takes away the sin of the world.' " The Blessed Lamb's great supper, or wedding feast, traditionally symbolizes beatitude, in which the blessed endlessly feast on the vision of God. (See Rev. 19:9.)

2–3 Cf. John 6:35: "Jesus answered: 'I am the bread of life. He who comes to me will never be hungry; he who believes in me will never thirst.' "

4–5 " 'this man receives / foretaste of something fallen from your table' ": The image derives from Matthew 15:27: "even house-dogs can eat the scraps that fall from their master's table." In the *Convivio* (I, i, 10) Dante writes, "And I, therefore, who do not sit at the blessed table, but have escaped from eating the food of the vulgar, sit at the feet of those who are seated, and gather of that which falls from them."

7–9 Beatrice asks these souls to " 'quench . . . somewhat' " Dante's " 'immense desire' " to know God, to partake of the fountain of His Wisdom, " 'that Source' " from which these souls " 'forever drink.' " Cf. John 4:14: "but anyone who drinks the water that I shall give will never be thirsty again: the water that I shall give will turn into a spring inside him, welling up to eternal life.' " (Cf. *Purg.* XV, 130–132.) Beatrice's request is replete with references to the Scriptures, whose fundamental importance as a basis for faith will be emphasized repeatedly in this canto.

13–16 The simile of the "clock's machinery" involves a series of cogged wheels of decreasing size. The "first wheel," the largest, moves so slowly that it "seems to rest," but driving a smaller wheel that must turn several times for each of the larger one's single turns, it causes that smaller wheel to turn faster than itself. At the end of this series, the last and smallest wheel moves so fast that it "flies."

18–19 "what their riches were": i.e., the degree of their beatitude, evidenced by their swiftness and splendor.

22–27 Beatrice's request (7–9) is fulfilled by the song sung by the sphere Dante "noted as most precious," (19) as it whirled around Beatrice. The impossibility of Dante's even recalling to his "imagination" (24) (equivalent to "fantasy" [26]; see *Purg.* XVII, 13–18, note) the divine song of the sphere is expressed with an image probably drawn from the craft of painting. In painting the folds of garments, not simply a darker but also a subtler color was required. Our speech and indeed even our "fantasy" lack the subtlety for "painting folds so deep"—for representing the subtlety and sweetness of "so divine a song."

34–37 This soul is that of St. Peter. See Matthew 16:19, where Jesus says to Peter, "I will give you the keys of the kingdom of heaven." (Cf. *Purg.* IX, 116–127.) St. Peter's appearance was prepared for in the closing lines of Canto XXIII.

37–45 Beatrice entreats St. Peter to " 'test' " Dante concerning faith. This is to be the first part of a three-part examination (occupying Cantos XXIV, XXV, and half of XXVI) on the three Theological Virtues, Faith, Hope, and Charity. Each part will be administered by one of the three Apostles closest to Jesus (see XXV, 30–34, note), each of whom is traditionally associated with the virtue on which he tests Dante. Thus Dante is to undergo a sort of entrance examination to the Empyrean, and as Momigliano observes, "it is natural that the first to examine Dante before he is admitted to the Empyrean should be the keeper of the keys to Paradise." The form of this examination (particularly in this first part), with its rapid succession of concise questions and answers, has its basis in the practices of the medieval universities, as do a number of the associated images. But as Sapegno notes, the actual character of the examination, far from being schoollike or pedantic, is, "on the contrary, ritual and one of solemn consecration and supreme confirmation of the moral and religious mission of the poet."

38 " 'the faith by which you walked upon the Sea' ": see Matthew 14:22–33. "Then Peter got out of the boat and started walking towards Jesus across the water" (Matt. 14:29). Later in the Gospel account, on feeling the force of the wind, Peter takes fright and begins to sink, and Jesus, immediately supporting him, says, "Man of little faith, why did you doubt?" But it is the first part of the account—the faith Peter shows in getting out of the boat and starting to walk—that Dante chooses to highlight.

41–42 " 'that Place . . .' ": the Mind of God. Cf. Canto XV, 61–63.

43 " 'this realm' " is Paradise, and " 'its citizens' " are the blessed.

46–51 In medieval schools of theology and philosophy, in the final examination for the bachelor's degree, the master would first submit a "question for discussion," and the bachelor candidate, after a brief interval in which to prepare himself, was expected to bring arguments to bear on that question. Later, the master alone would pass judgment on the arguments and decide the question.

55–56 Cf. John 7:37–39: "On the last and greatest day of the festival, Jesus stood there and cried out: 'If any man is thirsty, let him come to me! Let the man come and drink who believes in me!' As Scripture says: From his breast shall flow fountains of living water." Cf. also John 4:14 (quoted in 7–9, note).

57–59 The " 'Chief Centurion' " (*primipilo* from the Latin *primopilus)* was the commander of the most important company, or century, in the ancient Roman army. Dante applies the title to Peter as first head of the Church Militant (see XXV, 52, note).

61–62   Dante refers to St. Paul (who, together with St. Peter, evangelized Rome) with St. Peter's own words, from 2 Peter 3:15: "our brother Paul, who is so dear to us." And Dante is about to reply to St. Peter's first question, " 'What is faith?' " (53), with St. Paul's own definition (in his Letter to the Hebrews 11:1).

63–65   Dante himself, at St. Peter's prompting, will explain the significance of the terms of this definition of faith (70–78, and see note).

65 A thing's " 'quiddity' " is its essence (see XX, 92, note).

70–78   Eternal beatitude and Paradise (" 'the things we hope for' " [63]) " 'are hid from sight below.' " Not occupying space and time, they are not susceptible to human sense perception—but " 'from / the senses only can [the mind] apprehend / what then becomes fit for the intellect' " (IV, 40–42). These things are therefore hidden from man's intellect, so that he must base on faith alone his belief in " 'their being.' " Thus faith is the " 'substance' " of these things. Cf. St. Thomas: "In this, indeed, we hope to be blessed: that we will openly see that truth to which we adhere by faith" (*Summa theol.* II–II, q. 4, a. 1). Furthermore, while ordinarily we reason based on evidence derived from the senses, with regard to eternal truths, lacking any such evidence, we must reason based on faith. Thus in these matters, " 'faith is also called an evidence.' "

83–85   " 'this coin' " is faith. Its " 'alloy' " is what it is composed of, or consists of, its definition. Its " 'weight' " is what that definition amounts to. St. Peter now asks Dante, " 'Do you have it in your purse?' " i.e., "Do you have faith?" Dante's reply will deftly continue the numismatic metaphor.

86–87   Dante's " 'coin' " (his faith) is " 'so bright,' " because of the high quality of its " 'alloy,' " and " 'so round,' " because, not having been worn away, its weight is full, intact. It is unmarred by doubt.

88–91   " 'the dear gem' ": faith. On faith, "all virtues are founded" (cf. *Summa theol.* II–II, q. 4, a. 7).

91–96   The inspiration of the Holy Ghost, evident throughout the Old and New Testaments, makes them, as it were, the incontestable premises of a syllogism whose conclusion is faith.

97–99   St. Peter continues Dante's metaphor of the Old and New Testaments as the premises of a syllogism. Why, he asks, does Dante believe the Old and New Testaments to have been divinely inspired.

100–102   The proof that the Scriptures are indeed " 'the speech of God' " (99) relies, Dante says, on the miracles recorded in the Old and New Testaments—acts that nature (likened to a smith who lacks the means) could not possibly have produced alone. (Cf. Matt. 11:2–6.)

103–105   St. Peter points out a circularity in Dante's reasoning: how can miracles prove the veracity of the Scriptures when it is the Scriptures themselves that alone attest to those miracles? In other words, Dante is begging the question, by presupposing the truth of that which he is attempting to demonstrate. Yet such presupposition, though it renders the proof invalid from a strictly logical point of view, is in fact precisely characteristic of faith, and indeed, a proof of Dante's faith.

106–111 Dante aptly responds with St. Augustine's argument: "This one great miracle is enough for us: that the whole world has believed without any miracles" (*The City of God* XXII, 5; cf. St. Thomas, *Summa contra gentiles* I, 6). And this miracle is all the greater in that when Peter began his evangelizing, he was, like all the Apostles, "'poor / and hungry'" and "in appearance, contemptible in the eyes of the world, utterly without all those means which usually justify and procure success in the world" (Sapegno), in spite of which, "'the world / was turned to Christianity.'" Dante's criticism of the "'good plant'" of the Christian Church, "'once a vine and now a thorn'" (cf. XII, 86–87, and see Jer. 2:21), recalls his earlier criticism, voiced by Peter Damian, of the degeneracy of "'modern pastors'" in comparison with St. Peter and St. Paul (XXI, 127–135).

113 *"Te Deum laudamus,"* "We praise Thee, O God," are the opening words of the famous hymn of thanksgiving known as the Te Deum, which especially celebrates the Trinity and is sung at matins and on special and solemn occasions. Dante's responses have indeed exalted and "glorif[ied]" (45) faith, and the souls raise their hymn to God.

115 The title of baron, a rank of nobleman in the medieval feudal system, was often used by Tuscan writers to mean simply "lord" or to designate a great man (Casini-Barbi) and was sometimes applied to saints and to Jesus. St. James too will be called a baron, in XXV, 17.

118–123 St. Peter confirms that Divine Grace has lovingly responded to Dante's invocation (57–59). Now he asks Dante two final questions: what are Dante's own beliefs, and what was the particular source of his faith.

124–126 "'what you believed'": the divinity of Christ. For Peter's declaration of his faith, see Matthew 16:13–17.

126 Though Peter arrived at Jesus' tomb after John, it was he who first entered (as Dante emphasizes in *Monarchy* III, IX, 16). See John 20:1–9: "They ran together, but the other disciple, running faster than Peter, reached the tomb first; he bent down and saw the linen cloths lying on the ground, but did not go in. Simon Peter who was following now came up, went right into the tomb." "Dante here, as in verse 39 [see 38, note], adapts the sacred text to his own requirements" (Bosco-Reggio).

130–132 Dante now begins to recite his Creed, which contains the essential Christian principles: in this first part (130–132), the belief that there exists "'one God—sole, / external—He who, motionless, moves all / the heavens with His love'" (cf. X, 10–12) and with the desire for Him that He instills in the heavens (this latter point is specifically Aristotelian; cf. I, 76–77). Dante's Creed will continue in lines 139–142.

133–138 See *Summa theol.* I, q. 2, a. 3, in which St. Thomas presents and discusses five proofs of the existence of God. Dante has " 'proofs / both physical and metaphysical,' " but he has been well warned against the folly and danger or presumptuously attempting to penetrate with the limited, if not feeble, light of reason, the infinitely profound depths, the abyss, of God's ways and being: " 'Think: how, below, can mind see that which hides / even when mind is raised to Heaven's height?' " (XXI, 101–102). Yet Dante again emphasizes the importance of Scripture as a basis for faith. (On the "complex conjoining in Dante" of the "two often diverging paths: the path of intellect and the path of love," see Introduction, pp. XVI–XVII, and see "Dante in His Age," Bantam Classics *Inferno,* p. 321.)

135–138 These designations indicate the Scriptures in their entirety: in the Old Testament, the five books of Moses, or the Pentateuch; the Prophets, prophetic and historical books; and the Psalms and other Writings (the Hagiographa). This division of the Old Testament is used by Jesus in Luke 24:44: " 'This is what I meant when I said, while I was still with you, that everything written about me in the Law of Moses, in the Prophets and in the Psalms, has to be fulfilled.' " The New Testament is designated by the Gospels and the writings of the Apostles—those " 'who wrote words given to [them] by the Holy Ghost' "—the Acts, the Epistles, or Letters, and Apocalypse, or the Book of Revelation.

139–142 Dante continues his profession of faith, his Creed, begun in lines 130–132. His expression of the Triune nature of God echoes, in particular, the Athanasian Creed (one of the three ecumenically accepted Creeds, today the least known [cf. the Apostles' and Nicene Creeds], no longer ascribed to St. Athanasius, but evidently influenced by his thought). According to the Athanasian Creed, "this is the Catholic faith: we worship one sole God in the Trinity, and the Trinity in the Unity, without confusing the Persons, or separating the Substance." (Cf. XIII, 25–27.) God, in His Unity, may be spoken of in the singular, with "is," and at the same time, in His Trinity, spoken of in the plural, with "are."

142–147 " 'Of this profound condition / ... Gospel teaching / has often set the imprint on my mind' ": See, e.g., Matthew 28:19, John 14:16–17, 20, 26, 2 Corinthians 13:14, 1 Peter 1:2, 1 John 5:7, and Revelation 22:1. Once again Dante emphasizes the prime importance of Scripture for the revelation of truth—here, the truth of God's Triune nature. Cf. St. Thomas: "by natural reason those things can be known which pertain to the Unity in the Divine Essence, but not those things which pertain to the distinction of the Persons" (*Summa theol.* I, q. 32, a. 1).

145 " 'This is the origin, this is the spark' ": namely, the " 'profound condition / of God that [Dante has] touched on' " (142–143): His being at once " 'single and threefold' " (141). His Unity in Trinity and Trinity in Unity.

CANTO XXV

1–12 The opening of this canto gives pensive and pathetic expression to Dante's earthly hopes: his long cherished hope to return to Florence, and his hope of being crowned a poet, of meriting "[Apollo's loved] laurel" (see 9–12, note). But Dante's poetic, political, and religious missions were inseparable. His hope is that "this sacred poem" (1) (so near to completion at this point) might "overcome the cruelty" (4) of the "wolves that war on [Florence]," (6) the Black Guelphs in power in Florence, whose political condemnation of Dante had forced him into exile (see "Dante in His Age," Bantam Classics *Inferno,* pp. 322–329). For Dante nothing less than the confirmation of being crowned a poet "at [his] baptismal font" in the baptistery of San Giovanni in Florence will do—and this not from motives of vain pride, but in the absolute conviction of the justice of his threefold cause. Not long before his death, Dante in fact declined an invitation by the scholar Giovanni del Virgilio to come to Bologna to be crowned a poet (see "Dante in His Age," p. 329). And if he should ever return to Florence, Dante says, it will be "with other voice" (7)—a poetic voice changed and matured "through these long years" (3)—and "with other fleece" (7)—the white hair of old age, but also, a poetic material (in which the voice is clothed) substantially different from that of his youthful, pre-exilic works.

With Dante already " 'so near the final blessedness' " (XXII, 124), the expression of earthly hopes, in these opening lines, might at first seem somewhat inappropriate in a canto that will be mainly devoted to his examination on the second of the three Theological Virtues. Hope, whose object is glory in Paradise. But the tone of wistful contingency in these lines ("If it should happen . . . If this sacred poem . . . can ever overcome the cruelty")—the realization implicit in them of the possible futility of those long-cherished hopes and the possible necessity of resignation to the sorrows of exile—contrasts with those specific, earthly hopes. Furthermore, the central consolation of this canto lies in the hope of otherworldly reward: " 'the certain expectation / of future glory' " (67–68).

4–6 "The fair fold" is Florence, " 'the sheepfold of St. John [the patron saint of Florence]' " (XVI, 25). As in the beginning of Canto XXIV, the images here are biblical (cf. Ecclesiasticus 13:17, Jer. 50:6, and Matt. 10:16).

9–12 For "the laurel crown," the crown of poets, see I, 25–27, and 13–36, note. Dante's "baptismal font" was in the baptistery he called "my handsome San Giovanni" (*Inf.* XIX, 17). There he first "found entry," through baptism, to the Catholic faith. And for that faith, St. Peter "garlanded [his] brow" (see XXIV, 151–153).

13–15 "the first . . . of . . . His vicars" is St. Peter, the first pope; see Matthew 16:18: "So now I say to you: You are Peter and on this rock I will build my Church. And the gates of the underworld can never hold out against it."

17–18 The title of baron, also applied to St. Peter in XXIV, 115 (see note), is given here to James the Apostle, St. James the Great, son of Zebedee and brother of John the Apostle (see Matt. 10:2). Martyred under Herod Agrippa I in A.D. 44 (Acts 12:2), his body was believed to have been miraculously transferred to Santiago de Compostela in Galicia in northwest Spain, where the sanctuary containing his tomb was second only to Rome as a pilgrimage site in the Middle Ages.

22–24 "both . . . princes": St. James and St. Peter. (For the title *prince,* cf. *baron,* XXIV, 115, note.) The "banquet that is offered them on high" is God's wisdom. His love, His grace. (Cf. XXIV, 1–9.)

26 *"coram me":* Latin, meaning, "before me."

28–30 " 'our basilica' ": the divine realm. The Epistle of St. James (believed in Dante's time to have been written by St. James the Great, though today generally attributed to St. James the Less, brother of Jesus [Matt. 13:55]) speaks of God's generosity: "If there is any one of you who needs wisdom, he must ask God, who gives to all freely and ungrudgingly. . . . It is all that is good, everything that is perfect, which is given us from above; it comes down from the Father of all light" (James 1:5, 17).

30–34 Just as she had entreated St. Peter to " 'test [Dante] concerning . . . faith' " (XXIV, 37–38), Beatrice here entreats St. James to test him on the second of the three Theological Virtues, Hope. St. James " 'can' " (32), i.e., he is eminently qualified, well understanding the nature of hope, for on the three occasions on which Jesus chose the Apostles Peter, James, and John alone to be present at revelatory or decisive events (the restoring to life of Jairus' daughter [Luke 8:40–56], the Transfiguration [Matt. 17:1–8], and the prayer in the Garden of Gethsemane [Matt. 26:36–46]), it was James—according to the exegesis that saw the three Apostles as representing the three Theological Virtues—who was "the figure / of hope." Significantly, Dante named his sons after these three Apostles.

34–37 By sustaining the radiance of the blessed (or perhaps, in particular the radiance of the three Apostles), the soul (and in Dante's case, the living man) ascending in Paradise is strengthened and prepared for the sight of even greater splendors. (Cf. XXIII, 46–48.)

37 "The second fire": St. James.

38–39 "the mountains": i.e., the Apostles James and Peter. The metaphor derives from Psalm 121 [120 in the Vulgate]:1: "I lift my eyes to the mountains: where is help to come from?"

40–45 When, owing to God's grace, Dante will have seen the whole of Paradise (the " 'court' " of God, " 'our Emperor' "), even to " 'the inmost of His halls,' " the Empyrean, and seen those souls most blessed (" 'His nobles' "), then Dante's hope, and the hope of those " 'others' " who will hear his account of "the holy kingdom" (I, 11), may be strengthened and "'comforted.'" For the feudal terminology, cf. XXIV, 112, 115, and XXV, 17, 23.

46–48 St. James asks three things of Dante: that he tell "'what hope is,'" to what degree he has hope ("'how it has blossomed / within your mind'"), and what the source of his hope is. These three questions correspond to those St. Peter asked Dante concerning faith, in XXIV, 53, 85, and 89–91, respectively.

49–51 Cf. Canto XV, 54. Beatrice is sensitive to the fact that St. James' second question—to what degree does Dante have hope—might be "'hard'" (61) for Dante to answer because of his not wishing to appear presumptuous (Hope being "the certain expectation / of future glory" [67–68], or that it might, indeed, be "'cause for arrogance'" (62) in Dante, whose self-admitted worst failing was pride (*Purg.* XIII, 136–138, and note). She thus takes it upon herself to answer for him, though she will leave it to Dante to reply to "the other two points" (58).

52 The "'Church Militant'" consists of those Christians still alive on earth, in contrast to the Church Triumphant, the blessed in "'eternal / triumph'" (v. 116–117) in Paradise.

54 "'the Sun'": God (cf. IX, 8, and XVIII, 105), "'whose rays reach all our ranks,'" all the blessed of the Church Triumphant.

55–56 "'Egypt,'" the land of exile and bondage for the Hebrews in the Bible, traditionally symbolizes man's life on earth (cf. *Purg.* II, 46, note), and "'Jerusalem,'" "the city of the living God" (Heb. 12:22), Heaven.

57 "'before his term of warring ends'": i.e., while still alive, still a member of the Church Militant. (Cf. v. 117 and note.)

58–60 St. James questioned Dante "'not ... so that [he, St. James] may know,'" for he already knows; cf. XXIV, 40–42. Rather, he asked Dante to speak of hope because, in spite of the fact that the blessed no longer experience hope, the virtue remains dear to St. James (see 82–83 and note).

61–63 See 49–51, note.

64–66 Cf. XXIV, 46–51. The tone of the simile here seems somewhat more confident—Dante has been bolstered, perhaps, by Beatrice's auspicious words (52–57).

67–69 Replying to St. James' first question (46), Dante draws his definition of hope directly from the Sentences of Peter Lombard (see X, 106–108 and note): "Hope is the certain expectation of future beatitude, proceeding from God's grace and from antecedent merits" (*Sent.* III, 26). As Singleton notes, this definition continues: "Without merits, to hope for something is not hope but may be called presumption." St. Thomas emphasizes that although hope, to be justified, requires merits, it is not, properly speaking, caused by merits, but only by grace (*Summa theol.* II–II, q. 17, a. 1).

70–72 Responding now to St. James' third question (47–48), Dante

says that "'this light,'" hope, "'has come to [him] from many stars,'"
i.e., from many sources of illumination, from many authors of sacred
texts (cf. Dan. 12:3: "The learned will shine as brightly as the vault of
heaven, and those who have instructed many in virtue, as bright as stars
for all eternity"). The "'chief singer of the Sovereign Guide'" is David,
king of Israel (see xx, 38, and 37–42, notes), whose Psalms, so often expressing and praising hope, "'first instilled'" hope in Dante's heart.

73–75   A "'theody'" is a song of praise to God, a psalm. Dante is quot-
ing Psalm 9:10. As in xxiv, 90–91, implicit in lines 74–75 is the central
idea that "faith, by its very nature, precedes all other virtues" (*Summa
theol.* ii–ii, q. 4, a. 7; cf. ii–ii, q. 17, a. 7).

76–77   Dante is referring to the Epistle of St. James (see 28–30, note),
expressing hope in a number of passages. (See James 1:12, 2:5, 4:7–10,
and 5:8.)

78   "'your rain'": i.e., hope.

82–83   The blessed no longer experience hope, having already had
their highest hope fulfilled (see *Summa theol.* ii–ii, q. 18, a. 2: "hope, like
faith, ceases in [Paradise]"). Yet so ardent was the love with which St.
James burned, during his lifetime, for the virtue of Hope, that that love
remains unextinguished even in Paradise.

84   The "'palm'" is the traditional symbol of martyrdom. St. James
was beheaded in A.D. 44 at the order of Herod Agrippa I (see Acts 12:2).
"'my departure from the field'": i.e., from the battlefield on which
man's "'war of life'" is fought (see v, 117, note).

88–90   The Old and New Testaments speak of the ultimate destination,
or fate, of those souls whom God elects, and this fate (specified in lines
91–96) is "'what is promised us by hope.'"

91–96   Dante's interpretation of Isaiah 61:7—"Twofold therefore shall
they possess in their land, everlasting joy is theirs"—sees "twofold" as
signifying "'a double garment,'" the glorified body as well as soul,
worn by the blessed in Paradise. (This interpretation may have been suggested to Dante by Isaiah 61:10: "He has clothed me in the garments of
salvation"). St. James' "'brother'" (94), is St. John the Apostle and
Evangelist (considered one and the same, in Dante's day, with John, the
author of the Book of Revelation, or Apocalypse). In Revelation, John
"'treats of those white robes,'" the luminous bodies of the blessed (see
Rev. 3:5 and 7:9–17).

98–99   "'Sperent in te,'" "Let them hope in You," are the opening
words (in the Vulgate) of verse 11 of the Ninth Psalm, which Dante ad-
duced earlier (73–74), in answering St. James' third question. Now that
Dante has completed his examination on hope, these fitting words are
sung.

100–102   From December 21 to January 21 the sun is in the constellation Capricorn, which, in the zodiac, is diametrically opposite Cancer,
"the Crab." Thus when the sun (in Capricorn) is above the horizon, dur-

ing the day, the Crab is below the horizon, but when the sun sets, the Crab rises above the horizon. According to Dante's figure then, "If the Crab had one such crystal," that is, if one star in the constellation Cancer were as bright as this soul-light became, then even when the sun had set, that one bright star (in the newly risen Crab) would continue to light the sky as if it were day. There would be, so to speak, "a month of one long day." In other words, the soul-light became as bright as the sun. For a similar hypothetical and somewhat fantastic parallel, cf. XXVII, 13–15.

107 " 'those two flames' ": St. Peter and St. James.

111 The echo of "bride" from the simile of lines 103–105 suggests at least the possibility that these three souls, representative of the three Theological Virtues, are dancing and singing to honor Beatrice (cf. XXIV, 22–24). Compare the angelic dance and beseeching song of the three personified Theological Virtues in *Purgatorio* XXXI, 130–132.

112–114 " 'He who lay upon the breast / of Christ' " at the Last Supper, is John the Apostle: see John 13:23–25 and John 21:20. " 'From on the Cross,' " Jesus elected John to take Jesus' place as a son to Mary and to care for her as his mother. See John 19:26–27: "Seeing his mother and the disciple he loved standing near her, Jesus said to his mother, 'Woman, this is your son.' Then to the disciple he said, 'This is your mother.' And from that moment the disciple made a place for her in his home."

113 " 'Christ our Pelican' ": Christ was often symbolically represented by a pelican because it was commonly believed that the pelican could pierce its own breast and with its blood bring its deceased young back to life and nourish them—just as Christ, with the sacrifice of His blood, redeemed and gave eternal life to men (see John 6:54, 56).

115–117 Beatrice, exemplar of theological vision, gazes steadfastly at the dance of the three Apostles. Some interpret: Theology's task is to center its attention on the Theological Virtues; others, Theology must never turn its gaze from Holy Scripture.

119 "somewhat eclipsed," during a partial eclipse of the sun.

122–126 Deriving from the Gospel account (in John 21:20–23) of a rumor that arose among Jesus' disciples that John would not die (a rumor denied by John himself), a legend arose that John had been taken up to Heaven in body as well as soul. Dante, eager to see St. John in the flesh, "squints and strains" (118) to see within his brilliant splendor. But St. John discredits the legend in no uncertain terms.

" 'until / our number equals the eternal purpose' ": In the *Convivio* (II, v, 12), Dante says that God created mankind in order that with the souls of the blessed He might replace Lucifer and the other angels who rebelled and were cast out of Heaven (see XXIX, 49–51, 55–57, and 49–57, note). When this " 'eternal purpose' " is fulfilled, Judgment Day will come, and the Resurrection of the Flesh (see XIV, 43–45), but until then St. John's body will remain on earth together with other human bodies.

127–128 In Paradise only Christ and the Virgin Mary (who ascended back to the Empyrean, in XXIII, 85–87, and 118–120) already " 'wear / their double garment,' " their glorified body as well as soul.

130–135 "the flaming circle": formed by the Apostles Peter, James, and John (see 106–109). On Dante's simile for the reverent alacrity with which these souls cease their dance and song the instant St. John stops and begins to speak, Benvenuto comments, "there is no king or commander in the world, whose subjects obey him so promptly as rowers do the head of the crew."

CANTO XXVI

1–2 "with blinded eyes": as a result of his too intent gazing at the sun-bright flame of St. John. (On Dante's blindness, see 76–79, note.)

4–9 While Dante's examinations on faith and hope were both preceded by Beatrice's entreating the administering Apostle to test Dante (XXIV, 34–39; XXV, 28–31), here St. John charitably takes the initiative himself, first immediately assuring the "apprehensive" (1) Dante implicitly (4–5) and then explicitly (8–12), that his blindness is only temporary, and bidding him compensate for the sensory loss of his power of sight with the light of the intellect, in reasoned discourse. St. John then begins without delay the third and final part of Dante's examination, on the third Theological Virtue, Charity. He bids Dante declare the object of his soul's longing, the object of his love. Although St. John does not begin with an explicit question as to the definition of the virtue (cf. XXIV, 53, and XXV, 46), that definition is, in fact, already implicit in his question. For charity, says St. Thomas, is "love of God, loved as the object of beatitude, to which we are disposed by means of faith and hope" (*Summa theol.* I–II, q. 65, a. 5).

8–12 St. John assures Dante that his vision will eventually be restored by Beatrice, merely through her gazing upon him, for " 'within her gaze' " she has " 'that force the hand of Ananias had.' " Ananias, one of the first disciples of Jesus, was sent by the Lord to restore Saul's (St. Paul's) vision by laying his hands on him. Saul had been blinded when, while traveling to Damascus to arrest the followers of Jesus, Jesus appeared to him in a "light from heaven . . . saying 'Saul, Saul, why are you persecuting me?' " (See Acts 9:1–19.)

14–15 " 'the fire with which I always burn' ": the fire of Love, first instilled in Dante by Beatrice, through his eyes, the " 'gates' " to his heart (an image frequent in 13th- and 14th-century lyric poetry). Cf. *Purgatorio* XXX, 40–42 (and see "Dante in His Age," Bantam Classics *Inferno*, p. 320).

16–18 To St. John's question (7–8), Dante responds that God is the beginning and end (" 'Alpha and Omega' "), the origin and aim of all his loves, both greater and lesser. Cf. Revelation 1:8 and 21:6: " 'I am the Alpha and the Omega' says the Lord God, who is, who was, and who is to come, the Almighty"; "I am the Alpha and the Omega, the Beginning and the End" (cf. Rev. 22:13). The letters naturally suggest the metaphor of "writings . . . read out" by Love.

22–24   While a fairly general answer sufficed for St. John's first question, his next will require that Dante " 'sift with a still finer sieve,' " that he be more specific, that he particularize in his next answer. Considering that St. John's next question, analogous to those asked by St. Peter, in XXIV, 123, and by St. James in XXV, 47–48, would have Dante tell " 'who led [his] bow to aim at such a target,' " that is, who directed his love toward God, St. John's desire that Dante be especially particular and clear in his reply might be motivated by the fact that Dante's love had not always been directed with such perfect rectitude (see *Purg.* XXX, 109–145, and XXXI, 1–63). (For the metaphor of bow and target, cf. I, 125–126, and XV, 43.)

25–27   " 'philosophic arguments' ": i.e., " 'human reasoning' " (46); " 'authority whose source is here' ": divinely inspired Scripture (cf. XXIV, 133–138).

28–30   Insofar as the good is understood as being the good, it " 'enkindles love,' " and the greater the good understood as such, the greater the love it enkindles.

30–36   Anyone who discerns the underlying truth of this principle must love God (" 'that Essence / which is preeminent' ") " 'more than . . . all else,' " for God is the Highest Good (cf. XIII, 52–54, and XIX, 52–54).

37–39   " 'him / who demonstrates . . . that the first love / of the eternal beings is their Maker' ": Dante is probably referring to the author of the *De causis* (*Book on Causes*), widely attributed to Aristotle in the Middle Ages, though not by St. Thomas, and probably not by Dante (though Dante may indeed intend Aristotle here, with the *Metaphysics* [e.g., XII, 11] in mind). The idea is, in any case, basically Aristotelian. In the *Convivio* (III, ii, 7, 9), citing the *De causis,* Dante writes: "the human soul naturally wills, with all its desire, to exist; and since its being depends upon God, and is preserved by Him, it naturally desires and wills to be united with God, in order to fortify its being. . . . And this uniting is that which we call love." (Cf. also *Convivio* IV, xii, 14 [quoted in VII, 143–144, note].) A similar argument can be applied to the other eternal beings as well, the heavenly bodies and the Celestial Intelligences, or angels, since "each substantial form proceeds from its first cause, which is God, as is written in the *Book on Causes*" (*Convivio* III, ii, 4; cf. I, 76–77).

40–45   The " 'true Author' " is God Himself, who, after "Moses said 'Show me your glory, I beg you,' " replied " 'I shall show you all goodness' " (see Exod. 33:18–23 [Dante is translating from the Vulgate]). God is " 'all goodness,' " the all-inclusive and Highest Good, and therefore rightly to be loved " 'more than . . . all else' " (33). St. John, too, reveals this truth, at the beginning of his Gospel, which " 'more than any other proclamation' "—in particular, more than the other Gospels, which are less explicitly theological and philosophical than John's—" 'cries out to earth the mystery of Heaven,' " the mystery of God's nature and of the Incarnation of God, in which "the Word was made flesh" for the redemption of mankind, demonstrating God's grace and the boundless goodness that makes Him the true and proper object of man's " 'highest love' " (48). (See John 1.)

46–48 " 'authorities' ": scriptural authorities.

49–51 " 'other cords' ": i.e., other stimuli, other reasons. St. John, in this final question of Dante's examination on charity, continues to press Dante for particulars (see 22–24, note).

52 "Christ's Eagle" is St. John. The "flying eagle" is one of the four animals of the Apocalypse (see Rev. 4:6–7), traditionally used as symbols of the four Evangelists (the Lion for St. Mark, the bull for St. Luke, and the animal with a human face, for St. Matthew). The symbol suggests John's keen insight into "the mystery of Heaven" (45).

57 " 'the world's existence' ": cf. Psalm 19 [18 in the Vulgate]:1–2: "The heavens declare the glory of God, the vault of heaven proclaims his handiwork; day discourses of it to day, night to night hands on the knowledge."

58 " 'and mine' ": i.e., my existence. Cf. Psalm 8:4–5: "Ah, what is man that you should spare a thought for him, the son of man that you should care for him? Yet you have made him little less than a god, you have crowned him with glory and splendor."

58–59 " 'the death that He sustained that I / might live' ": Christ's sacrifice for the redemption of mankind. See John 1, and 1 John 4:9: "God's love for us was revealed when God sent into the world his only Son so that we could have life through him."

59–60 " 'the hope of all / believers,' " for eternal beatitude.

61 " 'living knowledge,' " that God is the Greatest Good, and therefore to be loved above all else.

62 " 'the sea of twisted love' ": i.e., love of an evil object or else (as in Dante's case [see *Purg.* XXX, 124–132, and 34–36]) excessive love of a lesser, or " 'secondary,' " good (see *Purg.* XVII, 94–102, and 97, note). The " 'right love' " is, of course, the love of God. The metaphor of sea and shore recalls *Inferno* I, 22–24.

64–66 All creatures in the created world, Dante loves in proportion to the good bestowed upon them by God. The image recalls John 15:1: "I am the true vine, and my Father is the vinedresser."

67–69 Dante's examination is ended, and his success is attested to by the "song most sweet," in which Beatrice, too, takes part. " 'Holy, holy, holy' " begins the song of the four animals of the Apocalypse, with which they "glorified, and honored and gave thanks" to God (see Rev.

4:6–9). In Isaiah 6:3, the same words are cried out by the Seraphim flying above God's throne.

71–73 Sight, in Dante's time, was conceived of as arising from the transmission by the visual spirit (the "spirit of eyesight," which ran along a nerve running from the pupil in the eye to the brain) of the image formed on the pupil, as on a mirror, by "brightness"—i.e., by light and color, conveying the form of visible things, passing successively from membrane to membrane (beginning with the eyelid) in the eye. (See *Convivio* III, ix, 7–10.)

76 "until his judgment helps him": i.e., by making sense of the confused image seen upon first waking. (Cf. *Purg.* XXIX, 49, and see 43–51, note.)

76–79 "so / did Beatrice dispel . . . the chaff / from my eyes"—restoring Dante's vision, just as St. John had assured him she would (8–12). The symbolical and allegorical significance of Dante's blindness, which has lasted throughout his examination on charity, and the restoration of his vision by Beatrice's gaze, is much disputed and is undoubtedly multiple, but Beatrice's words, and then Dante's, in Canto XXII, 124–138, seem to shed some light: "'You are so near the final blessedness,' / so Beatrice began, 'that you have need / of vision clear and keen; and thus, / before / you enter farther, do look downward, see / what I have set beneath your feet already: / much of the world is there. . . . I approve / that judgment as the best, which holds this earth / to be the least; and he whose thoughts are set / elsewhere, can truly be called virtuous.'"

By gazing too intently at the brilliant light of St. John in an effort to verify the legend that St. John had been raised to Heaven with his body (XXV, 118–123); thereby concerning himself with what is, for St. John apparently, a piece of earthly superstitious sentimentalism (see XXV, 122–123, 129), Dante was, so to speak, dragging his feet on the ground, distracting himself from, and interfering with, the process of refining his doctrine, which the examination is intended to effect. But there is no contradiction at all here in seeing Dante's blindness as divinely effected to facilitate the utmost absorption of thought as he strives to enunciate the nature and his personal experience of charity or Love. Indeed, that Dante's blindness, which is intended to insulate him from the realm of "'mere appearances'" (*Purg.* XXXI, 34), comes about as it does is proof that there is a need for that insulation; it aids him in perfect concentration on spiritual truth. His blindness is thus at once appropriate justice and a gift of God's grace.

It is fitting—now that Dante's doctrine has been thoroughly sifted and resoundingly certified pure and secure—that it should be Beatrice who restores his vision, for it is she who has been, in Dante's life, the principal vehicle of God's bestowal of illuminating grace upon him—though the force "within her gaze" (11), like "that force the hand of Ananias had" (12), is entirely God's.

83–84 The "'first soul'": the soul of Adam, the first man. At the side of the three Apostles representing the three Theological Virtues, which were imparted by God through Christ as gifts to man to guide him toward salvation from his fallen state, it is appropriate that Adam, who incurred man's fall, should appear—he who, " 'damning himself, damned all his progeny' " (VII, 27).

93–94 To Adam, the progenitor of all mankind, " 'each bride is as a daughter and/daughter-in-law,' " since she is both a descendant of his and the bride of a descendant.

101–102 Through a brightening or flashing in the radiance surrounding his soul, Adam showed his joy in "coming to delight [Dante]" through answering the questions in his mind.

103–108 Adam generously and paternally reiterates what Dante by now well knows: that the souls of the blessed are able to read Dante's thoughts reflected in the Mind of God (" 'the Truthful Mirror' "), upon which they gaze.

109–112 " 'how long... in that high Garden' ": i.e., in the garden of Eden (see Gen. 2:8). Earthly Paradise (on the summit of the mountain island of Purgatory), where Beatrice " 'readied' " Dante to begin his ascent to Paradise. This is the first of four questions of Dante's that Adam will voice aloud, afterward answering them in the order of their importance.

112 " 'just how long it pleased my eyes' ": i.e., how long Adam remained in the garden of Eden before he was expelled by God (see Gen. 3:22–24).

113 " 'the true cause of the great anger' ": i.e., the true reason for God's expulsion of Adam from the garden of Eden, the true nature of Adam's sin.

114 " 'what idiom' ": i.e., what language Adam invented and spoke.

115–117 Adam chooses to answer the most important of Dante's four questions first (cf. IV, 25–27)—the third question (113). "The cause of [Adam's] long exile" from Earthly Paradise and, after his death, from Paradise (see 118–123, note), did not lie in his tasting of the forbidden fruit per se (see VII, 25–27 and note), but rather in his trespass of the spiritual boundary set by God as proper to man. As St. Thomas explains, "man's first sin was in desiring a spiritual good beyond its proper measure. Now this pertains to pride.... The first thing man desired was his own excellence. Therefore the disobedience in him was caused by pride" (*Summa theol.* II–II, q. 163, a. 1). (Cf. VII, 97–102.)

118–123 Adam answers next Dante's first question (109–112). He lived 930 years (930 passages of the sun through the entire zodiac) and was then in Limbo (" 'that place from which your Lady sent you Virgil' " [see *Inf.* II, 52–74]) for 4,302 years, during which he longed for Paradise. Adam was liberated from Hell by Christ's Harrowing of Hell in A.D. 34 (see *Inf.* IV, 52–61, note); from then until 1300 (the year of Dante's journey [*Inf.* I, 1–3, note]) was 1,266 years. The total span was thus 6,498 years. Dante is following the chronology established by Eusebius of Caesarea (c260–c339) in his *Thesaurus Temporum*. (Cf. *Purg.* XXXIII, 61–63.)

124–132 In his earlier work *On Writing in the Common Tongue* (*De vulgari eloquentia* I, VI, 4–7), Dante had expressed the view that the Hebrew language had been created directly by God simultaneously with the creation of Adam, and that it was therefore unchanging and incorruptible (to be spoken for all time by the Hebrews), and had been spoken universally until, to punish man's attempt to build "a tower with its top reaching heaven" (the tower of Babel), God confused men's language, so that they could no longer understand one another. (See Gen. 11:1–9. Cf. *Inf.* XXXI, 76–81, and *Purg.* XII, 34–36.) But subsequently Dante's thoughts on the nature and origin of language changed and here, through Adam's response to his fourth question (114) Dante expresses his revised opinions. Although there is a natural predisposition in man to express himself using words, the particular words and way are for man himself to choose. (Cf. *Summa theol.* II–II, q. 85, a. I.) His language, like all products of human reason, is subject to change and extinction. In fact, says Adam, the first language was extinct by the time the Babylonians (under King Nimrod) attempted to build the tower of Babel.

133–136 Dante revises here his earlier opinion (in *De vulgari eloquentia* I, IV, 4) that the first word uttered by Adam was *El* (the earliest name for God among the Hebrews, according to St. Isidore [*Etymologiae* VII, i, 3]), though the earliest name of God, *I*, which Adam here says preceded *El*, is probably Dante's invention, undoubtedly prompted partly by the letter's significance as a symbol for one, or unity, the supreme attribute of God (Casini-Barbi).

137–138 The image recalls Horace's *Ars poetica*, 60–62: "As forests change their leaves with each year's decline, and the earliest drop off: so with words, the old race dies, and, like the young of human kind, the newborn bloom and thrive" (Loeb Classical Library translation).

139–142 Lastly Adam answers Dante's second question (112). " 'That peak rising highest from the sea' " is the mountain island of Purgatory (cf. *Inf.* XXVI, 133–135). Adam's sojourn in Eden (on its summit), including the time before his sin and the time after his sin but before his expulsion (" 'first pure, then tainted' "), lasted " 'from/the first hour' " of the day, 6 A.M., until the seventh hour, when the sun passes the 90° point overhead, i.e., between 12 noon and 1 P.M. In sum, then, Adam and Eve remained in the garden of Eden no more than a pitiably brief seven hours. Estimates as to the length of their sojourn varied considerably (the longest, perhaps, thirty-four years, the length of Christ's life on earth), but Dante adopts the very briefest, that of Petrus Comestor, Peter Book-Devourer (XII, 135), in his *Historia scolastica*, ch. 24.

CANTO XXVII

1–3 The blessed souls intone a hymn of praise to the Holy Trinity. The full text of the liturgical *Gloria* reads as follows: "Glory be to the Father, and to the Son, and to the Holy Spirit, as it was in the beginning, is now and ever shall be, world without end. Amen."

10–12 The four "torches" are Peter, James, John, and Adam. The "first to come" was of course St. Peter, Christ's first vicar.

13–15 Flushing with righteous indignation, Peter's light intensifies and changes color from white to red, as if the planet Jupiter had exchanged its silvery whiteness for the red of the fiery planet Mars. The unusual simile (cf. XIII, 1–18 and XXV, 100–102) is further complicated by the fact that it contains two levels of comparison—that of Peter's appearance to that of the planets' and that of the planets' to that of the birds'—the second of which may seem gratuitous. Early commentators, however, offer an explanation, pointing out that the planets' rays were technically referred to as their "plumage."

22–24 The threefold reiteration of " 'my place' " recalls the rhetorical repetition of Jeremiah 7:4: "Put no trust in delusive words like these: This is the sanctuary of Yahweh, the sanctuary of Yahweh, the sanctuary of Yahweh!" St. Peter was martyred and buried in Rome. His place on earth is usurped by the current pope—in 1300, Boniface VIII. So unworthy is Boniface of the office that, in the eyes of Christ, the papacy is vacant.

26 The " 'perverse one who fell from Heaven' " is of course Lucifer, otherwise known as Satan.

34–36 The reference is to the darkness that accompanied Christ's agony on the cross: "It was now about the sixth hour and, with the sun eclipsed, a darkness came over the whole land until the ninth hour. The veil of the temple was torn right down the middle" (Luke 23:44–45).

40–41 The " 'Bride of Christ' " is the Church (cf. XI, 31). Linus, pope from 66 to 78, was Peter's first successor and, like Peter, gave his life's blood for the Church, as did Linus' successor, Cletus, or Anacletus, pope from 78 to 91.

44–45 The early popes Sixtus I (117–127), Pius I (142–149), Calixtus I (217–222), and Urban I (222–230) were all martyrs for the faith.

46–48 Recent popes have divided the house of God against itself, favoring one faction (the Guelphs) over the other (the Ghibellines).

49–51 The keys of the kingdom of heaven, conferred upon him by Christ, symbolized the spiritual authority of Peter and his successors (see Matt. 16:19, [quoted in XXIII, 139, note]). The papal seal, with which venal and worthless privileges were being stamped, incorporates the image of St. Peter.

56–59 Cf. Psalm 44 (43 in the Vulgate):23–24: "Wake up, Lord! Why are you asleep? Awake! Do not abandon us for good. Why do you hide your face, and forget we are wretched and exploited?"

58–59 The generic plurals contain transparent allusions to individual French popes—Clement V (the "'Gascon'" of XVII, 82), pope from 1305 to 1314, who took the papacy into its Babylonian Captivity in Avignon, and John XXII, pope from 1316 to 1334, a native of Cahors. In *Inferno* XI, 50, the name of Cahors was used as a synonym for usury.

61–63 Publius Scipio Africanus the Elder led the victorious Roman legions against Hannibal in 202 B.C. (cf. VI, 49–52).

64–66 This allusion to Dante's "'mortal weight'" appears to confirm the fact that he conceives his journey as having been made in the flesh (cf. I, 73–75, note). St. Peter's solemn admonition to Dante to declare on earth what he has seen may be added to the similar injunctions of Beatrice in the Earthly Paradise (*Purg.* XXXII, 103–106, and XXXIII, 52–47) and of his ancestor Cacciaguida (XVII, 127–129).

67–72 The spirits drifting slowly up into the outermost Empyrean, after manifesting themselves to the pilgrim in the Eighth Heaven, are compared to flakes of snow ("frozen vapors"). Unlike our winter snow on earth, however, they fall *upward*. The sun is in the house of Capricorn ("heaven's Goat") from December 21 to January 21.

79–84 The last time Dante obeyed Beatrice's bidding and looked down at the earth was in Canto XXII, 127–153. He now discovers that, since then, his journey has taken him westward through an arc of ninety degrees, the equivalent of a quarter of the earth's circumference. In terms of earthly time, six hours have passed. He had been over the meridian of Jerusalem then, now he is over that of Cadiz. Looking west, he can see the ocean that Ulysses was punished for attempting to cross (cf. *Inf.* XXVI), and looking east, he can almost distinguish the shore of Phoenicia, whence Jupiter, disguised as a white bull, carried Europa away on his back to the island of Crete (see *Met.* II, 833–875). The ancient geographers and astronomers divided the northern hemisphere (the hemisphere of land) into seven horizontal sectors, or "'clime[s],'" moving out from the equator.

85–87 The same disparaging term ("'threshing floor'") was used for the earth in Canto XXII, 150. Dante is still in the constellation of Gemini, whereas the sun is two signs ahead (i.e., farther west), in Aries (between Gemini and Aries lies Taurus). Had the sun been in Gemini also, more of the earth's surface to the east would have been illuminated.

97–114 Gazing on Beatrice's smile, Dante is transported out of the Heaven of the Fixed Stars and the constellation of Gemini (named for Castor and Pollux, the twin sons of Leda, born from an egg fertilized by Jupiter, who had assumed the form of a swan—hence "the nest of Leda") into the Ninth or Crystalline Heaven, the Primum Mobile, Heaven's last and swiftest sphere. Beyond the Primum Mobile lies only the Empyrean itself, the containing heaven, purely of "light and love" (112) in which God dwells. (See *Convivio* II, iii, 9 [quoted in XXVIII, 43–45, note], and cf. II, 112–114.)

115–120 The motion of the whole universe is generated in the Primum Mobile, even as the number ten is the generated product of its factors two and five. Moreover, since time is a function of motion, time—whose effects we can observe in the other heavens, because, unlike the Primum Mobile, they contain the visible fixed and moving bodies of the stars and the planets, by which time on earth is measured—has its roots here too.

121–141 Here, from the most divine of the material celestial spheres, Beatrice elegiacally deplores the perversity of mankind, who turn from contemplation of the celestial and the divine to the greedy pursuit of fallacious earthly goods.

140–141 "on earth no king holds sway": See "Dante in His Age," Bantam Classics *Inferno,* p. 326.

142–148 Beatrice's regret, like St. Peter's bitter lament over the corruption of the Church, which, in the structure of the canto, it completes and counterbalances, ends on a note of hopeful prophecy: it will not be long before Providence sets things straight. In Dante's day the year was still measured by the Julian calendar, which set the duration of a year at 365 days 6 hours. Until the error was corrected, with the introduction of the Gregorian calendar in 1582, this meant that the actual length of the year was overestimated by about twelve minutes, or a hundredth part of a day. In the course of time (in about ninety centuries, to be precise) the result of the accumulation of these neglected fractions would be that January would no longer fall in winter but in spring.

CANTO XXVIII

7–9 "to gauge/if that glass tells the truth to him": i.e., to see whether the actual object accords with its mirrored image (here, the image of the twin flame of a "double candle" [5]).

11–12 "the lovely eyes...": Beatrice's. (cf. *Purg.* XXXI, 116–117.)

13–21 Turning from the image reflected in Beatrice's eyes, to the thing in itself, Dante sees "a point" (16), infinitesimally small and of the most intense luminosity. This point is a self-manifestation of God. (Cf. *Purg.* XXXI, 115–126, where Dante first discerned the dual nature of the Griffin, symbolic of Christ, by gazing at its image reflected in Beatrice's eyes.)

13–15 "What appears within that sphere [the Primum Mobile] when-ever/one looks intently at its revolution" is the vision, now appearing to Dante, of the intensely luminous point surrounded, as we are about to learn, by nine wheeling rings of fire (22–39). These rings are the Angelic Intelligences, which exert their influences on the natural world. It seems natural, then, that they should appear within that world, at its uppermost limit, here in the Primum Mobile.

16 Cf. *Convivio* II, xiii, 27: "for its indivisibility, [the point] is immeasurable."

22–25 The halo around a star is smallest when the "mist that forms the halo" is thickest. (Cf. X, 67–69.) Thus this first wheeling "ring of fire" is fairly close to the brilliant central point.

26–27 "the motion that most swiftly girds the world": the motion of the Primum Mobile, "heaven's swiftest sphere" (XXVII, 99).

31–33 "Juno's messenger" is Iris, goddess of the rainbow. (Cf. XII, 10–13, and *Aen.* IV, 964–966.) The seventh ring of fire, then, is "so wide" that "all of" a rainbow, that is, a rainbow imagined as completed to form an entire circle, "would be too narrow" to enclose it.

37–39 "shares most deeply": i.e., penetrates most deeply with its vision (as Beatrice will explain in lines 106–108) "that point's truth," the Truth of the light at the center that is God.

41–42 Beatrice's formulation recalls Aristotle's: "It is on such a principle, then, that the heavens and the natural world depend" (*Metaphysics* XII, 7). St. Thomas, in his commentary, elaborates: "Thus it is on this principle, i.e., the First Mover seen as an end, that the heavens depend both for the eternality of their substance and the eternality of their motion. And consequently the whole of nature depends on such a principle, because all natural things depend on the heavens and on such motion as they possess" (*In duodecim libros Metaphysicorum expositio* XII, lect. 7, n. 2534).

43–45 " 'burning love' "—for God. Note that the swiftest motion of the outermost of the material heavens, the Primum Mobile, is explained by Dante (*Convivio* II, iii, 9) in analogous but inverse terms: "Because of the most fervent appetite with which every part of this ninth heaven [the Primum Mobile], which is surrounded by [the Empyrean], longs to be conjoined with every part of that most divine and tranquil heaven, it revolves within it with such yearning that its swiftness is almost incomprehensible."

46–57 Dante, referring to the Primum Mobile as " 'this … angelic temple' " (53), has understood that the nine rings of fire that he sees before him are a visual manifestation of the nine orders of the Angelic Intelligences, the " 'blessed movers' " by whom " 'the force and motion of the holy spheres / must be inspired' " (II, 127–129). But what perplexes Dante is that this suprasensible, purely spiritual world (" 'the model' ") and the material world (the " 'copy' "—" 'earth and the nine spheres,' " which is the image of that spiritual world and bears its stamp) appear " 'not [to] share in one same plan,' " indeed, appear to be inverse in plan, for the material heavens become " 'more divine,' " move more swiftly, and burn with greater love for God, the more distant they are from the center (the Earth), that is, the closer they are to the Empyrean, which encloses the whole natural world (" 'the world of sense' ") purely with " 'love and light' " (54 [cf. XXVII, 112–114]).

58–60 " 'that knot' ": the mystery of the correspondence, the " 'wonderful accord' " (76), between the spiritual and the material world.

64–78 Beatrice proceeds to unravel " 'that knot.' " She begins by stating the principle that the size of each of the nine material heavens depends upon the power it contains—the power that, as Beatrice explained in Canto II (112–123), emanates from the Empyrean and is transmitted downward through the heavens. Her explanation is straightforward: the greater the power, or " 'excellence,' " a body possesses, the greater its blessedness; moreover, if a " 'body's parts are equally complete,' " that is, equally capable of, and disposed to, blessedness, then " 'more blessedness' " necessitates a larger, or " 'greater,' " body. It follows that the outermost, largest, and swiftest of the material heavens, the Primum Mobile, is the most blessed and therefore corresponds to the most blessed of the Angelic Intelligences, the innermost ring of fire, which " 'loves most and knows the most' " (72). It is solely the " 'power within' " (74) the Angelic Intelligences, their degree of blessedness " 'and not [their] semblance,' " or apparent physical size in Dante's vision, that must be considered in order to discern the perfect correspondence between the heavens and the Intelligences: each heaven is associated with the correspondingly divine angelic order.

79–82 The winds were often represented, in cartography, as human faces—one at each of the four principal points of the compass—with puffed cheeks, blowing three winds: one directly from the center, and one from each side of their mouth (each "cheek"). When Boreas, the personification of the three winds from the north, blew "from his gentler cheek" the northeast wind, it kept the rain and clouds away, and cleared the air of all obfuscation (Latini, *Tresor* II, 37). Cf. *Aeneid* XII, 493–497.

88–90 The distinct sparks are individual angels, who continue, however, to circle within the "flaming ring" in which they have appeared.

91–93 On the problem of the number of angels (already alluded to in XIII, 97–98), Dante notes in the *Convivio* (II, v, 5) that according to Church belief and teaching, the angels, "those noblest of creatures," are "almost innumerable." And according to Pseudo-Dionysius (*De coelestia Hierarchia* XIV [see 97–102, note]), the angels "exceed the weak and limited measure of our material numbers." (Cf. XXIX, 130–135.) Here Dante's estimate of the number of angels refers to an old legend, according to which the king of Persia was so grateful to the inventor of the game of chess, that he offered to grant him any reward he might ask for. The inventor's request seemed at first modest enough: one grain of corn for the first square of a chessboard, two grains for the second square, four grains for the third, and so on, successively doubling the number of grains for each of the sixty-four squares on the chessboard. But when the king attempted to keep his promise, it did not take him long to realize that all the corn in Persia, indeed all the corn in the entire world, would not be enough to fill the shrewd inventor's request. (The number of grains required would be $2^{64}-1$, about eighteen and one half billion billion.)

94 *"Hosanna":* a cry of adoration (see VII, 1–3, note).

97–102 The Church doctors and theologians held discordant opinions concerning the number and ordering of the Celestial Intelligences. Most adopted either the arrangement presented in the *De coelestia Hierarchia* (*On the Celestial Hierarchy,* a 5th- or 6th-century Neoplatonic work, erroneously attributed in the Middle Ages to Dionysius the Areopagite [see 130–132 and note]) or one of the two arrangements proposed by St. Gregory the Great (see 133–135 and note). Dante, in his *Convivio,* had adopted one of St. Gregory's proposed orderings, but St. Thomas had accepted Pseudo-Dionysius's. Inevitably, here, perplexities arise in Dante's mind, and Beatrice, as ever, perceiving his thoughts reflected in the Mind of God, responds by beginning her exposition of the true arrangement.

The first two angelic orders are the Seraphim and the Cherubim. (Cf. IX, 77–78, note.)

103–105 The third ring comprises the Thrones (so named, according to St. Gregory, because "upon them God sits, and by means of them exercises judgment" [*Homiliae in Evangelis* II, 34]; cf. IX, 61–62).

St. Gregory and Pseudo-Dionysius agree in seeing nine angelic orders divided into three hierarchies of three orders each. St. Gregory distinguished these according to their different offices or functions; Pseudo-Dionysius, according to their natural endowments; and St. Thomas, following him, according to the different ways in which they have knowledge of created things (*Summa theol.* I, q. 108, a. 1). But Dante, in the *Convivio* (II, v, 7–11), distinguishes the hierarchies and orders according to their contemplation of the three Persons of the Trinity and the essential attributes assigned to each of those Persons (though common to all): the first, second, and third hierarchies contemplate, respectively, the Father and His Power, the Son and His Wisdom, and the Holy Spirit and Its Love. Moreover, "since each Person of the Divine Trinity may be contemplated in three ways"—in itself and in relation to each of the other two Persons—"there are, in each hierarchy, three orders."

Lines 104–105, then, suggest that this third angelic order derives its name from being placed, like a throne, at the foundation, or bottom, of the first and most divine hierarchy, God's "immediate court" (Casini-Barbi).

106–111 The beatitude of the Angelic Intelligences is in proportion to the profundity of their vision of God, "that truth in which all intellects find rest." (Cf. St. Thomas, *Summa contra gentiles* III, ch. 59: "necessarily, the natural appetite of an intellective substance that sees the divine essence is wholly quieted.")

Thus beatitude " 'depends / upon the act of vision, not upon / the act of love—which is a consequence.' " Every act of the will (e.g., the act of love) has some object. But to have such an object, it is necessary that that

object be in some way already present to the mind, or intellect. Thus
there must be an act of intellection first, an " 'act of vision' " of an object, for it to be the possible object of an act of love (or any act of will).
(It follows that an act of vision which errs in understanding the nature of
its object will result in an erroneous act of love.)

Dante's position, aligned with that of St. Thomas (see *Summa theol.*
I–II, q. 3, a. 1–8, and *Suppl.*, q. 92, a. 1–3), differs in emphasis from the
Augustinian-Franciscan position of those Scholastics who maintained
that beatitude consists in the love of God. Nevertheless, it is an essential
part of this—Dante's—doctrine, that " 'the act of love... *is* a consequence' " of the act of vision of God. (See XXVI, 28–36.) There is no
beatitude without love. (Cf. Solomon's words in XIV, 41, and see 1 Cor.
13:1–13.)

112–114   The profundity of their vision of God is according to their
merit. And merit results from " 'grace and then... will to goodness.' "
God's grace must be met, or responded to, with the will to goodness,
through which one cooperates with that grace.

115–119   The " 'nightly Ram' " signifies autumn, that time of year
when the constellation Aries (the Ram) is opposite the sun, so that after
the sun sets, Aries is present in the nighttime sky. The "leaves" in
Paradise never suffer the fate of earthly leaves in autumn.

120–123   The three orders of Angelic Intelligences in the second hierarchy are the Dominions, the Virtues, and the Powers. (On their names,
see St. Thomas [*Summa theol.* I, q. 108, a. 5], who follows Pseudo-
Dionysius.)

123–126   The last hierarchy is composed of the Principalities, the
Archangels, and finally, the Angels—though Dante notes in the *Convivio*
(II, iv, 2) that "the common people call [all of the Celestial Intelligences]
'Angels.' " (On their names, see *Summa theol.*, ibid.)

127–129   In ecstatic contemplation of God, the angelic orders all are
"drawn... to God," by their knowledge and love of Him, and draw the
lower orders to God, by transmitting to them their own knowledge of His
workings.

130–132   Pseudo-Dionysius the Areopagite, who " 'beheld most
deeply / the angels' nature and their ministry,' " was among the eleven
souls presented by Thomas Aquinas in the Fourth Heaven (see X,
115–117 and note). The exposition of the hierarchies of the angelic orders in the *De coelestia Hierarchia* is, indeed, identical with Beatrice's,
and with good reason (as we are about to learn [136–139]).

133–135   St. Gregory the Great, pope from A.D. 590 to 604 (see *Purg.*
X, 75, and 73–93, note), "disputed" Pseudo-Dionysius, proposing, in
fact, two different arrangements of the angelic orders, one of which had
been adopted by Dante in his *Convivio* (II, v, 6). But " 'when Gregory
came here' " and beheld the vision of the Angelic Intelligences, " 'he
smiled at his mistake.' "

The following table summarizes Dante's earlier and revised orderings of the angelic hierarchies:

Heavenly Sphere	St. Gregory and Convivio	Pseudo-Dionysius and Paradiso
Primum Mobile	Seraphim	Seraphim
Fixed Stars	Cherubim	Cherubim
Saturn	Powers	Thrones
Jupiter	Principalities	Dominions
Mars	Virtues	Virtues
Sun	Dominions	Powers
Venus	Thrones	Principalities
Mercury	Archangels	Archangels
Moon	Angels	Angels

136–139 Pseudo-Dionysius affirms in the *De coelestia Hierarchia* (IV), that the truth concerning the Celestial Intelligences was disclosed to him by St. Paul himself, who had been "caught up ... right into the third heaven [for St. Paul, the highest heaven]" (see 2 Cor. 12:2–4).

CANTO XXIX

1–6 The elaborate opening simile, which conveys the duration of Beatrice's silence, is suited to the intellectual tone of the canto. The children of Latona are Apollo and Diana, the sun and the moon. The constellations of Aries (the Ram) and Libra (the Scales) are diametrically opposite each other on the circle of the zodiac. When the sun is in Aries and the moon in Libra (or vice versa), one "planet" rises while the other sets, at opposing points on the horizon. To the observer, the half disk of the rising moon and that of the setting sun—the lower half of each disk being covered, so that the horizon acts as a kind of belt—appear for a brief moment to hang in equilibrium from the zenith of the sky, like the pans of a balance. Then, little by little, they leave the belt of the horizon, one rising into the hemisphere above it, the other sinking into the hemisphere below.

8–9 Unlike Dante, who had been overwhelmed by its brightness, Beatrice is able to gaze intently at the Point of light (see XXVIII, 16–21).

10–12 Beatrice has see Dante's unexpressed question—actually a series of questions: about Creation, the rebellion of the fallen angels, the nature of the non-fallen angels and their number—in the eternal infinite Mind of God, the alpha and omega of all time (" 'whens' ") and space (" 'ubis' "—*ubi* is the Latin word for "where").

13–18 The Creation was an overflowing of God's eternal love. God Himself being Infinite Perfection, He had no need of Creation. Rather, by a spontaneous act of His Divine Will ("as pleased Him") and solely in order that those reflecting the splendor of His light and love might delight, like Himself, in the knowledge of their being (" 'might / ... declare *"Subsisto"* [i.e., I am]' "), He, like a blossoming flower, "opened into new loves," creating the angels, the incorruptible heavens, and primary matter.

19–21   The Creation did not represent a transition from idleness to activity on God's part, or from one state of affairs to another. It occurred outside of time and change. Only with the Creation did it become possible to speak of " 'before' " and " 'after.' "

21   Cf. Genesis 1:2: "And the Spirit of God moved upon the face of the waters."

22–30   These lines express the *simultaneity* of Creation, and are directed against those who, like St. Jerome (mentioned in line 37), claimed that it was achieved in staggered order. Pure form, pure matter, and the combination of form and matter (see note below) were all created at once, like three arrows shot from a single three-stringed bow, or like a light, which penetrates immediately and equally all portions of a translucent substance. (Dante believed, with his contemporaries, that the propagation of light was instantaneous.)

31–37   Along with the three created " 'substances' "—" 'form, matter, and their union' " (28)—was created the hierarchy among them. The angels, being pure form (or " 'pure act' "), were the highest of created things, pure matter (or " 'pure potentiality' ") was the lowest (cf. VII, 130–138, note), while the middle ground was occupied by the heavens, a combination of form and matter (or " 'act' " and " 'potentiality' ").

37–39   St. Jerome claimed that the angels were created long before the creation of the material world—an opinion contradicted by other authorities. Dante's view closely follows that of Thomas Aquinas, who cites in support of his argument the opening words of Genesis: "In the beginning God created the heavens and the earth."

40–42   The "scribes of the Holy Ghost" are the authors of Holy Scripture, the various divinely inspired books of the Bible.

43–46   Beatrice's appeal to the authority of revelation is buttressed, in the Scholastic mode, with an appeal to reason. If the Angelic Intelligences were created to move the heavens, then they and the heavens must have been created at almost the same time. Otherwise, the angels would have remained too long imperfect, lacking scope for their true function. The argument is borrowed from Aquinas.

49–57   No sooner had the angels been created, when a certain portion of them, led by the " 'cursed / pride' " of Lucifer, rebelled and were thrust down from Heaven, creating in their fall the cavity of Hell within the earth (where Dante encountered Lucifer, or Satan, in *Inf.* XXXIV). Of the four elements, earth was considered the lowest. Elsewhere, Dante estimates that the fallen angels were "in number perhaps a tenth part" of those originally created (*Convivio* II, v, 12). After the defeat of the rebels, the remainder of the angels took up their designated task of moving the heavens.

57   The modesty and humility of the good angels is in contrast to the presumption of the rebels. The good angels realized they were soon to be rewarded with the vast understanding required to move the heavens, and their patient fidelity was rewarded by the further generous bestowal of God's illuminating grace. Their will is constantly and fully in harmony with God's, because, since " 'affection follows / the act of knowledge' " (139–140), to see Him perfectly is to will only what He wills.

70–82 Beatrice adds a corollary on the nature of the angels, to whom many attribute the same three powers attributed to the human soul—understanding, memory, and will. The allusion is to a question discussed at length by theologians. Dante, who concentrates on disproving the angels' need for memory and does not go into the other two powers, takes the point of view that the attribution of such faculties to the angels is at best misleading, at worst pernicious.

82–126 The doctrinal point turns out to have been merely a prologue and leads into an extended harangue against preachers and teachers more concerned with their own ingenuity and success with an audience than with truth and divine revelation. Several modern critics are not at all at ease with this diatribe and seem to endorse the Romantic critic Tommaseo's observation that the Antonines' pigs (124–125) are unworthy of Beatrice and of Paradise.

97–102 One example of these overingenious inventions is the theory that the darkness from the sixth to the ninth hour at Christ's Crucifixion was caused by a specially engineered lunar eclipse of the sun. But there is nothing about a lunar eclipse in the Gospels, and the Gospels plainly say that there was darkness over *all* the earth (visible therefore not only to the Jews of Jerusalem but to the Spaniards and Indians too). A lunar eclipse would have been more local in its effects.

105 Lapo and Bindo, short for Jacopo and Ildebrando, were extremely common first names in Dante's Florence.

118 The " 'bird' " that nests in the fashionable preacher's cowl is presumably the devil. (For the term, cf. *Inf.* XXII, 96, and XXXIV, 47.) The ultimate purpose of the theatrical preaching style is to extract money from the ignorant.

124–125 The Antonine monks of the order of St. Anthony the Great (not St. Anthony of Padua), founded in the 3rd century, grazed their pigs on public land and fed them on the charity of the faithful. They seem to have been regarded as one of the more greedy and less scrupulous of the mendicant orders.

130–141 The final point regarding the angels, to which Beatrice now returns, concerns their number (which is incalculable) and their multiformity. Even Daniel's "A thousand thousand waited on him, ten thousand times ten thousand stood before him" (Dan. 7:10) is meant simply to indicate an astronomical figure and is not to be taken literally (cf. XXVIII, 91–93 and note). Moreover, among them, there are as many degrees of intelligence and charity as there are angels.

CANTO XXX

1–9   Though we do not become aware of it till we reach the word "So," at the beginning of line 10, the peremptory first nine lines of the canto, which, unlike the narration of the events in Paradise, are in the present tense, are actually the first term of an erudite and ornate (but basically simple) comparison. Dante compares the gradual disappearance of the nine luminous circles playing around the central Point of light (described in XXVIII, 22–39) to the disappearance of the stars in our sky at dawn. It is the hour when the sun has still a quarter of the earth's circumference (according to Dante's calculations, about six thousand miles) to cover before reaching the position it occupies at noon ("the sixth hour"). At the moment, the cone-shaped shadow cast by the earth when the sun illuminates it (cf. IX, 118–119) is almost level. It will be perfectly horizontal at sunrise. For now, the sun has yet to appear on the horizon, but already the color of the eastern sky has begun to change white, and many of the night stars are no longer visible. As the dawn ("the brightest handmaid of the sun") advances, the remainder of the stars (heaven's "lights") are gradually extinguished, until even the last star visible, Venus, the lovely morning star, is gone.

10   The "triumph" is the circling of the nine angelic hierarchies around the Divine Point.

11–12   The Point of light so brilliant "that anyone who faced the force / with which it blazed would have to shut his eyes" (XXVIII, 17–18), which appeared to Dante as the center of the play of lights, represented God. But God is both the Center and the Circumference, "not circumscribed and circumscribing all" (XIV, 30), and in fact encloses what seemed there to enclose Him.

28–33   Dante first saw Beatrice when he was nine years old, as the *Vita nuova* tells us. Since then, he now says, he has sung the praises of her beauty over and over, never despairing of conveying it to his readers. Now, however, he must admit defeat. He could never describe her as she appeared to him in all her perfect glory in the Empyrean.

34–36   That is, "I yield, and leave the description of Beatrice's beauty to a greater poet than myself."

38–39   " 'matter's largest sphere' ": the Primum Mobile. The Empyrean, "the heaven of pure light," is not material.

43–45   " 'both ranks of Paradise' ": the angels and the blessed saints. Dante will see the images of the latter (no longer "conceal[ed]" [V, 136] BY THE EFFULGENCE THAT HAD SURROUNDED THEM) JUST AS THEY WILL BE WHEN THEY ASSUME THEIR GLORIFIED BODIES ON JUDGMENT DAY.

46–47   The " 'spirits / of sight' " belong to medieval psychophysiology (cf. XXVI, 71–73, note). Dante's early poetry, like that of certain other contemporary practitioners of the "sweet new style," makes ample use of this scientific terminology.

52   " 'calms this heaven' ": the reader will recall that the Empyrean, unlike the revolving heavens below it, is still.

54   Cf. Proverbs 20:27: "Man's spirit is the lamp of Yahweh, searching his deepest self."

76–77   " 'gems / of topaz' ": the "living sparks" of line 64, the "rubies" of line 66. Since the ruby is red and the topaz yellow, the color of the angels does not seem to be the point—rather their brightness and their worth. The soul of Cacciaguida was addressed as " 'living topaz' " in xv, 85.

87   "may find our betterment": may increase our capacity for seeing and become better fitted for the final revelation of God.

88–96   As Dante bends toward the stream of light, bathing his eyes in its effulgence to perfect his vision, he sees the river change its shape and the flowers and the precious sparks transformed, like maskers who remove their disguises, into the blessed saints and the angels, " 'both ranks of Paradise' " (43), i.e., both groups of those who dwell in the heavenly court.

97–99   This is the canto in which the verb *vedere* ("to see") and its cognates reign supreme. Forms of the verb occur sixteen times. (See Di Scipio in *Dante Studies,* 98, 1980).

106–109   All of the immense circle of light derives from one great ray that emanates from the Light of God Himself and strikes the convex outer surface of the Primum Mobile (which thereby receives the life, or motion, it transmits to the spheres below and the power to influence the sublunar world, which it communicates to them) and is reflected from it.

114   "all of us who have won return above": the souls of all those mortals who have won a place in Heaven and have returned there from their exile on earth.

117   The metaphor of the Rose, introduced here for the first time, will dominate the next two cantos. The form of the Rose, as will become apparent, is that of a vast amphitheater. At one point, when the references to imperial Rome become unmistakably insistent, Singleton aptly refers to it as a celestial "colosseum" (p. 551).

118–120   That is, "My eyes were able to absorb the joyous spectacle in all its extension and intensity."

121–123   In the Empyrean, beyond space and time, the fact that something is near or far away does not make it easier or more difficult to see. The very notions of nearness and farness, so important here below, simply do not apply.

126   The "Sun," the warmth and light of whose love causes the Rose to flourish in the eternal spring of Paradise, is of course God.

132   There is little room left for more souls in the Rose of Paradise because, in Dante's opinion, as in that of most of his contemporaries, the end of the world is at hand. Cf. *Convivio* II, xiv, 13: "We are already in the last age of the world, and we are truly awaiting the consummation of the movement of the heavens."

135   " 'before you join this wedding feast' ": i.e., "before you die and come to take the place set aside for you in the Rose." The image of the celestial wedding feast also occurs in Canto XXIV, 1–2 (see note), and *Purgatorio* XXXII, 76.

136   " 'noble Henry' ": the emperor Henry VII, count of Luxembourg. Younger than Dante, he was born between 1270 and 1280. In November 1308 he was unanimously elected emperor and crowned king of Germany at Aix-la-Chapelle in January 1309. Accepting Pope Clement V's invitation to descend into Italy to put an end to factional strife there, he received the title of *rex Romanorum* ("king of the Romans") in Milan in January 1311. Dante followed his movements eagerly and placed all his hopes for the righting of Italy's and his own personal wrongs in Henry, saluting his coming with enthusiastic public epistles. Henry's triumph did not last long. He dissipated his energies attempting to quell the rebellious cities of northern Italy and struggling against the Guelph coalition incited against him by the treacherous Clement. In June 1313 he finally succeeded in being crowned emperor in Rome, but not in St. Peter's, which was under the control of the Guelphs led by King Robert of Naples. Called north to combat a further Guelph uprising led by Florence, he fell ill and died suddenly at Buonconvento, near Siena, in August 1313. Italy, says Dante, was not ready for him.

139–141   The *you* in these lines is a plural *you* and is addressed not to Dante but to the peoples of Italy.

142–144   The " 'Prefect' " of the " 'holy forum,' " or head of the Church, at the time of Henry's coming to Italy, was, as we have seen, Clement V, whom Dante considered to have tricked and betrayed Henry.

145–147   The death of Clement, which came a bare eight months after that of Henry, was seen by Dante as just retribution. It is hardly necessary to say that Dante had the pope earmarked for an eternity in Hell, in the Third Pouch of the Eighth Circle, among the Simonists, where he would succeed his predecessor, Boniface VIII, in the mouth of the hole in the rock, pushing Boniface farther into the hole on top of his predecessor, Nicholas III (cf. *Inf.* XIX). Boniface was born in the city of Anagni.

CANTO XXXI

1–3   The souls of the blessed, wedded to Christ through the sacrifice of His Crucifixion, many of whom Dante had encountered previously in the various heavens, are gathered all together here in their true dwelling place—the white Celestial Rose.

4–12 The angels form the other host—the bees that ceaselessly and lovingly toil in the garden of Paradise.

13–15 The description of the angels is not unnaturally an elaboration of biblical reminiscences: "Then I saw another powerful angel coming down from heaven, . . . his face was like the sun" (Rev. 10:1); "something could be seen like flaming brands or torches" (Ezek. 1:13); "His face was like lightning, his robe white as snow" (Matt. 28:3).

17–18 Shuttling back and forth between the Rose and the eternal dwelling of God's love, the angel bees share with the blessed the honey of His peace and ardor.

22–24 Cf. Canto I, 1–3.

26 The "people of both new and ancient times," as we shall see in the following canto, are the saved from the periods of the Old and the New Testaments.

33 The nymph Helice (perhaps better known as Callisto) was seduced by Jupiter and punished by Juno by being turned into a bear. Her son and Jupiter's, Arcas, encountered the bear on a hunt and was about to kill it, when his father intervened, exalting the transformed Helice among the stars as the constellation of the Great Bear and placing Arcas near her as the Little Bear (see Ovid, *Met.* II, 401–530). The barbarians hailed from the north of Europe, where the Bear is visible year round.

35–36 The Lateran Palace, first the residence of the emperors, then of the popes, is cited as an outstanding monument to the power and magnificence of Rome.

40 The concrete name of Florence, coming at the climax of a crescendo of abstractions, is thrown into bitter relief in Dante's last and most sardonic thrust against his ungrateful homeland.

55–60 As the awestruck Dante turns to seek his beloved guide, Beatrice, only to find that she has left his side, we are reminded of a similar moment in Purgatory, when, overwhelmed by the triumphal advent of Beatrice, he had turned to Virgil for comfort, only to find him gone (cf. *Purg.* XXX, 40–54). The difference in dramatic tone derives from the fact that Virgil had returned to exile in Limbo, whereas Beatrice has taken her rightful place in the Rose of Paradise.

60 This "elder" will identify himself in line 102.

80–81 Cf. *Inferno* II, 53.

102 The "holy elder" (94) now reveals himself to be the famous mystic St. Bernard (1091–1153), canonized in 1173, founder and first abbot of the Cistercian monastery of Clairvaux. (The Cistercians were a stricter branch of the Benedictine order.) The contemplative author of many works on the ascetic and mystical path to God, he was also an active preacher and reformer, the respected counselor of popes and princes, and the promoter of the Second Crusade. He was particularly noted for his restoration of the cult of the Blessed Virgin Mary.

102–104 Dante contemplates St. Bernard with the same eagerness with which a pilgrim from the remote outback of Christendom might contemplate the "Veronica"—the image of Christ's face imprinted on a piece of cloth preserved in St. Peter's Basilica in Rome, connected with the pious legend of the woman who wiped the face of Jesus with her kerchief as he climbed to Calvary. The term *Veronica* is actually a phrase of Greek origin: *vera icona,* "true likeness."

124–126 The comparison with the sunrise continues. The "shaft" or chariot that Phaethon misguided was the chariot of the sun (see XV, 13–18, note).

127 The "oriflamme" was the ancient royal standard of France—a red silk banner split at one end to form flame-shaped streamers. The term is used metaphorically to indicate the flamelike summit of the Rose, in the center of which is the place occupied by the Queen of Heaven. Unlike the warlike banner of the French kings, this oriflamme is a flag of peace.

CANTO XXXII

1–2 Though ardently absorbed in the contemplation of Mary, Bernard does not forget his task of instructing Dante.

4–6 The place of Eve in the Rose is in the second highest rank, or tier, at the feet of Mary. Eve was the woman who opened the wound of original sin, Mary the woman who closed it. Mary is in fact often called the second Eve, as Christ is called the second Adam. Dante chooses to mention the healing of the wound before its infliction, placing the emphasis, in this brief epitome of providential history, on God's love for the world rather than on His just vengeance, on the Redemption rather than the Fall. The reversal of the logical position of words and ideas, the rhetorical figure known as *hysteron proteron,* extends to the order of the verbs—one anoints a wound before closing it, and piercing precedes opening. (Cf. II, 23–24 and note.)

7 We were already told that Beatrice was "sitting beside the venerable Rachel," the second wife of Jacob and a symbol of the contemplative life, in *Inferno* II, 102. For Rachel and her sister Leah, see also *Purgatorio* XXVII, 100–108 and note. Beatrice is at the right hand of Rachel in the third rank of souls.

8 Below Rachel, in the fourth rank, is Sarah, wife of Abraham and mother of Isaac. Below her, in the fifth rank, Rebecca, wife of Isaac and mother of Jacob and Esau. Next, in the sixth rank, comes Judith, the beautiful heroine of the Book of Judith, who delivered Israel from the Assyrians by gaining access to the tent of their general, Holofernes, and beheading him in his drunken sleep.

10–12 The central place in the seventh rank is occupied by the great-grandmother of King David the psalmist—Ruth, wife of Boaz. David's "sinfulness" was his adultery with Bathsheba. " 'Miserere mei' " ("Have mercy upon me, O God") are the opening words of Psalm 50 in the Latin Vulgate, composed by David.

15–27 The vertical row of Hebrew women from the Old Testament continues below the seventh rank; the women, though, are not named. Together they form one radius of the circular Rose, a kind of a wall or dividing line that separates those saved under the Old Dispensation ("whose faith was in the Christ to come"), who are on Mary's left, from those saved under the New ("whose sight was set upon the Christ / who had already come"), who are on her right. Since the number of saved under each of the two covenants was to be equal ("both aspects of / the faith shall fill this garden equally" [38–39]), the seats on the left are all full, while on the right side a few vacancies still remain.

28–37 Radiating out from the center of the Rose, on the opposite side, is another wall or partition of souls, serving the same dividing function as the first. Together the two radii form the circle's diameter, and divide the Rose into two semicircles.

31 At the topmost rank on the other side, across from Eve, is St. John the Baptist, the precursor of Christ, of whom Christ said: "I tell you solemnly, of all the children born of women, a greater than John the Baptist has never been seen" (Matt. 11:11).

32–33 " 'always saintly' ": See Luke 1:15: "Even from his mother's womb he will be filled with the Holy Spirit." The Baptist lived in the desert and suffered martyrdom at the hands of Herod. Since he died two years before Christ, he spent two years in Limbo before Christ's Harrowing of Hell (see *Inf.* IV, 52–61, note).

35 The life of Francis of Assisi was recounted by Thomas Aquinas in Canto XI, while Dante met Benedict himself in Canto XXII. Some commentators have expressed surprise at the absence of Dominic from this brief list of founders. Augustine of Hippo (354–426), the famous Father of the Church, was born a pagan and became, like St. Paul, a convert to Christianity. His works, which Dante clearly knew very well, are among the most influential noncanonical texts in the Christian tradition. There is another passing reference to Augustine in Canto X, 120.

40–45 A further major division of the Rose comes halfway down the ranks or tiers. The places in the lower half are reserved for the souls of infants who died before reaching the age at which their reason would have made them capable of distinguishing between good and evil, and hence of exercising " 'the power of true choice.' "

49–75 The narrative strategy of the pilgrim's doubt serves, here as elsewhere, to underline an aspect of Dante's vision of the otherworld that is not in conformity with received theological opinion. In fact, Aquinas, along with most other thinkers who addressed the problem, concluded that there could be no difference in degree of beatitude among the infants in Heaven. The gist of Bernard's explanation is that no two souls are created equal and that there must therefore be qualitative and quantitative differences in the capacity even of innocent children for beatitude.

67–69 The twins in question were Esau and Jacob, who "struggled with one another" in Rebecca's womb (Gen. 25:22).

72 Unlike Jacob's, which was black, Esau's hair was red and, even at his birth, covered him "as though he were completely wrapped in a hairy cloak" (Gen. 25:25).

76 The " 'early centuries' " (the " 'early times' " of line 79) are the first two ages of the world—from Adam to Noah, and from Noah to Abraham. "Before the institution of circumcision, faith in the future Christ justified both children and adults" (*Summa theol.* III, q. 70, a. 4).

79–82 Circumcision was introduced by Abraham at God's command (see Gen. 17:10–14). According to St. Thomas, the male was circumcised because it was through the male that original sin was transmitted (cf. *Summa theol.* I–II, q. 81, a. 5). The rite was considered by medieval theologians to be an imperfect form of baptism: "Now, our faith is the same as that of the Fathers of old. . . . But circumcision was a protestation of faith. . . . Consequently, it is manifest that circumcision was a preparation for baptism and a figure thereof. . . ." (*Summa theol.* III, q. 70, a. 1).

82–84 The " 'age of grace' " is the Christian era. With the advent of Christ, unbaptized infants were consigned to Limbo.

83–87 In the Italian text the name *Christ* appears once more in rhyme with itself. This is the fourth time in the *Paradiso* that this has occurred (see XII, 71–75, XIV, 104–108, and XIX, 104–108, in the Italian).

85–86 Mary's face is most like Christ's because she was His mother, and because she is closest to Him in brightness and beatitude.

89 "holy intellects": the angels.

94–96 The "angelic love" is the Archangel Gabriel, the angel of the Annunciation. His words to Mary became the opening words of the prayer Ave Maria (Hail Mary).

112–113 The palm is a symbol of victory. In pictorial representations of the Annunciation, Gabriel is usually depicted as bearing a palm frond or a flowering branch.

116–119 The patricians were the aristocracy of ancient Rome. The heavenly court is frequently described in feudal or imperial terms. In the same paradigm is the word *Empress* used to designate Mary (the *Agusta [Augusta]* of the Italian text is even more Roman in its connotations). The empress Mary is surrounded on both sides by the highest members of her court—those from the period of the Old Testament on her left, those from the Christian dispensation on her right.

121–123 On Mary's left, in the highest rank, sits Adam, the father of mankind, whose tasting of the forbidden fruit caused his descendants to taste the bitterness of their fallen state. The play on the word *taste* is typically medieval rhetorical embellishment.

124–126 On her right sits St. Peter, to whom Christ gave the keys of the kingdom of heaven (Matt. 16:19).

127–129 To the right of Peter, in the top tier of souls, is St. John the Evangelist (identified, in Dante's day, with St. John the Apostle), author of Revelation, which recounts his vision of the persecutions and hardships of the Church, the Bride of Christ. Christ's sacrifice, by which he won his Bride, is indicated symbolically by the instruments of His Passion—the lance that pierced His side and the nails that wounded His hands and feet.

130–132 On the left of Adam is Moses. He led the Jews (who "murmured against him") out of the land of Egypt into the wilderness, where they were fed with manna from Heaven (Exod. 16).

133–135 Anna was the mother of Mary and died before the birth of Christ. She closes the semicircle of those who believed in Christ to come. This places her diametrically opposite Peter (who sits next to Mary on her right) and to the right of John the Baptist. From this position the proud mother is free to gaze for all eternity upon her daughter.

136–138 Diametrically opposite Adam (" 'the greatest father of a family' ") and therefore on John the Baptist's left, closing the semicircle of those who believed in Christ come, sits St. Lucy, or Lucia, the 4th-century martyr saint of Syracuse, patron saint of sight and symbol of illuminating grace. She was sent by Mary and in turn sent Beatrice to Dante's aid, in *Inferno* II, 97–102.

147–148 Before he raises his eyes to contemplate God Himself, Dante must pray to Mary (" 'that one who has the power to help you' ") for the grace of the vision and the strength to withstand it. His prayer will be spoken for him by St. Bernard.

CANTO XXXIII

1–39 The canto opens with St. Bernard's prayer to Mary, the Virgin Mother of the Second Person of the Holy Trinity. Like other familiar formulas of devotion—among them the Ave Maria (or Hail Mary)—this prayer falls into two parts. The first part (1–21) consists of a litany of her praises, her frequently paradoxical theological attributes. (In rhetoric, this part would be termed a *captatio benevolentiae,* a stratagem by which an orator attempts to capture the good will of his audience.) The second part (22–39) formulates the worshipper's request. The urgent liturgical antitheses of the first part—Mary's virginity and maternity, maternity and filiation, humility and exaltedness, presence in time and in eternity, etc.—bear witness to Dante's intimate absorption of the spirit and texts of Christian mysticism.

2 Mary's humility characterized her at the Annunciation: " 'I am the handmaid of the Lord,' said Mary 'let what you have said be done to me' " (Luke 1:38). Her own words in the Magnificat, the verses spoken by her to her cousin Elizabeth, are the first statement of her singular combination of humbleness and sublimity: "He has looked upon his lowly handmaid. Yes, from this day forward all generations will call me blessed" (Luke 1:48).

7–9 The Incarnation of Christ, the Word made flesh in the womb of Mary, made possible the Redemption of fallen mankind, and hence the salvation of all of the souls from the Old Dispensation and the New, who now form the Celestial Rose of the Empyrean.

14–15 That is, "God does not wish us to have anything that does not pass through the hands of Mary" (Bernard of Clairvaux, *"In Vigilia Nativitatis Domini," Sermones de tempore* III, 10).

16–18 That Dante is here at all is an illustration of the overflowing zeal of Mary's loving-kindness. It was she who set in motion the chain of intercessors who prevailed upon Virgil to come to his aid (see *Inf.* II, 94–96).

34–37 Bernard makes the same request for Dante that Dante himself made earlier to Beatrice (XXXI, 87–90): that when he returns to the world after his vision, he will maintain his faith and his Christian disposition intact. Some critics see a reference here to Dante's special need for grace to combat his tendency toward the sin of pride.

38 Our last glimpse of Beatrice (this is the last mention of her name) is of a Beatrice who no longer stands alone and apart, as she did until now, both within the poem and outside it, but who has merged into the chorus of exulting spirits.

58 Dante, the poet attempting to record his vision, is like a man awakened from a dream he does not remember, filled with the emotion of a dream, but with no clear recollection of its particulars. We are reminded of Coleridge's preface to "Kubla Khan," where the poem itself is presented as the recollection of a dream. Reading this last canto, it is easy to see how the Romantic poets were attracted by Dante. The stupendous tension of the remainder of the poem derives in large part from Dante's dramatization of his present struggle to recollect (i.e., imagine) and describe (i.e., create in words) the content of his final vision.

64–66 So the snow melts beneath the sun's heat, and so the divinatory verses written upon leaves by the Sibyl, the frenzied prophetess of Cumae, consulted by Aeneas in Book VI of the *Aeneid,* were scattered and lost upon the wind. "Deep in her cave of rock she charts the fates, / consigning to the leaves her words and symbols. / Whatever verses she has written down / upon the leaves, she puts in place and order / and then abandons them inside her cavern. / When all is still, that order is not troubled; / but when soft winds are stirring and the door, / turning upon its hinge, disturbs the tender / leaves, then she never cares to catch the verses / that flutter through the hollow grotto, never / recalls their place or joins them all together" (*Aen.* III, 579–589).

75 The exact meaning of the word *victory* in this context is contested. It could be simply a synonym of "omnipotence"; it may also refer more specifically to the victory of the Divine Vision over Dante's ability to describe it.

76–78 The words "gone astray" (in Italian, *"smarrito")* may recall the opening lines of *Inferno* I, where Dante first found himself "astray" in the dark wood of error.

85–87 The first metaphor Dante uses to describe his vision of God is that of a book. God is the book in which all of the separate pages, as it were, that we see scattered throughout the universe are bound together.

88–90 This tercet continues and repeats—in the technical language of medieval Scholastic philosophy—the notion of ingathering. A "substance" *(substantia)* is that which subsists in and of itself; an "accident" *(accidens)* has no independent existence but exists only as a quality or attribute of a substance; their "disposition" *(habitus)* is the way substances and accidents are joined together, their relationship to each other.

96 That is, "I can recall so little of the moment of my overwhelming vision that the twenty-five centuries that have passed since Neptune saw with amazement from the ocean's depth the shadow of the keel of the first ship, the *Argo,* on which Jason sailed with the Argonauts in search of the Golden Fleece, have not engendered more forgetfulness." The voyage of the Argonauts is still remembered twenty-five centuries later, whereas Dante, who is still alive, has already almost lost what he saw. The sublime parallel stresses once again the infinite incommensurability between the seen and the remembered, as well as inviting comparison between Jason's marvelous voyage and Dante's (cf. II, 16–18 and note).

109–114 God, the Living Light, is eternal and unchanging, always equal to Himself. The changes that Dante now witnesses, which are an attempt to translate into visual imagery the mystery of the Trinity, depend, not upon the object of his vision, but on his own increasing capacity to see.

118 The description of the three circles discerned within the single Light is theologically impeccable: all three are equal, the second reflects the first (the Son proceeds from all eternity from the Father), and the third (the Holy Spirit) is the fire of Love that is breathed from both ("that Love which / One and the Other breathe eternally" [X, 1–2]). (For a possible source of this image in Joachim of Flora, see Luigi Tondelli's edition of and commentary on the *Liber figurarum* of Joachim of Flora, 2 vols., Turin, 1953, and the recent article by Piero di Vona "Dante filosofo e San Bonaventura," in *Miscellanea Francescana,* Tomo 84, 1984, I–II, pp. 8–10.)

127–132 The second circle (the Second Person of the Trinity—the Son, the Logos, the Word, the "Idea") seemed to contain within itself our human form. The reference is to the mystery of the Incarnation. The human form of Christ is "painted" within the circle in the same color as the circle itself and yet is clearly discernible.

133–135 The problem of constructing or finding a square equal in area to a given circle is an ancient and proverbially insoluble mathematical puzzle.

BIBLIOGRAPHICAL NOTE

The foregoing translation and brief annotations are much indebted to the exegetes cited in the Introduction to the *Inferno,* as well as to many earlier commentators.

Throughout, the *Enciclopedia Dantesca* has been consulted—the six-volume work directed by Umberto Bosco, with Giorgio Petrocchi and (from Vol. IV on) Ignazio Baldelli as general editors, Rome, 1970–1978. The first five volumes are ordered alphabetically. The sixth volume includes: Petrocchi's biography of Dante; a unique collective series of essays on the language and style of Dante; a bibliography; and the texts of all of Dante's works—and works that may be Dante's. The *E.D.* is one of the finest examples of a collective scholarly-critical enterprise that our times have produced, but the special bibliographical section in Vol. VI is much less cogent and complete than many of the separate bibliographies at the end of the alphabetically-ordered entries.

Some of the commentaries that have proved most helpful are: Umberto Bosco and Giovanni Reggio, eds., Dante Alighieri, *La Divina Commedia: Paradiso* (Florence, 1979); Tommasso Casini and Silvio Adrasti Barbi (the latter revising the former after Casini's death, in 1917), *La Divina Commedia di Dante Alighieri,* 6th ed. (Florence, 1926); and the editions of the *Commedia* by Siro A. Chimenz (Turin, 1967); Hermann Gmelin (Stuttgart, 1954–1957); Daniele Mattalia (Milan, 1960); Attilio Momigliano (Florence, 1945–1946); André Pézard (Paris, 1965); Natalino Sapegno (Milan, 1957); Charles S. Singleton (Princeton, 1975). All references to these commentaries are *ad locum* (to the same place in the *Paradiso* at which the exegete is cited in these notes), except for Bosco-Reggio, where the reference may call attention to Umberto Bosco's preface to the canto in question.

Essays on the individual cantos of the *Paradiso* are to be found far beyond the range of the principal collective volumes—or pamphlet collections—of *Paradiso* readings. But the following compilations (with their separate essays on each canto, in the Lectura Dantis format that the *California Lectura Dantis* volumes, now in progress, will follow) have been both convenient and particularly helpful:

Letture dantesche: Paradiso, ed. Giovanni Getto, Florence, 1958 (now in the 1965 single-volume edition of the three *cantiche); Lectura Dantis Scaligera: Paradiso,* ed. Mario Marcazzan, Florence, 1967; the separate pamphlets of the *Lectura Dantis Romana,* ed. Giovanni Fallani,

Turin, 1959–1967; the third, fourth, and fifth volumes of the *Nuove letture dantesche* of the Casa di Dante di Roma, Florence, 1969–1972; *Letture del Paradiso,* ed. Vittorio Vettori, Milan, 1970; and readings of *Paradiso* cantos scattered through Vols. I–III, V, VII, and IX of the *Letture Classensi,* Ravenna, 1969–1979.

ALLEN MANDELBAUM's five verse volumes are *Chelmaxions; The Savantasse of Montparnasse; Journeyman; Leaves of Absence;* and *A Lied of Letterpress.* His volumes of verse translation include *The Aeneid of Virgil,* a University of California Press volume (now Bantam) for which he won a National Book Award; the *Inferno, Purgatorio,* and *Paradiso* volumes of the California Dante (now Bantam); *The Odyssey of Homer* (now Bantam); *The Metamorphoses of Ovid,* a finalist for the Pulitzer Prize in poetry; *Ovid in Sicily; Selected Poems of Giuseppe Ungaretti; Selected Writings of Salvatore Quasimodo;* and *David Maria Turoldo.* Mandelbaum is co-editor with Robert Richardson of *Three Centuries of American Poetry* (Bantam Books) and, with Yehuda Amichai, of the eight volumes of the JPS Jewish Poetry Series. After receiving his Ph.D. from Columbia, he was in the Society of Fellows at Harvard. While chairman of the Ph.D. program in English at the Graduate Center of CUNY, he was a visiting profesor at Washington University in St. Louis, and at the universities of Houston, Denver, Colorado, and Purdue. His honorary degrees are from Notre Dame University, Purdue Unversity, the University of Assino, and the University of Torino. He received the Gold Medal of Honor from the city of Florence in 2000, celebrating the 735th anniversary of Dante's birth, the only translator to be so honored; and in 2003 he received the President of Italy's award for translation. He is now Professor of the History of Literary Criticism at the University of Turin and the W. R. Kenan Professor of Humanities at Wake Forest University.

Born in Chattanooga in 1940, **BARRY MOSER** was educated at Auburn University, the University of Tennessee at Chattanooga, and the University of Massachusetts, where he did his graduate studies. His work as illustrator, designer, and printer, which includes the books of Pennyroyal Press, is represented in numerous collections, museums, and libraries in the United States and abroad, among them, the British Museum, the Library of Congress, the New York Public Library, the National Library of Australia, the London College of Printing, the Houghton Library at Harvard University, the Bienecke Library at Yale University, and the Firestone Library at Princeton University. Mr. Moser's illustrated books form a list of over sixty titles, including the Arion Press *Moby Dick,* the University of California Press edition of this translation of *The Divine Comedy*, and the Limited Editions Club of New York edition of Homer's *Odyssey*. The Pennyroyal *Alice's Adventures in Wonderland* was awarded the American Book Award for design/pictorial. An associate of the National Academy of Design, Mr. Moser frequently lectures and acts as visiting artist at universities and institutions across the country. His most ambitious work is the heralded Pennyroyal Caxton Bible in two volumes, with 231 engravings.

ASK YOUR BOOKSELLER FOR THESE BANTAM CLASSICS

GREAT AMERICAN SHORT STORIES, 0-440-33060-2
SHORT STORY MASTERPIECES, 0-440-37864-8
THE VOICE THAT IS GREAT WITHIN US, 0-553-26263-7
THE BLACK POETS, 0-553-27563-1
THREE CENTURIES OF AMERICAN POETRY, (Trade) 0-553-37518-0,
    (Hardcover) 0-553-10250-8
FOUR GREAT AMERICAN CLASSICS, (*The Scarlet Letter*, *The Adventures
    of Huckleberry Finn*, *The Red Badge of Courage*, *Billy Budd,
    Sailor*), 0-553-21362-8